naught's

had

vivian gerow

naught's had

a romance

EFG
PUB

efg publishing, Vancouver, Canada

ISBN: 978-0991-7977-6-9

efg publishing   **EFG**
10420 148 ST – 301   **PUB**
Surrey, British Columbia, Canada,
V3R 3X4
email: publish@efgpublishing.com

Or contact the author on the Naught's Had website:

http://naughtshad.com

Cover designs: Marvin Rayala & efgpublishing.
Cover photograph by Foster & Asher via DSTTSP.
Editors: K. Leach, N. K. Johel.
Proofreaders: Alan Potter, Karen Ngai, Alyssa Linn Palmer.

" ... this isn't your everyday romance — far from it."

Publisher's Daily Reviews

"*Naught's had, all's spent,*

Where our desire is got without content.

'Tis safer to be that which we destroy

Than by destruction dwell in doubtful joy."

Macbeth, Act III, Scene 2

naught's had

"now"

S ay?" The word tugs her back to life, making her remember – that was how she's always dealt with him: she's said – and said and said and said and said until she's filled up too many years – seven – with talk. And all the wrong talk – alcoholism, responsibility, self-image, life-style; words fall too easily into issues, into points with a beginning and an end. Nothing here is so neat and tidy – the words let it get away, and maybe that is why she has always used them: to escape it – to let him escape it, because he has always been too fragile to accept it. She looks at him, the glare from the lamp hitting her eyes – she's not standing half-naked in front of a man who just tried what he just tried, and telling him – insisting, because telling wouldn't make him believe it – that his existence depends on her – the laugh he'd have. She looks at the wall. Don't you have something to say? – what's she supposed to say to rape, to at least a rape mentality? She has to say something. Seven years demand it, and he's asked for it. She lets her jeans drop from her hands. *"Yeah, I guess I have something to say."* She doesn't know what to say. "You understand so little and that's what you want – you want to empty yourself of everything, and I don't understand it – and I don't understand how you can celebrate it when you should be fighting it. You'd rather hide in a bottle or a toke, and maybe you have lots of friends there, but that doesn't make you right, not by a long shot." These words don't fit, these words are letting it get away.

They come close, but just close enough to move them away from it, misdirecting. It has always been misdirected. Okay, there are forces around you, feeding you ideas. TV, the magazines you read, the store – Lord knows they really want you to be one thing in that company, from every angle, customers, employees, the bosses, middle management. When I was there, I knew that cashiers were supposed to be rather stupid, very pleasant and quite competent pieces of machinery. We were supposed to be able to blather on endlessly about the weather. We didn't have opinions about anything else. Of course we all felt personally and dreadfully about the high cost of food. And we had to be watched like hawks, because we were pretty stupid. But I didn't pay any attention to that, and you don't have to either. You don't have to be one of the boys. You can just refuse." She's getting closer, but not close enough. She can't make it real this way. "This mans-man act you're putting on, Al, it's a lie, a joke. I mean, if it was real, that would be one thing, but it isn't. It's not you. You know it's not, and that makes it just a failure, a way to make up for the fact it's not true. And the more you do it, the more it's going to be a failure for you, and the more you're going to have to do it." But she can't even follow what she's saying. How can he? "You see, I used to see some control there. A sneer, a smile, something that put it in perspective, that put some of you in it. Now it's all monkey-see-monkey-do, as if you don't know where you start and all those ideas and forces end. I mean, you're just like a sponge now, just soaking up all the crap in the world and trying to make it true. When did you decide that everything that mattered was outside? that you couldn't depend on you? You don't look inside yourself anymore, and when I come over here, I don't find you anymore." And that's it: he's not Alex anymore, not for her. "You used to talk about freedom all the time, holding it up like a god, and now you're the least free person I know. And you celebrate that – you should walk around in sack-cloth and ashes, not with a grin and a bottle. You don't have a clue anymore. You don't know where you

start, you don't know where living starts, you don't know where. . . ."
She can't say 'where loving starts,' not after tonight. It would be
too funny, too nightmarish, after tonight. But she should have
been ready for tonight, and she knows it. After all the things she's
heard about him, knew what he was doing, even talked to him
about, she should have been ready. But she simply never believed
that he would turn it on her – that part of him wasn't supposed to
be part of them. She looks around for her purse.

You keep me hanging on for a reason, and you should look to yourself
for that reason, come up with it yourself instead of making all the pain
mine. But no, you play 'on-again, off-again.' If you are really sadistic, if
that's the sex you want, why am I here – because you've had something to
do with my being here. Why else: 'don't you have something to say?' Why
else us?

She picks up her cigarettes and puts the shade back on the
lamp. It's true: the fact of them – seven years of them – proves his
life a lie. But the fact of his little display tonight proves they are a lie
– was that the purpose? Don't you have something to say? – if he'd
wanted her gone, all he'd had to do was keep his mouth shut right
then. He hadn't – that was the hook, the con man's hook, the way
to make her play the fool, because that makes her believe that he
wants solutions, that he wants to be reached, touched, moved. And
she wants to believe that, because she doesn't want to leave him. If
only words could hit – his do, always. Don't you have something to
say? and out flies the fury, the legitimate, necessary, even required
fury. She becomes the problem solver. She talks nicely to him,
about him. She doesn't make him pay. He's good. Very good.

"Is that all?"

And he's laying there grinning. She doesn't even have to look
to know that – won't look because she knows that. And a real grin
now too, the kind she'd wanted all night, not the cold and cruel
flick of the lips he'd played with before. Happy as a clam. Because he loves to hear about himself – given five minutes with
God, he'd talk about himself, not good and evil or faith and science,

but "What do you really think of me, God?" And he'd listen with that same smile. "I don't know how someone like you got so sucked in the first place. It's like you've grabbed would be truisms out of the air, and if you're dancing around with them like an Indian with a scalp in a B-rated western, and it's just not you. You have so much going for you. Why all the masks, all the roles, because life has a way of getting lost in the roles, Alex, just getting shuffled out of the way. I really can't believe you think masculinity comes from walking all over other people. I just don't believe that of you." She feels like a child tugging at some elbow for attention, whining. Because if the words were true, she wouldn't be saying them. But the words are true, and the faith is true, it's just − she needs her soul to speak. She needs that grand glorious moment, made of grand glorious phrases, that moment when the scales fall from his eyes and he cries "I can see, I can see." But souls don't speak. They stir, rustle like leaves in the wind, and no more. They leave the mind to search out the words. She laughs, It isn't going to happen. "If you think you're just going to trip over the right role one day, you're dreaming. It doesn't happen."

"If you say so."

It's a sing-song − she's going to rip his face off. She lights her cigarette. What can she say? There's no focus here, just the whin-ings of a mad woman. Anything she says, he can and will wipe out − he's had that down to a fine art for years: You say I Love you, I say I don't. You say it's sick, I say it's fun. It's not the truth that mat-ters to him, it's the escape. His infinite freedom to twist and turn everything into new shapes and forms. "When did you decide to buy into all the crap?" She wants him to say he didn't. "Did you just get lazy? Give up?"

"I'm not lazy. I'm not the one who works for the government. You're the bureaucrat, aren't you Kim? You know, we don't get ten people for every job out in the real world. We have to go out there, every day and work for our dollars." Alex laughs − he's rushed; he's standing on top of a cliff in a storm, standing at the edge, feeling the ripping winds and watching, splashed by, the up-roaring waters, until, for a moment – a flash, like lightening – he's a part of it. Feeling her strength, her belief, her knowledge, feeling her feeling him. And she'd thought she'd done with him – he'd thought she'd done with him. He laughs – he wants more, he wants to keep this going.

"What would you do without stereotypes, Alex? Would you be all alone and lost in the universe?"

"Is that like being up a creek without a paddle?"

Why don't you try it sometime? Go out there without the blinders on and see what's really there. But that wouldn't do, would it? You have to be all closed up, like a great wall."

"If you say so."

"Say that again, and I'll kill you."

"If you say so." He has to keep her stirred up, keep her in the midst of it, because if she fails out, he fails out with her, and they aren't there yet – the eye of the storm, that's where he wants to be. She's taking a long drag off her cigarette. "You smoke too much."

"You drive me to it."

"Do I? I must be a pretty powerful guy." And he laughs – he feels powerful now. He feels alive and rushed and awake. Because he's created confusion out of order: she should have left him, and she must know that.

"If you were, we wouldn't be where we are."

"Where's that?" He's daring her to admit it – nowhere – forcing her to avoid it.

"If you don't know, it doesn't matter much."

"Oh, I know. I just wanted to know what you thought." It's an-other invitation, because he can see that she is slowing down, and she can't slow down yet because they haven't gotten to it: what does she really think of him? He needs to know – she can't leave him like this. She has to forgive him, find him so captivating again – he loves it when she's in love with him.

"Figure it out for yourself."

"Think I can?"

"I have my doubts."

"Then you'd better tell me."

"I'm tired of telling you."

But he is watching her every move, and he can see that she's not empty of it yet, but searching. He just has to provoke her. "So you hate me in the morning, do you? Don't respect me? That's nice to hear."

"I don't recall saying that."

"That's what it sounded like to me."

"I hate the way you stereotype. I hate the way you want to crush people down into some shape just so that you can control them – you don't even control them that way. They go on being exactly what they are. You're the one whose lost. You're the one who's limited, not them."

He can feel the anger. It's a thrill on his skin.

"You would have made a perfect Nazi with your 'a place for everything and everything in its place' attitude, you know that? I mean you cannot limit things, Alex, all you can do is limit yourself, and you have that down pat. Does it make you feel like you're on top, or what?"

"I like it when you're on top, doing the work." To provoke more.

"Bad joke at a bad time, Alex. You just can't do that to people. You can't deny the whole world its basic humanity just because you don't know what to do with yours. And that's what you do, isn't it?"

He doesn't know. If he knew, he wouldn't need her.

"You just have to plug everything in to some strange . . . I don't know what it is, but it's wrong. It denies that people have gifts. You don't see what that means, do you? You don't understand why not to do that."

She's still struggling, searching. She's pacing the floor, around the bed. Slapping her thigh with each step. He can wait.

"You won't think for yourself. You buy it all because you want to. If some stranger came waltzing in here, wearing a three piece suit, and he said that everything that makes living worthwhile – happiness, success, confidence, all of it – depended on the business of your eyes, you'd buy that."

"Yeah, I would."

"Sure. Why not?"

"If I had brown eyes, I wouldn't, but I have nice blue eyes."

"Glints of steel."

"No, they're more like pools you can swim in."

"Someone tell you that, or did you come up with it all on your own?"

"What do you think?"

"Cute."

"I'm listening to you, aren't I?" He wants to remind her, to give her something to get her going again. Because she's getting further away, not closer, now.

"Are you? That would be a first."

"I always listen to you."

"And then you invert it all."

"What do you mean?" He sits up. This is new.

"I mean, you twist it and turn it around. You see what you hear to justify whatever you want to justify. You deliberately draw the wrong conclusions."

"How?"

"I don't know how. I don't know how your mind works. I'm not even sure it does."

But he doesn't believe that. She's on to something, she just won't say anymore. "I don't see that."

"That's what I mean. You don't see much, and you do it deliberately."

And she sits down, at the foot of the bed, her back to him. Slouched. Exhausted. He watches her. She doesn't move. Maybe they are there now – he doesn't know but he thinks this might be it: the end. Maybe that is all she thinks of him. A loser, a washout. Maybe she's finally come around to seeing it. He wants to hold her, to make it up to her . . . "So I didn't get it right. How am I supposed to know? You never tell me your fantasies."

"If you'd bothered finding out who you were in bed with the last who knows how many years, you'd have known not to. You should know me that well – and you should ask."

"So I'm asking."

"It's too late – you just can't – and I don't believe you just thought . . . you. . . ."

She buries her head in her hands, defeated. Leaving him defeated too. "Kim . . ."

'*No one knows what it's like, to be the bad man, to be the sad man, behind blue eyes –*' the song will not stop going around in her head. I have pretty nice blue eyes. How did they know him?

But no one has to tell him the bad news, because he has it lined up and at the ready. That was all tonight was: bad news to counter that 'I Love You' he'd let slip in the quiet of the night.

When I say spread 'em, you spread 'em. Women are just pleasure vehicles. Words of a man without dreams or a conscience. It is still too real, too cold. She can't talk to him while she's feeling that—can't.

"Did I have a sweater when I came in?"

"I don't remember."

"I don't either."

"Probably. It's cold out for just a coat."

"Yeah. Where are my jeans?"

"Are you getting dressed?"

"No, I'm still tap dancing, Alex." She snaps. She's through – he's won. He can lay there and be whatever sick thing he wants to be. She sees her jeans laying on the floor. She kicks them close to her.

He watches – she's hating him, he can feel it, but she doesn't have to. They could make love, if she wanted. He'd start with all the long deep kisses, because she loves them, and then, since she's getting dressed, he could undress her, slowly, the way she loves it. He'd draw back her blouse, kiss her breasts, holding her to him, rubbing his face so gently against her — her skin is so soft, so firm, it shows how much she looks after it, the care she takes, and he'd take that sort of care with her too — her stomach, so firm. He knows, he remembers, every part of her body, and he remembers her touch too. And he knows how to get to that touch, to make her want him, to make her have to reach out and caress him because she cannot, any longer, bear to have him touch her without touching him. And so gently, so perfectly. "Come back to bed."

"It's not that easy, is it?"

"Yes." He moves over to make space for her again beside him. And he fluffs a pillow for her.

"Alex."

"Come back to bed."

"I can't."

"Sure you can." He reaches over, patting her back.

"No."

She moves away from his hand. "What do you want, Kim? What am I supposed to do? Just tell me. I'll make it up to you." He remembers what it would be like if she would come. Her desire, her wanting, it was more than anyone ease's, somehow. . . .

"Don't plead, Alex."

"Then what?" He'll do anything, but he doesn't know what to do. He's in over his head with her — always has been. "What?"

"Just don't plead. Never plead." She's so tired. She can't think. She can't deal with anymore . . . doesn't he know not to plead, that she can't take it when he pleads? He should be strong, he should be what he used to be — should carry her away into that great force — fire and hope; it had been so wonderful, and it was so long ago now, and it is getting further away with every day that passes. "Alex." She turns around and looks at him. He is still the best looking man she has ever laid eyes on. He still has that innocence to him. "We have to talk."

"Okay."

Maybe he is all innocence, somehow — doesn't think things through enough to lose innocence, something. He looks so eager now. She laughs – she'd been wanting this for weeks, and here it is, and she has to say no to it. She reaches for a cigarette.

"Can I have one too?"

"Sure." He's so boyish sometimes – can I play with your toys, because if I can play with your toys, you must like me still. She passes him a cigarette, lights hers, and passes him the lighter. "I can't deal with it Alex. I just can't. Things have to change."

"I've changed. Come back to bed."

And his hand is out, reaching for her. And he's smiling so softly, his face so full of promise. It's tempting. She wishes it was that easy. "For how long?" She knows he can change with the wind.

"For now."

And he grins – he knows he can change with the wind too. His infinite freedom, and he'll insist on it. "Nothing permanent."

"I don't make promises, Kim."

But he's still grinning, promising. For now. But it's too hard to keep coming here, wondering who he'll be when he arrives. Especially after tonight. She drags a long drag from her cigarette, and exhales towards the ceiling. At the very least, she has to have his promise that he won't be that again. "I can't accept that."

"It's the way I am."

"It's the way you choose to be, because it's the way you can get away with the most. 'Now you see me, now you don't.' That's what it is. And I can't take it, not when it leads to where it's going." She's calm now. She can talk. I don't know where you get your ideas from, but I don't think I know why you get them, and that's the part I don't understand, coming from you. You don't need any of it – you have so much, how could you possibly need any of it? I mean, I know that everyday, and it seems in every way, people want you to be something for them – friends, bosses, TV advertisers, but when you have so much going for yourself, why do you bother with it all?"

She looks so sincere, so intent. As if she really believes it – believes it of him. How . . . when it isn't true? How can she not see that it isn't true? He can't take his eyes from hers. He can't believe that she doesn't see through him, doesn't see the games and the pain and the need to hide. "Some people need that, Kim."

"I know that. You aren't one of them."

Her voice sounds so hard, so firm, as if wishes could be real . . . does she believe that too? – does she know how to do that? He's wondered before.

"You're not. You never have been, and you're not."

As if saying it could make it true. But he knows what's true. And she's going to know too, one day – she's going to see it in spite of herself, her wants, because it is just the wanting that makes her see him that way, he knows that, just the fact that she wants him that way – the wanting him means he has to be that way, but it has nothing to do with him. And now she's going to see it herself one day, and she's going to insist he be there for it. Because wishes don't come true in the grown up world. He knows. He's wished, he's wanted too. She'll kill him for her wishes. She gets up and moves to the window. He breathes again.

"You should move into the other room."

"Why?"

"It has a view of the city."

"I don't care that much about the city. Can't see it for the smog most days anyway."

"Yea, that's true. I can see the river from my place."

"Can you?" He's never been there – he's not a part of her, and he can't let her become a part of him.

"Yeah, all the time. Sometimes at night I can see the boats, you know, the lights, moving up and down the river. It's nice. I'm glad I moved there."

"Good." But he wants her. He wants to hold that belief again, just once more, just tonight. "Coming to bed?" Hold it while it lasts.

"You have to learn to choose, Alex. Don't take things as they come, because they lie. Take the freedom, choose."

I live the way I want to." She wants him to choose her, and he can't – it would be a lie, when he knows, has known all along, that he'd never keep her – she'd leave the next day, as soon as she saw through him.

"No you don't. You adjust and adapt. It's been a long time since your lifestyle was a choice." She keeps looking out the window, watching the cars pass by. "you live the way you think you have to. Or something. I don't know." She doesn't want to talk about him. She wants to talk about them. But somehow, somewhere along the line, he became them, and what he does is what they are. It is as if she doesn't have any place here, as if she's just a mirror for him to check his luck in. "Because we aren't going to stay together much longer if you don't. I can't take it anymore. I just can't. I can't take coming over here and not knowing until I get here just who you are going to be, or what game you'll be playing. And I really can't take seeing you put on the act you were trying tonight. I won't."

"I was just trying to spice up our sex life."

"Bullshit." She knows exactly what he was trying to do: he wanted to humiliate her. When hell freezes over. "if you ever—"

"I won't. After this, you think I would?"

"If you ever, and I'm not kidding."

"I won't. Come back to bed and see."

And he's smiling his 'lets' smile again. And he's letting the blankets fall from his chest – sitting up to make them fall. And his leg drops to the floor. She's seen this somewhere else before . . . she remembers: the poses, in magazines that used to be – probably still were – in the coffee room in the store. *Playboy* and *Playgirl*. He thinks – she had to look away, get away from what he thinks. She smokes – she wants him, she was born wanting him, but it's him he wants, not just sex, and he won't understand that. Won't understand he doesn't need the poses. Won't understand that there is no moment in life like the moment when his skin dances under her touch, and hers under his. Won't understand that happens through who he is, even in all his confusion. On those rare moments when he lets himself through. "And another thing: it's not easy to make love to a man who has to go on and on about his cheating on his girlfriend and his guilt and the rest of it."

"I do feel guilty."

He doesn't — he doesn't even sound like he does. He's just saying it, because he thinks he should say it, thinks he's a better person because he's said it. At best, he feels guilty for cheating on his life, because when he's with her, he is cheating on his life. "The hell you do."

"I'm not easy, you know."

And he smiles, coaxing — having you does not mean nothing to me, wanting you does not mean nothing to me, I am not easy, come to bed. One hundred and forty times it would be enough, but to-night it isn't. She's thought these thoughts too many times, she's gone through it all too many times. She's a tired old river now, un-yielding, just going. "you and that slut are perfect together because you're both so easy."

"Where'd you hear that?"

"Who doesn't say it?"

"That doesn't make it true."

"But it is true. It's the attraction: you don't have to be faithful to her because the word 'faithful' isn't in her vocabulary. You leave her at the bar, and go off with someone else and you don't have to think twice, because all you are to her is a body and all she is to you is a body, and that's all the value that's there. You're not just into bodies, you want to be just a body. And then you say you aren't cheap. Maybe you aren't. Maybe 'cheap' isn't in your vocabulary either." He's not smiling now. She smiles to herself — he has to realize the contradictions. He has to see that his life is false. "But it's in mine."

She's caught him — she is seeing him, she is knowing him, and now she will leave him. He pulls the blankets up him. "What do you want?"

"I want to know that you want me here. I want you to be honest with me. I want — each time, not just when I push so hard that you have to or I have to leave, but each time, I want you to be here too. I don't want the games, Alex. I can't take the games, and little hints dropped here and there, they aren't enough anymore. Things are going to change, and if that's asking too much, then there isn't any purpose in being here anyway."

And she's caught him there too: he does that, he drops hints, he plays, he'll admit it. If that's all she wants. But it's not, he knows. "Does that mean I have to call you everyday and that stuff?"

"You never listen. I don't really care who calls whom and when and how often – I'm not the one who counts the times we've made love, remember. I just don't want to come over here and wonder all the way if I'll get hit or hugged when I come in. That's all. I just want to know that you care."

But he'd known that too, because he knows Kim: she goes straight for the heart, like a mad dog, and nothing less will do. "You've always known that I care." He's whispering, hoping – if she lets it be enough . . .

"I've always guessed, if that's what you mean."

She's yelling, and she's shaking, trembling. He can't be that important to her – she can't be losing it for him. "Are you all right? Do you have high blood pressure?"

"No – if I do, it's your fault."

"Oh." She's probably right.

"Guessing isn't enough, not when you have to get yourself good and loaded before you can feel anything. The only time you're yourself is when you're too drunk to stop yourself in time, and it just happens. The rest of the time, it's games.

He has to stop her. "You've seen me drunk plenty of times. You know me. And I'm here now."

Because I've yelled enough. It's like summoning up through demons. It's not fair to me. There's a wonderful person inside there somewhere, but I have to go through hell to get him. And when I do – this is the real killer – when I do, you turn around the next time and say that you were drunk, and you didn't know

– 16 –

what you were doing, and then, just to top it off, you say you don't even remember what happened. No more. Nope."

He has no way to stop this. "you take things too seriously Kim. I just do it to get a charge out of you. If you'd just laugh, then I couldn't do it."

"I don't think it's my responsibility to stop you from playing your games. I think it's yours. I don't trust you anymore, and I don't respect you, and just laughing when you 'try to get a charge out of me' isn't going to bring back the trust, is it? Trust and respect just don't pop out of nowhere, Alex."

She doesn't trust or respect him. He shouldn't be surprised; he's given her no reason to.

"Things are going to change. I will not be here for another night like tonight."

But things can't change. He can't give her promises he won't keep – he's never done that to her, he won't start now. And there's no other way to change things.

"I mean it. You have got to start to be honest."

But he can't be honest about things he doesn't know the truth of, and he doesn't know . . . "I'm confused."

"That one has run it's course, Alex."

"But I am." Because he's helpless in front of her – when she isn't there, the world, his life are fixed and fine, but then she comes and scorns it, and he isn't so sure anymore – the possibilities she insists on. . . . He looks into her eyes, hoping she will see into his, because he is being true, being as true as he can be.

"Yes, but I think by choice now. Or at least, because it's easier. If you are confused, sort it out."

"Does that mean you won't save me anymore?" Because that is what she has done for years for him: insisting that he see more, be more. You aren't one of them – she's done everything she can to make that true.

"What?"

"Won't you try?"

"What are you saying?" She thinks she's hearing him say that everything she hates about this relationship make up his reasons for keeping it going. She grabs her jeans off of the floor, and slips them on. "What do you mean?"

"That's what you do. You try to save me from myself."

Her blood has gone cold. She can't move, breathe. She just looks at him – everything she's said tonight has been a waste, because this is what he wants, this is what he likes, this is what it is all about for him. "It's not going to happen anymore. It's not."

"You aren't going to save me anymore?"

"I can't save you." She doesn't believe that this is being said. She's stepping back from him, picking up her purse. Because if this is what he wants, it's all been a waste. She's at the door. She doesn't think. She leaves – what can she say to someone who wants to hear it and hear it and hear it forever?

"So don't say goodbye." Alex grabs his robe, and runs after her. He can't let her leave mad, hating him. He can't stay in a room she has just left. He catches up with her at the door. She's waiting for him.

"What?"

But he has nothing to say to her. "You're going?"

"Yeah."

"That's probably for the best."

"Who knows?"

"This is true. This is true." He needs her. He slips his arms around her. "So."

"It's your move."

He laughs, scoffing himself. "I'm not making any more moves tonight." The whole night has been a disaster, and it is all his fault – he should have known, he should have thought, he never thinks. He holds her closer to him. He wants to feel her softening towards him, feel her comfort.

"Yeah, it's been quite a night."

She puts her head on his shoulder. He smooths her hair. I'll walk you to your car. It's late and it's dark, and some of my friends may be about, in the bushes." It's an old joke between them. He wants to hear her laugh at it. She does.

"They're still allowed out after dark?"

"Amazing, isn't it?" He can feel her relaxing against him. He relaxes with her, and he holds her tighter – he has to make her understand. "So much is new to me Kim, and it's not new to you. I don't think like you do. I don't think at all."

"Don't say that."

"I'm stupid."

"Don't say that. You aren't."

"I'm not good enough for you."

"Alex, don't. Just don't. Not now."

He bends down and bites her shoulder – he wants her, loves her, and she will never stay with him. But her arms tighten around him.

"You just have to trust yourself more. That's all."

He laughs again – he doesn't know what that means, how it's done. Let me think about things."

"Okay."

He kisses her forehead and lets her go. "Drive carefully. It's slippery."

"I will."

"Don't brake suddenly. There's frost."

"I won't."

"Okay. Just give me a couple of weeks."

"Yeah."

"Take care."

"You too."

"Bye-bye."

"Yeah."

He watches her walk down the driveway to her car. He waits until she's in it and on her way before he goes into the house.

S he wrapped herself in the familiar blanket of "hide in your shell.' Hearing the plaintive voice over and over again:

frightening . . . too beautiful . . . pride . . .

pain. . . love . . . help . . . me . . .

if I can help you. . . be . . . cool . . . fools . . .

Oh yes, that's what he does. It's exactly what he does, and he does it so well, and he won't believe that he's doing it all. And he won't know illusion because he doesn't know reality. And he won't listen, hear me. Damn – if he would listen, just listen, at least he'd hear what he's doing away with. Why won't you let me touch you, let me near you, feel you? Why won't you let me love you, why won't you let you love me? Why are you so scared? There is no need to be so scared. It's your emotions in the first place. Listen to them if you want answers. They will give you control too. Take control too. I only seem to be out of control, but you really are. Take control too. Don't lose it. No, don't lose it. Oh God, why does it always work out this way? I mean it God, I need an answer – I need to know, I need to stay sane: why does it always work out this way, him playing some game, me fighting some battle? All over a little "I-love-you" that slipped out because he forgot to choke it. He had to deny it. He had to destroy it. What is wrong with him. Tell me. He's your creation, not mine. Tell me why it is so impossible to love in this world – Your world, not mine. Tell me why it always turns to jelly or goes to hell. Your love, Your love is rumored to be so perfect. Infinite. Limitless. Boundless. Eternal. Everlasting. What didn't You give to us?– what did You hold back? Or must Your love be perfect, any less being too little to last one day, too little to last one hour, because our love is so imperfect? But that's where You gave us only half of the gift, and that's where I won't forgive You. You let us taste the power and the joy, and You let us feel the cares and the pride and all the world and even ourselves, our unease, our flaws, cease for us right within us, and You let us find them again, transformed, in him – all the hims and hers – but You will not let us have it, not have it, just taste it. A taste, a splash of water on the face, no more. And it's not that we're weak and hiding behind confusion, like Alex, because it's everywhere. Even in loving you, it's there, we have only seconds of pure view, if that, and only that if we search and plead. So it's not the undeserving or imperfect. You gave us only half of the gift. You gave us less than we need.–or maybe that's what we settled for. Maybe we can't believe in the whole gift. Maybe we can only believe in it when it's so fresh in our lives that we haven't had the time or even the inclination to put it under the microscope and tear it apart, to come to know it is a thing when it isn't a thing at all, and was never meant to be a thing. It was meant to live, and we can't let it live. We must control it. So maybe the problem is in us: don't see me, don't touch me, don't feel me, never love me. And so we turn it into the comfort of an old shoe. We even say that: "She fits me like an old shoe." We can rip over the heavens, but we want old shoes, we want to break people in just like shoes. Oh, blow it up. Why don't You blow it up? I would, if this were my creation. They don't want to change, they don't want to feel change experience. They want to be safe. Not lonely, only because there is someone in bed with them every night, someone nicely dead, as nicely dead as he wants to be because he is not different from those others except that he wants to take a strap to the body beside him and see the memory of life appear in her jerks and screams . . . it's not the memory of life, it is just another mockery, as if we don't have enough already. I bet he doesn't even know that. Another illusion before him.

You see how it works, and You probably have answers. You stay silent, no burning bushes. You make it all come down to Peter Pan and Tinkerbell, and clapping and saying "I believe, I believe," in our sleep. I've been clapping for seven years now, and I still clap. I just don't expect anything to come of it anymore. You see, we don't know how to love. He said that once, almost. He said, "I'm learning about love, I'm trying." Damn near killed me. You didn't give us enough of the gift.

— No, some do have it. I've seen it. Marriages that last fifty years, and still go on with quiet dignity. Unreal city. They can hold onto the taste, savor it, take more of it, never stop having it, live in it. But not enough of them.

I want so much from him. He could do it too, but there's something in him that can't believe he can. And then there's something in him that does anyway, that won't let him stop. I get stuck between the two, and I get hurt. It hurts so much, and I make it hurt more because there is something in me that believes that I can love, and won't let me believe that I can't, and won't let him stop me, even while he is stopping me, while he is holding my hands together so I can't clap.

But I don't want to hurt — is that his problem, once hurt, forever shy? But when did he take a risk and get hurt? No. It's that he doesn't know how and he's scared of failure to do anything that is not a guaranteed success. Lord, just give him a piece more of that love, just enough to learn from, a touch and he'll learn. He's just enough to learn from, a touch and he'll learn. He's starving too. But he cannot believe that all he needs to do is believe and then it's made true. He can't believe that he has that power. He has to find the answer, the pattern, the way. Someone has to give him the blueprint. That's the problem, and he doesn't want me running around proving it otherwise. Hence tonight, I know, I know. That's where it comes from. But even in that, he's trapped, because a thing doesn't have to be disproved unless it exists, threatens. So he tried to slap it down. Yes, he has to stand up and scream at me – only at me; the rest of the world doesn't matter because he can tell them any lie he wants and get away with it, but I can call him on it because I've been there with him and I know what he felt, and I know what this is between us. No sleazy affair. This has taken him places that so thrilled him that they scared him. This has taken him places that so thrilled him that he forgot to play his games for a while, that he knew he didn't need his games for a while. Yes, I know he has loved me, wanted me, needed me, and so it is me that he must scream at and me he must convince that it all never happened the way it happened, if it is to be denied. But he can't. I was there. I won't let him take the value away. No Alex. It happened. You are responsible.

Oh, how lovely it would be if love were truly a thing that I could hold. I could pick it up, and throw it at him whenever he started one of his games. I could toss it up and down, like a baseball: "Here it is, the thing that never happened. Look at it, and deny it, and deny the sky and trees while you're at it. Look. This is what we created. Tell me now that it doesn't exist." It works . . . it would crumble him.

I was praying, I forgot. I wasn't heard anyway. Lord, go to another planet and try again. Or maybe you already have. Maybe that explains the lack of burning bushes in the last few centuries. Ignore me tonight. I haven't had any sleep. You know all anyway. You know hell. Goodnight. Amen, and good night.

Because I have to figure this out on my own. So is there any left to hope on? Hope springs eternal. No, not right now it doesn't. Where is it—that jump I used to have? that knowledge I never had to learn, but came to me? all the things that have gotten me through all the nights of the past seven years? It goes when I talk to him – he only has to be in the room, that's all it takes, and I don't function anymore. I'm too aware of him, scared of myself. Not when we're fine, just now. When we're fine, oh the awareness, what a delight, no fear. I have to keep trying.

What did I say to him tonight? I think I said more than I have ever said before. I didn't feel it at the time, but now, I think I did. Especially near the end. What did I say to him tonight?

It was all so hard, so stuttered, as it always is when he is near and far—worse tonight, for I didn't expect that welcoming scene. I should have. I should have known that it would come one night. I should have had something ready to say. The way he played it . . . I wasted all my energy trying to forget, push away that, away and out of sight. I should have had something ready. I'd heard.

What did I do? At least I got up. It took me long enough. He looked surprised – he was surprised, he should have been me for a minute. I never thought I would. I did. That much is good. Then what did I say? Nothing. I was going to leave. He said his little "Don't you have something to say?" I couldn't believe I'd heard that. I would have left if he hadn't said that. He was asking me to stay. And I didn't know what to say. I started talking, about something . . . acquiescing, not choosing, that was it, and then forces. I don't think I said his friends though. That's good. That's good. It would have antagonized him. But they do want something from him. They put him in the role he plays, the great Don Juan and all that stuff. The more he scores, the better they feel. He'd never have understood that – never ever admitted it to me. That he has to figure out on his own.

What else did I say? I think I said the same thing a thousand times. I wasn't prepared. I went over there, expecting him, not Attila the Hun. It doesn't matter. All those nights I went over there prepared and said less. But I didn't make him talk. He won't talk. The best he'll do is admit to listening. He won't open it up.

It was very strange, the way he changed, so fast. That he even said "don't you have something to say." when I thought that he was going to open the doors for me on my way out – I thought that the whole thing was played to get me out because surely he knows me well enough now to know that there is no way under heaven that I would for one minute permit something like that. What I felt when he was doing it . . . he was betraying me, and he must have known that that is how I would take it, he must have. He is simply not that stupid – and if he was ever going to try anything like that, as a new thing for us, he would talk first, ask, or try it in a better way. No, that was power tripping. He did that to get to me. Well, he did. I hope he's happy now.

But he did change, right away–no, not right away, when I got up. He was calling me back when I was dressing. And then he said, "I've changed." I was too far gone then to care, and maybe that's for the best because if we're ever going to straighten things out, we have to stay out of bed to do it.

Those things had to be said.

Yes, I did get closer tonight. He makes it so hard because he'll lie anytime, anywhere, for any reason. He'll lie for the thrill of it – more power tripping. Yeah: 'You say yes, I say no, You said goodbye, and I say hello, hello, You say goodbye and I say hello' and around we go. Because I don't have the guts to say the real things. I dance around with cheap psychology. What I should say, should have said – I should make him explain it all to me instead of explaining it all to him. That would have been fun. Yes, Alex, you tell me, since you don't want this, since you really don't want this, why do you pursue it? Because you do, you know. And please tell me why you so carefully keep me around if you don't care. If it's all sex, and all guilt, and you're so guilt-ridden that you can barely look yourself in the mirror the next morning, and you're just using me – which doesn't make much sense in the first place because it isn't as if sex is hard to get these days, and it certainly has never been hard for you to get, never so hard that you would take all the crap I dish out to you just to get it – but you tell me why, if it's all that, you keep it going. Because you do, but he'll say he doesn't. He'll say I come over and pursue him, seduce him, take him at my whim. He'll deny any interest in it at all, beyond minor sexual pleasure – minor, too, he'll say. Then I can say, I can remind Mr. I'll-never-forget-a-moment-of-us, of all those times he's grabbed us back from the edge. Like the hand, sneaking around to hold mine, so gently. Like the plea: "I'm hanging around with hippies, learning about love." Like the last time we were together, the very night he wanted to destroy this time. What was it you mumbled all the way home, Alex? – no loving since me, we were Romeo and Juliet, something you don't know the true value of things until you've lost them – and on like that, making even me nauseous. You want to deny? I can give you plenty to deny. So explain away. Explain to me why someone who wants so desperately to be out of it would say and do things that keep him in it. I would love to hear that.

I could never do it. I don't have the guts. I've tried, I've wanted to, and something always tells me that it's wrong, that I can't do that to those moments, that I can't betray him like that, that it will all be gone if I do that. Even if I did it, he'd lie his way out of it anyway. Backed into a corner like that, he'd lie. I wouldn't blame him – and what could it mean to me to get him by twisting his arm behind his back until he cried uncle, because that's all I would be doing. He'd have no choice.

What did he say tonight?

He couldn't have had it planned because he was too stunned when I pushed him over and got up. So he was really trying a little power trip, as if I would be manipulated that way. Not a chance, Talon. Why . . . there is something terribly wrong, and not just between us because he does that routinely with Charlene, or at least Patty says so and she wouldn't say it if it wasn't going on, and she'd know if it was because Tony would know and tell her, so something is not right at all in him. Something that used to be so right in him is not right at all . . . why? – because he lost it. He's so impotent because he's lost it, and he won't act like a man, so he won't find it. Oh Alex—

What did he say tonight? What did he say tonight? "You've seen me drunk lots of times, you know the real me." You've got that right: I do know the real you. So why should I settle for less? And hearing that, you think I'd settle for that? No, no games, no copouts, no hints and teases. It's not good enough any longer. It should never have been good enough.

What else? – that was the problem with the whole night: I never knew what was happening, or why, or what I was saying or what I was supposed to be saying. I was playing catch-up all night. I did catch-up in the end. There was tenderness, then some love. The way he came charging out of that room, he couldn't let me go. It's funny, all the times I've known that dishing out ultimatums and walking to the door would not work, the one time I just do it, don't think about it, it works; he stops me. There was hope there. Then he said he was stupid: "I'm stupid." You're not stupid Alex, that much you're not. What you are, I don't know. Maybe just scared. But I don't fall in love with stupid men. Even the games you play, they aren't the games of a stupid man. They are too well played. Too subtle, too well balanced, kept so close to the edge. You're not stupid. Wrong, but not stupid.

What else – what else? Come on, think girl. I can't spend two hours fighting and not remember it when I get home. But it's all a blur. Let me think. Okay, I told him I couldn't be there anymore under those circumstances. What did he say? Nothing. Or something like did he have to phone me and make dates—he didn't understand. He thinks in those terms, and I don't care about dates and phone calls and all the trappings of that boy-meet-girl crap. I just want him there, the way he used to be. I don't want to be a part of his routine, or him to be a part of mine. I want him to be a lover, and the great lover doesn't understand that.

What else? I don't remember – I don't believe this. How can I know . . . he said that some people need to be led around, and he was one of them. No. He's not. He wasn't. How can I get him to feel like that again if he doesn't think he is anymore? I'm believing in him more than he is. It's all I can do. At least I'm making it a little harder for him to turn his life into some black farce.

He just won't understand anything; he doesn't want to. Even tonight, if I asked him to explain tonight, he wouldn't know what to say, he wouldn't know what he felt, or why he felt it, or what he wanted, and he wouldn't bother to find out. He'd say he felt guilty or bad or horny or something. He'd twist it until black was white and white was black. He's so much fun.

He didn't do any of that tonight. Give him some credit. Of course he couldn't tonight. I was saying goodbye, so he had to say hello. I was saying no, so he had to say yes. But he was being honest. He said what he believed about him—how can anyone believe such crap about himself? He can't, he can't . . . I won't let him.

Okay. He was loving me at the door, more than if we had gone back into his room and made love. He was moved. I didn't expect that. It came from nowhere at me. Never before, never anywhere near that much honesty from him in the past – no, lots of times, but not when he's knowing that he's doing it. That's what he doesn't understand about us, that way we can be that honest without knowing it – no, it's not that he doesn't understand, won't admit it, because he thinks that it's the admitting that's the commitment, not the having, so he won't admit it, but that doesn't make it go away, because it is the having that commits. And that doesn't go away. It doesn't. It's damn near a miracle, but it really doesn't. We hurt each other. We leave each other for months. Then we meet, and it is still there, in an instant it is there, without the hurting and the leaving touching it, until we do it again. Hurt and leave. But we wouldn't do it again at all if he would but admit that we have that going for us because when two people can do what we do to each other—what he does to me—and still find the glow of sparks not once, but each time we need to find them, then they have something special, something so special it can survive the abuse. Or maybe it is that special quality that causes the abuse, because maybe it is that special quality that is too much for him. Maybe when the pleasures come at him so fast, so strong, so real, he must run. Maybe he is that innocent of bliss.

I need to walk through his mind. Just for a few seconds. I would know then, I would sleep then. I would know if it's worth it or not.

What else was said? That saving him nonsense. I almost forgot that. Is that the way he sees it? I don't want to save him, I have no interest in saving him, I don't want to stay to save him, I don't get jollies from talking to him about his problems. I am not the female counterpart to Prince Valiant. He'd better get over that one. The one day we don't have to bother with all that crap . . . that's the day I want, that's the day we'll work. We don't work like that, on that level. If he thinks we do, he's missed it, he's missed it all. Does he really believe that I want that? I guess he thinks that's how I care. He's wrong. He'd be closer to the truth if he said I was there for sex. 'Cause I am, in a way. Not to save him.

I don't understand it. I don't know what happened there to-night. Did I say anything that made sense? Did he hear anything? I didn't know it was coming, that's the problem; I didn't know it was coming. I really didn't expect it. Maybe he was just cashing in on what I said about not liking rejection. Maybe he thought I would take it to avoid rejection. Probably. Thought he'd sneak it in by me, cash in on a weakness. But I know what I want. If only . . . I've thought that so much.

All the maybes and the if-onlies came down to one: if he would want it, recognize it, reach out and go for it. Sometimes he does, and I let that be good enough. But maybe it has to be good enough, because you can't have it all every time, and I don't want to be an ornament on his arm. But it's not good enough. That's what I tried to tell him tonight. And I did. I said what I wanted, and I said what had to be said, even if it sounded like cheapened psychology. That's the issue. All that stuff about him, all the stuff that he thinks I say to save him, that's all crap thrown in to keep us from having to deal with the real stuff – it's escape. It keeps me from saying "I want this from you," keeps us shadow dancing. Not now. He knows where I stand, what I want. I'm not going to back down – I would in a second if he said "I can't," instead of "I won't." That's loving him. I can't take space from him. I can't tell him he has to be a perfectly functioning adult simply because I require a perfectly functioning adult. Catch 22. And I can't force things from him either. I don't want to play the vice grip all my life. That's what his little girlfriend doesn't understand: she has nothing because he merely lets her hang around, he doesn't choose her. But that's the way he likes it, because then he always has that power. He'd let me hang around, get my claws into him, and not let go, but there's no commitment from him in that. It would be the same as now – worse.

I'd really thought he meant that night, and I'm still sure he did. Too much so – too much was revealed. He made me believe again when I was choosing not to. Damn – but he was all again. His chest, his heartbeat, his touch, his life, all there again. Make Love to me. Stay for me, please. I haven't had any loving since you and that was so long ago Kim. All the pain will go away if you stay. You Love me any way you want, you do anything you want, I'm yours. Next time it will all be for you, Kim, please. You should never have let me hear you say that. And the way you said it, not pleading – I couldn't have taken pleading – and not a little boy crying for comfort either. You were sincere, open. I wasn't going to have you. I was going to drop you off there and leave. I was going to let it be over between us, just like I was tonight, and you stopped me. And you were sober, or at least in the haze of breaking through. You knew, you knew all the consequences. But now: "hold yourself down, hold yourself down, why d'ya hold yourself down" . . . you are the world when you don't. And the risks never hurts until you make it hurt – you make it hurt us both for nothing.

Oh, God, how about some crisis intervention? It's always

worked before. We're great in a crisis. I should probably thank You for the few You've tossed our way. They make him honest. Unfortunately, we can't live in a state of perpetual crisis. And it wouldn't be good enough either.

I've tried to stay away from games Alex. I've never even tried to make you jealous, and that would be easy and likely effective. But I don't like games. I want you to choose freely, and I want to choose freely. That's so important to me. So know this: This is not a game. I won't be back if you back out now. This is an ultimatum, yes, but no game. I won't be back. You won't believe it. My past behavior will deny it. It will be true. I'm not taking anymore. I'm not losing sleep over you anymore. I'm not going to pick up on your little messages anymore. For once, when you make a decision, even a bad decision, it's going to stick. You don't have to believe this now, you'll believe it a few months or a year down the road. I just don't want you thinking you can say no and make me start saying yes this time. You say no, you'd better mean no. You need it written in blood? It is, and in tears and pain and seven years of history. Even tonight was just too much pain, too much confusion. You made me pay for your emotions. I wouldn't mind, if it helped, but it doesn't. It just goes on and on and on. No more. Tonight was my best shot, and if it misses, if you won't see me again. And that would be a great loss for you because I'm the only sober one in your life.

But you can't hear me.

Oh, God, let him hear me, give me that much of a miracle. I hear him sometimes, You give me that. Let me be near him, not him near me. Help me be near him, touch him. When it's knocking in him, touch him and let him know that it is good. Don't let him run.

When he said, "Don't you have something to say," I should have said, "Yes, I love you." Right in the midst of it – the risk, the denial, the games, the lies, the power tripping; I could have blown it all apart. No guts. Maybe I don't love him. I'm not always sure that I do. It shouldn't take guts, but it does. More and more as the years go by. I'm getting old. The risk, I know it better now. Pain.

Let it go, Kim, and get some sleep. There's nothing left to do now. If you didn't do it earlier, it can't be done. You left it in his hands. You didn't have to. You don't even have to bother with ultimatums, you could give him orders. But he's not worth much is he? No, I don't know what went down tonight. And I don't know why it went down. I don't think he does either. But I have to get some sleep. Maybe I'll understand it better in the morning. I think I can sleep now. I think I'm empty enough now. Relax. Let go. Don't think anymore. Count sheep. Count backwards. One hundred, Ninety-nine. Ninety-eight. Ninety-seven. Ninety-six. Ninety-five. Ninety-four. Ninety-three. . . .

3

Well, that was different. I sure let that get out of hand. Blew that – so she isn't going to take me anymore – 'we aren't going to take it anymore,' that's what I want to hear, yeah, a little *Tommy*, that's what I need. Where's that tape? Who's been fucking around here – that's it. There. What a night. He threw in the tape for *Tommy* – that's what I need, someone to cheer me – she should try to cheer me. That would be different, wouldn't it Kim, eh? Ever think of that? Just let me alone, let me feel good? – I can't save you – you should be with someone where you don't even have to try. I'm too stupid for you, I can't make it happen for you. Fuck, I don't want to listen to this side, it's on the last side . . . there. So she's not going to take it anymore. That's good. That's the way it should be. Yeah, I guess I don't give her much of a chance—I told her I'd change, I told her to come back to bed, she could have. She didn't have to go that far . . . she was getting personal. It's like summoning up through demons. What did she mean by that? You want to be just a body – maybe it's all I can clinch. Yeah, you may as well throw me back Kim. I'm too small fry for you. Keep fishing 'til you get yourself a bigger catch.

I shouldn't let her get to me—it's because I don't see things. *There are forces around you, feeding you ideas, but you can refuse. How?* She never gets to the how. Because there isn't any way. Because the world just won't take it. Water on oil, that's all her ideas are, that's all I'd be if I listened to her. You don't make it that way, Kim. You make it by feeding on those 'forces,' by going with it, because that's where the action is, where it happens.

And he reached for a joint to make it all go away.

"then"

4

He rushed up the stairs, taking two at a time, and again he wanted to try taking three in a leap, and again he didn't. Because he couldn't. In the newer stores he could, he knew, because he'd seen how they were built and they were built for speed; they were built so that a guy could get things done, could just move through the place, could show them all just how fast a job could get done, and could do it without being sorry about breaking his neck – weren't built to save maybe thirty cents on a light socket and about a foot of storage space while wasting maybe two minutes of staff time, per staff member, per day, like here. Here. He put his hands out against the wall and thrust himself up the last four steps; it was all he could do here.

He rushed down the hall too, stopping just at the door to the coffee room. And there he was: an abrupt cessation of movement, like a sudden splash, a wave. It suited him, he knew: it was the way he liked to enter a room. He didn't know what it was – maybe the air kept moving around him, rushing into the room still yet missing something because he didn't come in with it, and everyone had to look up then, and wait for what the air was missing; he didn't know, but he knew he looked good, and he knew if he threw on a smile just as he stopped sharp, he would pretty much catch them, whoever they were – young, old, male, female, they all always looked up and smiled, and waited for him to come in the room. While he stood there and took them in. Just like now. The girl had looked up from her forms, and was smiling and noticing, anticipating and waiting. He leaned against the door jam and took stock. She was a pretty thing – not as young-looking as he expected, but he'd never been a good judge of that sort of thing – with dark hair framing a small tanned face, and dark curls sitting on small shoulders. He liked her – he liked small firm girls, and she looked firm, although he couldn't see much of her with the table cutting across her. But he could see possibilities here. "Hi there."

"Hi."

The voice wasn't a disappointment either. It was clear and soft. He crossed his arms on his chest and smiled smugly. He knew how he was going to play this scene. He was going to have some fun. "So you're Kimberley Karris, and you're starting with us next week."

"Yeah, that's right."

She looked puzzled, her face and body, giving into that little turn that questioned: "how did you know?" He grinned and stood straight. This was the way he liked to start things off, because he loved to take them in, just for a moment, just long enough to have tricked them. "You'll be working nights and weekends until you finish school. One year left, right?"

"But I was only hired a minute ago."

And her eyes flustered around for a moment, asking how he knew. He laughed a little, and saw her smile – she was trying to smile with him, but she was still asking, he had her going now. "That's right. You were just hired about five minutes ago."

"Does news always travel this fast around this place?"

"It does if you're the right person in the right place at the right time." He leaned against the door jam again.

"And that's you?"

And now she was half-amused, her face changing into a teasing smile but not so sure to laugh. She'd caught him, and she was pretty sure of it, but not enough to bet. He laughed – he didn't care, didn't need to care because he didn't need to be "the man" to get a girl; he had a face that did it for him. He let his smile admit his tease – to charm – and he shrugged. "It's not that hard to be the right guy in the right place around here."

"Griffins said it was a small store."

"Yeah?" He walked into the room, and, turning a chair around so that it's back faced her, sat down across from her, drumming his fingers against the back of the chair. He liked her, so far. He wanted to know more of her. "What else did Griffins say?"

"Not much. Nothing that you haven't already said."

"No?"

"No. I think you've pretty much covered it."

Her eyes were gray, light gray and they stood out on her face: smoke. And they watched him now, closely, although she smiled and shrugged. He knew she was liking him, liking what she saw. He kept smiling.

"He said he couldn't promise me any hours."

"He could have. You'll get between sixteen and twenty hours a week. We're short at least that. We could use twenty-four hours." And his smile dashed to his eyes; he knew how to tease here too. "That should be enough to keep you out of trouble til June, right?"

"Could be."

"And you'll get all the lousy shifts too, because that's what we hire students for: the Friday nights and Saturdays and Sundays that everyone else phones in sick for." He was tilting his chair forward on its hind legs, and he was watching her face. "Griffins will give you just enough of them to break up your weekend. What do you think?" She looked amused – almost blushing. And he wanted to know just what wild-weekend thoughts he was bringing to her mind. "Aren't you glad you found work?"

"I better not complain since news travels so fast around here."

He laughed – he liked her. "So what do you do for fun?"

"Apparently nothing."

"This is true." He raised his eyebrows in a salute. "But what did you used to do?"

"Who are you?"

She'd asked quietly, flashing her eyes away from him for the second before, almost as if she was taking on the embarrassment herself. And he appreciated it; it was his mistake. "Alex, Alex Talon. It's Kim, isn't it? No one calls you Kimberley?"

"No one but my mom. She has to call me that all the time."

"Yeah?" He laughed. He had a mom like that. "My mom does that too – Alexander, she drags that up all the time when I go there."

"It didn't bother me when I was a kid, you know, because when she'd scream 'Kimberley Karris' around the block, it never mattered how mad she was, she couldn't sound it."

"Yeah?"

"I told her it wasn't my fault I always laughed when she yelled. I didn't name me."

She was half impulsed and half abashed; she was charming.

"But then she said that they weren't trying for that either. I was named after my aunt on my Mom's side of the family. That disappointed me – isn't that funny? I told them that that made them a lot less interesting people."

And now she as all abashment but she didn't have to be, because he knew what she meant. His name was the same way, but the other way around. His mom had chosen it quite deliberately, wanted a name that "called men to arms," as she described it. But he hadn't known that when he was a little boy, learning how to roll his name off his tongue, in French style, trying to create the sound of it: 'Alexander Talon.' He'd have been more than disappointed to find that that sound was some accident – he'd been proud to discover it wasn't. Even now, when his friends sneered it as "Alex-and-her-talons" – which didn't bother him because that was the way it was, and his friends were not able even to wonder why him while knowing why not them – even sneered, he could still hear that old sound of it. So he smiled at her, knowing. "Pissed you right off, didn't it?"

"I don't know. They did seem a lot less interesting after that."

He knew that she was going to make a life a lot more interesting around here.

"Alex Talon. That's like a voyager's name."

"A what?"

"A voyager. You know, one of those early explorers. Canoes, Indians, trade."

"Oh yeah." He'd forgotten about them.

"Your name, it is French isn't it?"

"Talon is."

"All those voyagers were French. All the ones I've looked at anyway."

"Oh, I get it. Yeah, I see what you mean." And then he caught the thought she was inviting – expecting – feeding him. He leaned towards her in the chair again. "Yeah, we were French when we came over. Maybe that's what we were doing."

"Sure be a lot more interesting than that pilgrim stock, don't you think?"

"Yeah." He hadn't ever thought about it, but now. . . .

"See, it's an assignment. For a class."

She was embarrassed again. He smiled.

"We had to choose between the pilgrims and the voyagers, were they 'civilizing influences?' I took the voyagers."

She was talking so fast that she was stumbling all over her words, but he didn't mind. Because he was stunned. Because she wasn't what he'd expected, but was a rush, and he hadn't even hoped for a rush – or thought of it. He'd expected a high school girl, either prim or punk. He hadn't expected to get charged, and he hadn't expected to connect – or even to want to. And here she was, feeding him things he knew – felt – but had never stopped to think.

"I bet you do your assignments the night before they're due."

"Sometimes."

"Yeah, I bet you stay up all night, cramming it together and then you get A's, right?" He dropped his chair back on its four legs.

"Sometimes."

"Yeah, I can see it." And he grinned at her, and she looked away, shyly. He laughed.

"Sometimes I just get B's."

He laughed again, but he knew he had to get going. He glanced over her shoulder, towards the door. Griffins would be coming up any moment to catch him. "You going to be around for a while?"

"I'm supposed to fill out these forms. You guys sure have enough of them."

"Yeah, ever since we got a personnel department. It gives them something to do." He was thinking. He didn't know how to ask her. "If it takes you about an hour, I get lunch then. You be around?"

"Um . . . yeah, sure."

She looked surprised. He was a little surprised at himself too; he didn't date the girls he worked with. "Good." He had to get going. He stood up and looked out the door, then back at her. "Meet me outside the store?"

"Okay."

"Right at eleven-thirty. That's when I go."

"Okay."

"I have to get back to work."

"I thought you were on a coffee break, or something."

"No." Then he remembered what he'd been sent up here for: the form. He took it out of his pocket and passed it over to her. "I brought this up to you. Griffins forgot it."

"Oh."

She was laughing. He shrugged. "I remembered before I got downstairs."

"Yeah."

"Could have been worse."

"Yeah."

And she kept smiling. He nodded at her, smiling too. He had to leave. He had to get back to work. "Eleven-thirty."

"Right outside the store."

"Right. See you?"

"Yeah."

And she bit her bottom lip a little; he liked her. He smiled again, and left. He had to get that work done. He rushed down the hall and then the stairs, taking them one at a time now, but bouncing his hands against the walls, for speed. And then he was back at work, thinking that he liked her.

He was surprised with himself, and he liked that too. It had been a long time – if ever – that a girl had had this sort of effect on him. But he liked her – liked it – and didn't just want to take her; he wanted to get to know her, and he was actually looking forward to lunch.

Because she was a bit of a rush – he knew it, felt it; sure be a lot more interesting than that pilgrim stock, don't you think and he knew too that she'd taken the voyagers because they weren't a 'civilizing influence.' He knew it from the way she had said it, the way she'd leaned forward just as she spoke, as if she was sharing a secret with him, and maybe she was; not everyone would say it, because not everyone could feel it, could feel the burst inside when the rules were dropped.

She'd brought something back to him – that was it – something familiar and forgotten, something he knew but couldn't reach to touch. It was a feeling, and it laid in the rush of her, and he hadn't even noticed that he'd lost it until now. He was glad he was seeing her at lunch. He wouldn't have long to wait. Lunch was just past these two skids of stock. And so he went at them.

Until he saw her leaving. She didn't see him, but he spotted her up front, talking to Griffins, and then heading to the doors. He stopped to watch her. He liked her walk. He liked the way she stood. He liked the movement in her body, and he was pleased to see that he'd called that right too. She was slim and small, had nice legs, and a nice ass. She looked like she exercised, kept herself up. He smiled and watched until she was out of the store. For once, he thought, he agreed with Griffins' choice, even approved. He wanted lunch.

At eleven-thirty, he walked out of the store, already looking around for her, and he saw her standing beside the shopping carts: She'd changed since she'd been in to apply. She wasn't wearing a skirt now, just gray pants and a light shirt. And she wore it well. She wasn't wearing a bra, and she didn't need one. He smiled. "Hi. Where do you want to go? I only get an hour."

"Where do you usually go?"

"To the cafe here. Is that okay with you?"

"Sure."

But he didn't want to go there. He was too known there. He wanted to be alone with her. He looked down the street and around the mall, but he knew there was nowhere else. "Yeah, I guess we have to."

"What?"

He hadn't realized that he'd spoken. He shrugged. "Let's go then." And he dropped his arm around her shoulders for an instant, just long enough to turn her into the right direction, and just long enough to assure himself that she wanted his touch. "It's just down there. It's not usually too busy around this time."

"You eat there every day?"

"No. It depends." He glanced at her beside him, and saw that she was nearly running to keep up. He was moving too fast. But he wanted to move. He wanted to dig his heels into the ground and push hard against the earth – thrusting his feet hard enough and fast enough into the earth to make the day's spin increase, to bring the moment to him now. Because beside her again, he felt it again, but stronger. Now it was in him in a way that it hadn't been since he'd stopped jamming with the guys in a basement – and that was the feeling; he recognized it: breaking loose. He reined himself in and slowed his step. "Sorry." But they were already at the cafe. He pushed the door open and ushered her in front of him. "We usually sit at the back, that table." And he sat them down at the table and started drumming his fingers on the table-top – what would she do? what would she open?

"You know, it's funny, but I don't live ten minutes from here, but I haven't been in here before."

"There's no salads or anything like that, but if you like burgers, the cheeseburgers are pretty good."

"Oh. Okay. I'll have a cheeseburger."

He looked around for the waitress. It was Sandy today, which meant it was Tuesday. Sandy wasn't too bad. Gracie would have been worse with all her friendliness. He motioned Sandy over.

"Hi there. How's it going today?"

"Not very busy."

"Bit of a break then?"

"Yeah. You two want coffee?"

"Sure." He turned his cup over and looked at Kim. "Did you want coffee too?"

"No, I think I'll have an iced tea."

Kim spoke to Sandy, smiling and polite, and Alex didn't like it. These two wouldn't get along, he knew it. Sandy wouldn't like polite, and Kim wouldn't like Sandy, and they'd both look at him, wondering. He didn't want them talking, not today. He wanted Kim to know him first.

"She'll have an iced tea."

"I got that. You two ready to order?"

"Sure. We're both having cheeseburgers – did you want fries Kim?" He looked directly into her eyes, forcing her to answer to him.

"No, I don't think so."

"Did you want something else instead. You have tossed salads, don't you, Sandy?"

"We have coleslaw if you don't want the fries, or potatoes, mashed."

"Did you want coleslaw?" He kept looking right at her.

"No, just the burger."

"She'll just have the cheeseburger, and I'll have the fries with gravy."

"Yeah, and you'll want apple pie and ice cream for dessert, I bet."

Sandy was looking at him with a friendly sneer on her face: she was bringing it out – showing Kim him before he'd had a chance to – and waiting for him to take the bait and say something about burning it off tonight. And if he didn't, she wouldn't just wonder why, she'd pass it around that Alex was in acting weird because of a girl. He played it casually, stretching out a little in the booth. "Hey, you can't pinch an inch here."

"What are you going to do when you lose that body and don't have anything to work with?"

"Hey, now, come on." He looked hurt, and she looked satisfied.

"Did you want the tea now or with the burger?"

"Now please."

"I'll be right back."

Alex watched her drop her checks into her pocket and go back into the kitchen. He quickly turned back to Kim, scanning her face for changes. She looked just the same, still shy. "I've known her since I started working here."

"When was that?"

"Bout a year ago, a year November, it will be. I started just before the Christmas rush got going."

"So what do you do there?"

"I'm the assistant manager."

"What?"

And now her face was changed. She was drawing back. She was impressed in all the wrong ways. He talked fast. "Yeah, we've had real problems with assistant managers. We had two in the first few months that I was here. You see the store is way out here, and when head office sent someone from town, well, they took it like a demotion, and wouldn't work. The last guy had all the boys sitting in the back room with him." He took out his cigarettes and offered her one while he talked. He wouldn't have this seem important. "So when he had to go, head office decided not to send anyone else, and I was there, and now I'm here. No big deal."

"They must have liked you to promote you like that."

"I know the business. My old man had me working in his store when I was eight." Sandy was back with Kim's drink. Alex lit his cigarette while she gave it to her; he didn't have to talk to her. And it worked. She simply left. "There's not really anything to it. I just do the stuff Griffins doesn't like. He's been around so long that he doesn't need an assistant. He runs the place even when he's off."

"He's been here a long time, hasn't he? Dad said something about that."

"He's been here years. I think he came with the store."

"So are you being groomed to take over from him or something?"

"No." He didn't want to talk about this. He wanted to feel that energy again. "I'm just getting through the day, like everyone else."

"It's just that you seem young to be assistant manager. I didn't think you were that much older than me."

And in that, he caught her. She was blushing; she was pushing herself back into the booth; she was recoiling from her blurting. He leaned towards her, smiling. "Just how old do you think I am?"

"I didn't think you were much older than me."

"How old?"

"Not twenty."

She'd decided to be brave.

"You're right, I'm not twenty."

"Then, how old are you?"

"Nineteen."

"That's about what I thought. It must be nice to know where you're going when you're nineteen."

"What do you mean? What makes you think I know that?"

"Don't you?"

"You're telling me I do."

"No – I just meant . . ."

She looked at his cigarette, but he didn't want her to stop. He wanted to get into that mind. "What did you mean?"

"It's just that this is grade twelve and they keep asking what we think we'll be doing this time next year. Didn't you get that?"

"No."

"Well, they keep asking, and it's only September and I know

that they're going to keep asking til June, and I never know what to say. You seem to have that."

He'd never looked at it that way, and now, hearing it, he had to laugh. Because if the school had asked him that, he'd have said, "not a grocer."

"I was just thinking it must be nice to know where you're going to be in a year."

He laughed out loud. "You think I know that?"

"Yeah."

"You think I'm sitting pretty, don't you?"

"Aren't you?"

"I'm not staying in the grocery business, I'll tell you that."

"Why not?"

"You really want to know?" He wanted to tell her. He hadn't told anyone else.

"Yes."

"Because everyone who stays here turns into an asshole." He watched her face. She looked interested, not shocked. "It's okay if you have your own store like my dad did – he was okay – but if you stay with the company, nope. You should see these guys come in. They really want you to scramble all over them. I'm getting out of this business."

"What are you going to do?"

"I don't know. No idea. But a year from now I won't be around here." He saw Sandy bringing their burgers over to them, and he leaned back to give her the space on the table.

"You want more coffee there?"

He'd drank the cup. "Yeah, that would be great, and a glass of milk with this, okay?"

"Be right back."

He looked down at his plate. He'd gotten an extra large serving of fries and extra gravy. He smiled; Sandy knew how to take care of him. And she brought him a beer glass of milk.

"Thanks, Sands."

"No problem."

He looked back at Kim. "This looks good."

"You must be starving."

"Yeah. I worked hard all morning, and I didn't eat breakfast."

He started eating. The food tasted great.

"It's good to have hot food for a change."

"You don't come over here all the time?"

"No, too expensive. I usually brown bag it or buy something if I forget to make a lunch. I probably come here once a week."

"I guess in a grocery store, it's pretty easy to get lunch."

"You have to buy the whole oaf of bread and a pound of butter and whatever else you want, so I try to remember to make a lunch."

"I never thought of that."

"And then if head office shows up and sees bags of groceries in the coffee room, they start to hassle Griffins and he passes it on to us."

"What?"

They were talking between bites of food, and Alex had to swallow before answering her. "We're not supposed to keep groceries around. If you buy something, Griffins is supposed to check through the bag and then staple it together with the receipt and initial it. And then he's supposed to check it on the way out to make sure nothing's been dropped in, you know. Head office sees all these bags of bread laying around – no one gets Griffins to check them because it's a hassle – and they come down on him for encouraging shoplifting."

"What?"

"That's what happens." She wasn't eating now. She was staring at him, almost through him.

"That's sick. That's treating everyone like a bunch of thieves before they've done anything."

"Studies show that most of the shoplifting is done by staff."

"And that's supposed to explain that? What do they think I'm going to do – stuff an extra carton of milk in with my bread?"

"Apparently – this happened before I came – one girl stuffed roast beef in with her bread. It does happen."

"That doesn't mean I'm going to do it."

He laughed. He wanted to be there when she saw the rules posted in the change rooms.

"That's insulting."

"That's head office."

"It's no bloody wonder that they have thieves working for them then. They ask for it."

"You think that's the way it works?"

"Probably."

"Maybe." He shrugged. "How's the burger?"

"Oh. Good."

She picked it up and started eating again. He started on his fries. "You want a couple."

"No, thanks. I'm almost full."

"You eat like a bird, then."

"I had breakfast."

"Yeah, you live at home still. I bet your mom makes you breakfast."

"No. She's working nights now. I have cereal."

"What does she do?"

"She's a nurse."

"That's a good job. Why don't you go into that?"

"It's Mom's job."

He nodded. He knew. "You want something for yourself."

"That's exactly right."

"I don't blame you. That's what life's all about, you know. Experiencing things for yourself. It's no good just to step into other people's shoes."

"Is that what you think you've done? Stepped into your dad's?"

"Sort of. Some days." He didn't know what he thought about his life; he hadn't thought much about it. "It's not a bad job, for the money. Customers can be a pain, but it's not a bad job. But it's a job, you know?" He watched her smile and nod and encourage him. "What you were talking about earlier, the voyagers, something like that, now that would be something." She was taking in the thoughts he was feeding her. He went on. "Being out there, really on your own, and making it or dying. That would be something. You had a chance then, you know?" He felt energies stirring in him, and he could see she felt the same. Her eyes – he could almost see the fires starting behind the smoke. "You went down a river, not knowing that there'd be a nice little safe town all set up with everything you'd want around the next bend, and you were all alone, with a couple of guys maybe who were no different than you. And you just keep going, and you had to be ready for anything. You could do it right there."

"I guess mountaineers have that today."

"But that's a hobby." Somehow, hobbies weren't enough. Life on the line wasn't enough. "You ever canoe?"

"Yeah. It's part of P.E."

"It's pretty good, isn't it? I went down the rapids once, in a canoe, and it was something else." And he remembered: he'd almost stopped breathing in that rush, it had been so incredible. He'd known then he was alive. But he'd come back, and told them, and they'd been so-what about it. "You ever try that?"

"No. We just went out on the lake."

"You should try it. You really should." He'd forgotten all about that until now. He'd been whipped around like a bull in a bull-fight, but he'd won. He hadn't been in a canoe since then.

"You want to go canoeing next weekend?"

"Sure."

But she looked startled. He laughed. He hadn't thought of asking her, but he was glad he did. It had been too long since he was out there with the water and the wind. "We can go on the lake, if you want."

"I don't think I'm ready for rapids."

"We can go Saturday. I have Saturday off this week."

"I'm in Saturday, for two hours to train."

"What? Did Griffins set that up?"

"Yes. Why?"

"Ah, there's really nothing else he can do. It's head office's policy, but it's stupid. It just closes a checkout for two hours at the busiest time." It was one of his pet peeves – too often customers had come to him wanting to know why 'that girl' wouldn't take their groceries. "What hours? – twelve to two."

"Nine to eleven."

"That's not too bad there. We can go right after that."

"Okay."

"Good." He nodded his head, satisfied.

"Actually, I have to get going."

She was picking up her purse. "Why? I still have some time. You don't have to go."

"I do have to. I have an appointment with the counselor in about two minutes."

"Oh, I see. Going to tell them what you'll be doing this time next year. Tell them you're going to be a voyager."

"They'd probably set me up in the space program or something if I said that."

"They're that bad?"

"She says she wants us to succeed. I think she wants me to suffocate."

"Don't let her crowd you."

"Right."

And she stood up and smiled at him.

"So I'll see you Saturday?"

Now she was shy again. He smiled. "Yeah, I'll pick you up at twelve-thirty. He can be up to the lakes by one, one-thirty. How's that sound?"

"Good. Do you want my address or anything?"

"I'll get it off your application."

"Oh, you look at that, do you?"

"Yeah, sure do." He grinned.

"See you later, then."

"Bye-bye." He watched her leave and then found Sandy standing beside him.

"You were sure running off at the mouth today."

"Jealous, eh?" He grabbed her around the waist and pulled her into the booth. "Where's my apple pie and ice cream, my dear? You're getting slow."

"Let me go and I'll get it?"

"And hurry it up too. I can't sit here all afternoon." He slapped her butt as she left, and then he called out, "And coffee, I could use a refill here."

S he needed a friend to tell of her find, one who would listen quietly– not one of those girls who'd talk and talk, interject-ing all the time with tales of lust, or worse, attributing to her those lusty motives – because it wasn't lust. Yes, she needed a2 friend who'd listen, nod, and go away, someone who'd let her tell it and still let her keep it close to her, safe. Someone to understand quietly.

She knew the understanding would be a lot harder to come by than the silence. All of her friends would be pretty quiet if they heard her now; none would understand. They wanted her to fall for the "right" guys, the ones who sat around talking about saving the world, feeding hungry and making justice more just. The future bleeding hearts. And she did like and admire those guys, but they were pretty dull dates. A little necking interrupting a stream of social consciousness. No. But her friends were going to have some trouble seeing her with the one she wanted. They'd never see his charm. They would just see that he would never be a bleeding heart. But that was part of his appeal, because it was part of his life, spirit. He could run away with things; he could dash and leap and lead.

She'd tried an appeal to Karen, her best friend. She'd told Karen that he was more than cool, that he was special, that he had it, that he made excitement – was excitement. That he could do.

Karen had said that he had looks – which was obvious to anyone at twenty feet away – but that perhaps he was not Kim's type, "in the long run," that perhaps he was "too ordinary." Ordinary. Some people were born to be old. Kim had smiled at Karen, politely, and left. Later, thinking it over, she'd decided that some people had some real problems living, that some people couldn't see some things at all, that some people were dull from birth, and that she had always known that about Karen.

So she went over to Patty's. Patty was a girl from work, not one of Kim's longtime friends. Patty, Kim had gathered from Alex, was one of the students that failed to quit after graduation. Kim liked Patty, genuinely. And it helped that Patty knew Alex outside of work. Alex hung out with her boyfriend. So Patty was her next and her best bet. Patty, she was hoping, would be a source of information, if groomed right. But first Kim wanted to sound Patty out, make sure that Patty wasn't interested in him for herself. So she sat there, across the table from Patty, drinking coffee she hadn't learned to like. "I'm working Thursday and Friday nights and all day Sunday."

"Those are lousy shifts. Students always get stuck with the lousy shifts, though, so don't take it hard. I'm in Sunday, so we'll be working together then, but on Friday you're stuck with Brenda, and since she thinks any late night is punishment, she's bound to be in one of her moods."

"The last few nights I've worked, it's been so busy that I haven't had time to know what mood anyone is in."

"That's good. The time goes by a lot faster if there's some people in the store."

"A couple of nights, there was no one in, and I felt like I was there forever. I watched the clock turn all night."

"Those dead nights are something else. You stand there and think of all the things you could be doing, especially if it's a Friday or Saturday night. That kills me. I hate that. It's bad enough working nights."

"This is true." She knew she had picked up that expression from Alex. She liked using it. "This is true."

"You sound like you've been around the guys. Tony's always saying that."

"No, no. I don't know. I just picked that up somewhere. Maybe at the store. Alex is always saying it, that and he says 'no problem' all the time."

"You've just noticed Alex a little bit, haven't you?"

Patty was laughing. Kim could feel herself blushing. She looked down into her coffee cup. "He works Thursday nights and Sundays, so I see him more than Griffins at the store."

"Yeah, right."

Patty was still laughing. Kim didn't look up.

"Here, let me give you something to look at in that cup."

"Uh?"

"A refill, more coffee?"

"No, I'm fine. Yeah, Brenda can be a bitch can't she? One night, she took a good half hour for coffee and left me to cover for her."

"She does that to everybody, and she'll be the first to start bitching if anyone else is late coming back."

"Good, I thought she just didn't like me."

"She probably doesn't. She doesn't like anyone."

"Thanks."

"You'll get used to her. We all ignore her. She knows that we can make life pretty miserable for her if she pushes too far, so she keeps her distance now. She'll leave you alone if you tell her you aren't going to take it. You have to stand up to her."

"I don't think I can do that." And she wasn't sure how she was supposed to pump Patty either. She didn't know any pumping techniques. She tried one. I guess I could ask Alex about it."

"No, you don't want to do that. It would be a bad situation to put him in. He'd just tell you what I told you anyway. Maybe you could let Brenda know that you're seeing him. That would turn her around. I'd like to see that. She's a real ass-kisser."

"I'm what?" Kim didn't know how Patty knew – Kim didn't know that Patty knew. "I'm seeing Alex?"

"Oh, you didn't know I knew that. Alex told Tony, and Tony told me. You don't want the store to know, do you? I won't tell anyone – I haven't yet."

"Good." Kim was still stunned. But now she had an opening. "So what did Alex say?"

"I don't know. Just that he wasn't coming out with us because you two were going to a show or something like that. He didn't really say anything. Alex doesn't talk much, at least, Tony doesn't say what Alex said."

"Oh. Well, good. I really don't want to be gossip for Marg and Robby."

"Yeah, they would love to hear about this. They sort of have crushes on Alex, if girls their age have crushes."

"Do they?" Kim didn't like to hear that.

"Yeah, most of the girls there like Alex. Pretty much everyone has gone out with him – not the old ones. They buy him a beer after work."

"You too?"

"No, I watch. I love Tony. I just watch."

Patty sounded as if she was talking about some sport she rises above. Kim was getting mad. Patty made it sound like she was vying to join some in-store harem. All lust, and it wasn't lust at all – not just his looks: himself, the way he carried himself, the way he looked with his eyes: gestures inside of his eyes, gestures in his smile . . . the way he moved, the way he talked, the energy of the guy, the . . . it, the it that no one else had ever shown her.

"Alex goes through a good number of girls."

"You sound like he's . . . like he's collecting notches on his bedpost or something."

"He is."

She's had enough, just like she's had enough of Karen. She gets up. "I have to get going. I have a lot of homework."

"You don't want to hear it. But he is. That's what he's like. That's how he thinks and he'll never stop being like that. I'm only saying this because you're a nice kid, and you should know."

A kid – Patty was only three years older than her, not enough to lay claim to the wisdom of the ages. And Kim didn't have to justify herself to anyone. She picked up her coat. "Do me a favor. Don't call me kid."

"Don't get all worked up. If you want to think Alex is God's gift to womankind, go ahead. What the hell? – he does."

"Thanks for the coffee."

"No, sit down. I didn't mean anything by it, really."

"I don't need—"

"I didn't mean anything by it. Okay, I said it. I thought I should say it, but you don't have to listen if you don't want to. It's cool. Sit down."

Patty was pouring her more coffee.

"I want to hear about it. You must really like him to get this worked up."

"There's a lot there to like."

"There is. He's a nice guy. I like him. He's a good friend of ours. And I was glad when I heard you two were going out. Won't hurt Alex to get to know a nice girl for a change. He doesn't have good taste in women."

"Thanks a lot."

"I'm really fucking up here, aren't I? I always put my foot in my mouth. Tony tells me that. If I was out of line, I'm sorry. You can like anyone you want."

"Yes."

"And I can see why someone would like Alex. He's exciting. He said he likes you."

She put her coat down, and sat down. She didn't plan to share with Patty now, but she wasn't leaving until she'd heard each word Alex had said about her. "When did he say that?"

"That's what he told Tony, that he liked you, that he thought you were different, and I think he's right. I think he may be in for some-thing he hasn't known before now. He always thinks he can teach a girl a thing or two, but I think you can teach him a thing or two."

"How's that?"

"He hasn't gone out with a nice girl before. He usually dates sure bets, you know, and some of them, even Tony wonders how he can get with them, or at least that's what Tony says to me."

"He's not what you say he is, not around me. He's really very sweet. He doesn't seem always on the make. He's not an octopus."

"Then I'm glad for you both. Alex could use someone nice and straight in his life. I just thought I should say something, because I didn't know how much experience you've had with men."

"I know what the guy I'm sitting across from is like."

"I'm sure you do. I was out of line. Can we forget it?"

"Yes, but I just want you to understand. It's not what you think it is."

"You've got it bad."

But Patty's voice was soft now. She wasn't knowing it all now. And Kim wanted to tell, she had to tell, she couldn't hold it in any longer. "He has a wonderful smile." She felt all the warm feelings coming back, as if he was there smiling at her now. "He's fun, he's easy to be with. He gives me something . . . ease. And, I don't know, moving, we're always moving, always doing something, and he does everything so naturally. He moves people, he shows people what to do. He can control an entire room filled with strangers. We went out for dinner, and he had strangers pulling up their tables and sitting with us, to be near him, because he gives some-thing. There's no pause, no break, no hesitation in him. He even has perfect table manners, you know? He eats so tidily, my grandmother would love him. I don't know how to put it. I just look at him and forget everything else. He knows what to do always. He gets everyone going, everyone partying."

"Yeah." But Kim didn't think it was the same thing. But she didn't know how to tell Patty it was different. She put her hands around the warm coffee cup. "His smile tells you that he knows how to live. He knows things."

But that wasn't enough to tell Patty where Patty was wrong. There was something missing. . . . Patty didn't seem to understand the importance of him. That was it: Patty didn't know what it meant to make things happen, what it really meant – Patty didn't understand power. Patty saw it as just as good time to be had by all. Oh, but it was more than that; it was life itself, it was the only way to affect life.

"You want that warmed up?"

"When I first came into the store, I was handed a bunch of forms to fill out in the coffee room, and I was doing that when I knew that there was something else there. I looked up, and there he was, leaning against the door jam, completely still, but, I don't know, it was like the air was rearranging itself around him. There was some sort of movement . . . I don't know. And there was all this energy. I really wanted to know him right then. I talked to him – I wouldn't have talked to someone else like that. I would have waited until I knew more, I would have tested the waters, you know? I was really uptight, and when I'm uptight, I don't go out of myself, not like that. I don't let anyone near me when I'm like that. I don't trust myself when I'm like that. That's when I make mistakes, But I knew not with him. And we went for lunch, I was uptight again, and that was harder, but when we went to the movie, I don't even know what movie it was. It was. It was black and white; it was at the old film festival. There were tall women walking around in hats, smoking and being arrogant as all hell, but I don't know the movie. I watched it, but I didn't. I could feel too much of him. That doesn't make sense, does it?"

"No."

"But it did to him. He knew. I didn't have to put it into words for him. He said, 'don't worry,' and he smiled and he knew. I could feel that from him. I guess that's sensitivity, but somehow that doesn't say it all. He knew, and he knew how to guide the whole night. And he did. And I just let him. I don't do that. I don't trust like that. And I get bored easily, but I wasn't bored."

"Alex isn't boring for sure."

Patty wasn't following her. It didn't matter. She was thinking, aloud, figuring it out as she went through it. "You see, you hear about these things – I don't know where you hear about them, books maybe – Wuthering Heights maybe; you hear about them, and you like them, and want them, but you don't believe in them. Until you feel them – I've never felt even one desire before. I've been interested in things, lots of things, lots of times. I'm on the grad committee and student council and I've been out there for peace, and all the women's' issues. None of that has been really satisfying. This could be. This makes me feel good – this makes me feel something of me. This is what I want."

"Sit down. You're making me nervous."

Kim hadn't realized that she was pacing around the table. She sat down. "Sorry."

"I told you what Alex wants."

"You said what you think." And she knew that this was the wrong place to be at this time. It was time to leave, and to cover her tracks. "I'm just rambling. I don't even know what I'm saying."

"That makes two of us."

"Well, I got to go. Thanks for the coffee. I'll keep in mind what you said. I don't know. I've only seen Alex a few times in the last couple of months, so maybe I don't know all there is to know about him.

"I didn't mean to upset you, but I thought I should say something."

"I get it, don't worry."

"Thanks for coming over."

"Yeah, let's do it again. I only see you at work, and you can't talk there."

"Not unless you want it all over the store."

"That place is something else."

"Ain't that the truth."

"Well, don't say anything to anyone, will you?"

"Of course not, and if you want to talk some more, come over again."

"I will." She put on her coat and went to the door. "See you Sunday."

"Right."

And she escaped, to think alone. She knew what she wanted now, but she wasn't sure how to go about getting it, or if she could just go and get it. How did one take a man? Was she allowed to take a man? But she had to. People had bored her and frustrated her for a long time now. She'd thought them gutless. She had been surprised at their lack of push, desire. She had wanted desires. Now she had them, and she had to go for them. Because if she didn't have the guts to go for them, if she sat back and wrapped herself up in fears, what good was she to life? Life would just burp her up, like bad air. But what about her reputation – she didn't care. She'd never cared about that. But what about honor? She cared about honor. She liked the ideal of honor, and integrity. But honor was being true to oneself: "To thine own self be true." And that was right. And nothing had involved or excited something in her that screamed "self" like this did, not ever. She had to get herself this.

She'd driven straight to the store. She wasn't surprised. She walked right in, and started looking for him. He was in the fourth aisle. She went to the dairy, and picked up a quart of milk. There was no gain in being obvious. She went back to him. "Hi."

"Hi. What brings you in today?"

"We needed some milk." She held the quart forward to show him.

"Buying where you work, eh?"

"Something like that. How's it been today?"

"Steady, all day. It's been a good day."

"Good. The more business, the more hours for us stuck down at the bottom of the totem pole."

"This is true."

"So." She had to make a move or leave. Now. But it was harder than she'd expected. She started to sweat. And she knew he didn't like talking at work. He didn't need more gossip about him either. But she wanted to see him tonight. "So what are you doing tonight?"

"Why?"

His grin, and his eyes, laughing at her, but she'd expected that. She wasn't being subtle. She smiled back, trying not to be self-conscious. "I thought I'd buy you dinner for a change. I don't have any homework tonight."

"'Bout time you asked me out."

"Does that mean it's a date?"

"What time are you picking me up?"

"I could cook at your place."

"Yeah? You want to do that?"

Now she had surprised him. "You could come to my place, but I don't know if you want to talk to Mom and Dad all night."

"No, you come over. That sounds really good. I'm off at six, so maybe at seven?"

"Seven. Bye-bye." She turned quickly and left, barely remembering to pay for the milk on her way out. She was nervous. She knew she was putting something into motion, and she wouldn't relax until it was done. If it was. She didn't know how to finish it. She didn't know how to make those sorts of moves. But if Patty was right, she wouldn't have to worry about it.

She stopped off at another grocery store and bought the stuff for spaghetti—in all the movies, a good spaghetti sauce took three hours to simmer. Then she went home to dress, and wait.

There, her mother and brother and sisters were buzzing all around her, going through their traditional routine of asking about school and fighting over TV 'rights.' She barely heard them. Their voices were removed, clouded, vague. She gave the appropriate responses: "I'm going out for dinner, you'll meet him later." And they faded away, like phantom forms from a phantom world. She liked that. She didn't want them tonight. She wanted to come into her own tonight. She took a bath to pass the time.

And then it was time, and she was standing in front of his door, with a bag of groceries in her hand. She stalled. She didn't knock. She was too impressed with what could happen next. Having him. She didn't even know what that meant, not in any practical sense, and a practical sense could very easily become very important, very soon. Having him: having life, holding the spark. She wanted that. And it scared her – the sum, the substance of her life and self would be tested here. Not just in bed, although that intimacy was such an intimacy to have with someone who knew so intuitively so much; not just in bed, but the whole relationship with him. Did she have enough life to have a relationship with him?

Too many thoughts were coming too quickly. And all sensation was far too strong. Her emotions were filling each nerve. She had to knock. His door seemed huge. It loomed, almost like a sudden tree in a forest. She knocked, and smiled. He answered.

"Hi. Come on in. I thought I heard a car pull up."

He took the groceries. She followed him to the kitchen.

"What are we having?"

He looked through the bag. She hoped he'd seen the same movies.

"Looks like spaghetti to me."

"If you like it. If you want something else, I could change."

"No, I love it. Who doesn't? You want a drink now, or do you want to start cooking right away?"

"I'll start this. It needs to simmer for a while once it's put together. Where are the pots?"

"Right here, everything you need. I laid it out. You want me to stay and talk, or do you want me out of the way?"

"I think I want you out of the way. You go drink and relax. I'll be just a few minutes. I just have to get going."

"Come on into the living room when you're done."

– 64 –

"Yeah." He left, and she started chopping up onions and browning hamburger. She kicked herself for not having thought of chopping up everything at home, but, then, how could she have? Her parents would have asked too many questions. But it didn't take long. She had everything into the pot within fifteen minutes. She went into the living room. "I bought garlic and oregano. I'll leave it there. You don't have any spices."

"There's some, somewhere. But you can leave it. I can use it."

She heard music in the background, rock and roll, but turned way down. And he was turning off the big lamp, leaving a little red lamp to cast a warm glow. He had seen the right movies. She relaxed. Things were in his hands now, and he knew it. She sat down beside him. "That's going to be a while. Gets flavor as it simmers."

"That's okay. You want a drink now?"

"No."

"You sure?"

She laughed at the expression on his face: shock. "I'll have a small glass of red wine, if you have it."

"I have it. You don't drink much, do you Kim?"

"No, not much." He sounded concerned, as if he thought all his plans would go out the window if she stayed sober. He was in for a surprise. "Drinking doesn't turn me on."

"No?"

"I don't like it. It's nothing special to me the way it is to some of my friends."

"I've noticed that you don't drink much."

"It makes me sick. I always throw up when I drink."

"That's the mixer."

"No, I don't think so. So." She wanted to change the subject. "What do you want to do tonight?"

"I don't know. You have any ideas?"

So he knew that too. "Not really."

"We could stay here."

"Okay."

"Or we could go back to that cafe, what do you say?"

He was laughing at her. She blushed. She knew the one he was referring to. It was a cafe near her place, and one night after work they had dropped in there for coffee. He had been accosted by a drunk teenager. The girl couldn't get enough of him. She couldn't have been more than fifteen. She sat on his lap and tried to kiss him, and she openly glared at Kim. Kim had finally threatened to phone the girl's parents. That made the girl move as far away as the next table. And sitting there, she'd been whispering in the loudest whisper had ever heard, rather disgusting things to Alex. Alex had been really quite shaken by it. On the way out, she could feel him trembling under her arm. All night he'd kept saying, "I didn't know what to do, I didn't know what to do." She tried to laugh it off.

He grinned. "I think you were just jealous."

"Jealous? Disgusted. That was disgusting."

"She was a little young, wasn't she? You sure moved fast. You knew what to say, didn't you?"

"You freaked right out, didn't you? You were scared."

"I didn't know what to do."

"You should have dumped her on the floor."

"I couldn't do that."

"No, you're too nice. You should have."

"You were just jealous. You came to my rescue to get me back."

"I came to your rescue because you were too nice to her. You weren't enjoying yourself, so I didn't have to get jealous, did I?"

"You only get jealous when I'm having fun?"

"I don't get jealous." It was funny, the way they talked to each other like this, as if there was a bond, a commitment – there wasn't. He was seeing other girls and she was free to see other guys. But they still talked as if there was a bond. She liked that – she felt a bond. "I rise above it all."

"I bet you do. I bet this is true."

And his face looked like he was contemplating that,

contemplating her in that light. She was glad he had a red lamp on, to hide her blush. Don't look at me like that."

"Why not?"

"Makes me uncomfortable." She brought her leg up onto the couch, and rested her head against her bent knees. His hand encircled her knees too.

"What would make you comfortable?"

"I don't know."

"You don't know."

"I don't know." She picked up his beer bottle and started ripping at the label.

"You want a beer?"

"No, I just like ripping labels."

"Violent, aren't you?"

"I don't know."

"You don't know a lot tonight."

She was staring into his eyes. He had such beautiful blue eyes, real blue, the blue of burning brandy. It reminded her of Christmas time, and watching the brandy burn off the dessert. She leaned forward and let him kiss her. "Hi."

"What?"

"Nothing." She was completely relaxed now.

"You going to give me back my beer?"

"Oh." She looked at the bottle in her hands. The label was scattered all over the couch. She handed him the bottle.

"I can see I can't trust you with booze."

"Not one bit."

"You sure you don't want a beer?"

"I don't like beer. I just like to destroy labels."

"I see that."

"I'll clean it up."

"Don't worry about it. Worse has happened to this couch."

"Yeah?"

"There's been more than one beer spilled over it."

"Beer soaks in."

"I'll get this stuff next time I vacuum."

"You vacuum?"

"No one else does."

She wanted him – how long was he going to take. She kicked off her shoes, and tucked her feet under her. She was still excited. And relaxed. Everything was perfect. She laid back a little, leaning into the arm of the couch.

"You want the whole couch?"

And he moved them around until she was laying back, and he was sitting right beside her. She could see his profile—his Bowie cheekbones.

"So, what did you do in school today?"

"You sound like my mother."

"I want to know. What do you study?"

"I studied monastic life in Western Civ."

"What's that?"

"Monks."

"That sounds lively."

He was laughing. She laughed too. But then she had to defend it – she'd quite liked the monks. "It's not that boring. Well, the rules and stuff are boring, but the rest is pretty interesting – what my teacher calls the intent. They protected civilization for years, you know, and they made beautiful things. The work they did was incredible." But her voice had lost its interest. She said the words, but paid no attention to them. She was looking at his expression again. He was seeing her, and he was liking it, and it pulled her to him. "They did strange things, but they really cared about them. Some didn't probably, but history doesn't remember them."

"I couldn't live like a monk."

She laughed – she had to laugh at even the idea – and she let her arms go around him. "No, you couldn't. You're meant for this world."

"What do you mean?"

A spark had come to life in him. He was listening to her words now. She had to think about what she was saying. "You aren't . . . you should be in the center of the action. Maybe when the center was in a little cell, you could have been there, but not now. Now you should have it all, because you do have it all."

"You think so?"

He looked at her expectantly – he was hanging on her every word. She tried to give him what he wanted. "Yes. You. . . ." The moment was too much for her. "Chastity would be a bit too much to expect too, I think."

"Yeah, I don't think I could get into that."

"And all that contemplating."

"Too much for me. I like action."

"That's right." She relaxed again. Then he moved, bending towards her, laying down beside her.

"How long to dinner?"

"It can simmer." She loved the smell of him this close up. It was almost intoxicating. She pulled him closer to her.

"You want to spend the night?"

As if he didn't believe it – not didn't want it; did not believe it. As if she was moving too fast for him. She wanted to laugh – if Patty could see him now . . . he looked so surprised, no conqueror here. "If you want me to."

"Have you done this before."

Now she did laugh. "You're funny."

"I was just wondering."

"No, but that doesn't mean anything."

"No, it doesn't. I just didn't expect this."

"You want to. . . ." If he said no, she was going to . . . kill him.

"Yeah. You want to go to my room."

"Then we should go to your room." He stood up and put out a hand for her. She took it and follow him. In the bedroom, he turned to her, holding her tightly, kissing her. It was all so easy. She was amazed at the ease. It felt so natural, so right. They seemed to fit together perfectly. And he took off her clothes, and it was just the way she'd thought it would be. And they laid down on the bed, and even then, there was no awkwardness; their positions met each other. And he started kissing her and caressing her again, and she knew that his hands were meant to be on her, and hers on him. And she wasn't shy. "I want you."

"Wow."

She laughed. What Patty didn't know about Alex. . . .

6

I f we don't vote strike, we're telling them that we don't have the guts to back up our demands. Saying we won't risk a thing is just the same as saying we'll take what they feel like giving, and I don't think even you mean that Kim. Hell, they don't even expect us to accept it. They'd fall off their stools if we accepted that offer – probably fire us all for being so stupid. No one goes on good faith until the strike vote is in. It's the way it works, girl."

"I don't see why. I always thought that a strike, or a strike vote even, was a last resort. You make it sound like the first step."

"Maybe it is, just maybe it is."

"Well, that stinks."

"Look, they've been talking for six months since the contract ran out and for about a year before that, and they haven't decided if they want tea or coffee yet. If it takes a strike vote to get some sense out of them, I don't see why you have a problem with that. Give the union the support. To kick them in the butt and get them moving."

"If they can sit around that long, then they don't need a strike vote, they need new negotiators."

"You just don't understand the way it goes."

"And you won't understand that if you vote strike, you could end up on strike."

"I'm willing. It takes a strike to get a decent wage, I'm willing."

"I'm not, not without the chance to vote on each offer. I'm not giving anyone a strike vote as a negotiating tool."

"You don't get it, do you? There's not going to be any strike. It's too close to Christmas. There's no way they'd let us go out now. It's their busiest season. They've got too many dollars starting to roll in to see us march out – in March, we'd be out, and they'd be singing 'tax break,' but not now. There's not going to be a strike. We'll give the strike vote, and then sign the contract. Why can't you get something that simple into your head?"

"I don't like it when someone asks me for a gun to hold to someone else's head, and I really don't like it when there's a good chance that that gun just might backfire on me."

"Well that's the way the game is played, and if you don't like it, you should think about quitting and find yourself a non-union store to work at for a few years. Then you'd be with us."

"It's a stupid game, and I don't want to support it. I really didn't think unions were like this. It's one step short of blackmail, and I think it's reprehensible."

"It's not blackmail. It's smarts, and that's what it is. It's the timing of the thing, and the union's figured it out for us."

"It stinks."

"Well, maybe you should remember that you're a young girl still at home, and you don't have a family to feed or a mortgage to worry about."

Outside the door, Alex almost groaned out loud. Brenda was such a bitch going on about her mortgage, but making sure the rest of the time that everyone in the store knew her mortgage was paid off. Two-faced bitch, thinking no one remembered, and once saying they'd remortgaged to make more investments. They'd paid off that mortgage a month after the contract was signed, or so the story went. The same game now and forever.

"All you worry about is new clothes and make-up. I have two kids with families of their own."

He knew how to shut her up (he thought). All he had to do

was leave the office and walk into the coffee-room, smiling at her – or Griffins; actually it worked best with Griffins. When Griffins walked in, she didn't just shut up, she started singing the company tune, and all Alex got was a dirty look and a change of topic.

"I wouldn't have been able to keep those kids in decent clothes while they were growing up if it hadn't been for the union. I know which side my bread is buttered on, and you'd better learn that too instead of coming here with ideas."

Brenda had a mouth that thought it knew it all, but in all the years she'd been here, she hadn't figured out that sound carried down a hallway, especially if she faced the doorway. Alex exhaled his smoke towards the ceiling. Brenda didn't know that Griffins sat in here – had for years – and listened to her, that Griffins even timed his entrance to the coffee room to put a stop to her just before she peaked, that he would make her change tunes at a precise time chosen to make her look like the biggest fool. No Brenda didn't know about the laughs.

"Yeah, I know the union wouldn't want members with ideas."

"They know what they're doing. They don't need you to help them."

"And you have no problem with that?"

"And neither should you. The union is ours."

More than once he'd wanted to let Brenda know—to see her face, to see if she'd quit then or go hugging to her union. He could see it: Brenda wouldn't know what to say, and her little cheeks would well up like chipmunk cheeks and explode with all that hot air.

"You think the company will just waltz forward with a good offer. That's not their job."

Or maybe he could just hint – enough to set her mind in that direction, enough to make her think it possible. She'd squirm. She'd sit in the coffee-room and want to yap, and hesitate – little eyes dashing towards the office, wondering – and she wouldn't be able to stop herself but would yap, and doom herself to spend the rest of the day searching out his eyes – Griffins too – for a sign, a clue: did they hear? He'd never show it, neither would

Griffins. But he'd enjoy it, and now was the time to do it, with the union hot.

"So it's all cheap manipulation? And you're just going to sit there and play it out?"

Kim was starting to get worked up. She hadn't been around long enough to learn about Brenda. He grinned. Kim wanted to have Brenda for lunch.

"It's power-tripping. You're power-tripping, and maybe you – your husband has enough money to get through a strike, but not everyone does around here and before you get all hot and heavy into your trip, you should think about that. You sit there like Little Miss Self-Righteous, and all you want is the taste of power in a strike."

He could see her too: blurting forth; and that was Kim.

"Mortgages and food on the table are what it comes down to, and if you really understood that, you wouldn't be sitting there licking your lips. There are people around here who would like a different way, not wanting to give a strike vote yet. It's a lot more serious for them than you think it is."

Each word took her on to the next one with a new force. He knew her eyes were glaring—steaming. He heard it in her voice.

"They don't want to play with guns either, it's just you and your sick little power-trip that wants that. A hell of a lot of people around here want more negotiations before a strike vote is taken."

"That's all your young people who haven't ever had it bad. Let me tell you when I worked and I didn't have any place to go. We used to work late some night, until fifteen past or thirty past the hour before we'd be able to leave, and we didn't get paid for that. That was just part of our eight hour day, and – "

Alex reached over and closed the door. He knew that Brenda would not let anyone stop her now – couldn't because she had to show Kim that Kim was wrong. She'd make Kim listen to each word when until Kim gave up from exhaustion. He stretched. He wished Emma was there. He liked Emma's whens. Emma and "my

George." Emma always liked telling him about George because she saw in him a modern George: *"Yes, you have a bit of the devil in you too, I'd say, like my George. George couldn't stop himself either – wouldn't, didn't want to, just like you, I'd bet.* And Alex would smile and Emma would wrap her arms around herself, smiling too, knowing that he understood, and she'd go on, talking he knew not just to him but to those memories, and to George too. *Oh! But he spiced up life, that boy did – for all of us. In and out of trouble. Nothing serious, mind. The officers were never directly involved. The father, once, after someone had made some sort of complaint, or so we heard. Someone must have, because the Father wasn't one to take the bull by the horns without some nudging from someone, you know, but we never heard who on what was said. We knew that the Father had a little talk with George. And the Father looked pleased later. But George, well it just went to show that the devil can charm the angels. Oh, George could charm. Your doubts just couldn't stay when his charm was in the room. Yes, George was after the forbidden fruit. Because it was forbidden, that was George. There are people like that, don't you think? They hear 'no' and they have to turn it into yes. At times I think he would have done better by us if he had forbidden cod liver oil on Brussels sprouts. Maybe then George would have done better for himself – but he wouldn't have been my George then, would he? I don't blame George, myself. After all, why buy the cow when the milk is free? And all the girls liked George. Oh, I'm not saying anything about the hanky-panky that went on then, because that's not for me to talk about, but I'll tell you that after the wedding night, more than one girl started giving George little smiles. I guess he was the forbidden fruit for the girls. Poor George. He wasn't happy—happy-go-lucky, but not happy. Never found what he wanted when it was right in front of him all the time. Maybe too much in front of him. He told me that once, he said, 'Emmie, I've not gone looking for it, but it comes to me, and what's a guy to do?' Well, I knew the answer to that, but I didn't say a word because I knew too that George wouldn't do it. He enjoyed it way too much—what man wouldn't with those looks? Oh, I wish my Edward had that touch of the devil in him sometimes. I know I shouldn't, but it's spice, don't you think, and plain potatoes all the time . . . not that Edward isn't good to me. Oh dear.* And she'd look confused and hurt, and Alex would change the topic, but he'd keep George stored in his mind.

He wanted to meet George. He wanted to know what Emma was like in those days. He wanted to know if they'd been lovers. He was sure they had. He smiled.

He reached over and opened the door again.

" – don't understand those things, because you haven't had to suffer them, but you will, if you keep tearing down the union. I should have retired by then, on a nice pension that the union won for us, and I'll sit there and laugh at all you guys cutting your throats."

Brenda was a long-winded bitch, he'd say that much for her. He stood up and straightened out his pants. He wanted to talk to Kim alone now; he'd thought of a way to impress her. He went into the coffee-room. "Any coffee left?"

"Yeah, there should be some left. Pull the damn thing and find out."

Brenda gave him the dirty look he'd expected. I thought you girls would have drank it dry with all your yapping." He turned around to the cupboard but not before he'd caught the sudden thrust of Brenda's eye. He smiled: she didn't know – couldn't know – what he meant.

"Just girl-talk, nothing to interest you."

"This coffee's like mud. Any cream left?"

"In the fridge, where it should be."

"That's what we keep you girls around for, just to keep putting things where they should be." He shrugged as he pulled the cream out of the fridge, and then carefully casually left it on the counter-top. "It gives you something to do."

"I would like to have one break where I didn't have to spend half of it making this room decent again."

He let her get up and put away the cream. He didn't even break a smile when she tried to slam the fridge's door. "But you have to know your place." She jerked back, her shoulders tense. He knew her blood pressure was shooting upwards. "So what's your problem today, anyway Brenda? What's got you by the goat?" He was going to drive her right out of the room. "Didn't get lucky last night?"

"You have a one track mind."

"Hubby losing interest in it?"

"Some men grow up, Alex, and make something of themselves."

"Is that what they're calling it now?"

"There are other things in life, and if you want to go anywhere with this company, you'd better think on that."

"You think so?" He half leered.

"You won't make manager of this place."

"You hope not."

"I know better. The company's not going to promote a man who can't keep it in his pants."

"I don't know about that, Brenda. Seems we hear plenty of steamy stuff out head-office. Seems to me I'm doing pretty much what the big boys are doing." He grinned at her and winked as he took a sip of his coffee. "Didn't that new girl there know old man Patterson pretty well before she got the promotion? Maybe you should think on that." And that was enough. Brenda picked up her purse and bristled herself right out of the room. Alex turned to Kim and grinned. Kim was shaking her head at him with laughter. "Aren't you going to thank me?"

"Thank you."

"I hear her going on when I came out of the office. I hear she always gets up on her high horse when the contract is due."

"She is so petty, I just can't believe it. Can you imagine spending your life like that? She's just seizing crumbs. I suppose you should feel sorry for her."

"Yeah, well, she makes that pretty hard." He remembered what he'd heard Kim saying to Brenda, and he knew she couldn't know that he was playing echo. "She's just getting off on a bit of power she thinks she has now – until the contract's signed. If she had her way, we'd be out there in the cold starving just for her cheap thrill. Steve told me that the last time, she volunteered to paint the signs before there was any call for a strike vote. And last spring when the union was calling for demands from us, she wanted them to work it so that coffee breaks started when you got here, not when you left the front, as if she ever takes only the fifteen minutes in the first place." Kim was eating it up. Alex shrugged. "I guess you're right. It's sort of sad."

"She won't even see, though. She won't even try to see. What's she so bitter about?"

"Been here too long, I guess."

"Remind me to quit if I ever sound like that."

"You won't." He knew she wouldn't, because he knew she was willing to break the rules, and she was willing to want. He smiled and reached over to take her hand. And there it was: a quiver right through her. She took in one deep sharp breath, her body shifting slightly, her eyes looked up to his, and her lips parted; she was right in the state he liked, and with such a little touch from him, it amazed him—a shock ran from his hand and stunned his body. He wasn't sure if it excited him or frightened him when it rushed him. His voice fell softly now. "You haven't asked me out lately."

"What?"

"I was just thinking it was your turn to ask me out. You haven't asked me out in over a month." She blushed, remembering he knew. She was strange. She could come over and take him, and blush later. He shook his head. There had to be two people in that one body.

"Oh right."

"So are you going to, or do I have to do all the asking around here?"

"Where shall I ask you to?"

"You could ask me to go driving after work." He couldn't ask her to his place, and her place was out because it was her parents place. Parking was all that was left.

"Would you like to go for a drive tonight, Alex?"

She was blushing and her voice was teasing. He was fascinated. "Yeah, that sounds like a good idea."

"Your car or mine?"

He laughed. "I'll pick you up. About seven?"

"Seven-thirty would be better."

"Right, right." He remembered all the things to do after work: home and eat, bathe, dry hair, dress; they'd need more than an hour. "Seven-thirty, you're right, that's better." He nodded and picked up his coffee cup. "I better get back at it."

"Okay."

"Bye-bye."

"Bye."

He nodded at her once more and then pulled his eyes from her and went back to work.

He couldn't get back to work. He listened until he heard her leaving the room. Then he drew the invoices in front of him, stacked them, and thought of her. There was something about her – she made him feel so good. She made him feel like he could do anything, and he didn't know what it was about her that brought that to him. Maybe it was in her eyes. She searched with those eyes, but she wasn't scared – no fear at all. She was pleased. And excited. He was slapping a pen against the desk. He wanted to know what tonight would bring.

– Not that he didn't know already. That was another nice part of Kim: she didn't lie about wanting, no games. But he felt a will in her too, and part of him said he just might be in over his head with her. And that was okay; there were times when that was the best place to be. Times when that was the thrill.

He looked back at the invoices. He should have had them posted half an hour ago. He'd do it now, and he'd do it fast, and tonight would come all the faster. He lit up a cigarette and picked up the first one.

As he drove towards the parks, he glanced over at her. Secretly he was glad she didn't like bars and parties the way he did, because this way, he never had to take her there. He knew he shouldn't feel that – that she should be disappointed, and she should push him into it – but he couldn't help it; there were so many advantages to this way. He had her, and no one knew it—no one asked about it or expected him to share it. No girls were put out by it. This was his, and his alone, and that was right. "You're awfully quiet tonight."

"I hated today. Some days, I just hate."

"Tired?"

"A little. Trying not to be, but I get that in me, and I get so mad, and, I don't know, it's just doesn't leave me with much."

"Yeah, I've had days like that."

"I think I'll be glad when that contract's settled and things go back to being blah."

"Is that the way you think it is around there? Blah?"

"Don't you think so?"

"I guess it is for you girls. All you do is stand there and ring in groceries."

"No, I mean the place. It's not exactly lively. Well, it is now, and it's getting worse, but in the wrong way. Usually it's just dullsville, you know. Sometimes we really do look a lot like a bunch of robots. You know they say that robots are going to take over our jobs one day, and I can't see why they shouldn't. We may as well be robots, even in the coffee-room."

"Gets to you, doesn't it? He knew what she was talking about. He'd felt it too, especially when he'd started there. It wasn't like his dad's store. It wasn't exactly cold because to be cold it would have to be something, and it wasn't. It was there, a building inside and out.

"That's probably all this is."

"Probably." He pulled into the park's road.

"It's nice out here, isn't it?"

"Yeah, nice to get away from the city sometimes."

"They keep the roads open all winter?"

"Just to the ranger's post. Go past there and it gets pretty hairy."

"Are we going past there?"

"Nope, we're going right here." And he pulled over into a spot that was fairly well cleared, one he knew he could get out of later. "What do you think?"

"I like it here."

"Good." He reached into the back and pulled out a bottle. "Something to keep the cold off?"

She was laughing. He smiled. "Something like that." He couldn't see her now, only her outline in the snow's glow. "You want one?"

"Sure, a weak one – you have mixer there?"

"Of course." He pulled out a bottle of pop. "I'm always prepared."

"Were you a boy scout?"

"Nope. I didn't need to be one." He laughed, and poured two drinks into plastic cups. "You see? We won't even have to wash up."

"Thought of everything."

He drank. "It's hard to see here." He moved out from the driver's seat, and dropped the glove compartment open. He had a table now, and he put his drink on it. His hands were free to ease her out of her coat. He played with her hair, dropping his hands down to caress her throat. She shivered. "Hands cold?" He started rubbing them together, blowing on them.

"Yeah. Now I know what to get you for Christmas."

"Gloves?"

"I think so."

"Sounds good." He finished his drink and poured another one. And he topped hers up a bit. "You're a slow drinker." He put his drink back, and wrapped his arms around her. "So." He wondered if she was still upset from work. She seemed tense. She wasn't simply drifting into him the way she did when they were alone. "What do you think?" He kissed her face gently. "How's school?"

"I saw the counselor the other day. Still the same."

"Yeah? You haven't decided what you'll be doing in a year yet? When are they going to stop asking?" He laid down across the car seat, resting his hand in her lap.

"June."

He laughed – her voice was so flat and angry. "Don't give into them, then."

"I'm not, I just don't think I should have to take it. They keep going on about what I should be, and I don't think that one of them knows the first thing about being or they wouldn't be there, and they wouldn't be like that."

And with that, she hit the core of her force, he knew, and waited. He liked Kim when she was like this: impulsed by forces she didn't know and didn't stop to think about.

"Life isn't knowing where and why and what you'll be in a year from now. Lying in a coffin is when you'll know that. They should be asking us what stars we want to touch, what sights we want to see, what we want to feel. You know, you can't live from the plan to plan like that. You have to be open to it all, don't you think? We aren't computers to be programmed. We're people, and we have things to discover as we go along, or there isn't any point in going along."

"Yeah." He said perfectly still. He wouldn't disturb her – she had to continue. Because each word gave him joy. I am the way – maybe not to everlasting life, but at least for a moment, a glint. Because there was a way to it, and she was right: must strike to find life. Must take the cold stones and hit them together until they sent off those sudden sparks, and then . . . then he'd have won.

"I keep thinking I should tell them that, but you can't tell them that because they're sitting there waiting to hear 'thinker, tailor, soldier, sailor.' and if you say 'all of the above,' they suspend you. And how do you tell that?"

Each word fell into his blood and pulsed through him. He wanted to take her, but not now, not until she was through. "Experiencing is everything."

She bent down to kiss him. He held her down and kissed her long and deep. Because he understood, and because he knew she spoke to him because she saw he understood. She didn't see him as a grocer, she didn't see him as a weekend, drinking Don Juan, but she saw him as he was, because she was the same way. She came from that same chunk of earth that he did – a piece from the core. "Lay down."

7

What the hell are you doing here?" Her heart was still pounding from the fright – how could she have known that she'd find him standing out there, not some burglar, rapist, night-stalker, gang member, but him? How could she have guessed that that sound was a deliberate attempt to get her attention? – she couldn't have known; she still didn't believe it. But there he was, standing below on the lawn. She didn't believe, but she loved it. She loved him. "You scared the hell out of me."

"Sorry."

But he didn't look very sorry at all. He looked a little drunk, and quite pleased with himself. She was pretty pleased with him too. No one had ever done anything like this for her before. She shook her head at him. "Do you know what time it is?"

"No."

"Do you care?" He didn't seem to care. He just looked up at her, so happy.

"Do I have to go?"

"It's four AM, Alex."

"Too late to call?"

She laughed – he wasn't that drunk, she could see that, and she knew he knew that she knew. "Why are you here?"

"To see you."

"You're lucky you aren't seeing the rest of my family."

"Are Mom and Dad up?"

"No, and let's hope they don't get up."

"Are Mom and Dad good sleepers?"

"I hope so. I've never tested them before."

"Then we'll be quiet."

"Good idea."

"Thank you."

"You're welcome." She was laughing and he was hushing her – shhh, shhh. "I think it will be easier if I come down."

"I could come up."

"You ever scaled a wall before?"

"No."

"Wait there. I'll be right down."

"Okay."

"And don't let anyone see you."

"I'll wait here."

She saw him flop down on the spot as she closed the window. He looked quite at home. She laughed again – she couldn't stop laughing, and she wasn't at all sure that she believed it was happening. Alex at her window at four in the morning. He really was something else, something irresistible, even drunk – maybe more so a little drunk, because he was looser when he was drunk. But she'd never seen him this loose before – completely dispossessed. It amazed her. And he was so normal about it, as if early morning visits were just the thing, and throwing things at windows was not much different than ringing a doorbell, and lawns were fine couches. So free and relaxed and strangely innocent. She could never have done it. The best she could have done was drive past his place at three in the morning, which she did once, but hadn't gone to the door – hadn't stopped the car. No, she could never have waltzed up to the window and . . . and his face, so eager and alive, and strong – sensuous, curious, caring. She'd not seen such a look on his face before. He wanted her, he wasn't hesitating. And she wanted him. She wanted to be outside, to dash right out there into that simple free play, to hold it and learn it and know it and leave all awkwardness behind. She tucked her shirt into her jeans, and ran down the stairs. "Alex—" but he wasn't still flopped on that spot. "Alex?" Had he left? "Alex, where are you?"

"Ssshhh, over here."

She saw a hedge move. He was underneath it, half crouching, half-laying. He looked pretty comfortable. "What are you doing there?"

"I'm hiding. You said not to let them see me."

"I did, didn't I? Come out from there."

"Come here."

She had to. He was irresistible. She gave him her hand, and he pulled her down to him. "Are you sure this is a safe place to be?"

"Your parents wouldn't look here, would they?"

"I was thinking more about the dog I saw around here the other day."

"He's gone now."

"But what did he leave behind? That's the question."

"Oh, nothing, nothing. I checked."

She didn't believe that. "You're too lazy to move."

"It's nice here. We can see the sunrise from here."

"No, we can't. We're facing west."

"Oh. We'll move before the sun comes up."

"Okay." She was squatting in front of him, looking at him. He looked so happy. "What were you up to tonight, anyway?"

"Oh, we had a party. You should have come."

"Where was this party?"

"My place."

"Oh."

"Really, you should have come. It was a good party."

"So I see." She didn't want him saying that over and over. She didn't want to go to his parties, and she didn't want to feel guilty about not going to his parties. "But I think one drunk here's enough."

"I'm sobering up."

"You don't look it."

"Hey, I walked over here."

"You what?"

"I walked. I went to get some air, and I came here."

He looked too proud of himself again. She shook her head. She had a good idea of what he had done: he'd told some girl that he was getting some air, and he'd walked over here. He'd left the car behind because turning it on would have made too much noise. "Alex." But she didn't mind. In fact, she liked it. He could treat any girl like mud if he wanted, as long as he was choosing her over and over. "You shouldn't have done that."

"Yeah, it was a long walk."

"Come on."

"Are we going?"

"Yeah." She stood up, and gave him a pull up with her hand. He bumped into her, almost knocking her down. "Oh, God, you smell like a brewery."

"I've always liked the smell of beer. Beer and smoke."

"Come on, this way." She started off towards the street.

"Where are we going?"

"I don't know. It's getting late – or early, whatever. People will be getting up soon."

"Who?"

She laughed. "We have neighbors who jog. I don't know what time they get up. Come on."

"Where to? I'll follow you anywhere."

"I don't know. You want me to walk you home?"

"Too far. I'm tired, Kim."

"We could go down to the park."

"Okay."

She steadied him, and started them on their way. They walked, holding hands, and he bumped into her a few times along the way. But she didn't mind. She laughed and looked around her. The morning was beginning. The sun hadn't risen yet, but its light was breaking through already. And there was no one else around; the world was theirs, unblemished. And dewed. Everything was fresh. And he was here. She slowed their walk, and breathed deeply. "This is really a beautiful morning."

"And you were going to miss it all, sleeping."

"I wasn't sleeping."

"No? What were you doing. You were home, weren't you?"

"If I hadn't been home, how would you be talking to me now, you'd be talking to my parents now, trying to explain yourself while they dialed the police."

"Nine-one-one."

"I think they know that."

"You think so, do you?"

He swung her around, into his arms, and looked at her, swaying her back and forth. She giggled a little, and put her arms around his neck – there was so much she loved about this guy. "Hi there."

"Are you just waking up?"

"I was awake. I told you that already."

"What were you doing awake?"

"I was getting ready for bed."

"No, no. Why were you still up?"

"What was I doing all night?" She wasn't going to tell him, but she had been listening to music and thinking about him. "You'll never know. Who was at this party?"

"Everyone but you."

"And a good thing too, or we wouldn't be here now, and this is very nice."

"You like this?"

"Yeah, I like being alone with you." And at last, he kissed her. She wanted him. She wanted to take him right then.

"Hold on, hold on. We're going to the park."

"Okay." She kissed him once more, and started them walking again. "Why are we going to the park anyway?"

"It was your idea."

"What I mean is, why aren't we going to your place?"

"There's a party at my place."

"Still going on?"

"Yeah, it's my birthday party, and they won't leave me alone."

She stopped. "When's your birthday?"

"Today – yesterday – Friday."

"Why didn't you tell me?"

"I didn't know there was going to be a party."

"You could have told me. I would have got you something."

"Don't worry about it."

"I wanted to have gotten you something."

"What?"

"You know what I mean. I . . . you should have said."

"Next year you'll know."

"Alex."

"Come one, come on, this way to the park."

She walked with him again. And she thought about it. He had
sought her out on his birthday – it shocked her, it delighted her; she
loved it. Because it meant that he really did want her – not just sex,
but her, and all that she was. She was special to him. He could have
stayed at home, at his party with his friends, and with all the girls
who were there (Patty had been right about the girls who flocked to
Alex; she was always seeing girls coming in to see him at the store,
and Marg and Robbie were sure to tell everyone about the ones she
missed). But he had come to her. "So how old are you now?"

"Twenty."

"Over the hill, eh?"

"How?"

He gave her a strange look. She laughed and kissed him.
"Nineteen is the sexual peak for men, you know."

"Who said that?"

"I don't know. It's just one of those things you hear."

"I never heard it."

"Well, it's true."

"What's it for women?"

"Thirty. We just keep getting better until we're thirty, some-times thirty-five."

"I don't believe you."

"Okay. Don't."

"You're kidding?"

"I don't know, Alex. I just heard it. Some things you take too seriously."

"Well, if you're not sure. . . ."

"Then we don't have to believe it, do we?"

"I don't believe it."

"Time will tell." He gave her a look – he was so put out with her; she laughed. They were in the park now, walking towards the lake and the woods. And soon they were sitting together in a grove. He was smiling at her. She drew him to her, and that was all it took to set off all the sparks of wanting in him, and in herself. It was so easy to be with him. The rest of the world just drifted away when she was with him. It was like touching the heavens. So free, so simple, so natural. She loved it. She loved him.

8

Kim, is that you?" He was sure he'd recognized her voice, but his fears forced him to whisper – what if he had awakened her mother or – did she have a sister? "Kim, are you there?" He swore that his heart was beating louder and louder by the second. She must hear it.

"Alex?"

"Hi." He breathed out.

"Speak up. I can hardly hear you. Its like long distance. Where are you? In a booth?"

"No." He cleared his throat. She didn't need to know that he'd be whispering deliberately. "I'm at home. So how are you?"

"Fine. Do you have a cold or something?"

"No." He cleared his throat again. "How's that? Can you hear me?"

"Now I can. I thought I was getting an obscene call or something."

"Were you getting all excited?"

"Until I heard it was you."

"Thanks a lot."

"Anytime."

"So what are you doing?"

"I just got in. I was going to bed."

"Come to bed over here."

"You been out drinking?"

"Well." He laughed; she'd caught him. "Yeah."

"Have a good time?"

"Yeah, it was okay, but, you know."

"Didn't get lucky, eh?"

"I could have." He knew she was only kidding, but she was serious too. She didn't want to think that he'd called because he'd struck out at the bar, and he didn't want her to think that either. "But I decided to come home and phone you. So you coming over?"

"You're so subtle."

But he knew he didn't have to be subtle with her. Between them, things were simple and there was no need for games. She'd let him know that he could depend on her want for him. "Do you want red wine or white?"

"I'm tired."

"You should have stayed in tonight and gotten some rest."

"So that I'd be nice and rested when you called?"

"What would have been wrong with that?" He would have liked that. He could see it: a rested Kim, all ready for the whole night. "I'd do it for you."

"You wouldn't have been rested, and you'd pass out on me and I'd get mad at you."

"You never get mad at me."

"Not even when you call at two-thirty in the morning, apparently."

"So when you going to be here?"

"A half hour, I guess."

"Good."

"Bye."

"Bye-bye." He hung up the phone and stood up and stretched. He felt good tonight – the boy had it tonight. And Kim was coming over. He'd known that she would, but somehow it still surprised him when she said yes – rushed him with heaven; he wanted to sing and dance. Because she was something else, this girl. He'd been right about her, on everything. She shared with him – he guessed this was called 'having an affair,' but it didn't feel like that, because it didn't have all the traps of that. This was simple sharing, no demands, no conventions, and all because she cared for him. And she knew him, and because she knew him, she didn't try to restrict him. She left him free, because she knew he couldn't be him without being free. As it should be. And she soothed him, and excited him. He had the perfect girl. He was starting to spend a lot of time with her, more than with anyone else – than with all of them together. And why not? She gave him more than the rest of them all together, and without the games. She was enough to send him dancing into the streets. He knew he'd fallen for her.

He shook himself and started moving. He had a lot to do before she arrived. He had to have a shower, and he had to set up the surprise.

It was nearly a full hour before she showed up. The wine was chilled, the lights dimmed, and the surprise ready. Tom was still up. He'd stayed up to be in on this, but he wasn't going to make it. He'd pass out before long now. Alex watched him, and watched the door. Finally, her car pulled in. Alex took a quick last look in the mirror. His hair was damp, but that was okay. Kim wouldn't make a big deal out of it. He heard her knock. He went to the door and let her in. "Come in, come in."

"Hi there."

He kissed her and ushered her into the living-room. "I've got a surprise for you."

"What? Oh, hi Tom."

Kim wasn't pleased to see Tom. He could see that. But there was nothing he could do about it. Tom wanted to stay up. What could he say to the guy? He couldn't tell him that Kim didn't like him as much as he liked Kim.

"Hey Kim. You made it. Happy birthday."

"Thanks."

She turned to look at him, asking him how Tom knew, how he knew. He grinned. "I've seen your application."

"You don't remember from my application. That was almost a year ago."

"Birthdays don't change."

"You don't remember from a year ago."

Which was true. Patty had told him last week, but Kim didn't need to know that. "You don't give me any credit. And I bought you something."

"What did you get me?"

Even the way she stood so close to him excited him. He grabbed her, and kissed her, and then guided her to the bar. There stood four crystal wine glasses. "I didn't get them wrapped, but I knew you liked wine."

"They're nice. That's sweet."

"The sales lady said it's a basic pattern – to add on to, you know."

"That's good."

"I thought you could use them, since you're eighteen and out of school, and you know, you could get your own place."

"Yeah, that's good. Thank you."

She kissed him. She was happy. He relaxed. "So let's sit down and you can tell me what you did tonight."

"I didn't really do anything. Had dinner with the parents, and went out with a couple of friends."

"That doesn't sound like much of a party."

"It wasn't. Birthday parties never work out to be much fun. You ever notice that? People are trying so hard to make it special, it just drops. I don't like that."

"Well, on your eighteenth birthday you're supposed to make it special. You're legal now, and all that. It's tradition."

"Best reason I can think of for not bothering. I don't like all those things imposed on me. I don't need to try to live up to all those expectations, and feel sick in the morning because of it. And then I wouldn't have been home when you called, right?"

"This is true. I'm glad you didn't make a big party out of it."

"This is a nice party."

"Yeah, let me fill those glasses with some wine. You like white, right?"

"Sounds good."

He got up and grabbed the bottle of wine from the bar.

"Is he dead?"

He turned around and saw Kim pointing at Tom. He looked. Tom was out of it. "No, he's just passed out."

"What did he do – the drinking for the both of you tonight?"

"He was more into it than I was."

"He looks it. I guess he'll just sleep it off."

"He'll be out of it until morning now. If he starts to snore, I'll kick him out of here." He gave her a glass of wine and sat down beside her with his. "So we'd better toast to your birthday."

"It's too late. It's not my birthday anymore."

"Yeah, I guess it's not." He knew this game. "I guess we'll have to wait until next year."

"I guess so – or we could toast next year now."

"No, we'll wait."

"We'll just sit here and drink."

And she drank her wine, so he drank his. He looked over at her at the top of his glass. She was sitting sideways on the couch, facing him with her arm draped on the back. Her eyes were on him, all full of that wanting of hers. Her lips were slightly parted. She took hold of his hand and played with his fingers. It was time to make his move. He bent his head to her lightly, just a touch to make her want more. "So what do you think?"

"I think you said something about bed on the phone."

Her voice caught in the middle of the sentence. She wanted him. Because she cared about him, he could see that in her too. He liked to tease her. "You want to use me."

"No—"

"Yes."

"Don't say that."

"Why not?"

"Because we're close to it, but that's not it, so don't say it."

In some strange way, he understood what she meant, and he

was glad to hear her say it. "Okay." He squeezed her fingers for an instant. "What should I say then?"

"You don't have to say anything."

"No?"

"No."

She leaned to him and kissed him, long, and demandingly. He pushed her down on the couch, still kissing.

"Let's go to your room."

He wanted her now. He kissed her again.

"No. Let's go. Tom's here."

"He's dead to the world."

"I won't be comfortable. . . ."

"Okay." He stood up and helped her up, grabbing to him as she stood up, feeling her breasts pressed against him — he liked her body.

"Come on."

She was leading him to his room. He flicked the light on as they walked in. "Take off your clothes and let me see you."

"In a minute."

She led him to the bed. He laid down on top of her. She felt so good. She smelled good too — she didn't wear perfumes, and he liked that. And he liked her touch. She was taking off his shirt, caressing him, kissing him gently all over his chest. He could feel himself rising. "You can stay if you want." It had just been a glimmer of a thought before, but now he liked the idea. He could see it: Kim could live here too.

"That's a funny thing to say now."

"I mean, you can move in. You can stay if you want."

"Three's a crowd."

She'd barely whispered it, but he knew what she meant. It wasn't fair because he could stop if he wanted to, and he liked the picture he saw. But she knew him, and she was wise about him. Still, he wanted her to know he meant it, and he wanted her to think she was all to him. "No, just the two of us. Tom could move out."

"Later, okay?"

She kissed him again, moving her hands to his waist. He took off her sweater. He kissed her chest, her breasts, her stomach. "Okay." And he let all his thoughts be killed by the wanting.

9

She lay down on her bed. Her mind was running on and on; and she let it go: It's the calm and the rush. That's what it is, that's what it's all about: a calming rush. That's all, the whole all. It's so simple. And he's so perfect . . . as if he knows her or has it so in him he doesn't need to know, because he can give it to easily, and completely, so perfectly. Something special, some special way of knowing how . . . Oh, Alex . . . Alex . . . who blessed you? Who blessed me? The magic – it's magic, magic, and so much magic that I can't escape it – I don't want to escape it . . . but I can't remember it as I should. It's a blur, a wonderful blur, hazy, and I can't say what it is, yet it is here, so much here I can't leave it – it doesn't leave me. It lets me relive it, and relive it. Hold onto the feelings, sensations . . . so calm, so relaxed, so alert and aware – how can all of that happen in one person at one time? And happen and happen? And he is funny. What did he do last night? He had that smile – the way he looks at me, one look and he has me held to him, right to him, and it's just a smile. It's so strange, so free. That time he came to my window, I didn't know it was him, but it was. Him, grinning, so proud of himself as if he'd discovered the world. I was proud of him too. It's contagious – he's contagious, any mood he has is contagious. One year now, I've known him one year now . . . the way he moves down to my breasts . . . there's something in that movement, something powerful . . . it's so sudden, the calm and the rush. No man has ever had that power before. Just one touch, one smile, one movement . . . the way he touches, taunting my hips with his hand, but it doesn't seem to be a hand anymore, not just a hand. No, it's a touch that pulls all of me into it. One touch, and I don't think, don't breathe. One touch and I have to be touching him, if only to be able to breathe again – the contact . . . it is too great, too great. How can the world cease so suddenly like that? How can I care so little about so much so fast? How can I forget? And it's not just when he's here, because I know I don't care about the rest of it anymore, not really, not like I did. What's to care about? School, grades, it's all mechanical nonsense – work even more that way. There's nothing there to care about, and nothing there to feel. It can all go on without me – will too. This can't, because this takes me – all, pulled into one simple movement, can that really happen? Was God that kind? Because it renews me every instant. I never knew that power before. How can one thing give so much strength, and energy? How can it work? If God ever takes this away, I won't forgive Him. To have let us have this – all strength, all happiness – and to take it away – no. This will last. It's going to last forever – what's that song? '*I'm in love for the first time / don't you know it's gonna last.*' Oh, that's old—'*It's a love that lasts forever / It's a love that has no past.*' I remember that. '*Don't let me know / don't let me down.*' It's a good song. We're gonna last. We'll last because we're good together, because we have it together. We have what it takes. Kim, is that you? I'd forgotten that. Oh, I shouldn't laugh. He'd be hurt if he knew I was laughing at him. But that was funny. Almost scared, very gentle, that's the store's Mr. Womanizer. That really was funny. I had to stop myself from laughing into the phone. That voice, whispered to me in the dead of the night. He sounded so anxious. It was funny. Yeah, Mr. Street life, right. He really is shy. Oh, and that time that kid was coming on to him, I'll never forget that, never. He was trembling. Actually trembling. I could feel it through him. He didn't know what to do. He really didn't either. And Patty thinks he has women for lunch. He's just not like that – he's not smooth enough. I can see that in his eyes, too. They're so blue, and alive, flaming, but they always have a question in them. Always . . . that's strange too. Even when he plays with them, widening them, and stuff, they still have a question in them. He's still looking and searching. Patty's not right. And all those rumors aren't right either. Maybe he is, but not to me. What was I thinking about – forgetting it all. Its not forgetting, not really. Wiping out, getting rid of, putting in the right place. Obliterating all that stuff. So it's more than forgetting. It's feeling something too. Because the forgetting comes through the feeling. The feeling dismisses the world. It's not really forgetting, because I don't decide to. So it's not really forgetting at all. Replacing. Sex with him – there's oh what a feeling for you. Too much almost. A person could drown in that. I'd panic if it wasn't so natural – it's not awkward; how can it not be awkward? But that's him. It's not me. Sometimes I'm so scared of touching him . . . its just that I don't want to spoil it. I shouldn't be scared. He said it's just relaxing and letting go and feeling it all – oh, feeling too much, feeling so much I have to do something to . . . to breathe. If he made me feel anymore, I swear, I'd throw up. That would be cute. Most unromantic. But then this isn't romance. This isn't peaceful sighs and long walks. This has its power, and sex has its power, and the two together is enough to overwhelm. Sex really does have its own like laws and dynamics, doesn't it? It's weird that way. So much a thing apart from life. Everything else carries over and it doesn't. Weird . . . but sometimes I just look at him, and I have to have him; that's it, I have to. I'm compulsive, I can't get enough of him. His hands, his face, his body, they aren't his then, but mine, a part of me that I've just found. How could anyone stand being touched by somebody if it felt like an octopus? Why would they? I have to get going here. I can't lay here all day. I have things to do. There's a list around here some place. I'm not going to get anything done if I don't move. Okay, stop enjoying him, girl. You had a great night last night, now go on. I can't I can't I can't. Just a moment more. How can he be so confident? He's confident, even when he's shy. How? I have so many fears. I doubt and I doubt and I wonder and think and worry, and he doesn't. I love that too – see, I'm not shallow; it's not all his looks. I should have said yes when he asked me to move in with him that night. I should have . . . but it really would not have been fair. He didn't really mean it – well, he meant it for that moment, but he didn't want to mean it. Not yet. He's not ready for that yet. As long as he feels it, he doesn't have to want to mean it. It's okay. I'll move in with him when he feels it and is ready for it. Maybe. Guys take so long to catch up with their emotions. And he's older than me. He'll be twenty-one pretty soon. I don't know. I sort of like him being a secret. Can't really call him a secret when half the world knows that we see each other, but they don't see us seeing each other much, and that's nice. It's private. There's something sick about everybody staring at you, wondering about your sex life. And they always think things are really quite different between us than they are. Even Karen, she doesn't get it. She gives me all the wrong reasons. That's why he's better as a lover. People expect all sorts of things from a boyfriend, but they don't know what I mean when I say 'lover,' so they leave it alone. Actually, I think they think that this is quite a wicked relationship. That's because they don't know. It's not. It's loving and laughing and loving and laughing and all smiles. It's special. Oh, it gives me so much. Not just the feelings, which I would take even if that were all, but also the – the strength – no, the enthuse – the energy to get through the rest of the day. Karen always says she can tell when I've seen him because I'm so much happier and relaxed and I don't take things so seriously the next day. She thinks that's all sex. She's wrong. It's something else, and it's important. She shouldn't sneer at it. Well, I guess I let her. I don't straighten her out. Always that excitement around him. I guess I melt. That's disgusting. No one would believe that I melt. But he melts too. It's not as if he's all in control and I'm all over the place, it's just that he flows and I flow with him. He loosens everything up. He lets the smiles and everything else come easy.

There's no self-consciousness there. It's like playing that way. We don't think together. We don't have to think. They want me to explain it, and I can't. They want me to justify it to them, but I can't. I don't have to. But they all think it's sex, and it's not, not sex in the way they mean it: all lust, and ripping off clothes and throwing them on beds or in bushes. I mean, that's there, but it's not all that's there, and it's not the reason that we're together. There's a connection between us. I know there is, but how can anyone else know it? Like that night he called. I thought he was going out with the guys – he said he was and he probably had been out with them; I didn't expect to hear from him. But when I came home, and I walked in the door, I went straight to the phone. I didn't think. I didn't wonder if he'd call. I knew he was going to call. I didn't even know that I knew, that's how much I knew it. I didn't actually have to think about it. I knew it the same way I knew where the phone was, and I acted on that without thinking on it first. I sat there and cleared my throat. It was strange. If I had thought about it, I would have gotten up and told myself not to be so silly. But I didn't. I sat there, and the phone rang. It really was a weird feeling. I guess it was psychic – must have been. It was weird. I'd forgotten how weird that was, but it wasn't weird when it was happening. It wasn't weird until the next morning when I thought about it. When he called, it just felt natural. So connected – almost too connected. Normal people do not have that, and yet they want me to tell them about it, or else they'll tell me it's all sex. It's not all sex. There's something very strong between us. Now it is time to move. I don't want to think about this anyway. Yeah, those people, they do ruin everything. I shouldn't have thought about them. It doesn't matter. I'll see him next week or the week after. Okay, on the count of three, get up and get going. One. Two. Three.

10

She was brushing up against him, breathing hard – harder than she knew, with more effect than she was after, he was sure. He could feel every heave against his chest, and he watched her eyes dance at him. Pretty gray eyes, with a hint of fire behind them.

"Well?"

He knew he should be enjoying this from her as much as he would from someone else, but he wasn't. Hot after sex – he didn't want her like that. It bothered him. Because she wasn't like that. Sex with her wasn't that. She had a touch, a way, a power, and this wasn't that. But what was he supposed to say? "You're a little hot minx tonight, aren't you?"

"Why not?"

Because he expected more from her. She understood more. "Maybe I'll scream rape."

"You do that, and we'll find out if Tom will come crashing through the doors to save you."

"I will. He will." He knew she'd leave if he did. She'd be too embarrassed to stay. She'd blush, and never forgive him. "Hel—" She'd cover his mouth with her hand. He pulled free. "Does that mean you're going to behave yourself?"

"What's your problem?"

"Maybe I'm not in the mood."

"Now that would be a red star – gold star today."

She'd hit him with that – a slap across the face that said he was easy and he hadn't even done anything. "You don't know anything." But that was too harsh. "You don't even know your stars."

"It's been a long time since I was in elementary school, and when I was, I liked blue stars best anyway."

She was still kissing him, crowding him. He twisted his body free. "You sure about that? You're sure acting like a school kid tonight."

"What is your problem?"

"You're over-sexed." He was barely keeping her at arm's length. She kept wrestling against his hands, her body jerking with greedy impatience. He pushed her back and slipped away, sitting in the lazy boy with his arms folded across his head and the footrest up and in her way. He nodded towards the couch opposite him. "You just sit there and behave yourself."

"You're just jealous."

"How you figure that?"

"You'd love to be over-sexed."

"Just sit there and behave yourself."

"Oh, so stern."

She sauntered over to him – he thought she didn't know that she was sauntering – and plunked herself down on top of him, her legs straddled and tucked in beside his. Her breasts were level with his face – so easy to bite. He kept his eyes on her face. "You call this being good?"

"It would be a hell of a lot better if you'd loosen up a little. Trust me on that."

He let her unfold his arms, but then dropped them, dead weight, by his sides. She picked one up and let it drop.

"I said loose, not limp."

"Did you?"

"A little cooperation would be appreciated."

"What's that?"

"You know what."

And she looked at him, pouting.

Her fingers only drummed against his sides now. She was backing down. He wanted her to back down a little more. "How would I?"

"Cute."

And she folded her arms in front of her and glared at him. He had to say something – he had an inspiration. "Baby, I think you're cute, but there's no substitute for love."

"What's that?"

"Don't you know that song? 'Baby it's a crying shame, this whole damned town thinks you're insane.'"

"This is a new tune, coming from Alex Talon, aka Sex Machine."

"Is that what you think?"

"That's what the whole town thinks. Talk about a whole town thinking someone's insane."

"Well, now you can tell them it's not true, can't you?"

"I don't think that's a testimonial I'll take to the streets, thanks."

She looked really put out. But then, so was he.

"My legs are going numb. You going to get off me?"

"No."

"What do you do? – take aphrodisiacs before you come over?"

"Sure as hell can't be anything you've done."

"That's right. I'm behaving myself."

"You sure picked a fine time to start."

"You have a bony ass."

"Good."

So she was going to sulk. There was no way he was going to win in this. And he did want her – he'd wanted all day, thought all day about her visit tonight. It was just that she came in like a typhoon. "You shake your hips child, like a rattlesnake, You make me jealous, make no mistake.'" She perked up a little, but suspiciously. "So you don't know Rod, especially his earlier stuff."

"I know the song."

"Yeah? He ran his hands up and down her back, but gently – a teasing almost-touch that made her shiver. He did it again. She tried to lean back and feel his hands, but he pulled them away. "We used to play that in our band."

"When were you in a band?"

"When I was a kid, sixteen, seventeen. I played lead guitar and sang."

"Center stage."

"We didn't get on stage. We just jammed together. I was working too much to do that scene too."

You would have been good at it."

"You think I would have found a few groupies?" He laughed and bounced her around a little with his legs. "It would have been a good time."

"You could still do it."

"Nope. I don't even know where the guitar is." He leaned forward and kissed her. Another scant touch. He could feel more shivers run through her. And she was getting that look on her face, the one which wondered too, not just wanted. "So, you want some cooperation?" He bounced her on his legs again.

"I want to hear about this group. What were you like when you were a kid? I didn't know you then."

"What do you think I was like?"

"Yeah, I can see you playing in a band, lead guitar. That fits. What else did you do?"

"I don't know. I did what everybody else did, I guess."

"No, I don't think so. I bet you were real cocky and arrogant and like that."

"I wasn't much different than I am now."

"Then you were cocky and arrogant and like that."

"Thanks a lot."

"It was a compliment."

"Yeah?" He took hold of her hands and stretched them out to

her sides, pulling her closer to him. "I didn't think you wanted to talk all night."

"I thought you did."

"I'd love to turn you on. We sang that too. We did a lot of their stuff."

"Everyone does a lot of their stuff."

He clasped her hands behind her back with his, embracing her. He started kissing her neck. "So you want to talk."

"I liked your last idea better."

"Did you?"

"Oh yes."

Her voice had so much breath in it – he'd turned her on. He turned her around in his lap and scooped her up. "What do you think? Can I stand up with you?"

"Going to try?"

"How much do you weigh?"

"About one hundred and ten."

"Yeah, I can stand up." He stood up and didn't drop her.

"Pretty good."

"Pretty damned good." He carried her to the couch.

11

She pulled up in front of his place, and her heart fell, here were too many cars around; his friends were over. So they wouldn't be alone tonight – why had he bothered phoning her and inviting her over if he had all these other people over? And he knew better – he knew she didn't like his friends – didn't want to spend time with them anyway. No, if she was going to sit around bullshitting, she'd rather be with her friends, friends she wasn't seeing much of these days between her courses and work and him and exams coming up in the next few weeks. And when she had time to see him, she wanted to see him, not him and his friends, because he was different when his friends were around; he was Mr. Cool when his friends were around, and that was an act she didn't care for. She got out of the car and tried slamming the door behind her.

And in the house, she found the worst: Lucy, Steven, Doug, Tom, and Wanda. Wanda was such a floozy of a name to begin with. And they were all drinking in the basement, with good old rock and roll playing away. It was a regular party. She wanted to leave.

"Bit of a party going on here."

Alex had come up behind her. She turned around to him. She didn't know if she was mad at him or not. "I see that."

"Yeah, everyone just showed up after I called you."

"Oh." She wasn't impressed with that explanation. He hadn't had to let them in. He could have told them, and honestly, that he had other plans.

"So."

And he hugged her, but Doug was turning up the stereo, and Alex let her go to run over there and turn it down again.

"Hey, this isn't the weekend. The neighbors will bitch."

"So invite them in."

"Just keep it down, will ya."

And he started bullshitting with Doug. Kim sat down on the couch. She looked around. She didn't like these people, and they didn't like her. She knew that and they knew that. There was a gap between them and her, and there always would be.

"We haven't seen you for a hell of a long time."

Wanda had sat down beside her, smiling at her, but Kim knew she wasn't really friendly. Wanda's tone was smug and bitchy. "No. So how have you been?" Kim knew that her tone was bitchy too – cold, uninterested.

"Pretty good. We've done so much partying lately."

There was something about that answer that really bothered Kim. It was as if Wanda was treating her like the new kid on the block, the kid who had to plead to join the group. Kim didn't even want to join the group. "I think I'll get myself a beer or something."

"There's a couple of cases in the fridge there."

Wanda pointed towards the fridge Alex had put in the basement. Kim snorted at her. "I know." And turned to bump into another one.

"So, how you been?"

Steven threw an arm around her. She moved back. "Pretty good. Yourself?"

"Hey, good, you know."

"Glad to hear it."

"So you still see Alex?"

"Sometimes." Kim didn't like Steven asking about her private times with Alex, but she was glad he had to ask. That meant that Alex wasn't telling everyone about them, and that was a sign of respect.

"Sort of surprised to see you come in."

"I was sort of surprised myself."

"The more the merrier, right?"

"Right."

"So."

She looked at him.

"I haven't seen you at work for a long time. You still working at the store?"

"Yeah, but weekends and nights now. I started taking some classes this year."

"I thought you finished school last year."

"I did. These are at a college."

"Oh, I get it."

"I'm just going to get a beer here, Steven." She got up and started for the fridge.

"I'll get it for you."

"No, that's all right."

"Hey, no problem."

Steven was tripping all over himself and her, so she stood back and let him get the beer. And she knew that she wasn't staying much longer. She couldn't take this – this – she didn't know what it was about these people that she couldn't stand, but she knew she couldn't stand them – she couldn't stand all the make-up on Wanda's face, and she couldn't stand all the lust on Steven's. And she couldn't stand the party – the let's-all-get-drunk-and-find-beds party that was going on here. Because it all seemed empty to her – what for? What was the point of it? Why was this happening? There was nothing here, no reason, no thought, just a bunch of half empty beer bottles. She took the beer from Steven and drank some. She hated beer.

"So, what's going on here?"

Alex was back, and had strung an arm around her. She didn't like it. She felt like she was being declared the personal property of ... as if it was some sort of clannish gesture. She shrugged the arm off, and decided to leave. "I think I'll skip this beer." She passed it to Alex. "Do you have any wine upstairs?" Because once upstairs, she could just walk out the front door, no scene, no explanation, no hurt feelings. And he could have his party.

"Sure, come on. We'll get you a glass there."

"No, I'll get it."

"It's my place. I'll get it."

So she followed him upstairs. She would have to explain to him. "Look, I can catch up with you some other time if that's better."

"What?"

He looked surprised. She felt worse. "You've got friends over, and I have exams coming up and stuff like that. So I can see you later."

"I thought we were going out tonight."

This was the first she'd heard of that plan. "But you have friends over."

"They don't care."

"Are you sure?" She'd never heard of that before.

"Sure. Why not? So where do you want to go?"

He was getting his shoes and coat. She put her coat on too. After all, if he was willing ... and she wouldn't stay here, why not? "I don't know. Where did you want to go?"

"We'll just drive until we see a place. How's that sound?"

"Fine."

"Then let's get going, eh. What's the hold up?"

And with a smile he was hustling her out of the house and into his car. And they were on their way, on the highway heading away from town. He was singing along with the radio, smiling at her, and bouncing his palms against the wheel. He didn't have any cares in the world. She wasn't so sure. Something still bothered her – those people, she didn't like to see those people. They reminded her about all those rumors about Alex. But this wasn't the time for that now: she had what she wanted. She should enjoy this. And there were things she had thought of telling him. "I wanted to tell you about this dream I had."

"What's this? A new approach?"

"What?" She looked at him and saw that old teasing smile on his face. "Get your mind out of the back seat for a few minutes, will you."

"Do I have to?"

"You have to." She spoke firmly. "Just listen. This was a really weird dream. I was flying up the river."

"That's supposed to be weird?"

"Will you listen? It was weird because it was so real and so simple. I was really flying. I woke up and I was surprised I wasn't. I flew up the whole river, even passed the lakes to the mountains and the streams. It was really strange. It was really weird."

"Were you tired the next morning?"

"No." She made the word a long sound. There was something not right here; there was something missing. "Actually, I was very rested. More than usually."

"You don't sleep well, do you? I've noticed that."

"Sometimes I do. Sometimes I don't." And she looked out the side window, away from him. Then she saw where they were going: the only thing up this way was the park lands. "Alex."

"What?"

"Where are we going?"

"I don't know. Where did you want to go?"

"I know where we're going. I didn't just move to town, you know."

"That's right. I forget. I guess 'cause I didn't know you then."

He'd reached over and grabbed her leg. "Yeah, well, we had a few parties up here when I was in high school, you know. The main grad party was up here."

"Yeah? So was ours."

"I think they all are. Some sort of tradition."

"Is that how it works?"

"Yeah." He was pulling into the park now. She didn't have long to decide what to do – decide; she knew all the decisions were made, had been made when she'd left with him, if not when he called her up. And it bothered her. She didn't know why – maybe it was seeing his friends again, or maybe it was because it seemed so plotted, or maybe because it was him; whatever, it felt cheap tonight. And she didn't want them to be cheap. And she didn't know what to do about it. Alex pulled into one of the first little spots along the lake.

"So."

He turned the engine off, and moved closer to her.

"What do you think?"

He was rubbing his hands up and down her arms, and bouncing his palms lightly against her now and then. He was full of energy, excitement. And she wasn't. And she knew that he really didn't want to hear what she thought. "What am I supposed to think?"

"You can think anything you like. What do you think of the lake? It looks nice, doesn't it?"

"Yeah." She took out her cigarettes and lit one up.

"You want to talk. We can talk."

He took one of her cigarettes and rolled down his window.

"What do you want to talk about?"

But that was a sham. He was playing a game, and it was an old game, the just-talk game. She wouldn't play that game. She blew smoke out her window.

"Well, you could tell me about all these other guys you've come up here with."

And that was another game, the tell-me-I'm-the-only-one game. It was a very strange game, coming from him, because he had made sure that this relationship was what he called free and what she called non-exclusive, but he didn't seem to be at ease about that. He always wanted to know if she was taking advantage of that. And that bothered her too. "What do you want me to say? There was the football team, and the basketball team, and the volleyball team, and let's see . . . yeah, the swim team, but you can't just add up the teams, you know. Some guys were on two or three teams."

"That's nice to know."

"That's what you deserve to hear. What a question." He was still caressing her. His hands were sliding up and down her back, almost massaging her. She let him.

"So, let's relax. What do you say?"

He was maneuvering her around until she was laying down beside him on the seat. He took away her cigarette. She knew what he wanted – and would get – from her tonight: they would have sex and go back to his place, where she would get into her car and leave, and he would go back to his party. The best of both worlds for him. She could smell him now, and she loved the smell of him. She breathed deeply, and pulled him closer to her, kissing his neck, shoulders.

"So you want to take off some clothes here?"

He slid out of his shirt and undid her bottoms. She lifted herself off the seat as he took off her skirt.

"You never needed a bra, did you?"

He was kissing her, pressing her against him. And he was moving down her front, to her breasts, to kiss and suck them. She put her hands on his head, and played with his hair. She wanted him – his touch, it still had those powers. But she knew she was still just letting him, not joining him. She needed more from him tonight. She needed words, words to help her relax. "Alex, do you care?"

"You've always known that I do."

His voice was almost a wince, not the passionate declaration of emotion the situation seemed to call for – not even the semi-outrage she'd half expected. A wince, and somehow that was more convincing. As if it was so deep in him, he didn't want to say it. She drew back his face up to hers, and kissed him.

"Anyway, you're the one who's using me."

"Am I?" He was smiling at her, teasing her.

"Yeah. You just want to use me up."

"Oh, yeah?" She ran her hand up his ribs and over his back. "Let's see how I'm doing. What do you say?"

12

He watched Kim as she knelt beside the campfire and stirred whatever it was they would have for dinner. Her face looked soft and sensuous in the strange light – she looked maybe a bit tired. For him, it had been a decent hike, but he knew that for her, it had been a hard one. She'd rest up. He grabbed a sleeping bag and laid it behind his head for a pillow. He watched and waited. He wanted his dinner. The hike and the fresh mountain air had added an edge to his hunger.

He soon turned his gaze to the sky. Darkness was slowly taking over. The clouds were already losing their punk glow and turning gray. A little pink – almost orange – was all that was left of the sun. And that would soon be gone. He smiled to himself and glanced at the trees. They were dense-dark now too. And the clearing was shadowed. The little campfire looked brighter. Kim was pretty by campfire. "Hey, what are you cooking there? Smells good."

"It's not going to be good."

"Why not?"

"I'm really quite a cook, and this doesn't cut it at all."

"Smells good."

"This is impossible."

"What is it?"

"Come on and find out. It's ready."

"That was fast."

"Fast food, but it's hot and nourishing. Are you coming before it gets cold?"

"Aren't you going to bring me some?"

"Self-serve tonight. I'm tired."

He pulled himself up with exaggerated fatigue and went over to her. "I carried it all the way up here and you won't even bring me a plate."

"Poor baby."

"You're hard."

"Tough as nails. Here you go."

She passed him a plateful of something. He bent down to the fire to see what it was. Noodles and corned beef. "This looks really good."

"The noodles are from a package, and the beef's from a can, so don't expect much taste. There's a couple of apples and some Parmesan cheese in the bag. You want to grab it?"

The bag was right beside him. He grabbed it and dug out the apples.

"Get the cheese too. It will help the noodles."

"Do they need help?"

"I told you: they're instant."

He grabbed the cheese and passed it to her. "This looks like a really well-balanced meal, Kim."

"Better eat it before it's all cold. The noodles are half-cold already. I couldn't keep everything hot over a fire."

"Next time we'll bring hot dogs."

"They'd be gone by noon."

"Yeah, we'd probably eat them on the way."

"No, I meant they'd be gone, be bad, rotten."

She was very cranky. "You want a beer? They should be cold now – or cold enough."

"Yeah, I think I do."

"I'll get them." He'd put the beers into a nearby creek to cool, but it had been light then, and it took him a few minutes to find them now. But he did, and he grabbed four and hurried back to her. A cold one was just about the thing she needed to revive her. "Here you go." He gave her one, put one by his plate, and stashed the other two away from the campfire. Then he grabbed the sleeping bags and brought them over to where Kim was sitting by the fire. "Here, this is more comfortable to sit on."

"Thanks."

"You're welcome." And he sat down beside her and ate his dinner. He thought it was a great dinner. He loved corned beef, hot or cold or somewhere in between. And the noodles were good, and the apple was a nice dessert. "You really did a good job on dinner, you know that?"

"I tried, but there are too many things you can't carry up here. It's hard."

"I think it was really good."

"Thanks. I got to go scrub that pot. I'm not going to heat up water. I've had it with that fire."

And she grabbed the flashlight and headed towards the stream – he'd forgotten about the flashlight. She'd been smart to put it in. It was pretty dark up here. The trees were just blobs now, and the sky was dark – no moon, few stars. All the light he saw was her flashlight bobbing around by the creek. He got up and went over to her. "Need a hand?"

"I knew noodles would make a mess. They always do. I think this pot's history."

"That's okay. I can buy a new one."

"I'll get this clean when I get home. For now, this is good enough."

"You need throwaway pots."

"You can't throw stuff away up here. It would be a crime. That's why I didn't bother with paper plates and stuff."

"I guess you're right." He wasn't right, again. She was sure in a bitchy mood tonight. "That dinner really hit the spot."

"You need something decent after being out here all day. Crap's not good enough."

"Well, it was really good. I appreciate it."

"You want to carry this back for me? It's as clean as it's going to get without hot water."

She passed him the pot. He carried it back to the fire and grabbed himself another beer. "Hey, where do you want me to put this?"

"Do you really want to know?"

"Kimberley."

"Stick it by the packs, anywhere, but don't put it in. It's not dry."

He put it down and laid down again against his sleeping bag, waiting for her to join him. The business of the day was done, and now they could just enjoy – if she would just snap out of it. And she would. "Grab yourself a beer while you're there."

"No."

She came over to him and laid down with a long sigh. "Tired?"

"Yeah. I'm going to grab a nap."

"What?"

"Just a nap. Wake me up in an hour."

And she unrolled her sleeping bag and laid down. "Are you that tired?"

"I'm tired. I'm cranky. I won't make it without a rest."

"You should be in better shape."

"You're going to be in dead shape in minutes. Now all I need is forty winks. I'll be fine if I can get a short nap. Are you going to give me a bad time about it?"

"No." Because that was all he could say to that, but really, this wasn't the way he'd thought tonight would go.

"Make sure you wake me up in an hour. Okay?"

She squeezed his hand for a second before she let go and rolled over. "Okay."

"That beer just put me out."

And she was asleep. He watched her for a while. He had nothing else to do. He knew he couldn't get pissed off about this, but this trip had been her idea, and if she couldn't take it, she shouldn't have suggested it. But, too, she was only asking for an hour's nap, and he knew what it was like to be tired – and a little snooze now would pay off for him later. But what was he going to do for an hour?

He was alone. The woods were dark. He could hear the stream rushing on its way, and a wind rustling the leaves. No birds were singing, but he could hear crickets. And there were a few other sounds that he didn't know. He should know all of them. A guy should know his way around the mountains. He didn't even know the types of the trees. He knew what poison ivy looked like. He'd checked on it before starting out. But that was all he knew – he wasn't even certain that those were crickets. He wished he knew more. Then, during the night, he could tell Kim that that was just an owl or a squirrel or whatever. Kim had known more than him. She'd thought of bringing a flashlight. He hadn't thought of that. They'd be out here with sleeping bags and beer and nothing else if she'd left it up to him. He drank his beer.

The fire was dying and it was getting cold. He got up and went over to it to throw in another log. He watched it crackle and burn. Then he stood up and dusted off his jeans. He wanted something to do – they should have come with another couple. Then the girls could rest, and he could play cards. But Kim wouldn't have gone for that. She'd have thought it too close to an orgy. He smiled to himself – he'd always wondered what an orgy would be like: would it be a thrill?

He started walking around the little clearing. Measuring steps. It was bigger than it looked, but not big enough. He grabbed a beer and sat down again. One thing about it: beer really tasted good up here. Those beer commercials didn't lie after all – they should have come with a group. He wouldn't be sitting around thinking about ads if they'd come with a group. In a group, there's a flow, a movement. Have a few beers, laugh. He lit up a cigarette and finished his beer.

How much time had passed?

He'd had two beers, one smoke. Half an hour, no more, maybe less. Eight minutes to the cigarettes (two to a coffee break). He'd call it half an hour after this smoke.

He knew that she took his being here as some sort of commitment – enough of one to feel free enough to go off to sleep, which she wouldn't have done a year ago. And maybe that was fine – maybe it was even true; he didn't know. He knew she was a very special lady. He put his cigarette out and walked over to her. He tried to see her face but he couldn't. She was hidden, as if she'd tucked herself up and put herself away. He smiled. He knew how to wake her – exactly what to do to get her back to him, and fast: one kiss. That was all it took with Kim. One kiss, and she'd be pulling him down on top of her with all that greed and impatience of hers. Hot stuff. But she'd been pretty cranky, and he'd let her sleep a little longer.

She was a very special lady, and he'd seen so much in her face at so many times that told him how special she thought he was. It amazed him. He didn't like to think about himself – never could get quite comfortable with it. But he liked what Kim thought about him. Even when he'd asked her to move in, and she'd said no, but she'd said it because she knew him, understood him, and was probably right about him; even then she hadn't hated what he was. That amazed him: she could love and not try to contain; she had other ways to show her want. No girl had ever been like that before. All of them had wanted to contain him, to make him into that boyfriend picture they had stuck in their minds – a gift from their folks. Kim didn't. Kim was stronger than that. If only she'd wake up.

He grabbed the flashlight and went to the creek for the last two beer. There was nothing else to do up here but listen to the night.

The bugs were starting to get to him too. Mosquitoes. Kim had nixed the Off, because it smelt so bad. That had seemed reasonable at the time, but now, he was beginning to wonder. He lit up another cigarette – smoke was supposed to keep them away.

"Is there any of that hiker's mix left? There should be some."

"I thought you were sleeping." He was delighted she wasn't but he had wanted to wake her up his way.

"No. I'm hungry. Too hungry to sleep."

"You've been sleeping for about an hour."

"Doesn't feel like it. Maybe twenty minutes."

"No way. Forty-five minutes at the least."

"Is there any of that left? Will you look for me?"

"I thought you ate it all on the way up." He grabbed the pack and started hunting for it.

"I put another bag in there for tomorrow. The way down, you know."

"You shouldn't eat it all now then if it's for tomorrow."

"I have to eat something. I'm so hungry. My stomach's growling."

"Here you go." He took the bag over to her. "Anything else?"

"I don't suppose you want to go over and get me some water?"

"Sure." Because that would give him a chance to clean up a little. He grabbed the flashlight and his toothbrush and paste, and headed for the stream. And he needed a convenient tree too. But he was only gone five minutes.

"Where's my water?"

He'd forgotten it. He confessed. "I'll be right back with it."

"No."

She grabbed his arm, holding him back.

"I could clean up a bit too. Pass the toothpaste and the flashlight, and wait here for me."

He laughed: so she'd seen him. But that was all right – it had given her the idea.

While she was gone, he rolled out his sleeping bag and zipped it up to hers. He wanted everything ready when she came back. He took off his shoes and kicked the bags out straight with his feet. Then he smoothed them out with his palm. This was the time he'd come for – this was their time. He unbuttoned his shirt and dropped his jeans and scrambled between the layers. And he laid back. And then he missed the pillows – they'd forgotten the pillows.

He sat up and looked around him. He couldn't see much, but he knew his jean jacket was around somewhere. It would have to do – what had she worn? She had a sweater, and he remembered seeing her with it when she laid down. She must have used it as a pillow. So it had to be near. He found it, and put it behind his head. That was better. He'd get his jacket when she came back. So everything was ready. He laid back between the bags and waited. She wasn't long – she was gone just long enough to miss his clumsiness, and he was glad of that. He knew that he looked calm and controlled when she came over. He flopped the top back for her: his invitation.

"I think I better put some wood on this fire first. What do you think?"

"Why bother?"

"Won't it get cold and wet tonight, up here?"

And he'd thought tonight would be strictly hot and wet – he couldn't say that to her, he smiled.

"Go ahead, and while you're over there, would you grab my jacket for me?"

"Sure."

He watched her – he just had to get her to lay down now, and she was his. And she looked good. He liked her body. She sat down beside him and passed him the jacket. He rolled it up and put it beside him quickly. He turned back to her. "So you coming?" And he waved the top bag's edge open for her. But she didn't move. She just looked at him. He propped himself up on his elbow and kissed her.

"Just give me a second to take off. . . ."

She was taking off her shoes. He rubbed her back. She slipped off her jeans. He moved over for her in the sleeping bag. And then she was there with him, and he rolled on top of her, kissing her and holding her, and feeling her hands grabbing his back. "So my dear, what do you think?"

"'Bout what?"

She was mumbling – she was getting into this fast. He tucked her sweater behind her head, for her comfort.

"Oh my God, I'd forgotten how beautiful they are. Will you look at that?"

Her voice had that strange charmed sound to it, and her hands had gone limp on his back. She'd stopped. "What?" He pulled up on his elbows to look at her – what was she seeing?

"The stars. They must have come out while I was asleep."

"Did they?" He tried to turn his head around for a peek. He didn't see much.

"There's so many. I've never seen so many."

"Yeah?" He kissed her neck. He knew how to get a girl's attention back to him.

"No."

She still sounded breathless because of those stars. He propped himself up again, and looked at her. She was right underneath him. She was all he could see. She was looking right past him. He moved his head to block her view. She moved away from him.

"I don't think I've ever seen so many. I wouldn't have forgotten."

Her voice trailed away into her thoughts. He didn't know what to do. He rolled off of her, and looked at the stupid stars himself. There were many up there, more than he'd seen at home. And then he knew what she wanted: romantic star-gazing. Of course – he could hit himself on the head. If she wanted that – she asked for so little – he was up for it. He pulled his jacket underneath his head, and put his arms around her. "So what do you know about the stars?"

"They say that there are more stars in the heavens than grains of sand on the earth."

"I doubt that."

"I do too, but when the sky's this clear, and the stars are right there like they are, it seems like it could be true. Don't you think?"

"Yeah, I guess." He curled her up to him, entwining his legs with hers, putting her hip against his – she was a little orb of his own, bunched up in his arms. He bit her shoulder. "So what do you think?"

"We used to go out at night, driving, and find good spots to look at the stars."

"So you know about them, do you?" He bit her ear lobe.

"No. Not really. Not like people who own telescopes. I guess I'm a dilettante. But they do something to my mind. You know?"

He didn't know. "What's a dilettante?"

"Someone who toys with something."

"Why do you say you're that?" He rubbed her shoulder.

"I don't try to learn about the stars. I don't know the constellations and stuff like that. I just pick up scraps of information as I go."

"Yeah? What have you picked up?" He undid the buttons on the cuffs of her shirt.

"Not much. Nothing really."

"Tell me what you know." He'd let her go on about it for a bit – get it out of her system. He rubbed her legs with his.

"I know about black holes. They're the most interesting thing I know about."

"I've heard of those. What are they?"

"It has something to do with density being more than gravity. I don't really understand that part. My uncle Bill explained it to me once, using a marble and a hankie. He knows all about the heavens. He has a telescope and all sorts of books. Dad says it's his hobby, but it's more like his life. He goes down to the south just to see the stars from there – he's the one who used to take me out in the car, looking for places to see the stars. He'd love it here."

Alex thought there was enough of him here already.

"Black holes are really neat. There's just something about them. They draw everything into them. I mean, they're just a theory, but if they exist, it would be a thrill to see one – even a picture. What are they – how can I put this? They're probably stars that collapsed, burned out and then fell inwards. I don't really know what that means. I think black hole pretty much says it all – but they aren't empty, but nothing can get out of them, nothing can escape them once it's been drawn in, and everything that comes near enough gets drawn in, or at least that's one theory. They may be completely closed. I've read that too."

"You sound like you're really into it." He could see the night unfolding before him: a lecture on astronomy.

"No – I know about sidereal time too. That's the time it takes for the earth to spin around the stars, the time it takes to return to the same spot, the same view of a constellation. I always liked that. We would stay out and watch it happen. After a while, the stars would seem to spin and be so alive. It was unreal."

Her voice was getting all excited, she was getting all pumped up, and it had nothing to do with him. He was being cheated.

He kissed her neck and bit her ear again. She barely noticed.

"You know, some of those lights we see now started towards us long before we were born, and some may not even exist now – we could be seeing a dead light, it's incredible. I don't remember all the light-years, but I know that Vega's twenty-seven light-years away. That's older than both of us. That's Vega there."

She pointed up to a bright star above them. He didn't look, just glanced.

"And those ones near Vega, two there, the light ones, you can barely see them, you have to look for a minute, they're about eight hundred light years away. That light started out to us practically before our history, in the Dark Ages."

"Yeah?" She paused, so he spoke.

"I don't know. It does something to me."

But he was supposed to be doing something to her, not the sky. He was supposed to be her thrill.

"Venus is an interesting planet. It spins in the opposite direction of the rest of the planets in the system, so its sun rises in the west and sets in the east."

She wouldn't stop. She wasn't going to notice him until sunrise.

"One day there is two hundred – no, more – of our days. They haven't had a lot of luck with probes to Venus. They break down when they get there. Could be the heat or something in the atmosphere, or little men. Who knows? It's sort of interesting."

He reached over for his cigarettes. "Well, all I know is that's the Big Dipper."

"Can you imagine naming a constellation after a kitchen utensil? I mean, it's not really a constellation, and that's not really what it's called, but still, telling kids to look up and see a kitchen utensil in the sky. The drone who started that should be shot. Not that it's very exciting in the first place. It's just a point of reference. There's one interesting thing about it though."

He knew he would soon know all about it.

"Look at the middle star of the handle. It's two stars. It's a binary system."

He didn't look – she couldn't see in the dark.

"Can you see? You can't really, not without binoculars, but it's two stars rotating around each other. I don't remember about that system, but in some binaries, one star's dying and the other one is growing. Now, either the dying one is feeding the growing one, or it's the other way around, the growing one is feeding on the dying one."

He was beginning to wish that he'd carried a tent all the way up the mountain.

"I don't remember, but there's some sort of attraction there – it could be both ways, with different systems. I know that if a star is with a black hole, the black hole can't be giving out anything, but has to be sucking up the star. I've seen pictures of that – not the black hole, but a star with a tail drifting behind it and going nowhere. The article said that there was all sorts of unnatural behavior – stuff not accountable for through some theory about some force. So they thought it was a black hole. It helped the theory about black holes."

He'd found a joint in with his cigarettes. He'd forgotten putting it in there, but he was sure glad he had. Pot was the surefire way of getting a girl horny. No-fail guarantee. "You want to smoke a joint?"

"No."

"Why not?"

"The last time I smoked pot outside – I was in grade eleven, and we were in the park, and I was swearing up and down that Bigfoot was hiding behind the closest tree. I heard him. Then I heard about that for about two weeks at school. That was the last time I smoked pot outside."

She wasn't telling him a story. She was brushing him off with a fact. The night was fast becoming a real pain. "Don't you think the stars would be a rush stoned?"

"I think they're a rush now. They don't need help."

He couldn't argue that with her, so he lit the joint and tried to pass it to her. She wouldn't have it. He smoked it alone. And he was pissed off. He'd never known her to be like this before, and he didn't like it. She didn't even seem to know that he was alive – or cared. She cared more about her stars than him – and she'd been the one insisting on this weekend, not him. She'd forgotten him pretty damned fast for someone who couldn't stand not being alone with him. "You don't care about me."

"Yes I do."

She'd turned to him as soon as he said it, and he hadn't even known that he'd said it. He'd thought he only thought it.

"And I'm sorry, but it was like seeing an old friend."

"It's okay." His eyes were seeing her – he could feel it right in front of his brain. He could merge right into her now. And she was leaning over him, blotting out her precious sky for him. And she was kissing him. She wanted him. "About time you remembered." He tugged at her shirt. "Take this off."

"Get up." He bent down and gave her a little slap. It was light. It was time to go.

"Go away."

"Get up, Kim."

"In a minute."

"You've been saying that all morning. Get up."

"You're mean."

She wanted sex this morning – that's what she meant by that remark. And he was mean. He meant to be mean. He'd been mad since he'd woke up this morning with the sun in his eyes. "I have to go to work tonight, you know. I'd like to get some sleep before that."

"Make some coffee."

"If you wanted coffee, you should have gotten up earlier. It's too late now. It must be ten."

"It's eight."

"By surreal time?"

"No, by my watch."

"It's still late."

"Okay, already."

He watched as she dragged herself out of the sleeping bag. He turned away as she dressed.

"So what are you mad about?"

"I have to get to work. Is there a problem with that?"

"No problem. We only have sixteen hours to get you there."

It took you that long to walk up here yesterday."

"Did not."

"Damn near."

"Alex."

He didn't say anything – what was the point?

"What are you? Hung over?"

"What I am is in a hurry. So move it."

"Oh, fuck, is this going to be a fun day."

He just rolled up the sleeping bag.

13

She'd quit. At the end of the summer, she'd given notice, and on her last day, she'd walked out of the store, and she'd made it clear that she was walking right out of the retail food industry. *It's not a happy place* – she didn't even have another job lined up. He didn't get it. He'd sat, and he'd listened, and he'd shrugged. He'd told her that he that was perhaps enough of a reason for a girl to quit work, but that it was a girl's reason. She hadn't even heard him – she didn't miss a bit the back-stabbing, the bullshitting, the bloody frustrations of all of them. *I don't need it, I'm tired of it.* So he'd told her that it was different for a guy. It could lead places. Sure, the girls were stuck up front, except for a couple of tokens, but it was different for a guy, and she had a girl's reason. And she'd looked a little apprehensive, but she hadn't stopped. There's something wrong with the place, and it's killing me. She'd kept it up for a good hour.

Griffins was pleased. He didn't like students who hung on after they'd quit being students. Not that he didn't like Kim, because Alex knew he did, but Griffins was strange sometimes, and he'd smiled when he'd told Alex – not for himself, Alex knew, but for Kim. It was almost as if he was saying "good for her."

It's even when I drive to work. I don't just know that something I like about me is left at home, I bloody well make sure of it. Who needs that? I don't want to be part of it now. I don't want to be a part of them, and I'm becoming one just with the hours I work. I'm beginning to sound like them. I don't even like them — what's there to like? What's there not to like? There's really not much there at all. That's just it: there's really not much there at all. She'd been pacing around the room, arms flapping with her mouth to emphasize all the words he didn't want to hear — not that he minded her quitting, but not like this.

They've got nothing, nothing. Nothing to call their own. Not when they get home at night. They didn't learn, they didn't care, they didn't experience one new thing during the day. They've just repeated every other day of their lives. I want more. I want something. Something for me, of me, something that makes me stand up — just that, no more than that. Something that makes me stand up once a day. Not unions or nostalgia or grandchildren. Not next week's schedule. Can you imagine being Margie? She's going to die with what? Nothing she's gotten from the last twenty-five years. She's going to lay there, surrounded by a family that she's bitched about on every coffee break for Lord only knows how long, and she'll probably be hoping that Griffins drops in to tell her that she has all early shifts next week, and then she'll die happy, thinking that she must have done good last week. He'd laughed, because she was funny, but he hadn't forgotten. Because he didn't have to imagine being Margie.

He knew Kim was just talking like that because it made quitting easier. She was trying to convince herself that night, not him. But she'd come to him because she expected him to understand her mood, and he had.

But she was wrong too. Work wasn't what she thought it was. Maybe it should be — he'd felt it should be once too, when he'd started there, leaving rock-and-roll for nine-to-five, because rock had been that and work wasn't. But work was work. That was why it was called that: WORK. And you played by their rules, and you developed a smile you kept for customers because customers didn't need more than that smile, and you kept your real smile for off-time. That was the way the world went around. And if you were good at it, you won time in the sun, and he would – had a shot anyway, he knew, because he'd seen it in their eyes, in the way they treated him; he could be their chosen boy.

But Kim was saying there was more to life than that, and something in him wanted to say, "yes." Like before. *You can't live from plan to plan*... and how do you tell that ... they sleep in the snow. Each word had been taken up by his blood. He'd said experience. And he'd meant it: life was got by living it all.

Tinker tailor soldier and grocer. She was right. There was no life in that, not a glint.

She didn't know she'd said that. But she would.

I won't die like that – he never said – thought – she would. Cold stones, that was death. Kim—he smiled—Kim was hot stuff. Getting it on with her, he knew he was with someone with a sex drive like his, and he knew that drive had the same source: wanting life, wanting every rush of sensation known to man, and coming up with a few never known before. His whole life was supposed to come from that – be that – and she was right: he was just repeating his days. And she would know that she had said it.

Somehow, he knew, he was jealous of her. He kept hearing her, and he wanted to hit her – how could she be so certain that she was so right? – because every word had been forced out as if a burning bush stood behind it; she didn't doubt, she quit. He never – not even spoken like that. He found himself jealous of that; caught.

He wasn't going to see her until he knew what to say to her, and he wasn't going to think about it long enough to find out what to say to her – couldn't, because each time he thought, he heard her again, and when he heard her, he felt it all over again, and he couldn't think and feel too. Because she was right and she wasn't right, and he wasn't quitting his job.

She was making him think too much.

Then she called him. He'd not forgotten her yet, just forfeited her, and he sat up when he heard that voice on the other end of the phone: "Alex? Hi." Kim. He played it casually, making his voice just drift into the phone: "No, I don't have anything special going on tonight, nothing I can't get out of . . . sure, come 'round . . . no problem . . . see you then . . . bye-bye." But what was he going to say when she was here?

It had been six weeks, he figured. Because that was September and this was November. So she'd ask about six weeks. He walked around the room. He didn't know how much she'd put together yet. He couldn't know what he'd have to say to her. He searched the call. She hadn't asked, she hadn't reproached. In fact, she'd been as casual as he had, acting – he started to breathe easier – as if there wasn't any six weeks, any silence. He sat down. Maybe she hadn't noticed. Maybe she just wanted him back.

She loved him. He smiled. Another night of hot sheets – if that was what was on her mind, she could come anytime. He grinned. He remembered her touch. She was so careful with her touch, not hurried or clumsy or heavy and insistent, but almost calculating – she touched almost like a man, touching not just because she felt his hands on her and had to move to escape that rush, but to drive him too, to rush him, turning him on and on and not letting him escape until she'd – and he'd – wrapped them both in sweating and wanting. He laid back on the couch and let his eyes close. "Gee it's hot, let's go to bed."

He still had that record. One he hadn't lost in the move.

He grinned. It didn't matter if Kim liked him, she wasn't coming over to be liked. She'd probably gone without it for the six weeks – she didn't sleep around for reasons he didn't ask about, why, or even acknowledged that she had, although he wasn't un-happy about her having them – and that was what was bringing her back: bees to honey. She was a horny little girl. He should have seen it right off.

He got up. He had things to do before she arrived. Shower, shave, maybe change the sheets, because Kim was coming back tonight. He stretched.

He was putting the wine in the fridge – tonight was going to be perfect, with everything set out, and everything the way she liked it, because then she couldn't ask, and wouldn't ask, because she'd see and wouldn't need to talk, or, if she needed to talk, wouldn't talk anyway because she wouldn't risk losing what she saw, which was just the way girls were – when he heard the doorbell. He glanced at the clock. It was a little early to be Kim – maybe she was anxious. He smiled. Even if it wasn't Kim, it didn't matter, because he could get rid of anyone. He opened the door: Lucy.

"You're going to close the door right in my face, so why don't you just do it? Go for it, just like you always say. You don't want me here, never have, never will, don't now."

Lucy, stoned, drunk, pained – making sure he couldn't turn her away – was slouched against the door jam, a half bottle of beer in her hand. He leaned his head against the door, and closed his eyes.

"You don't want me around, you just pretend you do so that you don't have to feel bad. That's all."

Her voice was nearly tears. She had him right where she wanted him. She didn't even have to ask him.

"You say you're my friend, but you don't mean it."

She wasn't pouting, or challenging him, or even looking at him – her eyes didn't look at anything, didn't seem to see. She didn't need to see, only to give him the words, because he'd been down this road with her before, many times, and she was just letting him know that they were going down it again. He took her beer from her and bundled her into the house. "I'll make you some coffee, Luc, and we'll talk it over. How's that?"

"You can if you want. I don't care what you do. It makes no difference to me. We all know you just like to sneak off into bedrooms. Nothing else matters to you."

But she didn't have to say that, because he already knew that she would never forgive him for not wanting her. Because that was her hold: they were friends, no more, and because of that, no less. He dumped her on the couch and went to make coffee. And he couldn't even hope that she'd pass out before Kim came, because he didn't know what drugs she'd done, or what an overdose looked like. He went back to her. "How we doing, Luc?"

"None of it's real. None of it's real. None of it's real."

She was half-sitting, half-laying on the couch, twisting her head around. A little foam gathered at one corner of her mouth. The hold she'd kept on her mind this far was leaving her now. She was letting herself slip deeper and deeper into it and leaving him to pull her out of it. "What's not real, Luc?"

"None of it, none of it, none of it."

"You have a fight with Steve?"

"I don't know any Steve."

Her voice was like that in a dream, distant and calm. He sat down on the floor beside her, and patted her head. "That's no way to talk about Steve, Luc."

"I just use Steve, like you use everyone, for sex. I learned from you to do that, and I don't get hurt anymore."

"Is that what it's all about?"

"It's not real, it's not about, it's not real."

"No?"

"If I say so, then it's not."

She fell all the way down to the couch, and started twisting around and around, holding her head in her hands. Alex wasn't sure how much of this was real. Lucy worked people and her hurt for all she could.

"You never use me, do you Alex?"

"No. We're friends."

"Yeah."

And she took his hand and kissed it, and closed her eyes. She looked out of it. Alex knew at least part of this was real – enough to be dangerous. Lucy had ended up in the hospital before.

"You say you are my friend, but you just stand there grinning. You say you're my friend, and you stand there grinning."

She was singing. Alex glanced at the clock.

"You've got a lot of nerve. I wish I had your nerve. And then I could stand there grinning."

He didn't like the way she was breathing. Too uneven. "Come on, Luc. You're tougher than this."

"I don't have to be tough 'cause nothing's real anymore. I don't have to be at all. I don't have to, don't have to."

"Luc." He spoke harshly. "Now come on here. Try."

"I can't fly, didn't you know that?"

"I'm glad to hear it. Now come on." He tried to pick her up. She had to start moving, even if it made her sick. "Come on. You're going to the can."

"No. You just want to lock me away in a small room. Then you can forget I'm there. That's what you want."

He let her drop back onto the couch. "I'll tell you, Luc, if you were in my can all the time, I couldn't forget you were there. Know what I mean?" And he grinned, and she looked up at him and grinned too. "See, you feel better."

"You always make me feel better."

"We're friends." He reminded her, to caution her, because he didn't want her grabbing at him again.

"Friends."

And she closed her eyes and appeared to sleep. He watched her for a few moments. Her breathing was a bit better. He relaxed. Because if Lucy slept, or even wandered into her own world, but one without screams, he could still work his way with Kim. He looked at the clock. Kim should be here. She was late.

He got up and looked out the window. Kim wasn't late, she was parking her car. He took in a deep breath and went to get the wine. He answered the door when he heard her knock. "Hi there. Right on time."

"Hi."

She was standing a few steps back from the door, as if she'd sprung back from her knock. And her face too, was nearly flinching.

She looked like she wanted to step further back, and further back, until she was gone. She was scared of him. He could see that she was asking him, *are you going to hurt me, squash me, tonight?* But not like a mouse, because mice didn't ready themselves to strike back. He thought he should reach for her and hold her. He couldn't – *how much will you demand from me to save me from hurting you?* – because I can't do it all and you won't settle for any less, will you? He'd been wrong to think he'd get out of tonight without facing it all. "So how are you?"

"Fine. You?"

"Good, good." He smiled, but she wouldn't relax.

"So."

"Oh." He moved back from the doorway to let her in.

"Yeah, come in, come in. Let me hang up your coat." He slipped her coat from her shoulders and hung it over a chair. She turned back to him, gray eyes steady and suspicious. "So." He was scared of her tonight – he wasn't going to let her demand all from him. "Long time no see." He said it before he could stop himself, and he saw her flinch. He kept talking, not letting space bring up that meaning. "I guess you've been busy looking for work. This is a good time of the year for it. There's lots of people moving around to different jobs, and with Christmas coming up, lots of people are hiring."

"I suppose it depends on what you're looking at."

"So what are you looking at?" He was casual.

"Is this a really bad time?"

"What?" She was skeptical of this little act – where had he slipped?

"I mean – "

And she made a little circle with her head. He looked around the entrance.

"Are we staying out here all night?"

"No, of course not." And quickly – too quickly he knew – he had her in the living room. "Come and sit down."

"I'm interrupting."

She'd stopped sharply and pulled her hand away from him. And every muscle in her face went tight – he almost expected to hear her teeth grinding together. He nearly laughed; she was jealous. "It's just Lucy, Kim. She dropped by a while ago. You know what they say, 'a friend in need is a friend indeed.' Come on, sit." He nudged her with his shoulder, and she came and sat with him. But her face didn't change, and he knew she'd thought she'd found the reason for the last six weeks. "We can sit in the kitchen if you want."

"Whatever."

"I've got some coffee on." He just remembered it. "We could have some coffee, or drink wine. Which do you want?"

"I don't care."

Something was hardening in her – she hadn't looked away from Lucy – becoming the insistence of a man who'd cast his line into the river too many times now to leave without catching what he came for, who'd forgotten he'd come for the fun of it. "Yeah, we'll sit in the kitchen." And he led the way. "So you were telling me about looking for work. How's that going?"

"I'm helping Dad out until I get something better."

"Oh yeah? What do you do there?"

He waited, but she didn't say any more. She was still sulky, and she was waiting for him to explain. "Oh, yeah, the wine. I forgot to get it. I put it in the fridge after you called." And he grinned, and winked at her, urging her to remember that they weren't strangers, that they'd spent plenty of nights alone, and this could be one of those nights, if she would. "It's a sparkling wine. I found it in the cupboard." He grabbed the wine.

"Slow weekend?"

But it was only an automatic response. She wasn't really with him. Two glasses were sitting on the countertop. He poured. "This is better chilled, isn't it, Kim?"

"Sure, I guess."

He sat down with her again, sliding her glass over to her,

watching for a look from those eyes. But she looked down into her glass. He bent his head down to meet hers. He saw a glimpse: fear, because it was all gone now. He wanted to talk – *remember when?* – *when you loved me and came running out the door? when you came to the store for me, the first time? when you left the stars for me?* – he wanted to will the thoughts from his body to hers and take them back to that. But she wasn't picking up on it, and he didn't say it – couldn't, because she would think he could do it then – follow through with words of love and actions, actions he couldn't do – a budgie soaring with a hawk. He wished she would see what she was doing to him, and leave. Because he hadn't meant to lie to her – didn't know then he was lying because he hadn't known enough of her, and couldn't have known that she could take it so far – and he didn't think he should have to pay this price. He drank his wine. She sat still with all her fears and commands oozing to him – she wanted it all tonight, he knew, because she wanted him to prove he had it in him. "Not bad, is it?"

"No."

"You got a smoke on you?"

"You out?"

"No, they're in the other room. I want one of yours."

"Sure."

She took a deck from her purse and tossed it over to him. He took one out for himself, and brought out matches, lighting hers first and smiling, still willing her to remember. "So, what do you think?"

"'Bout what?"

"Yeah, I guess Luc had too much."

"Looked it."

"Yeah, she's in rough shape." He took a drag from his cigarette. He couldn't gauge her reaction. He didn't know what she wanted from him, what she understood, what she wanted explained. "She gets like that sometimes, when things get too much for her."

"Alex – "

"She's only like that because she feels a lot, you know. That's why."

"That's nice, that's real nice."

And she glared at him. He giggled: at least he had her attention. "I didn't know she was coming over, and I couldn't turn her out."

"Alex – "

But this time she cut herself off, and looked away again. But he knew – had known all along, had known when she hadn't pressed for more, hadn't wondered about his life enough, hadn't wanted his life at all; and he had only been waiting for her to see it or say it or leave. And now he didn't even bother to tell her that he hasn't seen that much of Luc lately, or that he wouldn't touch Luc ever, because she is right: Lucy kept him from her. Because Lucy is a part of his everyday, and Kim wasn't, and as long as Lucy was, Kim wouldn't be. Because in the I-won't-die-like-that contest, Lucy could beat Margie hands down and by a country mile, every time. "We could take the bottle and finish drinking this in my room."

"Oh God."

She didn't have to look so beat. "Well, if you don't want to. . . ."

"For crying out loud."

"I don't know what you came over for, then."

"Right about now, neither do I."

And she glared at him again, as if she thought it was a threat. But he'd offered her the way out of it all, and it was all he could do.

"You're fucking impossible."

"Am I?"

"Yes."

"As long as I'm good at it." He laughed. He could hear her screaming not to my life, you don't, no, not here, not to me. "Pour me a real drink, will ya? There's a bottle of rye in that cupboard."

"Get it yourself."

"You're not nice to me, Kim."

"You're still alive, aren't you?"

He laughed. "This is true, this is true." Because he wouldn't have blamed her for killing him. He got himself the rye. "The problem with wine is that it only lasts thirty seconds, you know what I mean? But you can finish off the bottle if you want to."

"I think you know what I want."

"Bedroom's down the hall."

"Bastard."

"Yup." He laughed, savoring it. His head felt light now. He'd gotten away, escaped. And then he heard Lucy.

"I hear you knocking, but you can't come in. I hear you knocking, but you can't come in."

He looked over. She was slouching again, against the wall, singing.

"I hear you knocking, but you can't come in. I hear you knocking, but you can't come in."

"Come on in, Luc, and sit down. I've got some rye here. Have a drink with me, be a pal."

"Alex."

That was Kim, reprimanding him. "Yes, that's right. Sorry, Luc, but you're a disgusting drunk, and you can have coffee, but that's it." He looked at Kim. "Better?"

"Cute."

"I've always thought I was."

"I bet."

"You thought so too."

"Did I?"

He looked back at Lucy. "I was only joking, Luc. I'll put a good shot of rye in your coffee."

"You just want to get into her pants."

He stared. He didn't believe what he'd heard – why?

"I hope it's worth it to you."

And she sat down – plopped – on the floor in the doorway. And she started to moan. "Luc." But she gave him nothing. "Lucy."

Still nothing. "Come on, Luc." No response again, and he knew she knew what Kim must think of her. He got up and went over to her. "I'm your friend, Luc."

"Does not compute, does not compute, does not compute."

"You didn't hear anything to upset you because we weren't even talking about you."

"You just sneak off into bedrooms, and you don't care how you leave anyone else."

"That's not fair."

"You just sneak off into bedrooms, and you don't care if anyone else is having fun or not."

"When did I do that?"

"You say you are my friend, but you just stand there grinning."

"No, Lucy. Not again, okay?"

"Fuck off."

"Fine." Because he had had enough tonight too. He went back to his drink.

"She'll be all right in the morning, you know."

"Yeah." He looked at Kim. She seemed a little calmer. "If she wants to be like that, that's okay by me. People can be anything they want to be, you know."

"If you want to tell me something, say it."

"I'm not telling you anything." He wasn't. He was simply letting words run out of him. "People can do what they want to do and be what they want to be and you can't do anything about it because that's what it's all about."

"That's not functioning."

She pointed to Lucy. "That's her choice."

"Well, you're going to have to make a choice because I'm not staying here.

She took his rye and took a drink. He was wrong, she wasn't calm at all. She'd just been waiting for a chance to break.

"I don't have a clue in hell what's going on between us. I

haven't seen you or heard from you in over a month, and I don't know what you've been talking about all night. I can't sit here and not know anything. I really want to know what the hell is going on between us."

He looked at his rye. He always like the color of rye – scotch too.

"You don't like Lucy being here. I didn't invite her."

"I don't give a damn about Lucy. I want you. You have to decide yourself. You have to talk to me."

He looked at her.

"Now."

She meant it, and she'd wait until he did. He looked back at the table. He really hadn't meant to lie to her, and he didn't want to hurt her. But he couldn't burn up the world for her – he wasn't good enough for her. He couldn't because he didn't know how. But she would burn it up without even knowing that she had, never mind knowing how she did it. She was of that kind. And she should marry someone of that kind, like Captain Kirk of the USS Enterprise. And then she could boldly go where no man had gone before, and leave him behind, and he could get the rushes of his kind. "I love you." He was a washout. He didn't look up at her. "I've always loved you. Always will."

"Then leave with me, because I'm not staying here."

He looked over at Lucy. She'd curled up into a little ball. "Don't have to leave. Tom's out on the tugs."

"I don't care about Tom. I just don't want to be here. I want to be somewhere else, not here. Okay?"

"Okay."

"Then are we leaving?"

"Sure." He was watching Lucy get up. She was getting herself a cup of coffee. "It will be pretty strong by now, Lucy. Better put some cream in it."

"But you don't take cream in your coffee, Alex."

She was standing at the counter, taking the lid off of the pot. Steam rose. He was sure she'd burnt herself, but she didn't flinch.

She picked up the pot, and came towards him. And she was swinging the pot. She was going to toss it at him. He jumped up. "Go ahead."

"I heard every fucking word you said."

"So what?"

"I heard you say you loved her."

And then he couldn't blame her, because she couldn't know that he'd betrayed himself too. "Now, Luc." He took a step backwards, bumping into the chair. "You have to do what you have to do, but you don't have to do this."

"You have to pay."

"Luc—"

"Put that down."

Kim. She'd jumped between him and Lucy. He made sure he was right behind her.

"Tomorrow you're not going to get off saying you were drunk and you didn't know what you were doing, because you're not that drunk, and we know it."

And she took the pot right out of Lucy's hands.

"So just grow up. You're not throwing anything at anyone. Alex, I'm leaving."

"No." He was right behind her. He put his arms around her waist. "No, it's okay now." He watched Lucy. She was defeated. "You can go sleep in Tom's bed, okay?" But she didn't answer. She left, down the hall. And he was alone with Kim, and he could feel her trembling under his hands. "I guess that leaves us my room."

"Your friends are fun."

"It's just Luc, just the down-side, that's all." He hugged her tightly. We're going to bed?"

"Alex, I'm tired."

She fell back into him, resting against him. She was leaving the night up to him. He picked her up, and carried her to his room.

"So." He dropped her on the bed, and sat down beside her. "Quite a night."

"I don't want another one like it."

"You can say that again."

"I don't want another one like it."

She laughed, and he laughed too. "You don't have to do everything I tell you."

"Oh, okay."

And she stretched out on the bed, staring up at the ceiling. He stretched out with her. "So my dear." He wasn't sure. It wasn't so easy, going from that to sex; he needed something in between. "What do you think?"

"I'm tired."

"You're going to go to sleep on me now, aren't you?"

"I should have had some of that coffee."

And she laughed again – she was giddy. He stroked her arm. "It's still there, thanks to you."

"I don't even want to think about it."

She rolled over into him, and caressed his chest.

"I guess your shirt's still out there."

"Yeah." He dropped an arm around her shoulders. "So what do you think?"

"I don't want to talk about it, okay?"

"Sure, anything you say." He kissed the top of her head. "So you saved me tonight. I've never seen anyone move faster in my life." He had to talk about it. He had to know what she thought of him now. "You were right in there, like a dirty sheet."

"I didn't know what I was doing."

"You just couldn't stand there and watch me get hurt. That's the truth." He nudged her with his arm. "You weren't going to stand for that."

"I should have left as soon as I saw her."

"I'm glad you didn't." And he pulled her closer to him. "So what do you think Kim?"

"I think it is time not to think. I think it's time to do. What do you think?"

"I think you must hate me."

"If I hated you, I would have let her throw the coffee at you."

"This is true. Yeah."

"Turn out the light."

"I thought you were tired."

"Maybe I'm getting my second wind."

He moved her up to him, and kissed her, rolling on top of her. And he kept kissing her. They'd have tonight.

But she wouldn't stay over. She mumbled something about leaving him to "tend to his patient," but he knew she didn't want to wake up to breakfast with Lucy tomorrow. He got up and walked her to the door, hugging her before letting her go. It was all he could do.

And then he laid back in his bed. He was exhausted. He didn't believe the night. He was too tired to sleep. And thoughts were pounding in his head, thoughts he didn't want to have. But it was the first quiet moment, and he knew he had to think.

At least she'd stayed long enough to love him. There was something in that. But he's never thought he'd be the kind to need that – a part of the lie, but there never would have been a lie if there hadn't been her. His head hurt. He laughed – he'd thought she'd made him think too much before. "I'm a washout." Because he hadn't even dreamed what it was really all about. He'd thought that fast women and fast cars and fast parties would do it. Who'd he been kidding?

He got up and looked out his window. The night was gray and cold with winter moonlight. It looked more like November than October – none of the eeriness of a good old Halloween, nothing to say there was more than what there was. She wasn't coming back. She'd seen it all now, his life complete, and she'd been a fool to come back. He hit the wall with his fist. He couldn't make it happen for her because he wasn't good enough for that.

Because there was that part of her that saw those things. Visions. Some sort of vision that maybe she didn't even know she had, but that he knew he didn't share only felt a piece of, and even that little bit came through her, because he had it since he'd met her, not before – there were no lies before, none he didn't control. Because he'd been putting it on – but that was it: he'd been putting it on, strutting around with it, and she was taking it on, willing to risk for it. He was having a good time, and she'd die wise.

He went back to his bed and ripped the blankets off of it with one fling. He didn't know what he was thinking about anyway. None of it was real. Nothing had really happened here tonight. Kim had run into Lucy, and if she didn't like his friends, well, there was nothing new there. He flung his blankets back onto the bed and straightened them. He was glad he wouldn't be seeing her again, because then he couldn't feel this again. He went back to bed.

He heard a screech outside his window, and another. He knew it was a cat, some female in heat, screaming for it. Biological function functioning. He smiled. That was the way. No getting caught short there. Plenty of thrills. He snorted to himself. Maybe he didn't want it – never wanted it – and maybe just knowing someone else had it wasn't reason enough to want it – she didn't even have it, only some shapeless bright glint of it. He rolled over on his side. He didn't have to climb Everest just because it was there. Maybe he would if he saw it, but he hadn't seen it, not yet. Kim could come back when he'd seen it.

He closed his eyes. He needed sleep. Full day tomorrow. He got up and turned on the radio, setting it for sixty minutes of music. He'd be asleep by then.

14

On the verge. That meant on the extreme brink, edge, border. Verging on. That meant bordering on, approaching closely. She'd looked it up in the dictionary. For something to do. Because she was impatient. He didn't finish work until nine-thirty, and it was just past eight.

Breaking up. That she hadn't needed to check. She knew what it meant: tearing apart. And her stomach told her all she needed to know about that. And that that was what he was on the verge of doing to them.

That they were going to break up – tear apart – was obvious. Their time together wasn't working. He . . . something was bothering him. He didn't seek her out anymore. He was aloof, off-handed, even glib with her. And she cringed when she saw him. Together, they were tense at best. But why? – that was what she wanted to know: why – and how he could have moved so far away from her?

She'd come up with a few answers. One: he drank too much. Or, two, he was too scared of commitments? he was panicked. But really, she didn't know. She did know that he still loved her. She believed that—insisted on that, because the smell of him, his touch, the smiles, the knowledge, the power, all of that was too fresh still, and too good to be doubted: You've always known that

I do. And she did now, as she should know. He loved her. Each time they'd made love, each time he'd looked at her, each time his eyes had had that question in them, she'd known. Because those eyes did not lie – they were too vulnerable to be filled with lies. Not that he wouldn't lie—he liked to bullshit the world, and did it each chance he got. But no good liar ever looked scared. Lying, bullshitting, it was all a con, and cons took confidence. No, he had not been playing with her. He loved her.

But.

Somehow she just knew what he was going to do, and she knew it was for all the wrong reasons.

But then, there was the logical, objective view of it all. If she took that view, she had to admit that she wasn't losing much, because they didn't have much. She had hardly seen him since quitting the store – two, three visits, short, one trip, one "I love you" tossed in, but under distress. Before that, a lot of sex. Not even she could add that up to a grand relationship. So what did it matter? A formal ending to an informal relationship; what did that matter?

But she didn't believe that. She believed that something else was going on, something less honest than dying interest.

She did not want tonight. She did not like the idea of make-it-or-break-it evenings. She knew she wouldn't be any good at it. She would fall apart. She was falling apart already. Her stomach twitched and rolled around. She couldn't eat. She'd chain-smoked all day. She couldn't sit still. She paced. And it had been this way since seven. She dressed, putting herself through all the rituals of preparing to see her lover: showering, washing her hair, plucking her eyebrows, moisturizing every part of her, buffing, shaving, softening, dressing and dressing again until the right outfit was chosen, and putting on the bit of make-up that she wore. She wondered why she bothered. She knew what tonight would bring. She knew this would all be wasted. Still, it had passed some time by for her, and that counted for something.

She looked at the clock again. Nine-oh-five. She had dressed too soon. She had nothing to do now. She knew it would take her fifteen minutes to get to his house, including time to warm up the car, and more time to get up her courage. It would take him ten minutes to get home from work, and then another fifteen minutes to change and shower and all that. So she couldn't leave her house before nine-forty. More than half an hour to wait. To think, when she didn't want to think.

They'd missed Christmas this year. That bothered her. It didn't hurt her. She knew that he went out and bought gifts only because he was expected to, and that he bought only for his mother and brother. She didn't miss a gift from him, but she missed seeing him over the holidays. He'd partied a lot, she knew from Patty and Tony, and she was glad not to be a part of that scene, but it still would have been good to spend some time with him. She could have, had she called and arranged it, but she wasn't ready to do that. But then, it really didn't matter. It was too late now anyway. Six poor months couldn't wipe away those years. They had been filled with such a warmth, a closeness. And if they hadn't formed some recognizable relationship – going steady or something like that – what of it? He'd been her lover for two damn good years, her constant, secret, and passionate lover, and that was a fact. It was a fact that counted for something. It meant something. It gave them something. It probably gave them the very something that he was running away from. She felt sick. She was sweating. Everything told her that it was over, and that there was nothing she could do about it. She was going to hate tonight.

She'd tried to perk herself up for tonight. She'd said that there's always hope, but she somehow knew there wasn't, not really. To all appearances, he'd ended it already – a coward's way out. Still, nothing could be said to that. He had the right. Two good years didn't take any rights away from him. And bonds did weaken; that was a fact too. But for all the wrong reasons. That was the part she couldn't accept: he was ending it for all the wrong reasons.

What to say to him when she got there? – another problem. She didn't want to go in fighting. If it was going to be over, he was going to have to end it all on his own. But acting as if there was no problem was a lie, a cop-out, but walking in there and singing out, "Hi there, are we verging on to the end, or have we verged through it already, or is our love affair still intact, just lagging?" that was wrong too. So unless divine inspiration struck, and it wouldn't, she was going to walk in there and sound like an idiot. "Da . . . da . . . da . . ." It was not going to be a pleasant night.

So much was wrong. It made her angry – too much was wrong – shuddering wrong and for no reason. Because what was happening did not really have anything to do with them, but they were the ones paying for it. And she wasn't even sure what was happening. The loving was still there, that much she knew. It was there, because he had said it, and he wasn't the type to say those words easily – he was too scared of those words to say them easily, and he didn't need to say them to get sex. The loving was there, and they were breaking up. He was running away. It didn't make any sense. He wasn't the type to run. He went for what he wanted. This was all wrong.

She glanced at the clock. Nine-seventeen. She lit up a cigarette. Too much time before she has to leave. She stubbed out her cigarette, and went to have another bath. It was something to do.

Nine-thirty-two. Time for one more smoke, and then brush her teeth a last time, and she'd be off. She lit up again, and sat back in her chair. She listened to the house sounds, making sure everyone else was still watching TV. She didn't want to face a barrage of questions on her way out of the door. They were. At least that much was going her way tonight. She closed her eyes and tilted back her head. She wanted to build up some strength. She wanted to get past the trembling and foreboding. She let her cigarette burn down to the filter. Then she got up, brushed her teeth and hair, checked her make-up – she only wore blush tonight – and left. She still felt sick.

In the car and on her way, she felt a little better. At least things had started, and if there was a way to change his mind, she would have a chance to find it. He would show her the cracks. She just had to be sensitive, and look for them.

She liked the drive. She'd always liked driving. The time it took to go from A to B always seems to her free time, time between, time outside of the demands of life. All she had to do was drive. No worries until she got there. And on a night like this – snowy, dark, cold, typical for January – she enjoyed it even more. There was something about the dark and the cold that challenged her. As if the dark and the cold were there to be risen above.

Closer to his place, she slowed down. She even went around a few extra blocks. She didn't want to get there early. Late was better. But then she was there. She pulled in off the road quickly, and turned her car lights off before turning the car off. She didn't want him seeing her arrive. She didn't want him thinking: "I have only a few minutes. Now what I'm going to say is 'we're through, Kim.' That's all I have to say."

At the door, she took a deep breath and knocked. He answered before she had time to think.

"Hi Kim. I was just going to turn on the light for you."

"Hi." He was being pleasant – not considerate, concerned, or caring: pleasant, proper. It was as bad as she'd thought. She felt sick.

"Come on in. You're letting all the cold air in."

"Oh." She stepped in and he closed the door behind her. He gave her a pleasant smile.

"Come on. I've just made some tea. You need something hot to drink on a cold night, right?"

"Yes." But she didn't like that. Tea was a bad sign. Hot rum toddies would have been a good sign. She followed him into the living room, and sat down while he poured the tea.

"You take cream and sugar, don't you?"

He was forcing her to correct him. He was saying, *look what I've forgot, or maybe not.* "Just cream, thanks."

He passed her a cup, and taking his, sat down across from her, smiling at her, but not encouraging her. What was this – a Victorian stiffness from Alex Talon?

"So what can I do for you?"

She didn't believe it – that was the voice he used on customers. It was a slap in the face. It was cruel – meant to be cruel. It was so civilized . . . he was lying. He was denying before they even got to the words. He wasn't letting them get to the words. Because she couldn't say anything about them in this cold formal atmosphere. She stalled. "I thought I'd drop in and see how you're doing. I haven't seen much of you in a while."

"I thought there was something you wanted to talk about."

"No." She took out her cigarettes.

"Well, I'm doing fine. What about you? You got a job yet?"

"Yeah, since November, which was nice. Just in time for Christmas money, you know."

"Yeah? That was lucky. Where?"

"At Patterson's office."

"Doing what?"

"Answering phones, sorting mail, stuff like that for now, but when I finish studying, I should get more to do."

"Oh, yeah, you study. How's that going?"

As if he had forgotten that too – he was playing stranger. It was worse than she'd thought. "Pretty good. I did all right last semester. This semester, I'm taking a few history classes, and a political science course. It's really interesting stuff." She knew he didn't want to hear all this, but she had to say something – anything – until she could find a way to talk about them. "Next summer or in the fall – I don't know if I want to take a couple of classes in the summer or not yet – but anyway, sooner or later, I'm going to pick up a couple of skills courses at the college, like shorthand and stuff. For secretarial work. It will sort of complete things, I don't think I'll get a degree, not yet, and I want to move out. I think I could use more skills for the old job market."

"So you're a secretary now."

She smiled, mocking that little summary of his.

"Is it a happier place?"

He was almost sneering now. She felt cold. She didn't understand – why? He didn't have to do this. A simple "we're history," would have sufficed. Why this? It was almost punishment. And there was nothing she could do, as if he had poisoned her. But she couldn't sit there and take this from him. . . . "More things get done there. People who work there are involved. They don't waste their time backstabbing."

"Pretty active little office, is it?"

"You know who Patterson is, don't you?"

"No. I know the name. Should I?"

"You didn't vote for him then, did you?"

"Oh, that Patterson. You'd like that."

"I do." She drank her tea.

"So how'd you get on there?"

Family connections had gotten her the job, but she wasn't about to tell him that. "He needed help, I needed work. I heard about it from a friend."

"It worked out good for you then?"

"I like it."

"I'll vote for him next time around. Do my part to keep you employed."

"Gee, thanks." Because that wasn't support; it was patronizing, condescending, smug, vain, ego. She didn't need him. She finished her tea. She wanted to throw something at him. Anything. Something that would let them get at the words about them.

"So you just wanted to see how I was doing, eh?" – *so now you've seen, get lost*; she could hear it in his voice. Why? – resentment of what? what was the reason for this? If she knew the reason . . . but she couldn't know the reason while she was sitting there, taking it from him. And she wasn't going to take it from him; she wasn't going to curl up, repulsed, in a little ball and die.

She was going to make this as difficult for him as possible, and as difficult as she had to until he stopped it, and they could talk about them. "So how were the holidays for you?"

"Good. We had lots of parties. People were over here all the time."

"I heard that. People passing out and throwing up left, right and center."

"Yeah, they were really good parties. How was yours?"

"We had a nice family Christmas."

"I bet you enjoyed that."

"It was nice."

"Good."

And that ended that conversation. He looked so smug, controlled. She couldn't talk to him. But she had to try. She took a deep breath. "I did want to talk to you about – " her voice cracked. She cleared her throat. " – something, excuse me." She cleared her throat again.

"'Bout what?"

He was still controlled, pleasant – he had lines ready. She plunged on anyway. "About us."

"Us?"

As if there was no us. . . . "Yeah."

"What about us?"

As if there was no problem. . . . "We don't see much of each other anymore."

"Yeah, well, I'm pretty much in demand, you know."

As if they were just a part of his one-night stand scene. . . . She wasn't going to take that. "Are you really?"

"I don't have time to spend with one girl."

"I've noticed." What was she supposed to say to him? What the hell was she supposed to say to him? – tell him that they weren't what he was saying they were, and that was all she had meant to say to him? – in his proper and so civilized voice? Such a façade.

"That's just the way it goes sometimes, Kim."

"It's just a philosophical thing, is it?" She didn't know what she was saying, and she didn't care.

"It was fun while it lasted."

"Was it?"

"I had a good time."

"Did you?" It was charity from him: "Perk up, old girl, you had a good go." – And a good time, as if they were just a good time, when they had been more than a good time could ever be.

"I hoped you did too."

"If it's over, say it's over, Alex."

"I thought you knew."

"Say it." She was tired of the crap. She wanted to force the words, because once the words started, she could talk about them, honestly. They were going to be honest – she would make him honest.

"You know I don't give commitments."

"Not even to breaking up?"

"That's not what I meant."

"I don't recall asking for commitments. I didn't even bring a priest with me tonight."

"I know that."

"Say what you're saying, then, for Christ's sake. Cut the bloody crap all the time and say it."

"I guess we've broken up."

"Good guess." She took another cigarette. What was left to say to him now? She'd heard what she'd expected to hear. And she wasn't going to cry. She was going to let it happen; ineluctable; she couldn't struggle against it. But this . . . this she couldn't take. He owed her more than this. He was keeping it dry, dull, listless; he wasn't letting her – them be them. He owed her more than this. He owed her drama. Emotion. Hate. Anger. Or despair.

"It had to happen sooner or later."

"If that's the way you want it." She wanted him to know that the responsibility was his: he threw away what few he ever had.

"Hadn't thought about it until you brought it up."

"Is this what you want or not? Yes or no. Try to say something."

"It seems to be the way it is. Those things happen."

"Yes, right. God comes sweeping out of His heavens with a great magical broom, and stirs around in the cloud, creating a new atmospheric pressure, which changes all our lives, making what is was, and what was is, and no one is responsible for that whatsoever." She knew she sounded raving mad, but she thought he sounded no less mad, dispassionately mad.

"Uh?"

"Nothing." She smoked, looking away from him. She knew there was no point in getting all worked up. She knew he wouldn't understand anything he didn't want to understand tonight. And she'd known this was coming. This wasn't a surprise – the way he was going about it was a surprise, and that she wanted to change. If they were going to break up, she wanted them to do so on her terms, in her way, not this way, not his way, not as if they had never mattered, never had anything but cheap sex.

"Anything else you want?"

He wanted her to leave. "Yeah, a beer." She wanted time.

"I don't think I have any."

"Get serious. It's a beer, Alex, a lousy beer."

"You don't like beer."

He was so suspicious. "It's not asking for much."

"All right."

He went into the kitchen and she tried to think. Fast. There had to be a way. Wherever there was a will, there was a way. But, how could she turn this around? She wanted to take him to bed – if not to reunite, then to break up with some honesty, some respect for what had happened. But, how? She couldn't seduce him when he didn't want to be seduced. They had to show some respect, tenderness for what had been. She had to know if it was really over. He was back, with one beer. She took it from him. "You aren't having one?"

"No. That's the last one."

"Too soon after the weekend?"

"Something like that."

"You drink too much."

"Then it's a good thing I'm not having one now."

"So how's the store?" She was stalling again. "Big Christmas?"

"It was all right. Up from last year."

"I saw Patty over the holidays."

"What did she have to say for herself."

"'Merry Christmas.' That was about it. I just saw her in the mall, shopping. Been meaning to get over there, but you know how it is."

"She was over for a couple of parties."

"She looked a little hung over."

"Probably was. She parties a lot, you know."

He'd said that to draw another line between them, to remind her of his parties, to keep her separate from him, and she knew that, but she didn't know why. She picked up her coat. "Well, I guess you get to drink your last beer after all. I have to get up early tomorrow. I'd better get going."

"Leaving?"

"Yeah." She stood up. "Walk me to the door?"

"No harm in that I guess."

"Actually, it's only polite." She went to the door, and he followed, three steps back. He was so suspicious.

"So."

"Yeah." He looked uncomfortable. She wasn't going to make this easy for him.

"I hope you don't take this too hard."

"I was expecting it. Give me some credit for brains will you?"

"Yeah, I guess you would be. That's good."

But now she either had to leave, or make her move. She stepped closer to him. "We had some good times."

"Yeah."

"We could have one more good time – for the good times you know." She watched her hands. She couldn't meet his eyes. "Isn't that what the song says?"

"Kim."

"Alex."

"I don't think that would be fair to you."

"I don't think any less would be fair to me." She met his eyes now. She wanted him to see the stress in hers. "After more than two years, a handshake at the door is a little too cold. It won't cut it."

"I don't think it's a good idea."

She didn't think he thought at all – she knew he hadn't thought at all, or he would have seen that what they had was not the stuff one threw away, not even if one had blue eyes, dark curly hair, and a body perfect to complete the picture. But she couldn't say that now. She said what she had to say. "It's over, and when I leave we won't see each other again. I know that. I don't expect to change that. But there are ways of doing this, Alex, and I'm saying let's do it the other way."

"What do you mean?"

"I mean, one last time isn't going to cater to my delusions, if that's what you think." She moved her hands under his shirt, over his ribs, slowly. She was scared – she'd never tried to take him when he might say "No" before. "I mean, for the good times. I mean, because we did have something for two years."

"I – "

"Why not?" She pressed herself up against him.

"You know it's over?"

"Alex."

"Okay."

It was over, and it was sad, and it was over. She would let it go now. She didn't like to – she thought it stupid, wasteful, but it was his decision, and she couldn't stay when he said to go. So it was over, and it was sad, but she was willing to be sad for a while. She was willing to let go. Because if he could resist it, if he was not caught up in it, on fire with it, if it was so weak in him that a few doubts knocked it out, then she didn't want it from him. Then, he wasn't good enough for it. He was burned out by it. Simple. So she'd cry, and she'd hurt, and she'd go on. And she would go on, she knew that, and she knew, too, that she was more disappointed than torn apart.

15

We'll release you, but you will have to take it easy for a while yet. Rest in bed for the next week. Come to the office Friday, and we'll see how things are progressing. I've arranged for you to have a cardiogram on Wednesday, and if it looks all right, we'll talk about you going back to work. Now, while you're taking those painkillers, don't drive. I mean that. We don't need any repeats of accidents. Put your car keys away until you aren't taking any medications. Get a friend to drive you. Now, while your heart beat has settled, you may find that you experience palpitations if you overdo it. If that happens, start with the breathing exercises you were shown, and take one of these if you have to. Phone my office immediately if there is no improvement. With this type of injury, you can't be too careful. If you were an older man, I wouldn't expect you to come back from this so fast. You're young and that's on your side, but this would be a good time to stop smoking. Oh, yes, and stay away from alcohol while you are on this medication. You're still badly bruised, and you're going to be uncomfortable for a while, but there is no need for you to strain yourself. I was fairly happy with the results of your last tests, but that doesn't mean you can go on the way you're used to, because you are going to take it easy. You got that?

But he didn't even have any car keys to put away. Which just went to show what doctors didn't know. He didn't have a car now either. He was going to have to walk everywhere. Which would make him take it easy – he couldn't get to the good times.

But he needed them – just one. To break out of it. Because then he'd be himself again: healed. And it was so close – the music going on while he'd walk around with a beer and a girl (blonde, blue eyes, small waist, who never spoke but always looked at him) and he'd be wisecracking it up, not quite yelling over the music – "You think so?" and he'd take some beer and swing the girl close in to him, glance at her with a smile and a wink, and look back at his pal. "No, I'd say we were doing a hell of a lot closer to a hundred when we hit it. Maybe more. I mean, we were going down that highway," and he'd sway his beer around, "Hell, we'd have done it in record time if we'd made it. Maybe next time – what do you think?" and he'd grin, and swing the girl into him again, pressing her closer to him for a minute and then move them on to the next round. "Yeah, I'll tell ya, we were ready for it. Yup," and a drink, "I was moving that car. You should have been there. I mean, we were ripping up the highway, we were beating the wind," and over and over until he'd talked to them all, talked enough and danced enough and pressed her enough to take her to bed and leave everyone else knowing that the boy was back in town. Just one night, just getting back to the beat and the easy talk, and he'd be all right again. It would be gone then.

Because he was still stuck in it now. Hearing sirens, squinting at the flashing lights, smelling gas – tasting it too, in the back of his throat – and knowing, that he was in a position that his body wasn't meant for. He'd panicked. Reason told him not to move, not to make things worse, to wait until the voices with the sirens got him out, but they couldn't. He'd seen the engine blowing, and a hand coming down for him, and he'd started pushing at the door, the wheel, the seat, and squirming himself free. And he was still squirming.

Leaving the hospital had helped, but not as much as he'd hoped, expected. Because he didn't know what the doctor meant. He'd looked at the discharge papers, and he'd remembered the doctor talking, but he didn't know what that meant – was he all right, or not? And he hurt, and he thought he felt his heart flopping around. He could sit and feel it going at it. And he'd breathe and take the pills and he'd wonder if he should call. But he didn't call, because now out of there, he wasn't going back.

He knew it was all his fault. They'd told him that he must have been doing nearly fifty when he hit the median. The car had stopped on impact, crushing itself against the concrete. They'd told him he'd been pinned between the wheel and the seat. They'd told him that everyone in the car was lucky to be alive. They'd told him that, had they been tossed from the car, (why had they put their belts on? they never wore those things) they'd have been human hamburger all messed together. They'd told him that no charges were being made against him as he'd been unconscious before he'd arrived at the hospital. Then they'd stood there and looked down at him, as if they expected him to confess all then and there. But he couldn't confess what he didn't remember, and he didn't know what had happened that night. He'd smiled and kept his mouth shut. He knew he was lucky. Damned lucky.

The car was a write-off. It needed work anyway.

Everyone had walked away from it – Rex had crawled, but it was only a broken leg. Ron had a couple of broken bones too, ribs and an arm and a couple in his foot, and a good slash above the eye – a notch away from the eye, enough to be safe and no more. At least he'd taken the worst of it himself. He'd put himself into the hospital for nine days, needing more patchwork and observation. He'd bruised his heart – arrhythmia, they'd called it.

Everyone had been in to see him in the hospital. His mom, dragging his little brother with her, came in every day, which wasn't easy on her. Lucy too, every day, with Steve when he was working nights. Tom came all the time, bringing him stuff and joking that it was lucky only one of them was in the car leaving the other to fetch and carry. Patty and Tony had come down that night, and stayed until he came to. Been back a lot too. Everyone had been great. Once there'd been six or seven in visiting him and the nurses had chased half away. Ron and Rex were there then, showing off their casts and bandages. They'd been pretty hyped: We thought you were dead, man. *We were leaving you there when the cops showed up. You should have seen Rex, on his arms, pulling himself along like a big slug, you know. He thought the car would blow. We would have got to you, but we thought you were gone. Wait til you see the job you did on that car. You aren't going to believe it. I don't know man, you couldn't have hit the brakes at all.* He didn't know either, he didn't remember enough – maybe another car had forced him off the road; he didn't know. And he didn't believe that he wasn't dead.

But it was all over, and everyone was okay. He could breathe easy. He was home. No more strangers coming around, telling him what to do and where to do it, and poking him without asking him or telling him, and freaking out when he moved. He belonged to himself again. Not that he complained about the nurses. A couple anyway, were alright, smiling back to his smile, and teasing him: *We're going to let you go, but you behave yourself now because we like you and we don't want to see you back.* Which was nice, because they knew, even without charges, they knew that he had no right to their help.

He couldn't think about it: he'd done it to himself. He could hear such brutal whisperings in his ears: *You fucked up, Talon, just like you knew you would. You blew it and you knew you would. You're a prize idiot – you should be displayed, a sight for the circus.* And that was right. He hadn't taken any extra effort, but had done it by living the way he lived. And he couldn't stop living – where the hell was she? –because the panic was getting worse again. He was sweating and shivering, and cursing himself, hitting himself. And he'd have to get up, and walk it off. And he'd meet her face.

Last night hadn't helped the way he'd thought it would. Being back in the bar, with all his friends, he'd thought it would all fall back together, but it had fallen apart – he'd fallen apart and everyone had said that it was just too soon, and that maybe he shouldn't have come just getting out of the hospital that morning. But they'd brought him there, and then they hadn't helped. He'd had the jitters all night. Because they didn't really understand.

Kim would, he knew, and when it got really bad, he dared to glimpse her: in emergency, he'd thought she was running up to him, held back by the doctors. *You'll have to wait outside, Miss, until we're done,* and he'd relaxed and fallen asleep again; laying in that bed for those nine days, he'd been sure she was coming into the hospital, wearing her cut-offs and T-shirt – he'd seen her coming in and asking about him, and then coming on up to the ward and talking to the nurses, and then coming in around the corner, looking around the room until she saw him in his bed, and then coming over and closing the curtains off. On the way home, he'd seen her standing on the porch, waving as they pulled up, and coming to the car to help him out. It helped, and he didn't know why – maybe Bowie had it right: *"But our love comes from above – do it – let's make love!"* And she'd know it too.

He hurt.

—Because she knew things about him that no one else knew, and that made her his, and that meant her place was here, giving him what he craved – *You ever scaled a wall before? No. Wait there, I'll be right down. Okay. Why were you still up? What was I doing all night? – you'll never know. Who was at the party? No one, not you. Anyway, you're the one who's using me. Am I? I have only one lover now, all I need – 'cause I'm not alone – 'I'll have my share, I'll help you with the pain – You're not alone, Just turn on with me, And you're not alone, let's turn on and be (Not alone) wonderful, Give me your hands, 'Cause you're wonderful'* like a sponge dropped into the sea, she, drinking him in, growing drunk on his sweat, and he absorbed and making her live (he knew what he'd given her). She had no right to stay away from him. She had a duty to him. He was walking around again.

John had been around this morning, dropping in on his way to work. It had helped. He'd brought a couple of magazines and started a game of crib. *"Heard you guys had some party going up at*

*the bar last night. Wish I could have made it, but I was over at Ian's
and a couple of guys from across town showed up. I hung around. Ian
still has a bruise from the last time. Two by fours, the assholes. Nah, no
trouble. So if you're out tonight, come to Carol's. A few of us are
getting together up there. Should be all night. Yeah, she is, you got that
right. Hey, I got to get going. So I'll finish this tomorrow. Yeah –
anyone I know? I'll give you a call then. Yeah. So take it easy. Right."*
And Alex was alone again, set to watch another dreary day in.

It was better, this being home. At the hospital now he'd be
down smoking, watching soaps, in the lounge. Talking to other
patients too. He was tired of surgeries. So it was good to be home.
Just dull. Just boring when he wanted to live – *'You're not alone,'*
like a knife flashing through his gut.

He picked up a magazine and leafed through it. He snorted –
the doctor hadn't even told him if he should or shouldn't, *just take
it easy* when Alex was ready to take it any way he could get it. He
tossed the magazine away and stared up at the ceiling. She was
supposed to love him. Where the hell was she now? – she knew
he needed her now.

He knew it was planned by God – a sneaky way to send a message because it seemed too natural – too inevitable – except that
they'd lived, having put on those belts, which they'd never done
before, and wouldn't do again. God wanted him to know – not just
think, but know in his gut. God wanted him to face up to it – only
idiots were written up in that local rag, and God knew he wouldn't
stand in front of them all, proclaimed, but God knew too that Alex
wouldn't change because Alex loved the rush, and only washouts had
it. But God said – He'd used gas and sirens and pain to make it hard
to miss, but he missed it, because he couldn't see a way out, and he
wasn't giving in. He was walking around again, and his heart was
pounding again. He went back to bed and started his breathing
exercises. He was so alone – drifting away from himself in the solitude – losing it. He closed his eyes. The world was gray.

And he was still laying there when he heard the front door

open and close. He breathed out slowly and opened his eyes. Someone was here to save him. He wouldn't have to think. He watched the doorway . . . oh God, Kim—

"Hi."

— walking in, but stopped at the door. Hesitating. Readying to leave. He wouldn't let her. His hand reached out for her. "So what's kept you so long?" Impatiently. Because she had the right to stay away, and she should have been here sooner, and he wanted her to know it.

"I . . . I just walked right in because I didn't want to disturb you if you were sleeping."

She wasn't coming straight to him. She was weaving to the left, then the right. He leaned towards her, still holding his hand out. "So where have you been?"

"I was just going to come back later if you were sleeping."

He knew her too well to believe that one. If he'd been asleep, she'd have woke him up the way she did in the nights when she woke up wanting. He should have known, thought of it, faked the sleep. Too late now. But she'd come to him, and taken his hand, and sat beside him on the bed – sat gingerly, so carefully, as if the slightest bump would break him. He sat back into his pillows. "So what's kept you so long?"

"I didn't hear – I just got back – Patty phoned Sunday, but she said you were just about out of the hospital, and I called last night but no one answered."

She knew she should have been here. "Got back from where?"

"Holidays."

"You picked a fine time."

"I know, but I was going to come over Sunday or yesterday, but . . . I don't know."

"Yeah, you should have been here yesterday. I was here all morning and afternoon."

"I . . . I was too upset. You didn't need me here all upset like that."

"It would have been okay." It would have been bliss. He slipped his arms around her and pulled her onto his chest. She was shaking still, she was so worried about him. And her face – *'I'd lost you, and now I've found you; you could have died, and now I hold you'* – pain and joy so mixed together as to make one come from the other, but it wasn't enough. He wanted to hear it too – the forgiveness, the faith, clinging to words, to fill the lack. He brushed her hair back, and bent down to whisper in her ear. "So what do you think of me now?" He held his breath to hear the answer.

"I think you're alive."

"No." He let her sit up. He wanted to see her face. To search, and to show. "What do you think of me?"

"I think the same as I've always thought."

"What's that?"

"You really want details?"

She was embarrassed. "Now."

"I think you're . . . dynamic, and sensual, and what else do you want to hear?"

"I want to hear what you think."

"Well, that's it. I think you're not held back, and I wish someone had held you back that night."

"For a minute there, I thought I was doing all right."

"You're a hell of a lot more than all right, and if you ever do anything like that again—"

"I'm not going to. I've learnt my lesson."

"If you do, you better do the whole job, because if you don't—"

"You're going to finish me off, right?"

"You got it."

He clasped her to him again. She was perfect. She deserved so much more than him. "I won't. You can count on it."

"If you do, you're dead, and you can count on that."

"I'm sorry I upset you."

"Exactly what happened?"

And she freed herself. He sat up too. "I don't know. I don't remember any of it."

"I bet you were driving down the road with a beer in one hand and a joint in the other."

She was laughing a little, but he didn't want her saying or thinking that. "No—"

"'No?'"

"Well, maybe. I don't know. I don't remember." He wanted to dismiss it.

"I don't think you have to remember. I know you."

She was smug, but in knowing him, not hating, judging him. "Yeah, you do." He wasn't alone.

"So."

She pulled herself up and looked at him as if taking stock. He smiled, waiting.

"You didn't say how you are. What's going on with you now? Are you better, or well on the road, or what?"

She waited for a report. She was so pretty – almost a business-like slouch and still concern. He put up his hands around her face – *'You're not alone, let's turn on and be, (not alone) Wonderful – give me your hands'* – she'd turned it into a boast to the heavens, because they could, had, wanted to again. Her little face, so pinched, he loved it. He wanted more, and, during his days in the hospital, he learnt how get at it. He moved around and moaned. "I'm so sore, Kim." And she stared, sitting back, closer to the bed's edge.

"Stop that."

"I took a really bad hit." And he moaned again, half closing his eyes to mock pain, half watching her face.

"Don't do that."

And then she did jump off the bed. He laughed and moaned too, because it did hurt when he laughed. "Oh, Kim, I hurt."

"I think you're just wooing the sympathy vote."

"No, no. Could you get me a painkiller? They're there." He pointed at his bureau.

"Are you sure?"

"Why wouldn't I be?"

"Because you've had a lot. I mean, you're pretty stoned already."

"How you figure? I haven't touched drugs since I woke up."

"You're flying high up with the birds. Your eyes are like swimming pools."

"I haven't even smoked a joint."

"Those are drugs, Alex. All those things in those bottles are drugs."

"And I need another one." And he'd won. He grinned. "And a glass of water too."

"Anything else, while I'm up?"

"It's getting close to lunch, isn't it?"

"You want something to eat?"

"Yeah, that would be nice." He felt so warm now, and he could feel his eyes too, and she was right: they felt like swimming pools and he could melt into them. "I wish we could swim, Kim."

"You want to go swimming."

So she didn't know the song, but that didn't matter. She made up for it in other ways. "No, we don't have to. You make us lunch – you'll stay for lunch, won't you?" Because he hadn't asked, but just assumed.

"Sure. What do you have out there that's still edible?"

"Not much, I bet." He laughed. "Maybe Tom did some shopping while I was away."

"Let's hope."

"Just some soup. We usually have a can around somewhere."

"Okay."

"And then a massage." He was getting stiff with all this laying around.

"I'm not touching you with all your moaning."

He laughed – she'd caught him.

"You touch me right, and I won't moan."

"Used to be the other way around."

She'd burst on him with that one, and it took him a moment – it turned his head around – for him to see her grin and grin too. "I remember too."

"So you just want soup."

"And a massage."

"Tell you what. You go have a bath because that will help your muscles, a hot bath, and I'll clean up around here and get some lunch for us. How's that?"

She was taking over. "Good." He reached for his robe, and she was ripping the blankets off of the bed.

"So where do you keep the sheets?"

"Same place I keep the towels." And this time he got her: he turned her head and made her stumble. "You've helped herself to plenty of towels around here." And she blushed. He put his robe on, laughing. "A hot bath you say, do you?"

"Yup."

"Okay." He hugged her on his way out. She was so good to him – she let him rest, she made a home for him. He went to pour his bath.

But then he decided he wanted a shower, and he stepped in, letting the hot water spurt all over him. He leaned against the tiles. Because he could see it, feel it, know it – it was pouring through him with the water, and he was singing with David Bowie: "I will be king . . . and drink all the time."

And it would work. He could see it. She would scold, but like now, with all that joy in her face, and he would listen – Because she was out there, being so sweet for him. She was perfect, just being out there. And they would be so beautiful. Like dolphins. Not talking, not thinking, not doing anything but the doing, and they could, together, they could do – he could do – he could have been Bowie with her. She gave him that – let him have it just in being with him, because she didn't have to be with him. He closed his eyes, and let the water caress him as it turned cold. And when it was cold, he got out, and wrapped in a towel, went up behind her and took her in his arms. "You still making that bed? You're so slow." And he waltzed her around a little.

"Maybe you should have had a cold shower."

"Aw, you love me – you know it." And he pressed her tightly to him, kissing the top of her spine. "You know it."

"Your soup's ready."

"Go turn it off. I want my massage first." And while she went, he laid down on the bed. Fresh sheets, he loved fresh sheets. He should keep her around.

"So you need a good rubdown, you think?"

"Yeah." And he rolled over onto his stomach, giving himself up to her touch. And she was good. She rubbed his legs, up his thighs, and his back, shoulders, arms, and all around again, so slowly. "You are so good to me." And she did it all again.

"That better?"

"Oh yeah." He rolled over and stretched, and then pulled her into his arms. He was so relaxed, so tired. "Let's sleep." His eyes were closed. His head rested on the pillow.

"If you need to sleep, I'll come back later."

"No, no, you sleep too." He kept his arms firmly around her until he felt her give in to him. And that was right. They're lovers, and that was that. Her hair smelt so fresh. He cuddled up to her. He should have been a rock and roll star. – And he fell asleep.

16

They were watching TV. She didn't know why they were watching TV, and she couldn't think of a thing that would be a greater waste of time than watching TV, but that was what they were doing; that was what he'd chosen for them to do during one of their scarce evenings together. She didn't like it. She sat beside him, shaking her head.

"This should be a good show."

He'd said the same before each show started – some sort of justification, she guessed. She wasn't impressed. She leaned over and lifted his wrist, feeling for a pulse.

"We could watch something else if you had something in mind."

"Nope." She dropped his wrist, and yawning, stretched her legs out in front of her.

"Well, we'll see if this is any good."

"And if it isn't?"

"We'll change the channel."

"Oh goody." She moved over to the arm of the couch, and stretched her body out on the couch, flopping her legs over his lap. And she watched him. He smiled at her, and started rubbing her shins under her jeans. She wanted to lift her leg and let it drop back down into his lap, hard. And all she would have to say was that her foot had fallen asleep and she was simply trying to get the circulation going again. It wouldn't be such a lie. But she knew she wouldn't. She'd sit back and watch him all night instead, until he deemed it bedtime, and took some interest in her.

She didn't like this. She felt like some sort of wooden Indian, displayed: "see us sit here, the perfect picture, the ideal and sum total picture of togetherness." And on the surface, it was. They sat together on the couch with popcorn on the coffee table in front of them, and he gently and constantly caressed her legs; he'd smile, she'd smile, and he'd watch TV and rub her legs. Even the lights were dimmed. Anyone walking in would think it was tender. For others, maybe it was, but it wasn't them; it had nothing to do with them.

But it wasn't only that the evening was lifeless. It wasn't only that he was wasting her time doing things that she could do without him. It wasn't only that he seemed totally absent from the scene. What bothered her was that he wanted it this way. He was choosing this for them, he was keeping them at this level. Indeed, he was creating the bloody pretty picture. He had all the requisite gestures of the picture down perfectly – his smiles, the little caresses, the popcorn, the cokes; she knew he did this with no one else. This was not his typical evening. No; he was creating this for them. And she could think of a few interesting things he could do with it.

Stupefied: that's how she felt, and that was what she thought he wanted them to be. Because he had stopped reveling with her in them, but was still holding them together. At first, when she had walked into his room after he had been released from the hospital – *What kept you so long?* – those words had sent her to cloud nine faster than she had thought possible. She had expected to hear that she was not wanted, not welcome, but to hear that reproach in his voice for not being there soon enough . . . she'd heard him dismiss their break up as inconsequential, and she'd soared. And he'd soared with her. To come down to this – they hadn't even been this dull before they'd broken up. She wasn't ready to come down to this. She still felt all of the energy and feelings that she'd felt that day, but now she had nowhere to live them. They stuck inside like smoldering ash, denied air to burn, hot, incessant, desperate.

"You want another coke?"

"No thanks."

"I'm going to get myself one."

She smiled at him as he lifted up her legs, and put them back on the couch as he had left. And she smiled again when he came back, picked up her legs, and put them back across his lap, patting her shins again.

"You're sure you don't want anything?"

"I'm fine." She still wanted to hit him. He smiled at her again. But it was a smiled smile, not his smile. Why had he backed off? She'd searched for the answer to that question each night since he'd started this – *why don't you move in?* – that haunted her too, and had for three months. Maybe she should have then, but it hadn't seemed right at the time. But why wasn't he still asking? What had blocked all of those feelings of his? Her feelings hadn't changed. Her feelings wanted to live. They smoldered and prickled inside of her, waiting for that moment when they would live.

She'd thought about it. Every night she'd thought about it, and the one possibility that never left her thoughts was the nightmare: he didn't care any longer; it was lifeless because it was dead. She didn't want that to be – she didn't believe that was the truth. But it was a possibility. When she watched him, and when she thought about him and the way he acted, she could see that he wasn't acting as if he really cared – he wasn't sharing, not anything but his bed, and he'd share that with anyone, anytime, any place, or so the rumors went. So she had to wonder if he was simply being nice because she had been nice to him while he was sick. Duty, obligation, cowardess, or a combination of all three: it was possible. Alex did not like to hurt people, and he was sensitive enough to feel duty and obligation. And all he had said about them was that they were lovers, which meant nothing, or rather it could mean too much. It could mean that they were in love and loving. It could mean that they were having a long series of one night stands. It could mean that this was one of those vague and indulgent affairs that had all the right feelings, but for some reason never went anywhere. It meant nothing. And that meant that they could well mean nothing to him.

But she knew better. You've always known that I do. She still heard him saying that, and she knew it was true: she always knew he cared, if only she would clear her mood of fears and wants. There were just so many moments that were so caring. *Are Mom and Dad up?* – as if her parents were his parents. That was so long ago, but that closeness wasn't gone now. It hadn't been gone after the accident. At that time, she had known that he was going to call. That night had been so strange, it had felt so strange because it had felt like nothing – no dramatics, no revelations, just the knowledge of him. She knew he cared. She'd always known that he cared, just as he'd said. But she also knew that something was keeping her from the mystery of him, and that something was from him, because he was the force that kept the distance.

And that brought her back to the original problem: what was the block in him, and why did he want to block them? She knew the easy answers to that. She could blame the drinking and the drugs. She knew enough about substance abuse to know that no one could drink and do drugs every weekend and not lose something of himself. And she knew he partied every weekend, and sometimes during the week. And his friends, they had problems too (she had not forgotten Lucy, and would not forget Lucy for a long time yet). Overall, she would have to say that his social life was pretty dangerous stuff. It was his choice now, but she'd heard many times how choices become habits and habits become traps. But Alex wasn't the type to get his personality out of a bottle. He had too much personality to need a bottle. Yet, she had to admit that each time he had been so free and easy in his caring, he'd been under the influence of something or other. Even just out of the hospital, he'd had some sort of pills around.

Another answer came from looking at his self-image or self-concept. Play Psych 101 on him. She'd done this with one of her friends from that class, Colleen. She'd talk to Colleen about that time he had said, "Think I'm ready for the big leagues?" because that had really got to her. She hadn't known what to do with it, how to take it. It had seemed so wrong, coming from him. Colleen had agreed that it revealed a certain lack of self-esteem. Colleen had even suggested that it spoke of some real ego problems. Kim had thought about that and found that it made sense when she put it into the whole picture. If he was in that state, he would not be able to make a commitment or give of himself – and he should not be expected to do so. And what other state could a person be in and say something like that in that serious way he had said it? What right did he have to be crying inside when he had so much magic inside?

In her thoughts, at night, she'd solved the problem a hundred times or more. She'd seen herself sitting down with him, explaining the facts to him: "Drinking may be fun, a rush, but it is also inhibiting, because it impairs judgment, and thus the ability to act, to determine, to decide, and thus all possibility of growth and fulfillment is gone, because growth comes from acting and determining and deciding and making your way, not falling into it, or muddling around in an alcoholic haze. Add all to that the dependency, because even if it doesn't become a physical addiction for you – it can, it does, just the same as any drug – it can become a psychological crutch. You pour yourself a drink instead of drawing on yourself and your mind, imagination, when you want to have a good time, and soon enough you don't know how to have a good time without it. And you don't need that, Alex, you have too much going on for you." Or, "if there's something you don't like about yourself, change it. Take responsibility for it, and change it. Know that you don't have to be anything you don't want to be; know that you create yourself; know that you have it all in you, because I know that you do, and I've known it now for three and a half years, without doubting." And he would see, and they would kiss, and all would be right between them.

But something happened to that fine thinking and those easy dreams when she saw him. They left her. As they had tonight, as they had every night, no matter how much she had planned to talk to him and say it to him. She would stand or sit or even lay with him, with so much to say, and saying nothing. Not because she was less certain when he was near, but because she knew he didn't want to hear it. He wanted to sit there and keep them wrapped up in his limbo. Emotions, ideas, solutions – anything that would lead to any movement of any kind, he didn't want any part of. She could feel it from him, and she knew what would happen if she pushed: *I don't think we should see each other anymore.* She could still hear him saying that, it bothered her that he had said that, now more than when he had said it, because now she knew that he hadn't meant it, not in the long run. But he had said it, and she had no guarantees that he wouldn't say it again. If she pushed, he might – he had to show how very good he was at denial. She wasn't going to invite that again, and she wasn't going to hear that again. It hurt too much.

But how to stop him, or start them? And she was going to somehow. She had too many feelings in her to let this go on much longer. She watched him. He glanced at her, smiled, and looked back at the TV. She opened her mouth, and let out any words that would come out. "Have you ever heard of the Milgram experiment?"

"What?"

"The Milgram experiment. Colleen was telling me about it the other day. She's doing a write-up on it." Kim didn't know where this was coming from or why she was saying it, but it seemed innocuous enough. It wouldn't offend him, it wouldn't make him all defensive.

"Colleen is a little flaky."

"Yeah, she is, but this is really an interesting study. It is supposed to show insights into all sorts of things, from Nazi Germany to, well, to social dynamics and stuff like that. You see, he set up this experiment to see how people reacted to authority figures. He had it set up so some people were teachers and the rest were students, but the students were in on it. Anyway, the teachers were told that they were testing a new teaching technique, and that they were supposed to give the students a shock each time the students gave a wrong answer, and increase the voltage each time so the shock would get greater and greater, you see. Now they were on different sides of a screen and the teachers could only hear the students. So they started – I think Colleen said one man walked out right then, but everyone else was willing to go along with it – yeah, they started, and the students who were in on it started to fake pain as they got these shocks. And it went on and on, the shocks getting worse and worse, and the students putting on quite a show until some were screaming that they were having heart attacks and others were just screaming and some were completely silent, as if they had died or passed out from the pain. While all of this was going on, there were these men wearing white coats and carrying clipboards playing authority figures. Whenever the teacher people would hesitate or start to wonder if he should go on with these shocks, the guys in the white coats would tell them that they must go on, and that they – the guys in the coats – took full responsibility for anything that happened. Over sixty percent of the teacher group went all the way, even to the point of continuing to administer these shocks after the student had stopped responding at all – when the students were faking unconsciousness or death."

"This is what you study in school?"

"Colleen." He looked puzzled. She knew he wasn't getting it, but then she wasn't sure why she had told it. Maybe she just hoped that some thought would sink into his brain by the way of osmosis. "It shows how far people will go when they don't have to accept responsibility for their actions, when an authority figure tells them what to do. Their instincts or value system or whatever told them not to. They didn't want to, but they did."

"Really interesting, Kim."

And he looked back at the TV again. She didn't really blame him. She didn't know why she had told him that, except that it interested her when she'd heard it. In fact, it had set her off with a thousand rippling thoughts, and she'd sat there with Colleen for three hours talking. But Alex wasn't Colleen.

She sat, fiddling. She was trying to think of something to say, something about responsibility, about not copping out, about believing in oneself, about following through instead of running away. But it was too scattered in her head – too much mattered here and she couldn't think here.

Then it was eleven o'clock: bedtime. But she had to say something first. "Alex, we have to talk." But she cringed as she said it – she'd said that once before.

"Yeah? 'Bout what?"

"About us." She still didn't know what she was going to say, and he'd folded himself into his little "I-am-an-island-unto-myself" posture: arms across his chest, back stiff and straight, one leg over the other, no expression. It was just as she'd expected. He wasn't going to talk. But she had to. She knew they were falling apart. She had to do something or say something. "I don't think we're doing so well here."

"You come over quite a bit."

"That's not what I'm talking about." And this was going as she'd expected, too. He was reading all sorts of things into this that weren't a part of it. He was thinking that she wanted him as a regular boyfriend, which she did not. All she wanted was more of him, not more time or exclusive time, but time with him, just him, when she was there.

"So what do you mean?"

"I mean. . . ." What was she supposed to say to him now? She didn't want to say anything. She wanted to hold him, and take him. But that wouldn't be any good unless she said something first, something that would bring them together again. Why was it that they weren't together again? – she couldn't remember all that thinking she had done. "Don't you ever worry about your drinking?"

"I don't drink that much."

"You drink every weekend, and other nights too. You even say that the bar is your home away from home and I don't think that's so hot. I think that's something you should think about."

"That's what you wanted to say?"

"It's not that simple. Drinking like that can screw you up." She took in a deep breath. "You can lose yourself in a bar, you know."

"No kidding?"

"Alex." She didn't know if she was pained or exasperated or both. All she knew was that she didn't want to have any part of this talk, that all she wanted was more of him. And she wanted to say that he was hurting himself, which she believed he must be because he was hurting them – he was less in them – and he wouldn't stop hurting them until he stopped hurting himself. Self image, she remembered that word. "You have to believe in yourself and what you're doing, Alex. You have to. . . ."

"If you want a commitment, you should know by now that I don't give them. Variety is the spice of life."

Back to that theme. She hated the way he dragged this down to that all the time, as if she wanted to take away all his freedom, as if all she wanted was the dull and boring stuff of that routine. She hated that stuff. She knew too many couples who were caught in it, and who would think tonight was some sort of special evening simply because they had spent it in the same room. And she didn't care about the girls he was screwing all the time. He could screw all of them, she didn't care. It meant nothing to her, as long as he was here when she was with him. Because she had always thought that they had something special happening between them, and she wanted that back. It had been so good, so free, flowing, easy love. She wanted him. But words weren't going to tell him that. His look, his posture, his infernal "variety is the spice of life," his entire perception of everything she was talking about was stopping everything she was wanting. But she knew other ways of reaching him: shortcuts. She stood up and went over to him. She straddled herself on his lap, and pulled his arms off his chest. He looked amused.

"Make love not war, eh?"

"You don't listen."

"Should I?"

"Couldn't hurt."

"Yeah, you're right there. Never hurts to listen."

He was bouncing his hands against the bones of her hips. "Never know, you might learn something."

"This is true, this is true."

She leaned forward, resting her head against his. His hands moved to her back. Hers went around him.

"Is that comfortable?"

"Yeah."

"You don't have any bones, do you?"

"If I sit here much longer, you'll be feeling them."

"I bet."

And he laughed. She smiled. She was tired now. But things were softer now, and easier. It was always easy to hold him, it just didn't solve anything. It was all she had for now.

"So you want to go to bed."

"If you want to."

"It's up to you."

She leaned back and looked at him. His eyes . . . he really had incredible eyes. "Up to me, is it?"

"I don't want you to hate me in the morning."

"What makes you think I'm waiting until morning?"

"Hating me now?"

He was laughing gently again. He knew, he knew it all. He

knew how she felt, and he knew why. This was his answer to it. Not quite an apology, but regrets, and gentleness, and some sort of connection even while he refused to say he wanted her. "You are really strange."

"Am I?"

"You are. You play strange games."

"Do I?"

"You know you do."

"You think so, do you?"

"I know you do." And it was enough for now. It had to be, because it was all there was.

"You were right about your bones. Move a bit."

She slid back onto the couch.

"So you want to go to bed."

"Sure, why not?" Because the "I-do-if-you-do" game was a silly game, and it wasn't a game she needed to play. She knew, and he knew, and maybe it was unspoken and not wholly satisfying as an unspoken, but it was all there was for now. And she did want him, she always wanted him, and she loved the way he took her in his arms and closed the door behind them as they walked into his room. So she would make that trade for now.

17

What was a guy to do? He didn't know – he knew, just didn't want to know since knowing always ended up in doing, and he wasn't going to do it. Not that he cared that he'd be wrong in the long run; he couldn't be, he knew because he'd been wrong once (twice actually, but the second time was the same mistake, merely repeated, so he didn't count it) so he couldn't be wrong now. No, he wasn't leaving her (not that she gave him the chance to leave her but kept coming over, making him take her or repel her, which was altogether different than leaving her – effort, while leaving could mean—usually meant—just staying away) because he wasn't ready to give it up yet – it was a lie, he knew, every moment with her was a lie, but without her, it wasn't even that, because it wasn't there anymore: without her, there would be no one who'd understand the lie enough to believe it. Besides, she didn't think it was a lie – that was the difference between the first mistake and now: then he'd thought that she knew too, or was about to know, so he had to give it up before he'd been caught in it, but now he knew she didn't admit it was a lie – wouldn't give it up. And that was the excitement, the rush: watching her dodge the truth of the lie. And that was why he wouldn't know yet, and wouldn't do yet – why should he when she wouldn't? And who knew? Maybe she'd find a way to turn it all around and upside down and make her truth the truth, and his lie a lie. And in the meantime, there was the rush. He wouldn't give it up yet – soon, but not yet, not now.

She'd have left for here by now, and he'd had things as ready as he could. He had a nice wine out, just for her. He'd put off all of his friends, and unplugged the phone too, just in case. A couple of candles were handy for later. And he looked hot. He'd showered and shaved – she complained that he never shaved anymore, but it was that he shaved in the morning for work and not five minutes before she came – and brushed and flossed his teeth – he loved his pearly whites, and he kept them pearly white – and trimmed his nails and grabbed on his favorite shirt – plain blue, because it brought out his eyes, or so he'd been told (or was it that telling that made it his favorite shirt? – he smiled). He knew he looked good: fresh and on the move. He couldn't look better – it always surprised him how little it took for him to look this good.

He checked himself in the mirror one last time. He had to grin. The guy looking at him was acting like some green kid – was one, all over again, with the same nervousness, the clumsiness, the not-knowing. His friends would have a good laugh if they saw him now – giddy, and they'd say it was the girl, but it wasn't just that. This was the trip down the stairs in the dark every night a Christmas gift came in, and this was stumbling over a cave along the beach when he was alone and the cave was dark, because this was a rush. This put knots in his stomach, and this made sure he still had it in him – the power – because that was what she saw, and that was what she came for. He smiled at himself. He'd do it. But this time he didn't know what it was.

And she was here. He heard a car pull into the driveway. He went to the door but waited until he saw her hand coming forward to knock. He pulled the door open. She almost reeled backwards. "Hi. I thought I heard a car."

"Oh, God, I was just going to knock. You scared me."

"Oh, sorry." And he smiled – showing too much of his pleasure, he knew, but she merely shook her head a little, and smiled too. She knew, but wasn't sure – at best, suspected, but couldn't know. "So come in, before all the cold air gets in." And now he took the time to look her over, and he saw that she'd spent some time on herself. She wore a bomber jacket and jeans that clutched her hips and thighs – the tight fit of jeans fresh from the dryer. Her hair was thick and bouncy and shiny, betraying its fresh wash, her shower. He smiled. She had only a little make-up on – blush and eye stuff – and as he leaned over to help her off with her coat, he could smell her, and she smelt like soap and Kim. He breathed it in. And he saw her nipples catch against the felt of her shirt: she was bra-less and firm under that shirt, he knew. He wanted to rush her now, take her, but he couldn't. He choked – what if she didn't believe now, if she laughed? – she should laugh, and he should break it up, and it was the shoulds that turned his arms into lead. She was taking off her shoes. "Oh, you got your shoes wet."

"You have a puddle right in front of the house."

"Yeah, I know. I made sure I pulled up past it."

"I didn't see it until it was way too late. I didn't even look, you know. I guess I just don't think of puddles when I see the snow there."

"It's melting, but it will freeze over tonight."

"And isn't that going to be lovely tomorrow?"

He laughed, and she sat down and rubbed her feet. "You should have worn boots."

"Tell me about it."

He laughed again, and motioned towards the radiator. "Put them on the heater, and they'll dry." But she was already doing it. He turned and went into the living room to fill the wine glasses – he was useless to her already, and she was barely in the door. And she came in the room. He passed her a glass. "Here you go."

"Thanks."

And she sat down beside him on the couch, but curling her feet under her, and leaning back away from him. Posturing for a nice polite conversation. "I guess I should have had brandy out tonight, you know. A glass of brandy, nice and warm."

"To swirl."

And she smiled, and waited again. But a woman wasn't supposed to make a guy feel so restless, or have him thinking about himself so much. She wasn't supposed to step into his house and explode with sounds and visions – she hadn't yet, tonight, but she was waiting to – to stir him up and whirl him around. She was supposed to do the opposite: make him feel at rest, make him feel so at home inside himself that he needn't ever think about himself again. But Kim – and he couldn't have her any other way. "So, how's our government doing these days? Keeping you busy?"

"It's acting like a chicken with its head cut off."

"Oh? How's that?" He acted pleasant, interested. He wanted her to relax.

"It's an election year. Patterson's trying to decide whose ass to kiss."

"Kim." He was surprised. She usually had so much enthusiasm.

"Don't pay any attention to me. I just don't like what's going on. Right now, there are two projects waiting for funding, and both are really needed, but they aren't good public relations, because they give money to people who don't have any, and these aren't people you want your picture taken with for the front page. But it's a real need, and he's hedging, hoping he can put it off until after the election. It just bugs me."

And she drank her wine and looked past him, at the wall. Because she was only saying this because it was on her mind – it was impulsed out of her, not shared. Even she only half expected him to understand. The other half admitted he wouldn't. "So you going to vote for him?"

"A vote for Johnny is a vote for my job."

"That's pretty cynical, Kim."

"Yeah, I know. I don't really think that – well at times. He is good. He's just a politician."

"Yup, you're sounding cynical to me, my dear." And he drank down the last of the wine he had left and refilled his glass. Because he did understand what she said, just not the passion – interest – she had in it.

"You're right. I don't know some days." And she smiled and waited on him to say more, but he didn't know what he was supposed to say to help her keep her interest up in something he didn't see as interesting in the first place. He leaned over and topped up her glass. "Yup, there are days like that."

"Yeah."

And she stared past him again, at the wall. She couldn't stare at that wall for hours – minutes, really, he knew, but she turned them into hours; she was hating him. And she had every right – it was all a farce, this wanting her. *I could have been Bowie with her.* He almost winced in front of her, just remembering, but he'd been stoned, like she'd said, and he didn't have to own what he'd felt then. He just had to make her stop staring at that wall. "Yeah, I was thinking of getting a picture for there." The idea had just occurred to him. "Went out looking, but I couldn't find anything that really did it for me."

"What were you looking for?"

"Oh, something with a ship. There were a lot of, you know, flowers and sticks in vases." He'd seen some like that on Patty's wall. "But I was looking for something more, I don't know – a ship, fighting a storm, or something."

"There's lots of those around."

Of course she would know. It was probably one of her favorite pastimes. "Yeah, I saw some, but they weren't right."

"You should try the auctions. Sometimes they have really nice paintings for next to nothing. My friend got one that way. It's really old, and I've never seen anything like it – it's original. It's birds, and they're attacking a tree. It's really strange."

"It sounds it."

"It is. If you want something that's not 'off the rack,' you know, you should go to an auction."

"It's an idea. Maybe I'll do that." But he couldn't see himself going, and he knew she couldn't either. "When I get some time."

"There's a good one out at Freelake every Sunday. You should try there."

"Yeah. I could."

"But you might have to go a couple of times, because sometimes there's nothing there. If you want something special, you really have to work to find it."

"I guess you would." He refilled his wine glass. "I'm not working Sunday. Maybe I'll check it out."

"Sure. What have you got to lose?"

"Maybe my shirt, eh? I hear you can lose your shirt at one of those things — getting into the bidding."

"I guess it happens."

He lit up a cigarette and threw the match into the ashtray. Why was he bothering? She wasn't talking to him, but testing him, pricking him, daring him to go. Because she wanted him to be the type who spent weekends at auctions, milling about 'paintings,' not pictures. But they both knew what type he was. "Probably best to go sober, don't you think?" And there it was. She shivered as if he'd put an ice-cube down her back.

"Couldn't hurt."

And she gave him a dirty look, a warning. He laughed. "I don't know. Sundays I usually go out to the park if I'm not working. Cheap beer. You think I should waste my Sunday that way?" He was flaunting it — the difference, the objectionable — waving it like a red flag in front of her.

"You could try."

She had that hard edge in her voice now. She was feeling it — his life: *that's not even functioning you have to make a choice* because that was how she was it. But he knew better — he knew the rush, the thrill, the speed of the night, the party. And he liked it — the edge and the life that poured through him when he didn't — couldn't — know what would happen next. Breaking the rules to find out what they hid . . . he wouldn't get it. "Nah, I don't think so." He finished the wine in his glass and refilled it. The bottle was almost empty. "I can't see it. Unless they sell beer there?"

"Keep it up."

He raised his glass to her. She looked about to break hers in her little hands. He leaned over and poured the rest of the bottle into it. "Think I should?" He smiled into her eyes, watching, testing — he'd turned the tables and he pricked away at her now — little jabs to get her going, to get her bitching, because this was the fun, the rush.

"If you'd like to die."

Oh, she looked so serious, put out and ready. He laughed and sat back against the couch. "I don't think auctions are that dangerous, Kim." He was the matador, slipping away behind a fence, letting her rage at the dirt, because this was the way to play it: "now-you-see-me-now-you-don't." Because he wouldn't own up to her fury; he wouldn't show himself. "Maybe if they were, I'd go. I like a thrill you know – now and then."

"You have to make something out of everything, don't you?"

"Like hell."

And she glared at her wall, because she couldn't glare at him, not while he smiled and denied. Because she couldn't ready herself while he escaped. He watched her – she was filled with it now, that bloody vision of hers, and anger too, when he wouldn't play (couldn't play, he knew, wouldn't play was just her version). He wondered when she would burst. He waited – he'd done it; he'd made her feel him just as if he'd reached out and wrapped his arms around her, just as if he'd won a sigh, a moan. And it was a rush. She looked back at him – pained, but his face he kept so calm and casual.

"You just keep choosing it, don't you? And when it's not a choice anymore, you'll pretend it doesn't matter."

"What doesn't matter?"

"Your problems."

"I don't have any problems."

"No, none. You have a deep and meaningful life built on casual sex and drinking buddies."

"If this is the one about building your house on sand or rock, I've heard it already. In Sunday School." Still casual, unmoved, because that was the power, the thrust.

"You can't feel good about yourself when you never use anything that's in you to do it. You just can't. It's not possible."

She was up now, pacing. He followed her with his eyes.

"If you depend on booze and drugs and sex for it, then you're going to have to keep running there for it, and sooner or later, it's going to get harder to find."

"That's why variety's the spice of life, you know. Keeps me from getting bored." He watched her nipples grab her shirt as she raised her chest with her breath.

"Right. Always right. Okay, take it. See where it gets you, but at least have the decency – ability, mind – to see it when you're there."

"When I'm there, I'll let you know. How's that?" How'd she do it? how could she lay herself so open like that? How could she let herself want so badly? He loved to watch her love him – those energies, so steamed up, all trying to find a little crack to escape through, all for him. Her hand was in a fist, hitting her thigh – how could he be that important?

"You're hiding, and you know it."

"Am I?"

"Yes, and I don't know why."

"Then you don't know much." Because he didn't want to hurt her – he didn't want to love her – and he wanted her to see and to leave. "What you see is what you get."

"You think you are so free, and you're as tangled up as a guy can be. You can't be free when you don't think or figure out where you're going, and you don't even answer to yourself for what you do. Freedom has nothing to do with that."

"'Freedom's just another word for nothing left to lose.'"

"The hell."

And she sat down again, violently, her arms crossed on her chest. And the look she gave him. He wanted to push her on, he wanted her to tell him. He laughed.

"If you can't make any decisions about our life, then you're no freer than a guy in prison, because that's what prison is, not just four walls, but being told everything, never thinking nothing. It's accepting things that aren't from you. It's . . . it's not doing for yourself when you could and you know it, and you do – you know it, feel it, but you don't do it."

She had him. Wrestled right down, hog-tied and gored. Because he did know it – she'd brought it back to him – that gift, that charm, that part of him that wasn't the same as everybody else. He could lead them, he knew it. He could hold them and whirl them around in his hands. Because he had a power. He'd felt it, but he couldn't hold it in his grasp – them yes, but it, the power, it wouldn't stay, like butter in his hands on a hot day. But Kim saw it too – he'd thought he'd found the right part of the world for it, but she was right. He hadn't. Because the mockery laid on him. They weren't virgins drawn and convinced, but there because 'why not, eh?' and he had the right face. He knew it – she didn't have to bring it to him, or if she did, she should do it in victory: his head on a silver platter. Because this way killed him. Because if she was right . . . if she could give it to him – the way, the doing, the power . . . at times – he hated to admit it – times buried in the night, times after she had left, he prayed she was, and he prayed she'd tell him how. But he knew she wasn't, because he didn't know how. But he knew she wasn't, because he didn't know how – wouldn't the gift, the charm, the power itself be the way? She was trying to make him see too much and he couldn't see anything anymore.

"Why don't you go into the kitchen and grab us a bottle? There's another one on the countertop."

"It's your house. You play host."

"I just thought you might want to do something nice for me for a change." He needed her to be nice now.

"You put it that way. . . ."

She tossed her head and grinned a little, and did it, or at least brought the wine and corkscrew to him. "Why didn't you open it?"

"Because every time I try to get a cork out, it ends up in the bottle, in little bits and pieces."

"You're swift, aren't you?"

"Oh yeah, real swift."

And she sat down beside him, laughing, as he opened the bottle and poured the wine. And then they were quiet. He saw her hand sneak over to his, and she started gently playing with his fingers, entwining and caressing and stroking his fingers with hers. He watched her drinking his wine. He twisted her ring around her finger, and again. It was such a strange sorrow, and it laid on him. He could hear the rest of the world out there, passing by in cars, and he knew they – strangers, family, friends – didn't feel it. They talked and drank and yelled and were free. They never stopped to think – he'd have known everything she'd said if he'd ever stopped to think it through, but thinking wasn't the stuff of his life was made from, and he couldn't be expected to know. He should have thought. She was making him think too much too late. He poured himself another glass and topped hers up for her. "So." He raised their clasped hands for a moment. "What do you think?"

"Did I tell you I was moving?"

"No. Where to?" He'd never been to her place.

"We found a basement suite across town."

"Yeah? When's the big day?"

"The fifteenth, just a couple of weeks."

"Why'd you decide to do that?"

"Well, I'm moving out on Karen. I'll be sharing with Julie."

"Oh yeah. I met Julie once, didn't I?" He remembered a fairly tall, country-looking girl, who seemed to have a lot on the ball – not like any of Kim's other friends.

"A couple of times. She was in the store when I was there a lot, and she was at the beach with me once."

"Right. I remember her. Why you moving out on Karen?"

"She's driving me nuts. She's reading these articles to me all the time, and every month there's a new one. This month it's SAMMs, which is Sensitive And Masculine Males. It's really nauseating, and suffocating, and I just am not going home to hear about it anymore. I've been walking around dreading the week when the magazines come out for so long now, I finally decided to leave."

"I don't blame you."

"Jul's is sane. It will be a lot better. And it's a nice place too, and cheap – it's a steal, really. I'll be able to save lots of money now."

"What are you saving for?"

"A trip. To Europe."

"Oh." He should have known. She was one of those who'd get something out of Europe. "You'd like that."

"Yeah, I think so. We have an incredible view from this place. It's built on a hill and we can see the whole valley and the river. That's what really sold me on the place, because we had a view like that at home, and I've missed it."

"Sounds good." She sounded tired, and so, he knew, did he. He stretched. He had to get things going here.

"So, what's new with you? You never said."

"Didn't I?" He thought for a minute, remembering. He'd been the same – partying and all of it. "Nothing." He laughed – he'd met a new girl, she had a waterbed. "Nothing you'd want to hear about."

"Probably not."

And she laughed, too. They were okay now – they weren't going to touch on it now. He squeezed her hand, and pulled her closer to him. "Nothing changes me, you know."

"'Neither the devils nor the angels, 'cause the devil thinks you're his already and the angels are too charmed by you.' I remember Emma saying that. She used to say that a lot."

"Yeah?" He'd heard Emma saying that, but he didn't know she'd said it to Kim. "You didn't believe her, did you?" And he laughed, nudging her.

"So how's she doing?"

She was blushing. He laughed. "You know the store. It goes on."

"And on and on and on, and never has a reason. I know."

And she sighed. There was too much between them, he couldn't keep up with it all. He smiled and smoothed back her hair from her face. She was a pretty girl. "So you're moving."

"Packing and sorting and packing, and all the rest of it. I've got boxes at Mom's too. I've got a lot of stuff."

"It piles up, doesn't it?"

"Unbelievable."

"So." He stood up. He had to get things going here.

"You're getting a soft belly, you know that?"

"What?" He looked at her – he didn't expect Kim to . . . to notice that – to look before . . . she wasn't into bodies, she didn't notice things like that.

"You're getting a paunch."

And she reached her hand out and patted his stomach.

"Betcha I could pinch an inch."

And she was grinning. He didn't know what to say. "I can lose it. It's just the winter."

"Oh yeah."

"I never knew you noticed." He took her by the hands and pulled her up. "Come on. I want to show you something."

"What?"

"You'll see."

"Where are we going?"

"You thought we were going to my room, didn't you?" He laughed. They were heading the other direction.

"Disappointed?" He laughed again and hugged her to him a moment. Because he had an idea now – a flash – a way to get back to everything – the thrills, the satisfaction, the perfection. It wouldn't be mechanical tonight – it was time to unfreeze tonight.

"Where. . . ?"

"You'll see. Be patient." He opened the door to the basement. "I bet you didn't even know this was here."

"No."

She looked puzzled – he hugged her again. He'd surprise her, delight her. He turned on the light and led her down the stairs. "Be careful now. These stairs are pretty bad."

"Why are we going down here?"

"Wouldn't you like to know?" He laughed again and stepped up and kissed her lightly. "You'll like it."

"Like what?"

"You'll see. Oh, I forgot the wine. You want to go get it? Be nice?"

"I guess."

And she half laughed, half frowned. She didn't know, hadn't

figured it out yet, and he was almost shaking with it. He watched her go back up the stairs, and then turned and looked around. There were enough boxes around to make a maze, just like he'd thought. And she'd never been here before. He dragged a sleeping bag out from under the stairs and spread it out on the cement. And he sat and waited for her to bring the wine. She wasn't long. "That was fast."

"Are we having a picnic?"

"Sort of." He let her sit down beside him, and he poured the wine into the glasses. And he let her have one drink before he pumped her arm, and the wine spilt. "Oh, I'm sorry." And he dumped his glass on her jeans. "Oh God." And he moved right back from her and looked at her. She'd have to take everything off now.

"Terrific."

"Just go up and wash it out and you can put on my robe." He was talking to keep the smile off of his face. "Just use what's in the bathroom, and my robe's on my bed." He was shaking. "It should come out if you get it now, don't you think? Just grab my robe. They'll dry – do you want to put them in the washer? I think I have some of that stain remover stuff around somewhere."

"I'm just going to get out of this."

"Do that." He nodded.

"Maybe I will use your washer."

"It's down here."

"Yeah, I'll be . . . I'm going to wash it out."

"If you have to get it dry-cleaned, I'll pay it."

"I'll wash it. I like this blouse, you know."

"I like it too." They were standing at the bottom of the stairs, and he took her arm and urged her upwards. Because he had to get things ready. "Go see if it comes out."

"Yeah."

And she went upstairs, frowning and looking at her front. And he looked around. He really only had time to make a wall, not a whole maze – he should have thought of this earlier, had it ready.

He started piling boxes. He really only needed one end up, the end near the light switch – she didn't know where the downstairs switch was, so that wouldn't give him away. He stopped and listened so that wouldn't give him away. He stopped and listened for a moment. Water was running. She wasn't on her way back yet. His wall was done enough. What else could he do? He grabbed the sleeping bag and wine and put them behind the boxes. What else? – the candles were upstairs in his room. It didn't matter. The water stopped. He looked around. It would have to do. He dropped his clothes on the floor, where the sleeping bag had been, and laid down behind the wall. And waited. It was cold here. What was taking her so long. He breathed slowly, trying to be so quiet he could hear her footsteps on the rug. He got up – it was better if he was ready to turn off the light, and she couldn't see behind the boxes. He heard her step onto the stairs. He started counting. There were twelve stairs, twelve creaks.

"Alex?"

She was halfway down the stairs. His heart was pounding in his chest – what if she looked over and saw him before she was all the way down? He swallowed, and moved closer to the boxes.

"Oh."

Had she seen him? She only had two more stairs to go. He waited. She was down. He turned off the light. And it was dark. He hadn't thought of that. He couldn't see his hand in front of his face. He heard something fall. He didn't know what it was. He peeked around the box. He could see her standing in the light from the upstairs hall. She was looking around. Her clothes were at her feet, beside his. He drew back. She'd find him. And he heard her moving around.

"I know you're in this room."

He breathed slowly, quietly. He was sure she was coming this way. He could sense her steps. She was moving slowly. He could hear her breath – he could hear his heart. And now he could see her, she was coming around the boxes. And she'd dropped the robe. He should have gotten the candles. If he could light a candle now, and go up to her, and look at her, let the candle show him her shoulders, then her breasts, and stomach, and then he could drop to his knees and hold the light to her hips and run his hand through her hair, and thighs. She was with him and he pressed her against him, and ran his hands up and down her sides and back. Kim – she smelt the same as when she walked in the door, but with sweat and wine too. And smoke. He inhaled. Her hands were on his now. He kissed her neck and ears, and cheeks and mouth. He wanted her – he wanted to build up all her desire in her. And he didn't blame her for anything – not the bitching, not the knowing, nothing. She dragged her nails slowly down his ribs. He moaned and murmured, "Aren't you tired of babysitting?" Because she knew more than him.

"Hush."

"I'm trying, Kim, I'm trying to learn about love. I met some hippies—"

"Hush up."

They say down and he picked up the wine. She was so close – wasn't he only getting what any guy would take? He wasn't enough. He wanted her. He kissed her, he took her breast, he squeezed his thoughts away.

— 18 —

C almly: that was the way to go about it. She knew that. Nicely, and friendly, and calmly. With all the patience of a saint – patience was a virtue, and not for nothing; it was hard. Still, patiently, calmly. She could do it, if she would do it, but she didn't think she would do it after all.

The storm had knocked any pretense of calmness from her. Its power, its glory, its demanding and still stirring chaos excited and impressed her as she drove over to his place. She watched it. She saw it take trees and winds and leaves and rain and road and shadow and darkness and mix them so together as to make them nebulous to her eyes, and she changed her mind. She did not want to be calm, or nice, or friendly: she wanted more – wanted that electric mix, that power she'd known before. And nicely, friendly, and all that crap would only get her nicely friendly and all that crap back. She didn't want that. No one who could want Alex could want that. He wasn't about that, and neither was she. Nor was she a wet nurse. And she wasn't going to take it anymore.

The night was dark – genuinely dark, not city-dark. The usual street lights and porch lights were knocked out by power failure, and the moon moved in and out of the clouds. She loved it. It was eerie. Her knuckles were white around the steering wheel. It was a one in a million night. She poked her eyes out into the night – was that a person? was this a curve? where was the road? That was a bush. The thrill ran through her back.

She shuddered under a strike of lightening, and counted to the thunder: one two three four five six – the heart of the storm was near the mountains. She breathed out and relaxed. Even though she'd always wanted Novembers storms more than July suns, she shrank away a little when they came. Because of their power and noise and life. Such life – such intensity, she could feel it run through her, penetrating all of her, even through the protection of the car. That life promised that all things were possible tonight: all things could be willed if the will was strong enough, and all desires made content, if the person would want enough. That she could and would do.

At last, parked in front of his house, she relaxed and rubbed her fingers. She looked at his house. What was she going to do when she walked in there? She had no fight with him; this was not a fight. This was limbo and lingering. She was going to break that open. She was going to put a stop to his game, and bring back some sign of life to them.

She thought that she could do it. She thought that she had the will and strength to push it through, and that he had in him whatever it took to respond to that. Because with or without a god and a church, people still had sparks in them, and she did not believe – would not believe because believing it would kill her life – that a man, a man in love, touched, would act in a way other than true to that spark because that spark was himself – himself to mean not self-interest or self-promotion, but soul, emotion, center. Nor would she believe that dishonesty and dishonor and all the games that came with those two were facts of existence. Such was all merely mistakes made in foolishness, and could be stopped by revealing the foolishness. Therefore, while he had every right to linger or even to run, and while she would be perhaps not wise, but at least politically astute to let him and wait it out calmly, she felt no compulsion to do that. She saw other options and one had great appeal: challenge him on it, and force him to return from his thoughts to his spark – self. Hurry the process. And having gathered those thoughts, she stepped out of her car.

The wind and rain and darkness were harsher here, and she had to brace herself with every step. His driveway and porch were lightless. She moved slowly and carefully. She was soaked when she reached the door and knocked.

He opened the door and grabbed her inside quickly, saying, "I didn't think you'd come. You get that wet just walking to here?"

"It's pretty dark out there. I almost tripped."

"The power's been out for a while now."

"It's off everywhere around here. All the houses on the way were dark, just firelight or candles in the windows."

"We have a fire going. Come on in and dry off. Bring your coat. It can dry too."

She picked up her coat and followed him into the den. There the fire was burning behind the screen and Tom sat on the floor. A backgammon game was set out in front of him. A shot glass was on one side of it, and a bottle of beer was on the other, beside Tom.

"Hi Kim. You look like you could use a towel."

"Yeah, I think I could Tom. It's pretty wet out there." She shook her head, sending droplets of water all over Alex.

"I'll get you one."

Alex sped out of the room, as if, she noted, he was making up with speed for not having thought of the towel himself. And he was back as quickly, flopping a towel over her head, and roughly drying her hair. Then he took her coat and laid it near the fire. And he sat down, in his spot by the game, and patted the spot next to him, inviting her to join him. She did, relieved by his welcome, but unsure of what she would do now. The fire she liked; Tom, she could live without.

"I was just whipping him here."

"You're green, are you?" The board showed green ahead, with half the men home.

"You play?"

"Alex." She looked at him, amazed and a little hurt. "I used to play with you and everyone else on our breaks, remember?"

"Oh, yeah, that's right. You were still there when Steve brought it in."

"Yeah, I was there."

"You weren't very good at it."

"I beat you my share of the time."

"I've had a lot of practice since then."

"So you're good at it now?"

"You want the chance to find out?"

"You going to give me the chance to find out?"

"You going to give me the chance?"

"If you want to risk it . . ."

"You're on."

"Okay."

They were looking at each other with smiles. She was settled in beside him, and watched them finish their game. Alex won, but before she could move or speak, they were setting up again, for the tiebreaker. Alex leaned over to her.

"You see, I've set him up. I let him win the first game to get his confidence up, and I took the second, so now he has something to prove. And now I raise the bet. Right Tom? What do you say?"

"How much?"

"How much you got?"

"Make it twenty."

"That all?"

"That's all you got on you."

"You think so, do you?"

"You said you were down to your last twenty."

"Yeah, that's right. I am."

"So get it out here."

"We'll let Kim hold the money."

They both gave her twenty dollars. "You guys are betting on this?"

"Gotta keep it interesting."

She took the money and put it to one side, and settled in again to watch another game. But soon it was too boring. It was toss and count and toss and count and she didn't care who won. She looked around her, and the fire caught her eye. "Fires are nice."

"It's dying. Tom, put another log on it."

"I'm making a move. You do it."

"Maybe I'm making a move too, eh, and maybe my hands are full."

And his hands were on her, and he was grinning at Tom from behind her. She gave him a funny look, and found his eyes playing with hers for a moment. She liked that. "Pretty bad, Alex, pretty bad."

"It was all I could think of. It was bad, wasn't it?" A smile.

"Anything not to get up and toss a log, eh?"

"Yeah, that's right." Tom broke in. "Alex is pretty lazy, isn't he, Kim?"

"Sometimes he is, sometimes he isn't." She was playing with his eyes now.

"You think I am?"

"I think I've been here long enough to be offered a drink."

"Hey, I'm sorry. What do you want? There's um . . . rye and vodka and some scotch – you don't like scotch. There's wine in the fridge, I think. You like that. There's some red wine in the bar. What else— "

"I'll have some red wine."

"While you're over there, you want to get me another shot here?"

He had that expression now, the one that made her want to dance, and he was so close to her, just an inch or two away. "You're supposed to get the drinks."

"You do it."

A half-plead, a half-command. "This once." She stood up.

"While you're up, could you grab me a beer, Kim?"

Poor Tom, she felt sorry for Tom. He was doomed to be ignored tonight. "Sure."

"No." Alex objected. "You get your own girlfriend."

"She doesn't mind. You don't mind, do you Kim?"

"Hell no, and while I'm up, I may as well throw a log on the fire, right?" Alex grinned, and Tom looked back at the board. Kim started towards the kitchen. Alex called her back.

"Hey – no. We put all the beer in the bar when the lights went out."

"Warm beer?"

"It was just going to get warm in the fridge anyway."

"You guys are expecting a long power outage."

"Tom didn't want to have to keep going into the kitchen. He's lazy, you know."

"You should have some candles or a flashlight, or something to see with."

"The fire's enough in here."

"Well, I can't see back here." She was trying to find the rye bottle among all the other bottles.

"There's a couple of candles back there somewhere."

"Why don't you have them out?"

"We didn't need them."

"It's just that you guys are guys and you don't think. You should have put one in the window, and I would have been able to see where I was going up the driveway. From that side, the house is dark, you know. What if someone else comes over?"

"No one's coming over tonight."

He sounded so smug – she knew: he had made sure that no one was coming over tonight. It had nothing to do with the weather. She should have known right off. He had his plans, and he'd made sure that no one would screw them up. That was Alex. Sometimes, at the best of times. She grabbed the drinks and went back to their little circle. "So how are we doing?" She looked at the board. The game was still going.

"I thought you were going to get some candles."

"You said you didn't need them." She kept looking at the board. "Whose turn?"

"His."

Tom's. "It's always his turn."

"Because he's slow, you know."

Alex was leaning over to her, looking into her eyes again. She looked at him and drank her wine.

"That's good wine, isn't it?"

"Must have cost you over two dollars a bottle."

"You saying I buy cheap wine?"

"I'm saying your wine is a danger to my stomach."

"Gut-rot, you're calling it gut-rot."

"Yup."

"That's not. That's a nice wine."

"Yes, it is."

"You going to play or what here?"

Tom, poor Tom.

"Hey, my turn? Okay."

Alex rolled the dice, and Kim lit up a cigarette. She watched them play.

"Hey, I know, let's smoke a joint. Tom, roll us a joint."

Alex was in a high flying mood tonight. She laughed.

"There's some rolled there. Kim can get them."

"Do you mind?"

He was looking so inquisitive. She kept hold of his eyes. "I just love visiting you guys. I get treated so well here, just like royalty, never have to lift a finger."

"You forgot to put the log on the fire too."

"Did I? You'd better do something about me. I'm not working out as the maid."

"Get us a joint, hey?"

Almost all a plead; sweet talking now. She stood up. "You guys really have something against moving."

"You're just so nice to me."

He'd grabbed her hand. She laughed at him and got the joint. "Here you go." She passed it to Alex.

"No, here, you light it up."

He gave it back to her, but she wasn't sure of the look on his face. There was something behind this. "Why?"

"Because that's the good part."

"Is it?"

"Yeah, that, and the roach. You get a lot."

"Do you?"

"Yeah – go ahead, light it."

She did, and passed the joint over to Tom. Alex was still watching her and smiling to himself. "You want to let me in on it now?"

"Pot makes women horny."

She looked at him and tried not to blush. "Who told you that?"

"Maybe I found it out for myself."

"Doing a little experiment?"

"Something like that."

"You're something else, sometimes. You know that?"

"Am I?"

He still looked pleased. She drank her wine.

"Your turn again."

He was pushing the joint at her. She took it and passed it over to Tom, but Alex reached back for it, and gave it to her again. She took it, smoked it, and passed it to Tom. "You're really trying to be a great influence in my life, aren't you?"

"If you're going to talk like that, you aren't going to have any more."

Now he looked put out. She drank her wine and let them finish the joint. And they kept on with their game.

She knew she should be enjoying this evening, and she was. But she was restless too. She was tired of watching them play – she felt like she was on the sidelines again. She hadn't come over here to be on the sidelines. And she hadn't come over to visit Tom. And she knew that Tom was there still because Alex had told him it was okay. Tom would not be there at all if Alex had not wanted him there. Tom would have gone out if Alex had asked.

She stood up and wandered around the room. She poured herself another glass of wine and got the guys more drinks too. She put a log on the fire, and poked around the ashes, sending sparks flying up the chimney. She emptied the ashtrays. She looked out the window.

The rain had stopped, and the wind was less. The clouds were dispersing. A cold dim light shone from the moon onto the wet world, making it look wetter still. Darker too, somehow. The trees, and some leaves still fell, the last of the autumn leaves. She shuddered. She looked back at the guys. They were still playing. She looked back at the remains of the storm. She was cold now, and lonely, but she stayed at the window. She'd made resolutions at the door, she remembered, and she'd not followed through. Because this was nice. He was nice. The fire was nice. He'd made sure that no one else was coming over, and that was nice. He wanted her, and that was nice too. But none of that answered any questions and none of it brought them closer to what she was seeking here. *Pot makes girls horny* – she didn't need pot to want him: she wanted him every moment.

She wanted him to come over to her and stand beside her – no, stand behind her, and hold her and look out the window with her, and then to turn her around to him and pull her close to him, and want her, and be with her. Simple. Easy. And not likely to happen because he was too busy playing games.

She'd finished her wine. She went to the bar and filled her glass with rye. Alex held up his, as he would to a barmaid. She took the bottle over to him, let him squeeze her hand in thanks, and then went back to the window. Sipping the rye, she simply stared out. There wasn't anything else to do. She was just putting in time until they finished their game, which she understood was their way of putting in time tonight. So the whole world was just putting in time now, not living, making, but waiting, filling. Or so it seemed. The thought depressed her. She thought of leaving, walking out of this boredom. But she knew she wouldn't. She didn't see enough of Alex to ever leave him. So she stayed, and drank, and stared out at the wet world.

"You want to play now? Kim?"

She looked back at Alex. "Who won?"

"Don't ask."

She laughed. "Tom, your money's right there." She pointed to the bills she'd left beside Alex.

"Not so fast, not so fast. Want to make it double or nothing?"

"You don't have any more money."

"So you'll give me credit. Double or nothing, what do you say?"

"You're on."

"Let's make it Crib."

"You want to change the game?"

"Yeah, let's play crib."

"I know I'll beat you at Backgammon. Set up."

"You're pretty sure of yourself, aren't you? We'll see. I'm still green."

And they were going again. She watched him. He looked happy. He'd look happy all night; things were going his way. He had his plans, and, somehow, he thought they were all working out. And they were, she had to admit that much: he would get what he wanted. And she wouldn't, or, at least, wasn't. What she wanted . . . she'd seen him ecstatic because of her – she'd been ecstatic because of him. She'd seen him dancing about and clapping his hands because of her. She'd been there when he needed someone to pick him – needed her to pick him up, to tell him that it was all right – *So what do you think of me now?* – she'd given him that too.

Tonight was nice, and she knew she shouldn't complain. She should be relieved. He hadn't played some of his favorite games. He hadn't gone cold or aloof. He was being nice. He was probably being what he should and could be, given the circumstances. But it wasn't enough. And the circumstances were made by him.

So the sweet normalcy was a lie. He was playing at being a good boyfriend: *Get your own girlfriend.* If that was supposed to be an act of possession, that warmed the cockles of her heart, it failed. She wasn't his girlfriend. She wasn't his girlfriend.

She went back to the guys. "The rain's stopped. The power should be back soon."

"We're just about done here."

Alex was pulling her down to him by her hand. She flopped down and picked up the rye, refilling her glass. Alex gave her a strange look. Kim looked right back. "What's your problem?"

"I've never seen you drink straight rye before. There's some 7-Up in the fridge."

"Don't need it." She drank the rye. "Mixer makes me sick."

"Yeah, it can."

He looked confused. She laughed and picked up her smokes. "So how's this little game going? You beat him yet, Tom?"

"Just about."

"Good."

"Good?"

Alex looked hurt. She giggled.

"Thanks a lot Kim."

"You should have stopped at the twenty. Now you're going to have to give him forty."

"You sure have a lot of faith in me."

"I remember the way you played at the store. Why don't you just hand over the rest right now – write him a check." She smiled at him, and he looked back at her, stunned.

"I really need a girlfriend like you, don't I?"

And that was another one of his little messages, just like his earlier one. She wasn't impressed. "Then it's a shame you don't have one."

"So you're not my girlfriend?"

"What'd you think?" That was a trick she'd learnt from him too: avoid direct answers to any and all questions while putting the onus on the other person.

"I think you've had too much to drink."

"Can't be. I've known you too long – how long? – oh, a lot of years now, and after all that time near you, I can handle my liquor."

"You should stick to wine. The hard stuff's too much for you."

"I'm surprised Alex, and disappointed. With all the drinking and driving you do, I expected you to know that there's no difference between a glass of wine and a shot of the hard stuff."

"You're not driving tonight."

"Oh, so moral. So proper."

"You're not having anymore."

"I'm quite happy with what I've got, thank you."

She tilted her glass towards him and then drank up. And she sent him a little message. "Anyway, you have lots of girlfriends."

"I'm not seeing anyone."

"What happened to 'variety is the spice of life?'"

"I'm not seeing anyone special then, if you want to put it that way."

"I could think of more flattering ways it could be put."

"Well then, think of them."

And that was another message from him: think of all the ways she could be special to him. Think of them because he'd never say them out loud himself. "Sworn to fun, loyal to none. You should have that tattooed on your chest, and then all the girls would know and be forewarned."

"What did I do?"

He looked so surprised. "What did you do? How could you have done anything when you have not done anything down to such an art?"

"You think that, do you?"

"Hey, I can think anything. That's the beauty of this: I can think anything because nothing is ever said."

"What do you mean?"

"Forget it. Play your game." She motioned to the board, but he picked it up and put it on the coffee table.

"We can finish this tomorrow. Let's just sit here and talk."

"Okay." But she didn't want to talk to him. She turned to Tom, and stared at him until he started to talk.

"So you still working at Patterson's office?"

"Sure am."

"What do you do there?"

"Good works, we do good works. We're all pure as the driven snow and as high-minded as God Himself, and we do good works. We are the select who do good works. Poor helpless constituents write or phone us about all their dull little problems with all our dull little bureaucracies, and we put our little heads together and get them in touch with the proper agency, or get in touch with it ourselves. We oil the wheels of solutions – that's Johnny's phrase, his favorite and daily phrase: wheels of solutions."

"I was thinking of getting into something new."

"Were you Tom?" She leaned towards him, in her counseling posture. "Tugs getting you down?"

"No. I was just thinking it would be good to get into something else – teach little kids, or something."

"You should join Big Brothers."

"That's an idea."

"I can easily put you in touch with that organization Tom, and then if you really like working with the kids, you could go and get a teaching certificate. There are scholarships for the training."

"I'll remember that."

"You do that." She gave him one of her sweetest smiles. She didn't believe him for one second. She knew Tom, and Tom's type. The type that never actually did anything. The type that never even dreamed anything, but sometimes had fleeting thoughts: "Wouldn't it be nice. . . ." And most of what he was saying now, he was saying to impress her: "I'm not a loser, not really, I have these thoughts." She wasn't impressed. She smiled. He smiled. She laughed. As if she was such stuff that she needed to be impressed. What if he met someone who really knew things?

"Hey, what about me?"

Alex. "I thought you were going to get me another drink."

"I want a scholarship."

"For what?"

"I was thinking of getting some business administration training. It would help at work. You got scholarships for that?"

"You would start it and you wouldn't finish it."

"Thanks a lot."

"It's the truth." She felt quite brave now – and mad, too mad not to be brave. "That's the way you are. You make promises, and you get the whole world looking at the wonderful promise of you – you are full of promise and so full of shit. And you think that as long as you keep everyone looking at the promise, they won't see that the result is all shit, and if someone does see it, you drop them, or laugh it off. That's your life." She knew she'd gone too far. She didn't care.

"This is what you call support and love?"

He was laughing it off. She went on. "Love and support? You don't want love and support from me. If you ever got it, then you'd have to show results, wouldn't you? Not stop at shit, right?"

"So I'm just using you?"

He thought she was drunk, and he was amused by her now; she knew. And she was drunk, but that only let her say these things, it didn't invalidate them. "You have no ego at all. You want the world to prop you up, like some puppet, and you use booze and sex and your face to get it."

"You think you know me pretty well, don't you?"

"No one knows you like I know you. I've known you for years, more years than most, and I've known you well. And you know it's easier for me to know you than for you to. That's what they say."

"Sounds to me like you've thought a lot about me."

"I don't have to think much to know that you hang out with a bunch of losers because it keeps the pressure off you. And I don't have to think much to recognize a support group around you.

Don't have to think to see that you promise myths about yourself so that you don't have to try."

"I think she knows you pretty well, Al."

She was surprised to hear Tom's voice. She'd forgotten that he was there. But that explained Alex's coolness, as Alexander Talon never lost his cool in front of witnesses. She laughed.

"Thanks a lot Tom. You two going to gang up on me now, eh?"

"No, I'm heading to bed."

"No, stay, gang up on him." Because that was something she would love to see: the pot calling the kettle black. And Tom was worse than Alex. Because Alex did have all that in him. Alex had a spark. Tom didn't.

"Let him go."

"Take a candle Tom. Don't forget a candle."

"The lights are back on Kim."

"What?" She sat up and looked around her. There was a light on in the kitchen. She hadn't noticed. "Why aren't the lights on in here?"

"You're supposed to turn off all the lights and stuff when the power goes off so that you don't blow another major fuse when they get the power going again."

"Uh? I don't get it."

"I thought you knew everything."

"Just tell me what you're saying."

"If you have everything turned on when they get the power going again, you create a demand that can cause another blackout. "You see? Too much power surges."

"I've never heard that before."

"So why aren't you nice tonight?"

They were alone, and he looked serious – kind too, but mostly serious. He wanted to know and maybe she did owe him that. She shrugged. She didn't have an answer. She hadn't meant to . . . she'd just said it. "How nice do you want me to be?" She put her arms around his neck.

"You can be as nice as you want to be."

"Can I?" She didn't think so. She thought there were quite defined limits on what she could do and what she could say over here – he scared so easily. She never said she loved him, not once, because she truly thought she couldn't. And she wanted to.

"Why do you look sad?"

"Because I haven't had a drink for awhile."

"You've had enough. You're going to make yourself sick."

That would be cute. She'd look just like Lucy. She couldn't have that. She was supposed to be the alternative. How'd that come about anyway – she hadn't meant to set that up. The whole thing was such a mess – all these superfluous notions around them, like so many flies. It was such a mess. That they were together at all amazed her.

"You look like you're going to cry."

"No."

"You sure?"

"I'm fine. How are you?"

"I'm fine too."

"Good." She patted him on the back. "You know, you really are – fine."

"I know."

He laid them down on the floor. He propped himself up on one elbow, over her. His other hand was on her stomach. She took it and played with his finger.

"So what do you think?"

"I think it's all a fucking mess."

"What all?"

"Nothing." She kissed him – he was here, she didn't care about the rest for now – she didn't have answers for the rest for now; but she loved to kiss him. He was the only man she'd met that could kiss, and it amazed her when he kissed her. And he kissed her for a long wonderful time. And then he kissed her neck, her shoulders, and he was taking off her blouse. "Are we staying here?"

"It's the warmest room in the place."

"That's a good consideration." He was on top of her now. She unbuttoned his shirt and took it off him. And she loved doing that, she loved the sudden sight of his chest and the feel of his flesh all at once against hers. He was kissing her again. He could make the world cease with just a kiss. She couldn't hold onto her thoughts now. But she loved him, and she wanted to tell him that she loved him. She looked at him, at his blue eyes and they had that little question in them again. She wanted to tell him, but she knew she couldn't. Alex wouldn't want to hear. He wanted her to feel it, but not to say it. He liked it unnamed. And maybe that was all right after all. This was so much easier than working it all out. This was together, and this was fun. But . . . she shouldn't have said what she had. "Alex."

"Huh?"

"I'm sorry."

"For what?"

He was still kissing, caressing, loving her. "You know."

"You don't have anything to be sorry for."

"I shouldn't have said that."

"You can say anything you want."

"I didn't mean it."

"I don't even know what you're talking about."

He was dismissing it. He was taking her. She stopped thinking about it. "You know, it's funny. I've always sort of wondered what you'd look like by firelight."

"You have?"

He looked at her. He was surprised. "Why? Don't you think about you?"

"Why didn't you tell me?"

"Because I didn't have to now." She was looking at him, and she liked what she saw. And it was true that firelight was nice to skin. "You look good." He came down on top of her, kissing her again.

He sat still, his body an almost perfect slope, with his arms crossed on his chest, and his weight resting on his heels. His back hurt. "So." He smothered a yawn. She didn't excite him. She didn't even try. "The place is sure clean."

"Yeah?" He looked around as if he hadn't noticed. He let her wonder who'd clean it for him. He knew she'd remember (she who remembered everything she'd ever known about him, who kept every moment of his life never more than a couple of seconds from her mind) those girls, two or three or four over the years, who'd he'd let stay around long enough to clean for him. He hoped she suspected a new one. And he hoped she suspected this one excited him.

"So are you going to offer me something to drink?"

She tried so hard to be pleasant, to keep things so pleasant between them, as if pleasant would do it for him. It didn't. Never had, never would, because he liked his thrills, his feelings – sensations – the rushes when there was something new, something different. Stuff she didn't have and didn't think of – too much of a lady ever to think of, and if she did think of it, would be sure to crush those thoughts back before they were whole thoughts. "You can make yourself tea if you want." She smothered another yawn. "Better make it coffee."

"You did invite me over, you know."

"For last night, and you phoned." He wasn't owing her. He wasn't letting her lay claim. And he'd wanted her here just to show her that.

"So are you going to tell me what this is all about?"

"What is all about?"

"This hostility."

"I don't know what you're talking about."

"You've been miserable since I got here."

"That should tell you something."

"It tells me that you're going to be negative about everything all night."

"Well, if you make me feel that way. I guess I'll be that way, won't I?"

"Oh terrific. Just terrific."

And she looked at the wall. He took a cigarette out of the deck and played with it. He wasn't being negative, not in his book. He was being practical, reasonable. Because he was tired of the farce, of playing at fitting together when they didn't fit, when there was no excuse for them but one and that one she insisted wasn't true. Tired of pretending that was in the cut of things when it wasn't. Because the truth was that in his world the land might fall away and in her world the land might lie high, but that was just talking about the cut of it – not a choice, but the cut of it: the make. He lit his cigarette.

"So are you going to tell me why you're being like this or what?"

"I don't see how I'm being any different. I'm the same as I've always been." Because that was his plan. He wasn't swinging in the wind for her anymore. He was what he was, and he'd bring it out tonight for her to see – strut on the stage, and show, not adjust, adapt, try.

"Oh, right."

"I don't know what you come over for anyway." He was baiting her. Because he knew she had to see there was only the one thing going on between them and no more. She had to see that she was no different than any of the other girls who clustered around him.

And she had to stop masking it with talk of loving and caring, because there wasn't any. Because love meant doing, and he couldn't (not wouldn't, couldn't: was not even able to imagine how to) meet her in that doing because there was nothing for them to do together — not even nothing, because they couldn't do nothing together, not even that—and her too, never meeting him in the doing, never trying for him but looking for him to try for her.

"Visiting. Seeing how you are."

"As long as you didn't have anything else in mind." She came over to get laid. He knew it and she knew it, and it wasn't going to happen anymore — he'd promised himself that much: he wasn't going to give into her fantasies anymore, because they weren't his fantasies. He took a deep drag off of his cigarette, and exhaled slowly. She looked so puzzled, so worried, so defensive. He smiled. "I thought you were going to make some tea or something."

"If you want some."

"I thought you wanted some. I thought you said your mouth was dry. What were you doing before you came over? Hey Kim, what were you up to before you came here?" He laughed, she glared — she was not amused, she was so not amused. But he was — the words went through him like whiskey flaming his throat. And he savored it. "I bet I know. I bet I can imagine what you did." He was laughing.

"You're really cute tonight, aren't you?"

"Yup, you were out there cutting around, weren't you?"

"You want to die young?"

"Only the good die young."

"Then you have no fear of it, do you?"

"That's right." He smoked, and grinned.

"What the hell is your problem tonight?"

"I don't know. I thought you were the expert on my problems."

"You're being too strange for me to understand."

"I don't think I'm strange at all."

"Have you been drinking?"

"Not a drop, not since last night. Hey, I bet that's some sort of record for me."

"That's what this is about, isn't it?"

"What?" He looked at her sharply, innocently, with his lips parting opened and his eyes expectant. Because he knew she couldn't say it, not when he denied even knowledge of it.

"There's nothing like a little honesty, isn't there?"

"I'd agree with that." And she smiled, relaxed. Because this was as honest as the day was long. This was him. "I thought you were going to make some tea."

"If you want me to."

"I told you I don't care. If you want some, make some. Don't just sit there."

"I don't believe you tonight."

And she stood up and left, with one last glare his way. He laughed. She would believe him soon enough. He watched his cigarette burn, watched the smoke swirl upwards. She would see it tonight, because he wasn't going to let her pull him out of it tonight. He was going to stay firm, be stern, because he was right: they didn't fit, never had, never would. And when it was stripped down to its nakedness, it was sex, and if she wanted sex, she could get it on the same terms as any other girl: his terms, his way. She was back. "Don't let the kettle boil dry."

"It will whistle."

"No, it won't. You didn't even notice, did you? Pretty dumb. It's a new kettle. The other one was left on too long."

"How can you forget a pot that screams like that?"

"How do you think?" He laughed. "We were going to make coffee, but we didn't make it that long. You know how it goes." But she didn't know, and they both knew it – that was his everyday stuff, and she made sure she knew nothing about it. "It made a mess." He stretched. His back was aching. "Took Lucy most of the next day to clean it up. She had to buy all new stuff for us."

"I bet."

"But we had a hell of a good time that night." He grinned. "It was a hot time in the old town that night. You want to hear about it?"

"You really are going out of your way here, aren't you?"

"What? I'm just telling you about a good time I had. Visiting. That's what you came over for, right? To hear how I am?"

"Oh yeah."

"So we had, oh, eight or ten beers down at the bar before we drove out to this house party we'd heard of, and it was pretty good. We took a couple of cases with us so by the time we got back here, well, we weren't worrying about kettles, you know."

"Alex."

She sounded so tired, put out. "So you don't want to hear about my good times? Okay." He took a last drag from his smoke and put it out. "I thought that was what you came for."

"I really don't like this mood you're in."

"No?" He laughed – he knew girls who wouldn't talk, but who'd do something, who'd change his mood, who'd make him feel good, make him want. "Well, maybe if you did some bumps and grinds, you'd put me in a mood you'd like better. What do you think?" She started to fidget, squirm. She didn't even like the image. He laughed. "No, eh?"

"Why don't you just talk to me instead?"

She was so condescending. He grinned.

"You'd rather sulk."

"You call this sulking?"

"Yes. What else can you call it?"

"Well, I don't call it much of anything. I don't call it a good time, I'll tell you that."

"Neither do I, right now."

Right now, as if there'd be a difference later on. What was she going to do – list the things that made him right? There was nothing she could do about him tonight.

"So."

"What?"

"Let me know when you finish sulking."

"This isn't sulking."

"What else could it be?"

"Maybe being realistic. Or didn't you think of that?" Because that was all he was doing: bring a touch of reality to them.

"So what's 'being realistic?'"

But he wasn't falling into that trap tonight. Words were exacting cruel bits of fact – labellers, that never said what was meant, but always divided and multiplied, like worms, until there were so many of them wiggling and squirming around that no one could know where they'd all started or where'd they'd all end, but everyone was swamped – not even caring anymore about what was the thing itself, just wanting out, wanting to step on them all, and squash them down. That was what she wanted: swamp him with all her words: *alcoholic responsibility bars traps promise and shit* until he couldn't think through it all. No. Experiencing; that was where the charm laid for him. "I knew you'd forget that kettle. It's dry now."

"Oh, fuck."

"You shouldn't use that kind of language. It's not becoming in a lady."

"Oh, fuck."

And she was out of the room. He stretched. He was getting stiff just sitting here for so long. And he heard a car pull in – Tom. And Kim was in the hallway looking at him. She knew too: it was all over for her. He sat still until he heard Tom come into the house. Then he called out, "Hey Tom, in here."

"Hi Al. Oh, hi Kim."

"Hi."

And she sat down in her spot, glaring, sulking. He let her alone. "So what are you up to tonight?"

"Rob and Ron are coming over and we're heading to the bar for a few."

"Oh yeah?" He watched her and she stiffened up like a board. He toyed with the idea. "Who else is going down?"

"I don't know. We were just talking."

"You should grab us a couple of beers while you're waiting."

"Sure. Kim?"

"She's got herself a pot of tea out there." He didn't give her the chance to answer. He wasn't letting her drink tonight – include herself.

"I'm fine. Thanks Tom."

"Okay."

Tom left for the beers. Alex grinned. She glared and shook her head. But there was nothing she could do. His world was wrapped around him, and she couldn't budge it, couldn't fight it. And he knew what he was going to do next. He called out, over his shoulder to Tom, "Hey, you should give Steve a call, and maybe we could get a game going tonight."

"Yeah, that's an idea."

"Not much else happening around."

"This is true."

Tom passed him a beer. Kim sat perfectly still, her eyes trained on him. She wasn't enjoying the performance, but she was getting it, and that was the thing. "Give him a call, and maybe Bob too. What do you think?"

"Sure."

And Tom went to call. Alex grinned at Kim. "We clean those guys out every time. Last time, we won about sixty bucks between us."

"Sweethearts."

"Yeah. We cheat. We have a system."

"Real nice guys."

"Yup." She reached for her cigarettes. "Pass me one of those."

"Yours are right beside you."

"I want one of yours." He wanted to know if she would give him one.

"Don't tell me: 'variety is the spice of life.'"

He grinned – he hadn't thought of it that way, but it worked. "Glad to know you've been listening. So are you going to give me one?" She threw the deck at him. He caught it. "What's that – top-spin?"

"Whatever."

It was sweet. He smiled. And Tom came back. "What's the score?"

"They're coming."

"Good. We got a fresh deck around?" He smiled at Kim. "They think we mark the cards but that's not it."

"Yeah. I picked one up after the last game."

"Good." Kim wasn't saying a word. "You should have been here for that one, Kim. It was a real animal house. Game ended about seven when Jerry ripped up the cards. He was loaded, and we cleaned him out."

"Sounds like a real good time."

"It was."

"Good."

She glared. He smoked. "Hey, Tom, we got enough beer, or do we have to make a run? Kim could go for us."

"Steve's picking a couple of cases up on the way over and we've got some in the fridge."

"What about chips and dip and stuff? Kim could get us that."

"Steve's getting that too."

"Feeling rich, is he?"

"He was paid today."

"Oh. That's too bad, Kim. We don't have anything for you to do."

"Right."

She was like deadwood in a stream: inert. But what was she think-ing she could do? Because she wasn't staying just to be bumped around. He watched her. And then she heard a car pull up. "That will be Ron and Rob. Better go out there and tell them we've got a game going, Tom."

"Yeah, I got it."

And Tom was gone. "So." Was she leaving, or staying, or what — and why?

"So."

It wasn't hope on her face, or fear or urgency. And she wasn't worried or puzzled now. She'd seen, she knew. And she looked grim, set. What was she going to do — what could she possibly do? She couldn't do a thing. That was the beauty of it. She couldn't tell him he wasn't while he was. Her hands were tied, she was forced to admit it all — not only the fact of the difference, because she had always admitted, that, but also the truth of it: he was exactly what he was, and she wasn't and that was that. But she didn't. And he was curious. But it sounded like the game was ready to start. Steve and Bob were here, and they were calling him into the kitchen. "Yeah, I'll be right there. Just deal me out this hand." He looked at her. "So, are you going or what?"

"What do you think?"

"Well, these games go on all night, so you may as well go."

"Right."

But she didn't move. Or, if she did, it was only to settle more solidly into the chair, like a rock sinking to the bottom of the pond. And she smiled sweetly – a show of teeth. He saw: she claimed her time upon the stage. But there was nothing she could do – she couldn't deny a slap on the face, but . . . he smiled; this was Kim and there was no telling what she'd do. That was her charm. He heard his friends – he couldn't let her do it here because what he could hear from here, they could hear from there. He yawned, he stretched, he stood up. "I don't think I'll play after all. I think I'll head to bed. You should have made me that coffee."

"Your friends are going to love you for that."

"They don't care."

"Tom might, if he loses."

"Got to lose sometime." And, with a shrug, he turned and left the room, going straight to his bed, dropping his clothes on the floor beside him. And he waited. Because she was exciting to him now – making him curious. What did she think she could do to convince him – because that was the difference now: she had to convince him, not just state that she wasn't convinced, but to convince him, make him want. And she didn't have a prayer. Unless she wanted him enough to play it his way. He watched the doorway. He straightened out the sheets. Finally, he saw her coming down the hall. Lumbering almost. She came in the room. "Could you turn out the light for me?"

"No."

"Why not?"

"Because I want to talk to you."

"Well, you'll have to talk to me while I sleep. That's about all the listening I do anyway." And he grabbed the blankets up around his throat.

"You're not sleeping."

She leaned against the wall. He rolled over, turning his back to her and the light. "I would if you'd turn out the fucking light."

"That's a sure way to keep the light on."

"You could be nice and turn it off."

"Nice doesn't seem to count around here for much."

"It counts to you, doesn't it?"

"Not right now."

"That's sort of hypercritical, don't you think?"

"Right now, I'm not thinking."

"No?" He glanced at her over his shoulder, squinting into the light. She looked grim. "Turn out the light."

"Do it yourself."

"If you're going to be here, the least you could do is be useful, you know."

"No. I'm not here to be 'useful,' or anything else you want."

"This is true, this is true." He laughed and rolled back to face the wall. "Nothing new there."

"Oh, aren't you cute."

"Aren't I?" He snuggled into the blankets and closed his eyes tightly. There was nothing she could do to stop him from proving over and over again that they simply didn't fit, and truthfully – without the lie laying between them, like a birthday cake – she really didn't like him. And he didn't like her. "Okay, leave the light on. See if I care."

"Oh, fuck."

And the light went off. He rolled onto his back and stretched. "That's better." He could see her in the darkness. There was enough light shining in through the window and the door. "Close the door." And it slammed. Now he could see her form, not her face. She was standing upright, like a little soldier.

"We're going to talk, you and I."

"Nope."

"You're not sleeping."

Because sleep would be the ultimate insult, the final truth. He fluffed his pillow.

"If I have to recite everything I've ever memorized, you're not going to sleep. Not until you talk."

"Go ahead." He closed his eyes.

"'Once upon a midnight dreary, while I pondered, weak and weary. . . .'"

"I've heard that before. If you want me to keep up, you're going to have to be original."

"Once upon a time there was this obstinate male who insisted on indulging himself in the dumbest of games."

"And?"

"And they found him butchered in his bed one morning. Cut up into the littlest pieces. They suspected he was killed by an irate lover who was only there in the first place because he'd asked her."

He laughed. "You trying to give me nightmares?"

"Just keep on your toes."

"Well." He yawned. "This isn't doing it for me. Good night."

"Don't you think it's a little early to go to bed? It's not ten."

"I'm a hard working boy, not like you bureaucrats. I was up at six, and lifting stuff all day."

"Right."

He felt her sit down on the bed. He opened his eyes. She was sitting beside his knees, her legs crossed, her arms folded in her lap. Now he only had to wait to see how she'd work herself into his bed. "So go to sleep." And he rolled around, getting himself comfortable.

"Alex."

She moved up the bed and a hand grazed his shoulder. He shrugged it off. He wasn't going to make this easy for her.

"Don't you think this is a bit ridiculous?"

"I think it's rude, you keeping me up like this."

"Oh, I'm rude?"

"Yup."

"And you're a sweetheart, right?"

"What do you think?" But she didn't answer. She simply turned her head away – she didn't want to think what she was think-ing about him, he knew. And she really didn't want to stay, but she'd stay, he knew that too, because she couldn't leave things like this. "Why don't you just go to sleep then?"

"Christ."

And now she lay down beside him on the bed, but still on top of the blankets. "Go to sleep."

"You're not going to sleep."

"Yes, I am."

"I don't believe how stupid this is."

She wanted to provoke him into making a move, but he wouldn't – he knew she'd come to him, because it was all she could do, all he's left for her to do. Because if she was whom she claimed to be, if she loved him the way she claimed to love him (she'd never said it, he'd noticed that, she always left it implied, as if her pre-sence was proof enough, as if she wouldn't be there if she didn't, as if she was above lust when her sex drive bested half the guys he knew) she wouldn't walk out but would change it. He tossed her a pillow. "Here. Now sleep."

"Alex."

It was half a plea and half a command, and another hand strayed to him. He pulled the blankets up again. "That's not sleeping Kim." She crawled in under the blankets.

"We're not sleeping, Alex."

But she still had her clothes on. She was still thinking he'd take them off, still hoping for a neat romantic interlude. "You can't sleep in those jeans – I don't even know how you breathe in them, you wear them so tight, but I'm not having them rub against me all night."

"Tough."

And both of her hands grazed his chest, and she moved closer to him, her hair falling on his face. He waited. He wanted her to undress, to press her flesh against his, to excite him. He could feel her breath. And she kissed him. He lay passive, not even letting his breath betray him. "Sleep."

"No."

And she kissed him again. And this time he took her – swept her close to him with the power of his arms, rolled her under him, wrapping his legs around hers.

"Wait a minute."

"Why? I thought this was what you wanted." He buried his head in her neck, but she pushed him back with her hands against his shoulders.

"You wanted this all night? Right? You were waiting for this?"

He grinned. He kissed her quickly. "Maybe. What's wrong with that?"

"What's wrong with that?"

"Sometimes a guy likes to be pursued, you know." And it felt so good, her exciting him, her touching him, her wanting him, that he had it all back – the life, the rush, the not-alone.

"You could give a girl a little space to work in."

"What do you mean?"

"I mean making it seem impossible doesn't make it happen, you know. I almost left."

"It makes it more fun, my dear, it makes it more fun." And he scooped her up to him again, and tugged at her jeans. "You going to take these off?" He unzipped them.

"I don't believe this."

But he loved this. "We could switch roles, you and me. You could be the guy, setting things up all the time." He could see it. Because it wouldn't be a horror anymore, he wouldn't fall with every move, he wouldn't have to prove anything to her.

"What?"

But he ignored her, because he could see it: she'd have what she wanted, she'd know what pleased her, she wouldn't be pressing him anymore but would move them on so smoothly.

"Alex?"

He came back to her, smoothing off her jeans. She had such nice legs, firm and smooth thighs. "Let's make love, what do you think?" And he took her shirt off too, kissing her breast. She had a wonderful body. He kissed her ribs, and her stomach twitched underneath him. And he didn't care about anything else – where her hating left off and her loving started, or where or how her wanting was started at all. Just the wanting. They were good at the wanting. "And we can have a slow morning too."

Urgent and essential. Maybe to her, but it was nothing to him. She could leave messages all over town if she wanted, and it would still be nothing to him. Even before he knew what it was, because urgent and essential was impossible between them; there wasn't enough between them to shake the world — his world or her world. Not in his mind. *At last. You could bloody well return your calls, you know. I have to see you. It's important. It's urgent and essential, so stay there and I'll be there in five or ten minutes. It won't take long.* He really didn't know why he was hanging around. He already knew what the little girl wanted. It didn't take much thinking to know: he hadn't gotten together with her for a while, and she was going to squawk. That was all — she hadn't gone and got herself pregnant because she wasn't the type for that. The ones who had to be watched for those tricks were the ones who had to tell a guy those "I-love-yous" all the time. Kim was more the ultimatum type: "either-or." She'd probably noticed the time slipping by and got herself all upset about it, and decided to put her foot down: "Either we are going, or we're stopping. Which?" But she wouldn't do it when she got here. Because he wasn't going to give her the time of day.

He looked out his window. It was a beautiful evening. Cool and warm at the same time. Springtime. Everyone would be sitting around on the porch, drinking beer, passing the night. And she was already late. He wasn't hanging around much longer, and he wasn't giving her much time when she arrived.

It was bothering him more than it would, he knew. He should be amused, he knew – little girls calling him up to demand he fulfill their dearest fantasy of a full parade wedding, or, at least, a full march courting. As if he could. But that was it; he couldn't – she wanted to bring him into the couldn't again, the way she always had to insist he admit . . . he wasn't going to do it. He was going to sit, hear it, and shrug it off: *Well, Kim, maybe we haven't seen each other for a while, and maybe we should let it go at that.* And he'd purse his lips and nod, not leaving her anything much to say but *you bastard* and that was fine, because that was true.

"Hey, Al, Kim's here."

"Yeah, thanks, Tom. I'll be out." He rolled off the bed, and checked himself in the mirror, shrugging a couple of times. And he strolled out to the living room, looking unimpressed with the whole thing. "Hi." She looked worried, furious. He flopped down into a chair.

"I have to talk to you."

"So talk." He watched her. He yawned. "What's this all about?"

"Alone, Alex. I think we should talk alone."

"Oh." He expected as much. He stood up and grinned at Tom, winking, making her little demand just prove his charms. "I guess we could talk in my room." And he walked out, leaving her to trot alone behind him. He was comfortably propped up on his pillows when she came in the room. And he was ready for it: he'd give the girl a taste of himself, of life his way. He lit a cigarette. He took a slow drag. She was looking at him, not quite glaring; she could feel him already. "So what's so urgent and essential?" He showed his amusement with those words.

"You gave me V.D."

"What?" The word flung out at him – a baseball bat had hit his stomach. He looked at her, searching her – he hadn't heard it right, hadn't heard what he'd though he'd heard.

"You want me to shout that out good and loud?"

"No." And he was up and the door was closed because Tom was out there and could pass by the room. And he looked at her again, and there was not denying it. His heart started pounding – everything was falling away from him, all control, all plans, his very I-am; he'd been stripped of pretense, he'd been struck into reality. "But I haven't been with you in weeks." Because this wasn't going to be true.

"So?"

But he knew that. He knew everything. It was just that he didn't want to know, didn't want to admit to that knowing because once that was true, too many things were true – proven. He smoked. *You people just don't understand the medical consequences. You people think you can do what you want and so what.* He remembered those words, and he remembered sitting there, knowing – forced to know, admit – that the doctor had a right to know those words, that he couldn't stop them – had no right, no way – what could he say? – that he didn't? And he'd learnt what V.D. was: a slime, a gangrene that was shared among friends, a rot that festered with freedom because it was always earned by those who had it. Because what goes around comes around, like the man said. Everything had collapsed inside him then, and everything was collapsing in him now. He didn't look at Kim. "You're sure?"

"Right."

Of course she was sure.

"Go see your doctor."

But he wasn't doing that again, not a second time. He could still feel the nurses sneering behind his back. *We know all about you.* It was what they thought – everyone. He knew, he'd been there. They took that fact and they caught every bit of a guy's life in it. And they were right, because he'd entered slime, possibly eaten it too, and then he'd given it to all the girls he knew. What else mattered when that was known?

"Well, that's all I came over for."

"What?" He hardly heard her – couldn't yet, not until he had a hold on this. But she was standing, leaving. He wasn't letting her leave. She was all he had in this. "How'd you find out?"

"I had tests."

"Why? Did you think. . . ." He didn't want her to have thought, to have sat down and thought that.

"I had problems. I went to get them checked out. I didn't think . . . when I heard what she said, well, maybe it was lucky that you weren't home yesterday."

"What problems?"

"I'm not getting into that with you."

"Oh." But he wanted to know. He had to know all the facts that he could.

"If you want a silver lining in all this, you know that we're through."

But he didn't have time for that yet. "Wait here." He'd find out what he needed to know himself. There was a medical book somewhere – probably in the kitchen. He went into the kitchen and started going through drawers. Tom would know where it was, he knew, but he couldn't ask him, because Tom would figure it out – Tom had taken Kim's messages for him yesterday. The book had ragged corners, he remembered, and a stain on the front cover and back cover, and no back cover, and it could only be in – should be in – one of three places. He found it behind the pizza place fliers.

"So, I'll get going."

Kim was standing in the hallway. "Go back to my room."

"What for? Nothing we can do there."

"We'll read this." And he tucked the book under his arm, and took her by the arm back to his room. "Close the door." He was looking the section up in the book. "Here it is – there's a whole bunch of kinds here."

"Look up gonorrhea."

"Was that what I gave you?" He didn't look at her. There'd be time for pain later, now he needed facts.

"Yes."

"How do you spell it?" But he found it. "Here it is. It says symptoms show up quickly, in two or three days. How come you didn't know sooner?"

"Because – how come you didn't know at all?"

She was right. He kept reading. "Says you can get meningitis or arthritis from it, or go sterile."

"I really don't know why you're reading that. You just have to see your doctor tomorrow, and in a week or two, it's history anyway."

"It says it's an epidemic."

"So make sure you tell everyone you think you could have given it to, or gotten it from. Every girl you've had in the last six weeks for sure."

The girls – they'd hate him. He could see them, their faces all around them, spinning, accusing, laughing. "Oh, fuck."

"Just go to your doctor, Alex."

He wanted to die/disintegrate, not to be there anymore. Because he wasn't going to go through with it. He wasn't going to go face doctors and nurses and then girl after girl after girl with this, shaming himself over and over again, defenseless to what they would and must think of him. It was too much to ask. It was too much. He dropped his head down and rested his hands on his legs. V.D. For six weeks. He could practically feel the rot under the flesh of his legs. He pulled his hands back. "What did you do about it?"

"I had some shots. Penicillin."

He looked back at the book. "Yeah, that was what it says here too. Penicillin. How'd you get it?"

"The doctor."

"There has to be another way." Because he wasn't going to his doctor. In fact, he wasn't going anywhere where he was known at all.

"There are probably clinics in town."

He looked at her. He was almost hoping. It sounded perfect. "Are there?"

"I don't know."

"Why not?"

"What? – you think I'm up on all the V.D. clinics in town? I'd think that'd be more your style than mine."

"Don't you people give them grants?"

"Alex, we give everyone and their dogs grants. I don't know about it unless I've worked on it and I can't remember all the things I've worked on."

"Well you should."

"Look it up in a telephone book."

"He went to the hallway and grabbed the yellow pages. He took them to Kim. "What do I look up?"

"You could look up V.D. or venereal, or hospital, and see if there are clinics listed."

He'd found it. "There's one on eighth."

"So there you go."

"Let's go."

"What?" She looked so shocked. "What? Don't you think they'll be open?"

"I don't know."

"I guess we should phone first."

"You go ahead."

And he did. He let the phone ring and ring and ring.

"Aren't they answering?"

"No."

"Then they're probably closed."

"No. They're busy." Because it was going to work out this way. He was going to get cured – clinics didn't take names, he was sure of that, and even if they did, even if they asked for ID, it didn't matter because it was away in town and he'd be here. "We'll just go there."

"Why bother? They're closed."

"No, I don't think so. It's a clinic. It will be open."

"You're talking about an hour's drive at least."

"That's okay."

"Well, have a nice trip."

"You're coming too, aren't you?" She had to see him through this, because he needed someone, and she already knew.

"I happen to have plans for tonight."

"Nothing erotic, I hope." He laughed, a giggle, and reached over to squeeze her hand.

"If I did, you already put a stop to it."

"This is true. This is true." He laughed – he was going to be fine soon, and only Kim would have known.

"I'm visiting a girl friend."

"You can get out of that."

"If I wanted to, sure, but I don't."

"Sure you do." He passed her the phone. "Just give her a call." He pressed the phone into her hands. "Just tell her something came up. That's all you have to say."

"Alex."

"Just tell her you'll be late, that you have to help put out a friend." He put the receiver in her hand. "Go on. Just tell her that." He knew she would. He could see her deciding to. He nodded, encouraging. And she dialed.

"Hello, Deb? Hi . . . yeah . . . well, somethings come up and I'm going to be late. . . . I don't know how exactly, but two and a half hours, I think. . . . What's that? – nine thirty? Yeah. . . . Thanks. . . . . Good-bye."

And she put down the phone. He smiled. "Everything fixed?"

"It's all right with her."

"Good, we can go then."

"I guess. Make sure you have the address down. Eighth is a long street."

"It's Eighth Avenue, I think."

"What? That's on the other side of town."

"Yeah, here it is, it's Eighth Avenue."

"Oh terrific."

But he knew she wouldn't back out now, and he simply passed her her purse. "We better get going then, before they close. Get your car keys out."

"I'm not driving. You're driving."

"No, no, you'll drive." Because that was the point to her going along: she'd drive and he'd be free to collapse. Because he was exhausted, and he couldn't get himself in there – didn't even know the roads the way Kim did. "Do this for me."

"You know, you're asking a lot, and I don't think you're due any favors right now. Eighth Avenue is a good hour and a half without traffic, and there'll be traffic this time of night, because there's a concert at eight in the stadium tonight."

"I'm sorry." And he was – had been since she'd told him, but had forgotten it. "You know I didn't mean to."

"Yeah, I know. Okay, I'll drive you."

"Thanks." And he ushered them out of the room. "We'll just get our shoes on, and we're on our way."

"Did you write down the address?"

"No."

"Well, go get it, because I'm not driving up and down eighth, I'll tell you that now."

He went back and ripped the page out of the book and stuffed it into his pocket. And less than two minutes later, he had them in the car, ready to go. "Let's move it out." He drummed his fingers against the dashboard, and bounced up and down in his seat. And he watched her put the car in drive, look over her shoulder, and pull out onto the road. "We taking the freeway?"

"Yeah."

"Good. That's the fastest way."

He nodded up and down, and looked back, at the house they'd passed. They were on their way. It didn't have much longer to be true. "Good." He watched the road – she wasn't going very fast, she could do better on this road if she wanted. "If you cut across here, just that street, the freeway's just a couple of blocks around the corner."

"I know."

"Yeah, I guess you do. You've lived here for a long time, haven't you?"

"Will you relax. At least sit still. You're making me nervous with that bouncing."

"Oh, sorry." And he sat still, looking at her. She drove straight on, without even turning her head to him – where was her reaction? – *You people think you can get away with anything, but you can't, can you?* She'd said something about them being through, he remembered, but not much, nothing she couldn't beat on a bad day. *You live a lifestyle that begs for it, don't you? You deserve it.* Where was that? "I'm sorry. You know that, don't you?" She had to understand at least that much, that much if no more, because however sure as fate it was, he wouldn't have had her in it too.

"You've said it, if that's what you mean."

"And I mean it."

"I'm sure."

But she was just dismissing him, because if she really cared, she'd have yelled by now how can you say you're sorry when we both know it can happen again next week? *how can you say you're sorry when you can't promise me that it won't happen again?* because when she cared, she yelled. He looked away. There was nothing he could say to that. "I've seen you since Easter, haven't I?"

"You don't know? That's sweet. I'm driving a guy into a V.D. clinic when I should be somewhere else, and he's asking me when we've been together. I don't believe this."

"We have been. I remember now. It's just that time sometimes gets lost, you know – you must have had that too."

"You want dates and times and places and circumstances?"

"No, I remember. You don't have to do that. You see, I'm sure it was that Easter weekend. There was this girl from out of town."

"I don't want to hear about it."

"But she was from out of town."

"I don't care if she was from Mars. I'm not sitting here listening to your list of girlfriends."

But he didn't mean it that way. He only meant that she was from out of town. He looked out the window. She was pulling onto the freeway. It wouldn't be long now. He nodded – he was sure it was that girl from that weekend. Charlene McSomething, and she wasn't from around here, just down visiting her mother.

He was sure it was her. He should have known then it was her, because she'd been something else. He grinned – it must have come from her, and what a way to go. There were ways to go and ways to go, and that was the way to go. She'd taken the belt off his pants – was that the Friday or Saturday? – and then crushed it into his hands *tie me*. They'd been loaded, and he hadn't known what to do so he'd done it – she'd put her hands behind her back, waiting, and he'd trembled, because he didn't know what to do, and didn't believe that he could do this. It was pure fantasy, and to meet a girl who'd give it . . . he hadn't had a night like that since that first night when he'd been sixteen and she'd been twenty-two and she'd taken him in the back seat of the car. She'd been all body, all his – her breasts all his, and her thighs all his, all breast and hip and thigh and hair just like dough in his hands and there was nothing she could do. And he could remember spreading her thighs and playing with her while she squirmed and begged, but he'd had all the time in the world. He sat up sharply. "So." He wasn't going to let himself think about that for a few days. "What do you think?"

"About what?"

"Nothing." He wanted a cigarette. He'd left his behind. "You got a smoke there?"

"In my purse."

"You mind if I have one?"

"Go ahead."

"Thanks." He took the deck out. "You want one?"

"Sure. Why not?"

He lit one and passed it to her. And then he remembered. "Maybe I shouldn't have lit that for you."

"I don't think this is intimate sexual contact."

"No, I guess not." He lit his own. *Intimate sexual contact – that was the catch – your intimate sexual contact is about as intimate as the day at the market, ain't it boy?* And what could he say? He looked at her. She took a drag from her cigarette and drove. She was thinking that too. And she had every right, too, just like the rest of them, because she wasn't like him – she never would have had it if she hadn't had him, because he was the only part of her life that could bring it to her, because she had intimate sexual contact. He snickered sickly – this only proved there was a god, and that god was Murphy: "anything that can go wrong will and the worse will be the first," or however it went. Because with anyone else, all this would merely be a game, a cover. "I'm sorry."

"I don't know why you keep saying that. It's gotten you what you wanted, hasn't it? So why be sorry?"

"How's that?"

"You wanted us apart, and we are."

And that was true – there wasn't much he could say to that. But he never wanted it this way, not with her thinking what she was thinking. Because this was more than truth, this was fact, and a guy had a lot less to work with fact. "Well, Kim, we haven't been seeing much of each other anyway – you don't come over much – so maybe it's just as well we let it go at that."

"We don't have to 'let it go,' it's gone."

"Yeah." And that was what he couldn't stand, not the hating, because he could stand it if she hated him for what he was, if she hated him because she saw that he wasn't what she thought he was, but not now, not this way – for this he needed her to forgive him. Because this he had never meant. He looked around. "So how far is it now?"

"Far."

"Oh." He looked out the back window. "Not much traffic yet."

"No. Maybe we're behind it."

"That would be good."

"Yeah."

She didn't want to talk to him, and he couldn't blame her. He watched her. He didn't think her face had changed its expression since they'd gotten into the car. "You're going to get a sore jaw."

"I've had worse."

"Yeah, I guess you don't want to hear from me."

"Doesn't seem to stop you."

"Yeah, I guess you think you've had enough of me for one night."

"Something like that."

"That's probably good." And that was true. Because she shouldn't be having anything to do with him. He'd known that all along. The shock was just on her part. Because he'd been right all along: a guy couldn't get out of what he was. He could lie about it, fake it, but he could never get out of it, not really. Because he'd never know how. Because if he knew how, then he was that much already, and then not what he was. But Alex was what he was, and this was just the lie catching up with him – and with her too, because she was the one who wouldn't believe that he was what he was. At least this had made her see. "So this is all I had to do to break us up."

"That does it."

And she started pulling over. "What? What are you doing? You can't stop here."

"Watch me."

"Why are you doing this?"

"Would you rather I just open the door and push you out? Because that would be fine with me right about now."

"What – why?" They were stopped.

"Get out of my car."

"Why?"

"Just get out."

"You aren't allowed to stop here."

"If you aren't going to get out, then you are going to be quiet the rest of the way in."

"Okay." He put the gear-shift back in drive. "Let's go."

"Because I'm not going to drive you all the way in and listen to you go on and on about girlfriends, and have you insult me, or anything else."

"Okay." He looked at the road. "There's just a couple of cars coming and then you can go."

"Not until you promise to shut up."

"I promise."

"Fine."

And she glared, and started up again. He watched her – she would have done it, he knew that. "You couldn't push me out anyway. You're too small."

"You kept that promise for all of two seconds."

"I've said I'm sorry. And I am. What can I do to make it up to you?"

"Shut up."

"Okay." And he sat still with his hands clasped together in his lap. He watched the road. They were pretty close to the city now. The sun was set, and he could see the lights. It couldn't be much longer. "Mind if I turn on the radio?"

"Put a tape in."

"What one?"

"Doesn't matter."

"Okay." He couldn't read the tapes anyway. He slipped one in. The Stones. "That's good, that's good." And he listened to the music, and watched the lights get nearer. And then he looked back at her. He didn't need her back, didn't want her wanting him, but he needed something. He looked out the window again. It wouldn't be long now. He looked back at her. She was still driving straight on, one hand on the wheel, the other resting on her thigh. The one near him resting on her thigh. He moved a little closer to her. She didn't seem to notice. He moved his hand towards hers, slowly. She didn't look. He took her hand in his. She didn't pull away. She only glanced out at her side-view mirror. She didn't hate him. He breathed out. "So we're through." So she'd know he didn't expect her to come back – didn't ask for more than this.

"History. Have a party when you get home."

"Not for a few days."

"Yeah, right."

He let go of her hand and stretched. "So I don't have to worry about you anymore."

"I didn't know that you did."

"Well, you know, you wanted to catch me and take me off the market."

"Is that what I wanted?"

"Isn't it?"

"I don't know."

But he did, because he was remembering it. Every minute of it. It had been so sweet – she'd been so sweet. It was sort of sad – he could remember the first night, when she'd proved a little more than he'd expected. And after that, when she'd known every thought – had it had the same time. And her body – she was a good memory. He was glad he'd known her. He'd always remember her. "I'll remember us." And he would. And they were in town now. "How far now?"

"Not far."

"Good."

"I don't know why you're so anxious to get there. It's closed."

"No it's not."

"Yes it is."

"What do I do if it is?"

"Go back tomorrow when it's open."

"Yeah, I guess I can do that." But he didn't want to spend the night knowing. "I'm sorry."

"Forget it."

"I wish I could."

"Well, you will, I'm sure."

"You think so?"

"We both know it."

And she was right. He sat still until she pulled into a parking lot. "Are we here?"

"Yes, and it's dark, so they're closed."

He looked. The place was dark. There were no other cars in the parking lot. He got out. "Come on."

"For what?"

"Come on." He waited for her and she came, and they went over to the door. It was closed. He felt sick. He drew her close to him. "Oh, fuck."

"So you can come back tomorrow."

"I guess I don't have any choice. That's stupid." He glared at the posted hours. "What good's that?"

"So be here at eight sharp."

"I guess I don't have any choice."

"Come on."

They went back to the car. "Oh, fuck."

> "'The very deep did rot: O Christ!
> That ever this should be!
> Yea, slimy things did crawl with legs
> Upon the slimy sea.'"

And she was laughing. "That's gross, Kim. That's really gross."

"I know. It's been running through my head since yesterday, you know, the way songs do."

"Where'd you hear that?"

"School."

"It's sick."

"Get in the car. Tomorrow you can laugh too."

"Will you come too, tomorrow?"

"I have to work."

"Oh, yeah." He got into the car. You could take the morning off."

"As a taxpayer, you don't mind?"

"No."

"Why can't you go yourself?"

He didn't know, he just wasn't going to – maybe because it looked better with a girl there, maybe because she could make jokes, maybe because he knew she'd know what to say; he just wanted someone there. He grinned a little sheepishly – he was a washout, but he was still a good looking washout. "Do you have to know why?"

"Alex."

"Just come. For me." And he smiled, urging her. And he watched her decide: she would. He still had it.

"Okay, one last favor, for you."

"For the good times."

"But you have to be ready to go at seven, then I won't be too late."

"I will." And he reached over and squeezed her hand for a second. She was a genuinely nice person. He smiled – he could still be irresistible when he wanted to be. And he made himself comfortable in the seat. It was a long drive back. He was tired. She drove. He put on another tape, and soon fell asleep.

21

The bar seemed dark and somehow clammy, but then bars always seemed dark and clammy to her. It was part of the utter estrangement she felt when she walked into one. Because she couldn't understand why these places existed, or what these people were about – why would any living, feeling, self-respecting person permit such grunge near him? And it was grungy and they were grungy, and they spoke a language that she didn't understand, and they didn't mean what they said, and they all smelt like burped beer, and no one seemed to be having the perennial good time that was supposed to be happening here. There just seemed to be a lot of anger here, and the anger made it clammy, and the hopelessness made it dark.

The women bothered Kim more than did the men. In fact, they bothered her so much that she had had to develop a theory about them. She'd decided that they had all come to accept a man's way of thinking about women, that they saw themselves through the eyes of the men. In that, they were no different from the women in the business world she'd met who clearly lived in a man's world by thinking in male patterns. Except that this was more dangerous: these women had lost more. They'd lost any female sense of their bodies, and were mere sexual commodities, packaged, primmed, and now displayed. And dead – it was in their eyes. They hated other women, because other women were other possible objects for the men to collect, to chose over one of them. Another woman could make any one of them history, if she was just a little prettier, a little livelier, a little hotter – a little more attuned to the wants of the men. Really, they weren't much different from hookers fighting for a spot on a corner, save that these women weren't getting paid for it, not in cold hard cash. Kim wondered if they wouldn't be a little happier if they were getting paid. At least then, they would have some vengeance. Today they had nothing.

—Not that the men had much. Kim didn't see much in the lives of the men that she would want for herself. But they weren't as uptight as the women – they weren't so busy victimizing themselves. They were there for that perennial good time, and they weren't giving up on having it. They seemed to share camaraderie. Perhaps that was what the women wanted, to be a part of that group and that security. But it wasn't a healthy group. They didn't come together out of strength, or working together towards strength; they drank together, and forgot together, and fought each other. And they would have to stay together, because no one else would want them. No, unless a person had some strange desire to go partying in strange basements, and to watch – nightly, because this was nightly or close to it – watch people drink themselves into a state way beneath human, and to end up in a strange and almost uncomfortable and possibly diseased bed, only to lie the next morning ("Hi, I'm Jill and you must be Jack"), this was no way to live.

Julie had dragged Diane and her here after work. Her invitation had been short: "Put on your oldest jeans, and let's go checkout my roots tonight." Julie was from here, "emphasis, please, on from." Not that Julie wasn't proud of it. She was quick to remind people that it took something to get out of here, and that she had had that something. Tonight, Julie was testing Diane: could Diane handle herself among the animals? Kim didn't really approve of the entire thing, but she had her own reasons for coming tonight.

Julie didn't know any of the people in the place. This wasn't "her" bar. "Her" bar was one hundred miles away, in the town where she'd grown up. But, as she'd said, "any port in a storm." They sat down at an empty table. It was still early, and the place was only half-full.

Before they'd taken off their coats and settled in, three guys had joined them. Jerry, Donny, and Sam. Kim didn't know which name went with which face, and she doubted that it mattered. All three wore jeans and plain plaid work shirts. All three smoked, and all three drank beer – all three smelt of it. One was the best looking of the three, and he was clearly the leader. He did most of the talking, while the other two agreed and grinned and chug-a-lugged. Kim let Julie handle them.

Alex wasn't there, but that didn't surprise Kim. He could be working late. He usually worked late Wednesday nights. If he was coming, he'd be here in two or three hours. She told herself that she could relax until then.

The beers were on the table, twelve of them. It was the habit here to order at least two rounds at once, since no one was sure when the waiter would get back, and no one wanted to be left waiting. Kim ignored the beer. She sat and listened while Julie bullshitted with the guys.

"Na, na, na. Where I lived, we had the greatest bar. It was the tablecloths. They were perfect. They were red, really an ugly red, and sort of a corduroy, and they had this elastic that wrapped them around the tables. So whenever the cops showed up, you could see the whole place reach under the table and stash whatever they had between the cloth and the table. The elastic would hold it, right? You could never be caught holding in that place. You'd have to be pretty stupid. If you got hassled, well, you'd just sit down, and how were you to know who put what where and when? How could anyone know? Right? It was sweet."

Kim saw that Diane was impressed. Too bad. Rule One in these places was to act always as if you knew it all, or knew even more about it. Rule Two was to have a good line of bullshit ready if you were caught breaking Rule One.

"So what are you ladies up to tonight? Hear of any parties around?"

That was the good looking one talking – making his move. Kim wanted to laugh.

"If we knew of a party, what would we be doing here?"

"I hear there's one up North Road. What do you say?"

North Road, the old name for 226A Boulevard. Not Kim's favorite area of town. She wasn't going.

"Is there? Do you know anyone going up there?"

"We'll find that out when we get there."

"Well, what do you say?"

Julie was asking Diane. Kim jumped in. "No, not yet. It's too early for a party to get going. Maybe later. Have a few beers first." Julie looked pleased with that answer, and Diane looked relieved.

"Hey, smart thinking. How'd you get so smart?"

"It was one of the friends – Sam? Kim smiled at him. Smart – she could show him smart if he wanted. She could ask him his feelings on building a shelter for beaten wives in this area: did the suburbs need one, or was that just a slum problem? Or she could congratulate him on doing such a good job of keeping Rule Three, which was to be smooth, and to appear to agree and to stay 'in.' "Just luck."

"Come on, let's dance."

He'd grabbed her by the arm, and was pulling her to the dance floor. She went. Why not? It was something to do for a while. So she danced.

"So where you from?"

"Around here."

"How long you live here?"

"A while."

"I haven't seen you around here before."

She shrugged her shoulders and stepped back deeper into the crowd, where it was harder to hear, and harder to talk. And she danced three or four dances, until she sensed a slow song coming up and led them off the floor.

"I need a beer."

"You're a good little dancer."

Because she usually went dancing in places a bit nicer than this. But she wouldn't say that. "Thanks."

"Yeah, we can sit down a bit."

"Have a beer." Kim was looking at their table, and she saw that Julie was gone. Diane was sitting alone with the other two guys, and Diane looked ready to bolt. Kim sat down beside her.

"He said that I have bedroom eyes."

Diane had grabbed her arm sharply and was whispering into her ear. Clearly, Diane was scared, and impressed, and lost. Kim knew the feeling. There was something about a come-on . . . it did something to existence that was really strange.

"What should I do?"

"Why do anything?"

"Nobody's ever said any—"

"Hey, what are you two girls whispering about?"

It was the good looking one, reminding them of his existence. Kim wondered if he was the one who had said it to Diane. He was really quite good looking. "Nothing. Just wondering where the 'Ladies' is."

"Right past the bar."

He was pointing to the other side of the bar. "Thanks." She dragged Diane up and took her in there for a little talk. "Okay, so they want to get lucky. That's not news, and that line isn't new either. They want to get lucky, and they aren't going to throw you over their shoulder and cart you off to the cave anymore than anyone else would. So forget that. It's lines and smiles and beer, and if you're going to take it so seriously, you're going to wake up tomorrow in a strange place."

"You don't think he meant it?"

"I don't know. I don't know if he knows what bedroom eyes are, or if he's just seen a lot of Paul Newman movies. If you think he meant it, say 'thank you.' If you think he was just saying it to come on, say 'no thank you.' Best of all, don't say anything because he'll do all the talking then, and when Julie comes back, let her lead."

"Okay."

"Look, just don't feel obligated, okay?"

"I don't."

"Good." And she went back to the table with Diane. Julie wasn't back yet, which left Kim to take control. "So what do you guys do?"

"Work at the plant."

"Good wages there."

"Yeah, but not enough work these days."

"Oh yeah, it's closed for a couple of days. I read that in the paper. Too bad."

"Ah, it will get going again. What 'bout you ladies?" You all work together?"

"Yeah." She didn't want to tell where. She wasn't worried about a political argument, but that the guys would guess what the three of them were doing tonight. "You come here a lot?"

"I really think I know you from somewhere."

"It was the one she'd danced with. "I haven't been in here for a while."

"Were you at that party on the bus last weekend?"

"No. I haven't been at any parties on buses."

"We were parked down at the tracks. It was a riot. You missed a good party."

"Sounds good." Kim didn't know what else to say. Hell would have to freeze over before she went to a party on a bus – broken down and filthy, likely – parked down beside the railway tracks.

"Hey, it was really different. People were coming and going all night long. You sure you weren't there?"

"Yeah, I would have remembered that." And she wondered how they managed to get through the night without someone being run over by a train – she could just see the drunks laying on the tracks. She looked around the bar for Julie and caught sight of her over by the pool tables. She should have known. It was one part of a bar she was quite happy to leave to men only, but it was Julie's favorite spot. Julie liked to hustle, and Julie was good enough to hustle a few dollars. To-night she was playing a beach boy blond type, and he wasn't smiling. Kim grabbed her purse. "There's Julie. I think I'll watch the action."

"She plays?"

"I don't know. That's what I'm going to see." She went over there. Julie was playing a good game, but not winning. The kid (up close, he looked about seventeen) was good.

"How'd your friend get so good?"

Kim didn't know the guy who was talking to her. He had just come up and stood beside her. And she didn't know how he knew that Julie was her friend. "Practice, I guess. Same as everyone else."

"Who taught her?"

"I don't know." Kim knew: Julie's brother, who was a hustler himself. But that wasn't anyone else's business. "Maybe a boyfriend along the way."

"Yeah."

And he wandered off. Kim kept watching the game. Julie was having a good time.

"Here's a beer."

It was one of the guys who'd sat down with them. Not the good looking one. Kim looked and saw the good looking one–Jerry?– talking to Diane. Diane looked a little scared, but it was clear that she was also absorbed by it. Diane was naive. But it wasn't just that, and Kim knew better than to dismiss it with that. She knew that there was something in a come on, especially if you weren't used to it, as Diane wasn't. There was a moment, when, as a complete stranger told you about yourself, you were that person he said you were. And then you had to make a decision about who you were. Diane wasn't making that decision. But that was okay. It was an experience she would have to go through herself. Kim wasn't here to hold her hand tonight, and she didn't know if Diane would welcome more advice. Kim didn't really know Diane. Kim let it go and watched the rest of Julie's game.

Julie lost two out of three, and it cost her ten bucks. Kim was a little relieved, and Julie insisted that she'd thrown the game.

"That kid has problems. He is not a good loser. If I'd taken him in front of his friends, I don't know. He has to live here after I leave, you have to remember that. How old do you think he is? They seem to be getting younger all the time."

"You should have told them who your brother is. That would have explained why you're good."

"That kids going to be a hell of a hustler one day, if he stays half-assed sober. Your little town's going to sport one hell of a player."

"That should put us on the map." They were back at their table, and Kim tried to see what was going on with Diane. It seemed that Diane was taking her advice and not talking, making him do all the talking. And now he was trying to get her to go outside to smoke a joint with him. Diane wouldn't go, and Julie broke in with talk about all the types of marijuana around now. She was beginning to wonder if Alex would show up at all. Then she heard the voice at her shoulder.

"Kim, hi. How you doing? What are you doing here?"

It was Patty, which meant that the crowd was beginning to congregate, which meant that Alex would be here soon if he was coming at all, which was something Patty would know. "Hi Patty, grab a chair. How you doing?" Kim was all smiles.

"I came over to get you. Come have a beer with us."

Kim followed Patty's nod, and saw Tony and Alex – his back to her too – and some others sitting around. When had he come in? – during the game, she'd stopped watching the door then. And he was sitting there with his back to her. So that was his reaction to her being here – she wasn't going anywhere near him tonight, not now. "No."

"Come on."

"I don't think—" but Patty was bending down to whisper in her ear.

"He's been watching you for ten minutes, since we got here from work. He's been pretending not to, looking around saying, 'who's here tonight,' but he's been looking at you. I think he was waiting for me to see you. He wants to see you. Come on."

Patty was excited. Clearly loved playing this role. Kim wasn't so impressed. If he wanted to see her, and he had seen her, then he could move his butt for a change, and not send a girl to round her up. Kim wasn't going to see him if he wasn't going to do that. "Did he send you?"

"Not right out, but you know."

Kim didn't know. She wasn't sure that Alex would want her here at all— if she should be here because these were his stomping grounds, his home away from home, his place to be with his friends, the place where he was the person all the rumors were about. "No."

"What's wrong?"

"We broke up a while back, in May."

"But that doesn't mean anything."

"It means something. To me."

"Don't you want to see him?"

"No." Of course she wanted to see him. Would she be in this stinking hole if she wanted to avoid him? But she wasn't going to him. Couldn't, because he had to have that freedom to choose, or else... or else she wouldn't know what she was getting. He could be anything he wanted if she went over there hat in hand and on his command. But if she didn't go at all, what would he think? "Say 'hi' to him for me."

"But he's there."

Kim could see that he was there. Sitting there, his back to her: the most sought after male in the universe – in this bar anyway; the ultimate desirable one, the one who never sought but always found, the shining example of young manhood, the best and cheapest manipulator in the game. "I don't care. If he wants to see me, he can come over here."

"You want me to tell him to come over here?"

"I don't know." And she didn't, she couldn't think at all. All she knew was that if she wanted to go to him, she could have gone over to his place anytime in the last three months instead of going without sex all that time. She hadn't, because she was tired of getting nothing from him. She was tired of showing up looking for that love of his and fearing scorn and knowing she should be scorned because something as easily had as her would not be valued – couldn't be. She was tired of the two hims, the one that wanted her and the one that wanted all women to want him. She was tired of all the fucking games, and she didn't know how to play them anymore. He'd had his chance, his major moment of truth: he could have backed down in the car, but no, he'd had to agree that they were through, and sneak his hand on hers while she drove – and then to ramble on and on about being irresistible, and having to make a thousand calls when he got home. As if she wanted to know about his phone calls, as if she was one among. . . . "You let him do whatever he wants to do."

"Who, what, who? What are we talking about?"

Julie was sticking her nose into it too. "No one, nothing. Why don't you get another game of pool going?"

"Who?"

Julie knew. Because Julie knew quite a bit about her and Alex– not all, but enough. Julie had heard all the complaints and all the excuses. But Julie had never met the man himself, and wouldn't know him.

"It's Talon. Where?"

"Not here."

"Introduce me to him."

She was asking Patty. She didn't have that right. Kim wanted to throw her beer at her. "Don't you think you should introduce yourselves first? It might feel kind of strange standing there while Patty tries to guess your name."

"I'm Julie. You're Patty. Let's go."

"I don't know?"

Patty was looking at Kim. "Don't do it Patty. She just wants his body."

"No I don't. Patty, just point him out. I'll meet him myself."

"May as well take her, Patty. Let her satisfy her curiosity."

"It's not like that Kim."

"The hell it isn't."

"Let me handle this, okay?"

"No."

"Just take me there, Patty."

And they were gone. Kim looked in the other direction, and started talking to Diane and that guy again. "So we getting some more beer here or what?"

"We're going to head up to that party."

"What?" Kim looked at Diane in surprise. She'd more or less expected the guys to leave when Alex showed, because that was the way it worked – prior claims – but she'd thought Diane would stay. "You going too?"

"I thought I might."

"Oh."

"It might be fun."

"Live and let live, I guess." Her respect for Diane was leaving quickly. "You going?"

"Yeah, I think so."

"Have fun." She watched them leave. Diane was all over the guy. And Kim didn't like Diane anymore. But then Julie was back.

"Where'd they go?"

"To the party up on 226A."

"Quite a surprise."

"The mouse left with the rat."

"I didn't think she had it in her."

"I think she's about to find out what she does have in her."

"It doesn't matter—Alex is coming over."

"What?" Kim didn't believe it. Julie should have known better. Julie of all people should have seen that Kim was meeting him halfway just by coming here, and the other half was up to him. And Julie should have known that Kim wanted Alex to make that choice. But Julie had wasted all that. She'd given Alex exactly what he needed to hide behind: "Your friend invited me to join you."

"You invited him?"

"You weren't going to."

"For a reason. Did you stop to think of that?"

"You want him."

"That's my business – how I want him matters too."

"Well, you better decide how you want him, because he's coming in a few minutes."

Who was coming – the idiot with the beer in one hand and the joint in the other who'd smashed his car up? the sleaze who'd passed around VD? Good-time Charlie? or her Alex who really only existed in the dead of night in his bedroom with her – he wouldn't be like that here.

"This is your chance to make it up with him. Face it, Kim, you're nuts about the guy."

"I'm nuts because of the guy. There's a difference."

"You came here to see him tonight. I knew that when you said you'd come."

That had been a mistake. She didn't have the right to be here. Her heart was beating faster and faster. She picked up her cigarettes. "Shut up."

"Give the guy a break."

"What the hell do you think I did when I walked in here? That's enough of a break. Let's go."

"Too late. He's coming."

"That's a miracle in itself." Because she really hadn't believed that he would come over at all, and she still didn't believe that he wanted to.

"Hi there. Sit down."

And he was there. But so were his friends, Doug and a guy were with him. She should have known he wouldn't come alone– this was going to be a long night.

"You girls have got to get some beer on this table. Hey Glenn, bring a round over here. Make it ten, will you?"

He knew the name of the bouncer. She should have known he would. And she could see the bouncer had bounced him out once or twice.

"So you're a friend of Kim's"

He was looking at Julie, and he sat down beside Julie. He hadn't even looked at her. She looked at the wall.

"Yeah, and so are you, I hear."

She could kill Julie for that one.

"So what brings you girls down here tonight. Seeing how the other half lives?"

That he had directed at her. She'd noted the change in the direction of his voice. She didn't look at him. Julie had invited him, Julie would have to handle him.

"We're just out having a beer. I came to play a little pool. You play?"

"You played pool here tonight?"

He was surprised. It didn't fit his vision of her friends. It served him right.

"Sure did. There's some hot shot kid over there. I played him."

"How'd you make out?"

"Lost ten bucks."

"Yeah, sounds about right. Some of those guys play all day. That's all they do. They get pretty good."

"That kids going to be very good one day."

"Yeah? You think so?"

He said it as if Julie had no right to have an opinion on that. Kim let him know differently. "Julie's brother is one of those people for whom that is not a game, but a form of self-employment."

"Oh. You must be pretty good then."

"I didn't lose fifteen bucks. But I'm rusty. I don't play much anymore. How good are you?"

"I play."

"Much?"

"We'll have a game sometime. It looks pretty full there now."

That was a classic Alex move. Kim almost laughed out loud.

"So you like working with Kim?"

That really was too much. Kim got up and left the table before Julie could answer. She went to the washroom. But she couldn't stay there. She knew Julie would be in any minute to tell her off. So she brushed her hair, and went back to the table.

And there she turned to Doug. "So Doug, I haven't seen you in a long time." She'd met him once, for about thirty seconds, and she doubted if he even remembered her.

"Hi."

"So how you been?"

"Pretty good. What about you?"

"Fine." She heard Julie and Alex talking to each other still. That was fine with her. Julie had invited him. Let him be Julie's problem. Because Kim wasn't having anything to do with him.

"I met you once at Alex's, right?"

"Yup."

"I don't see you around here much."

"She's just here to see how the other half lives."

That was Alex, and he sounded sullen. She didn't care. She ignored him. "So, Doug." She couldn't think of anything to say to him.

"You work in the government offices, don't you?"

"Yeah, for Patterson."

"Not in Motor Vehicles?"

"No. Having problems?"

"They lost my record."

"And he wants to keep it lost. You should see it. You think I'm a bad driver?"

More Alex. He was listening to them as he talked to Julie. She didn't care. She talked to Doug. "I don't know anyone who can help you."

"It's a drag."

"You working still?

"Oh yeah. It goes on you know, it goes on."

She didn't know what he meant. "Yeah, I know."

"It's a drag."

"It sure is." She was glad that Doug didn't work for her. But then Doug was pretty drunk now, and she could see that he was stuck in the solitude of too much beer.

"Can you figure things out?"

"Uh?"

"I can't figure it."

She was sorry she'd started this. "What?"

"You know, my mother poured battery acid on my clothes. Why do you think she did that?"

"I don't know. What did she say?"

I didn't ask."

"Why not?"

"I didn't hang around that long. I moved out."

"When was this?"

"A couple of years ago. Just before I moved out."

"I see." She didn't know what to say. "I think I would have asked about it."

"She was going for me next."

"Then I would have left." She wasn't going to continue this conversation, and she wasn't going to talk to Alex. "You want to dance, Doug?"

"Uh?"

"Dance?"

"Sure."

She led him to the dance floor.

She led him off the dance floor when she saw Alex leave the table. But Alex's other friend was still there, and he was giving her knowing looks. "Something I can do for you? Who are you anyway?"

"George."

"I'm Kim."

"I know. Alex has told me all about you."

She doubted that. She didn't think Alex would tell anyone all about her, because, in that particular story, he didn't come out looking so great. "What did he say?"

"I don't think I should tell you that."

"Then don't." She didn't like George. He looked like an oaf, and he sounded too smug.

"I'd like to hear your side of it."

"How's that?"

"Then I would see how it works, you see."

"I don't think so."

"But I already know his."

"And that's all you're going to know."

"That's all right too."

There was even a note of approval in his voice. She snorted – as if she cared about approval from him, as if she was so desperate, she'd gossip with him. Yet she was pleased to note that Alex had said something about her that made her unusual enough to his friend that his friend was more than a little curious. Indeed, she found that quite interesting and encouraging.

"Come one, all of you, get up. Up. Let's get dancing here, let's go."

It was Alex. He was standing behind her, leaning his hands on her shoulder. She tensed up.

"Come on Doug, get moving. You have to dance with Patty here. Tony's deserted her."

Kim turned around and saw Patty standing beside Alex. So that was where he had gotten to. She wondered – she couldn't have known if he had to meet a date here tonight or not.

"He just went to work."

Patty was telling her. She smiled and nodded.

"Up."

Alex was shaking her shoulders. She knew he was hyped now. His energy was scattering out of him, all over her. She went to dance with him.

She didn't look at him, not really, no more than she had looked at that guy she'd danced with earlier – Donny, Sam? But this time it was because it mattered too much; she didn't know where he was at yet, and she wasn't sure she wanted to know. It didn't help that he wasn't looking at her. He was looking around him as much as she was looking around her. And so they danced.

The next dance they changed partners, and she found herself dancing with George. It was Alex's doing, he'd told them, he'd put them together. He was dancing with Patty. She watched him for a few moments. He looked happy. He was full of life tonight. If only she knew where that was coming from, and where it was going to ... but then she was dancing with him again, and George was off with Patty. The song hadn't changed, but he had switched. And then she knew that he had arranged that. She liked it – it was a game, she knew, and he even had the nerve to look surprised to find himself dancing with her, but it was also an indication, and since she never knew with him – she didn't even believe that he knew – she'd take the indications that came, no matter how clumsy and awkward and forced they seemed. Because that was the only way that they were going to find a way to come together tonight.

Alex kept everyone dancing to the next song. He set Patty with Doug again, and Julie back to George, and danced with her himself. And that was fine. But only a moment into the song, he stopped dancing, and took her off the floor with him. They sat down at the table, alone.

"You want a beer?"

"Sure."

"I didn't think you liked beer."

"I don't. It just seems to be the going drink here."

"I could get you something else."

"No, I'll have another beer."

"I'll be right back."

She watched him go to the bar. He stopped a few times to talk to friends. And did the same on the way back with the beers. She understood that: he was known at the bar, and he couldn't ignore his friends or they'd all be asking "What's wrong with Alex?" But she wanted him back as fast as he could come. Things had to be settled – established – known – figured out between them, and that had to come from him, and before their audience was back from the dance floor. Then he was back. He sat down in the chair beside hers.

"So what do you think?"

He was nervous. That surprised her. She hadn't noticed that he was nervous too. "I don't know. Are you supposed to think in a bar?"

"We think sometimes. I was thinking tonight."

That was an invitation, one she wasn't ready for. And she didn't like the way he was talking. It was too close to his favorite "I'm-not-like-you" theme. No good had ever come out of that. "How's things at the store?"

"Things never change there."

"That's true. I don't know how you stand it."

"I have other things that excite me."

Girls, drinking, partying, this place; she didn't need to hear about that now. "You go to that party on the bus last week?"

"What party was that?"

"On a bus parked by the tracks."

"No. I missed that."

"Some guys were talking about it earlier."

"Oh."

"It sounded very weird."

"Yeah, it does. So what about you? What's new and exciting with you these days.?"

She knew all the questions in that question. And he knew or should have known the answers by now. "Not a lot, nothing in particular."

"Have a good summer?"

"Pretty good. What about you?"

"Went south for a while."

"Have a good time?"

"Yeah, we were in Phoenix."

"Must have been hot."

"Yeah, it was. Like an oven."

Then George and Julie and Patty and Doug were back with them. Alex talked to them. Kim looked away, and sipped on her beer. It was such a mess of a night. She should have stayed home. She wanted him – she'd wanted him for three months now, and she wasn't going to let him leave, but how to come together. He didn't know either, that was clear.

"I didn't mean anything by it."

Alex was whispering to her. She looked at their friends. They were talking amongst themselves. She looked at Alex. He looked so good. And his eyes were so blue. And wide tonight, wide open. Those eyes could suck all of her existence into the one face of him – and were tonight, because she found that inquisitiveness in him again. She didn't know what to say to him. She leaned closer to him.

"I didn't mean to. . . ."

His tone was pained.

"I don't blame you for not forgiving me."

And then she knew that he was still stuck on that. "I forgave you for that one second after I knew because I never had the right to hold it against you. It was a consequence I knew would happen. That's all. It's not that."

"What then?"

"You could have phoned."

"I thought you'd call. You've always called before."

All that innocence . . . and all that pressure, in the same breath, dumped on her, it was too hard to take. She didn't know what to do. She wished he would do something. "You play so many games."

"I didn't mean to."

She believed that. "But you do."

"You know me."

"Sometimes I just want to forget that I ever knew you." She hadn't meant to say that. It was because he was so confusing. Because he kept her stuck in the flux of his look.

"I'll never forget knowing you. I'll always remember every moment between us."

"Alex—" She knew that he meant it; he was sincere. But why couldn't he be that strong on wanting her? – why wouldn't he do something that would let him keep her, and not need the memories? And why did she have to wonder about all this all the time? "I'm so tired of shadow-dancing with you."

"I'll think about things. Okay?"

Even that was confusing: if he wanted to remember so much of what had happened between them, what was there for him to think about? "What do you mean?"

"Give me some time to sort it all out."

"I can't say 'no' to that, can I?"

"You could."

"How long?"

"Six weeks."

"What?"

"Do you want me to try?"

He was pleading. And he was so close to her that he was almost on top of her. She wanted him. She lifted up her hands, and played with the color of her shirt. "Fine."

"I don't want to hurt you."

"You don't hurt me. I'm a big girl. I can take care of myself."

"I don't make you happy."

And that was true, but it was by his choice, because of his lack of choosing; she knew that. She knew too that he could make her happy if he wanted – happier than anyone else under the sun. He had it in him to have her dancing in the streets. "You don't try anymore."

"I don't know how."

"Forget this." And she stood up, and picked up her purse. "I'm going to get some air."

"You want me to come with you?"

"You can come if you want to." She walked out of the place, and he went with her. They stood in the parking lot.

"We could leave."

"Yeah." She was exhausted. She wanted to sleep.

"You want me to go back and get your coat?"

"No." She didn't trust him not to stay inside once inside. "Julie will bring it with her, or else it will still be there in the morning."

"This is true."

He led her to his car, and held the passenger door open for her. That amused her – she knew he did that for no one else.

He drove to his place. She sat with her eyes closed. She didn't know – was she relieved? Did she care? It seemed to take too much to care these days. And he didn't have answers . . . she didn't have answers either. She wasn't even sure of the questions anymore.

They were at his place. He helped out of the car, and held her. She could see his eyes under the street-light. She did want him. He kissed her.

"Let's go in."

"Okay." But she held him back for a few moments. She wanted to keep holding him. She wanted him to reassure her. He kissed her again, and she let her wanting take over. Three months of wanting him finding in him three months of wanting her. And uncertainty too, both his and hers, impelling each other to hold the other a little tighter, in case the other started to slip away, as others can and will. But he didn't. He took her inside.

22

Patty was basically harmless. Patty was nice enough, full of only good intentions, and therefore, except that one possibility of inadvertently saying the wrong thing at the wrong time – some attempt to be helpful, to be sure – Patty was a safe risk. Patty was pliable too; she pretty much believed what she was told to believe. Pliable and moldable and present, much like putty. Actually, Kim thought it a lack of personality: Patty would never take the initiative because Patty would never think of a thing until someone told her about it. Which meant that Patty had a definitely limited understanding. But Patty had her uses too. Unimaginative or not, Patty was a damned good source of information. The parts of his life that were alien to Kim were everyday facts to Patty. And Patty liked to ramble on and on about Alex, and Kim liked to take notes.

Kim needed to take notes. She needed to find out, to figure out one way or another, just what his problem was. Because something was. And because that something was, something was gone from them, and they wouldn't get it back until he had done something about his problem. Or until she had. One of them. Whichever. Whichever could. Because they were very close to being over, and getting closer and closer to it all the time. That scared Kim. Whatever they had – and they did have something (Kim hated the business of having to justify over and over again to herself and to her friends her belief in them, but nonetheless, she had to, as circumstances did seem to defy that belief: few people would accept that two people who saw each other less and less all the time, and who seemed to share so little to outside eyes, could have anything of significance taking place between them, yet they did, and she felt it – she even thought it possible that they saw each other less and less because what they had was so much and the risk became greater and greater) what they had between them was special, precious, or else they simply wouldn't be bothered with each other at all, as the pain and anger had taken its toll too. Her anger and hostility – sometimes she wanted to kill him, to slip some poison in his beer and be done with it. But his risk, so plain on his face at times, in his eyes, in his questions . . . he was not the sort who easily left himself open to hurt, and he was doing that with her, and if she ignored that, placed no value on that, and asked for more and more, what sort of insensitive bitch would she be? But . . . and . . . but . . . and around and around her mind would go, and where it would all stop . . . she hoped Patty would know.

But Patty was strained tonight. Patty hadn't even mentioned Alex, and she kept giving Kim the funniest looks. Kim had a good idea of what it was: the old "What's-a-nice-girl-like-you-doing-with-a-guy-like-him" theme. Patty had never asked her that before. Julie had, and Diane had made the assumption that Kim wasn't such a nice girl after all and would want to know all about Diane's little ventures into slime (which were becoming quite frequent) simply because she knew that Kim dated someone from a bar sometimes. Even Colleen, who should have known better, had told her all about some syndrome, and had dragged out some dead person's writing on why the worst men get the best women, all for her benefit. Such was the price of being involved with a man not known to anyone but her. Kim was willing to pay it. She didn't care what they all thought, because vanity didn't matter. Having him was that important. She'd swallowed a little pride. She wouldn't walk out on him simply because she wasn't having it all right now – not as long as she believed she would have it all again one day. And she wasn't a slut, and he wasn't getting away with using her for sex, and appearances could be deceiving, and depths couldn't always be seen. Not that she really had to justify anything to anyone. She didn't. She merely believed that somethings should not be left easily, because some things would not come your way again, and that this thing was one of those things. And why did everyone want her to accept less anyway? She loved him. She didn't feel degraded by the set-up. She didn't think that he was stretching things to the breaking point with all his games, but that was a problem, not a reason for leaving. So if Patty really wanted to know, she'd tell her. That was if Patty ever worked up the courage to ask. "Pat, something on your mind?"

"Well, it's none of my business. . . ."

Kim took a deep breath and made the invitation. "If something is really bothering you, you should talk about it."

"It's really none of my business, and Tony told me to keep out of it."

"So I won't tell Tony you said anything."

"You and Alex. . . ."

"What about us?"

"You two still see each other sometimes, don't you?"

"Of course." She couldn't envision herself not seeing Alex.

"But lately too?"

"A couple of weeks ago. Why?" Something in Patty's look told Kim that this would be about more than social inequality. Perhaps it would be about that something was his problem.

"How lately?"

"What do you mean? What are you getting at? Is something wrong with Alex lately?"

"No, no, nothing like that, but you two still see each other, right?"

"I said that."

"And things are good between you two?"

"I don't think that things are in any way solid between us, not right now." Alex had said he would think about things, that he needed six weeks to think things over. That was three months ago, and he hadn't said a word more about it. Kim didn't think that was good. Indeed, that was making her quite nervous. "But then they haven't been for a while now."

"I was just wondering how you two were doing."

Kim didn't buy that. Patty wasn't the sort to dream up things, or take things on herself. There was more to this than she knew, as yet. "Are you going to tell me what this is about?"

"It's not really about anything. I just was wondering about you and Alex, if you two still were, you know, staying together. I've always thought it was real romantic between you two. Like undercover."

Kim had to laugh at that. Undercover was one way to describe them; under covers was a better way.

"No really, aren't you like that? I've always thought of you two as being like that, you know, standing alone, private, just the two of you. Like in your own world."

Patty looked utterly earnest. Kim was intrigued. This perspective was one she had never though of, not once. Romantic? Fights at midnight? "Why did you think that?"

"That's always how it seemed. At least to me. Aren't you?"

"I don't know what you mean. We don't go walking around in the dark and hold hands or anything like that."

"Oh, Alex would never do anything like that."

"No, Alex never would. Why did you think we were romantic?"

"Because you keep to yourselves – and that night in the bar, remember that? He didn't take his eyes off of you, not once after we walked in and he saw you, and he watched you dance with Doug. He looked so jealous."

"I didn't see that."

"Oh, he did. He looked right put out."

"I wish I had seen that."

"And when you two were talking and touching and he was looking at you like I'd never seen him looking at anyone else. And you two were in your own world, and the rest of us didn't exist anymore. It was real romantic."

"And here I always thought that we lived in our own world because we didn't have any place else to go."

"Oh, don't be like that."

But it was what she thought. After all, she wouldn't go to his world, and he wouldn't go to hers.

"Don't you think you two are romantic?"

"Honestly?"

"Yes."

"No, I don't, not for one minute." Kim knew why: they were never settled enough to have romance, because they were too intense together, because everything seemed to matter when they were together – every word, every gesture, all of it mattered so much, they never relaxed and enjoyed what Patty thought they had. "It's a hell of a lot closer to hell, if you want to know what it's like."

"Really?"

"We don't know what we have and we don't know what we're doing with it. We fight. I'm so aware of him I can't think, and he doesn't think, and we don't get along. It's not relaxed, it's not easy. He's ... I don't know what he is sometimes. He's confused, if you listen to him, but I don't know if you should listen to him or not. I don't know. I don't know what we are – I don't think he knows either."

"But you two want to be together?"

"If we wanted to be together, we would be. Don't you think? And if we wanted to be apart, we would be. It's not hard to be apart." She didn't know, she didn't know, she didn't know. She had no way of knowing, not without hearing from him, and that was his favorite game of all: no words, no commitments. And even thinking about it was like stepping into a whirlpool, and going around and around and deeper and deeper into all the possibilities, and all the maybe's and the might be's and the rest of it until she was so sick and dizzy she couldn't think of it any longer. "And it's not hard to be together. Well, maybe it's hard. Who knows?"

"But you make him happy."

"A lot of things make him happy."

"No, that's not true. He's not happy. He's not a happy person — he's fun, and he's funny, but he's not happy."

"You don't think so?" Kim wanted to hear this. So far, it fit one of her theories, the one where he wasn't as happy in his life as he was pretending, the one where his life was just a habit turned trap.

"He always seems so alone. He sees girls, but he still seems alone. He didn't seem alone with you there."

That was music to her ears. That fit, it fit just right.

"It was different to see him like that. That was what I wished for him. I think you're good for him. I always thought that."

"I'm not really trying to be good for him. I just want him, you know. I just want things to settle down between us."

"Then you know about this girl he's seeing?"

That came out of nowhere at her. "Girl?" She knew that this was what Patty was getting at all along.

"Charlene MacGregor."

"Who's she?"

"You're not going to like this."

"He's seen other girls before." Which was true enough. She'd outlasted maybe ten now. Yet it bothered her. She took out a cigarette. The idea of Alex with another woman frightened her — always had, although she'd never admitted it because those sorts he went with seemed to low to acknowledge. But even that had frightened her. She knew that in being with her, he was not in his element, and that being with them, he was, and that one day he was going to have to choose between the two, and that he hadn't chosen yet because he hadn't met anyone in his world yet who satisfied him the way she did — not in bed, she didn't mean in bed because she was sure that some of the girls he went with had more exotic tastes than she did. She was betting that there was no one in his world who would satisfy him, that would make him feel as good about himself as she could, because there was no one in this world whom he respected as he respected her. Still, each new one was a threat. "So what's she like?"

"That's just it, what she's like. I shouldn't say this, but she's a slut.

And she's dangerous. The guys don't see it. They know she's a slut, and, like Tony calls her easy-streets, but they don't take her seriously. She started with Alex before Jessie dumped her, and she was going with other guys before that too, probably with her engagement ring on right in bed with them. But she would never have left Jessie, because she doesn't leave after she gets her hooks in them."

"Sounds charming."

"No, you have to do something."

"What can I do?"

"You have to fight for him."

Kim stared at Patty, uncomprehending. She didn't fight for men – she didn't know how anyone fought for men, because the essence of being with a man, Alex, was being wanted, chosen, by that man, and no one could force that choice and still value it. "He's free to do what he wants to. I have no commitment from him."

"You can't do nothing. I tell you, she'll have him married to her."

"Patty, calm down. Alex is a grown up."

"You don't know what I'm talking about."

"Then tell me."

"You aren't going to like this."

"What – what?" Kim's heart was starting to beat faster.

"They're into kinky sex."

"What?"

"They tie each other up, and stuff, or he ties her up and hits her."

Kim felt as if Patty had just hit her, right in the stomach, with all she had, and knocked the wind out of her. Alex? Like that? Her tender vulnerable Alex, hitting someone in the midst of the act of love? It rang so true in her – she knew it was true, and she knew it was destructive. And she didn't want to hear anymore. "There's nothing I can do."

"Alex told Tony."

"There's nothing I can do." Kim looked at the wall.

"He said he was hot for it. And she told me that they were into each other's bodies pretty heavy."

"She told you that?"

"She seemed proud of it. I told you she was a slut. But that's the way she works, too. I don't know if you know it, but Alex talks like that too sometimes, and she's working her way in, like a worm."

"There's nothing I can do."

"You have to do something."

"No." She knew it was true. Alex was doing those things. That part of Alex that wasn't hers, that she didn't even like, that was all the worst of him, that part of him was doing those things, which meant that that part of him was growing. She would have to do something. What could she do? There was nothing she could do. He liked being cheap. He liked being no good. He escaped all responsibility and all expectations by being as low as he could be. That was his way. He felt cold and nauseous. "I have to go."

"I'm sorry. Maybe I shouldn't have told you."

Kim looked at Patty, chubby little Patty. "I'm okay."

"You could talk to him."

"I can't talk to him. He doesn't listen to me."

"You could try."

"Patty, he'd just think I was jealous, don't you see? He'd get a kick out of it."

"Maybe you could talk to him without seeming jealous. You're smart. You could figure out a way."

She knew a way. She could start talking to him about his poor image problem, because this seemed to fit into that. She could start talking about ways to feel better about himself instead of feeling worst all the time. Because that's what this meant: he was feeling even worse about himself than before. His pain was growing. Love was failing in him. Something sick and hopeless was taking its place. She could feel it, and she could feel its pain. "I really have to get going here."

"Okay."

Kim picked up her coat and went to the door. She saw a car pulling up. "Looks like perfect timing. Tony's coming home."

"That's not just Tony. Who's with him?"

Kim saw five people get out of the car. One was Alex. She drew back. "The front door?"

"You can't. He's seen your car."

"The hell I can't."

"She's with him – look at her, running after him and grabbing his butt, like a dog in heat."

"I'm out of here." It was too much. To hear and see in the same night was too much. She couldn't do it. Wouldn't. But Tony was through the door, and everyone else was right behind him.

"All right, Kimmy's here. Come on Kim, we're going to have a party. What do you say?"

"Hi Tony." Alex walked in with a case of beer. He'd known she was there. He looked like he was going to turn and run. Not if she could first. "I was just heading out."

"Nah, you're staying. We want you here."

Tony was hugging her. Charlene walked in. Kim knew it was Charlene. She was all over Alex, very much like a dog in heat, and she wore too much blue eye-shadow. "I can't Tony, not tonight. I told Julie I'd be home soon."

"Stay with us."

"No."

"Phone. Say something came up."

"Can't." She wasn't mad, and she wasn't hurt. She wasn't feeling anything at all, except an overwhelming need to be out of there. She still had her coat in her hands. "Another time."

"You don't look so good."

She looked at Tony. He looked concerned about her. So it was showing. She couldn't let it show, not in front of Alex. He wasn't to know how much this bothered her. "I'll have a beer with you. How's that?"

"Let's go downstairs. Everyone, downstairs."

Tony herded his friends along down the stairs. She hung back, and Patty stayed with her.

"You all right?"

"I'm fine."

"You went completely pale when he walked in."

"I'm fine now." She had only seen them for a second anyway – Alex had been the first to escape downstairs, and he had pulled his girlfriend down behind him. So they were gone. "It's not important anyway."

"What's not important?"

It was Alex. He was back in the room with them. He'd come back. For what? She didn't want to talk to him. She sat down at the table again.

"You two girls having a nice chat up here?"

She didn't say anything, but he was looking at her, not Patty.

"Kim's really great to talk to, isn't she Pat?"

He sat down beside her, his hands folded in front of him on the table, and he was all smiles. She wasn't impressed. She wasn't going to talk to him. She wasn't going to let him think that she forgave him. Because she wasn't.

"Did I ever tell you what a fine lady Kim is? She's the best you know."

He was blithering on like an idiot. He could keep it to himself. She wasn't impressed. And she wasn't going to pretend that these little messages made it all right. "Gee, thanks."

"I mean it."

"Who cares?"

"Can I get you a beer? You said you'd have a beer with us."

"I lied."

"Come on – wine. Patty, Kim prefers wine to beer. Do you have any wine in the place?"

"Why don't you go downstairs and drink with your girlfriend?"

"You're my girlfriend."

And he looked so sincere, as if he couldn't see how true that couldn't be with that other one in the basement. She almost felt sorry for him. "I don't think so."

"Sure you are. You always have been."

She wasn't going to let that work, not this time. Maybe because seeing was believing or maybe seeing was too much all in one night. She looked away.

"You are, you know. You should know."

It was almost insulting. He really expected her to believe that.

"Al. Al."

It was Charlene's voice, coming up the stairs. Checking up on him probably. Kim turned to look at her. She was about twenty, five years younger than him. She was blondish. She was a type. Blond and cold. Her hair cut blunt, cheaply styled; her face, all makeup, no face. Hard, and not all that stupid in a survival sort of way. Kim knew the type. The worse type for him.

"Al, what are you doing?"

"Talking to my friends."

Alex stood up and moved behind Kim, resting his hands on her shoulders. She shrugged, but he stayed there.

"Why don't you two come downstairs?"

Kim was not going to socialize with this person. "I was just leaving."

"I'm Charlene. Hi."

Kim looked at Alex.

"Char, I'll be down in a minute."

"Okay."

And the little slut left. It had been a good act, but Charlene's eyes moved too fast. She wasn't being friendly, she was watching over her claim.

Then the slut was back, just to kiss Alex. Kim saw. Alex put his hands on her hips, and reassured her with a look. Kim saw. Kim knew that with that look, he'd tightened his grip on her hips. And that hurt. She picked up her coat again, and walked to the door. "I'll be talking to you later, Patty."

"You okay?"

"I'm fine." She turned to Alex. His girlfriend was gone. "You better get to your party."

"I didn't mean to do anything. . . ."

She didn't respect that little fear from him. "No, I guess not. I guess it was timing that got you this time. Fated maybe."

"Don't be mad."

He was walking towards her, and she just knew he was about to try that same move on her he'd just put on that slut. He wasn't going to let him touch her now. She stepped out the door.

She drove home. She tried not to think about it. She watched the road. She watched the world. It was dark and wet, and the leaves were all over, done with their autumn dance, left wet, now mush under the car's tires. Streetlights and neon illuminated nothing, but were there, announcing themselves. And the houses, some dark, some cheery. The world was going on. And a little voice inside of her was growing louder: "I am a person, and I count, and I do not deserve this, and I will not accept this; this will not be."

At home, she wasn't so sure it had been. It had happened so fast, like a nightmare. She had only fleeting impressions of people appearing and disappearing, and functioning, and herself there, robotically responding to it all. So civilized. She was sorry that she hadn't exploded. She should have made him pay – she had no right, not even the right to get mad, because she had not commitment from him and he could date if he wanted to. She'd had to take it, and she had. She'd stood there and let him pretend it wasn't really so when she was seeing it was so: he'd betrayed her, and he'd betrayed that betrayal. And she felt like the whirlpool starting to suck her in again. Her mind was whirling. She needed to calm down before she blew apart.

She sat in the living room, and put the lamp on its dim setting. About her were her things: her pictures, her books, her couch, her records, all things that he had nothing to do with because he had never set foot in the place. *Did I ever tell you what a fine lady Kim is, she's the best*—as if he knew, as if he had the smallest glimpse into her; he didn't even know her. Kim prefers wine to beer – he thought he knew her, but he didn't really. *You are, you know, you should know.* How could he have said that when he was with someone else? How could he have made such a mockery of it all just like that? If he had meant a word of it, he would have left Charlene. But he was still there, partying, the prelude to screwing. And she was crying.

Oh God—

She'd tried, she'd tried, she'd tried. She'd stayed far far beyond the point where others would have left. She'd not fought his freedom. She'd let him . . . she'd stayed because they loved each other. *You're my girlfriend* – one of the many wasn't good enough, not by a long shot, and one of two was somehow worse. She wasn't going to stay for it this time. *You're my girlfriend.* No. That was the simple truth of the night: she wasn't. Because he didn't have the guts to back up his emotions. She'd tried to be – she'd let them mold them, not tradition, not what was usually done, not what should be, not anything outside at all, but them, their ways and their needs, and their wants, and desires, and limitations and possibilities. She'd been sensitive to him . . . and this was the reward. She'd been true, and he was leaving her, killing her. She'd never be held by him again, and never feel so much at once again, and never know the skies again, the bliss, the touch, the all that he could stir in her, the spark of her – of him, all gone. She screamed. She couldn't stay sane.

And she knew he thought she'd be back because she loved him, and she knew he thought she'd take it because she loved him. Because he knew she loved him, because he knew she knew him, because he was used to having it all his way, because he knew her.

She had to get away from thoughts. She quickly went into the bathroom, and poured a bath, a bubble bath. When the tub was full, she turned off the bathroom light, and stepped into the water. The first touch was too hot. She had to grit her teeth to bear it, but soon she had inched herself into the tub, and was comfortable. The heat was relaxing. She closed her eyes and closed her mind, and took the silence in for a while.

Then she was bored – it wasn't enough. She bent her knees

and submerged the whole of her back into the water, turning her neck about, twisting her head side to side. That was better, as the tensions were easing even more. She kept her eyes closed, and let her face dip in and out, in and out, of the water. That felt good too. She was feeling better. She rocked her body, making waves in the tub. She enjoyed the feeling of the collapse of the water underneath her. She stayed there until the water cooled.

Wrapped in a towel, back in the living room, she remembered other ways of forcing relaxation into her body. She started taking deep breaths of air. She filled her lungs completely, held it for a count of ten, and released the breath slowly, imagining all her tensions leaving her with that used air. She did it ten times. And then another ten. And she wasn't trembling any longer.

Now she knew she could think about it. That one thought that had been tormenting her since she saw that woman: Charlene was worse than all the others, because Charlene was meant for him. They were meant to be together, they were destined. Charlene had that energy: a stubborn refusal to lay down and die. She'd seen that right away, and she'd seen it meeting something in him when he looked at her, when he touched her. Charlene would last. Charlene was the dark side of his mind. Kim held the best and the light of him, but Charlene would always have the dark, and Alex liked the dark better – not death, not Lucy, but the dark, and the refusal. He had found himself the perfect woman. He had found himself the one woman who would let him – help him be what he wanted to be. So they were over. Done. She was left empty. She stared at the wall.

The phone was ringing. She answered.

"I bet you're mad as a bear caught in the beehive."

"What?" It was Alex. She should have known it would be him. "I thought you'd be in bed by now."

"Without talking to you tonight?"

His voice sounded so nervous, it was almost giggly. She didn't know what to think. "Are you going to ask me my permission?"

"We can talk about this."

"Can we? Do we have anything left to talk about?"

"You could come over – "

"Now? Would you like me to drop in now?"

"I was thinking that next week – early next week would be good."

"And so you phoned me at what—" she looked at her clock, "almost two o'clock in the morning to ask me."

"I knew you'd be up."

"Is that all you wanted?"

"Just call before you come, okay?"

"I'll think about it."

"Take care."

"Right." She hung up. She wasn't going to let him make it up to her – there was no point as long as he had that Charlene. And she wasn't going to pay any attention to the meaning of that call – to phone her while he was spending the night with someone else – to phone her just before hopping into bed with a girl when he knew that she knew that he was about to do that? And an act just short of coming over, just short of making any sort of commitment or decision, an act that was just a way of keeping things the way they were. Typically Alex. She started pacing the floor.

It wasn't fair. He could do that so well, and he could always do it just right so that she couldn't question the sincerity behind it. Just like before – the hand holding in the car, the edginess in his eyes, the timid smiles, the *You are so good to me* and *You've always known that I do* and *What took you so long? What do you think of me now?* and all the other moments that had kept her around this long. And now a concerned call.

"What are you doing?"

"Uh?" It was Julie. She'd forgotten about her.

"You're pacing in the dark, wearing a towel. What is going on here?"

"Where have you been?"

"In bed."

"I didn't hear you come home."

"You were in the bath. I heard the water. Something's wrong, isn't it?"

Kim could feel the tears pushing around her eyes. She couldn't talk about it. "Nothing."

"Then it's Alex."

"Go back to bed."

"If you're all right."

"I'm all right."

"If it's Alex, give it time. The way you two are together, he'll come around."

The tears started their flow down her face. She didn't want to think about it – she wasn't talking about it. She ran to her room, and shut the door. And she knew he had gotten to her again. In the morning, or maybe the morning after tomorrow morning, she'd decided to see him. She'd find some strength from that call, and she'd go to him. But tomorrow, not tonight. Tonight she was too scared.

He opened the door, looked at her, and turned back into the house. Not a word; no welcome. She knew he'd changed his mind since that call. She knew he was going to play the victim, an innocent caught up in her insistence. Her stomach dropped, and she followed him into the house. "You said to come over."

"Yeah, I guess I did. I said to call too, didn't I?"

He was hoping to escape it through that route. She shook her head. "So crucify me. There were no cars outside, and your girlfriend works tonight."

"You seem to know an awful lot."

She shrugged. She'd seen the slut working in a beauty salon not fifteen minutes earlier. She'd known that they weren't going to be interrupted. And she wasn't going to explain that all to him – did he think that she was looking for a scene? "Do you want to talk?"

"I'll listen if you have something to say for yourself."

He sat down and folded himself up into his favorite little pose.

She dropped her purse on the couch and sat opposite him. "If I have something to say for myself." He was trying to put everything onto her. She wasn't going to let him do that – she came over, yes, but not to plead. "What the hell is your problem?"

"I don't have any problems."

"And birds don't fly."

"If you say so."

"For crying out loud." She looked away from him. She didn't believe he was doing this, but she knew she should have seen it coming – it was so like him. She looked back at him. He hadn't moved a muscle. "This is getting us nowhere fast."

"Maybe that's where we should be."

"And what does that mean?" She looked right at him, challenging him to go ahead and say it.

"I don't think we should see each other anymore."

Now she could deal with it. "What brought this on?"

"Nothing brought this on. It's just the way things should be."

"You phoned me at two o'clock in the morning to have me come over to hear this?"

"I've thought about it since then."

"And what did you think?"

"Love should be a two-way street. I don't love you. I shouldn't use you."

That hurt, but she didn't have time for that hurt now, not if she wanted to change things. And she did, because she didn't believe him. She thought that he had thought about it and saw that he had put himself into a no-win situation and was backing down now, but that he didn't love her, she didn't believe that. "So you've been using me."

"Good. You got it."

"I think you're a coward."

"Think whatever you want."

"I don't have a minister sitting in the car, you know."

"I know that." He snapped at her.

"I never said that you did."

"You're acting like you think I do."

"No I'm not."

"Then what the hell is all this?"

"I don't feel good about us, okay? That's all."

He was looking tense and annoyed. She knew he was retreating from that phone call. It had said too much. He had left himself too open. And this had all been planned, probably the next morning when he'd realized what he'd done (he'd been drunk on the phone). She wasn't going to let him get away with this – she wasn't going to feel that pain, not when he had called. "You just feel good about us when you're drunk?"

"Doesn't that tell you something?"

"But sober you don't have the guts to feel what you feel when you're drunk." She took a cigarette out.

"Don't make yourself so comfortable."

"I will, thanks."

"I like drinking. It's a good time."

"Right." She smoked, taking the time to find some thoughts. She knew what this was about. They had come close to this road before. But how far was she willing to go down it? So much of what she could say he could attribute to jealousy, and ignore it, escape it that way. So she couldn't attack it head on. "You know, Alex, people have choices in life, and you aren't very good at making the right ones."

"You can think that if you want."

"One day it's not going to be a choice anymore, because all the other avenues will be too far away."

"I don't know what you're talking about."

But the way he said it, he knew. "You know what alcohol does to you, and your precious body. You know that it kills the brain cells, and pickles other precious organs. And you know that it can be a crutch psychologically. You know it closes doors, and they don't open easily again."

"Maybe that's the thrill."

"It's a dangerous cycle."

"It's my life."

She was stumbling around, and she knew it. The words wouldn't take what she wanted them to say – she didn't have the guts to say what should be said. How could she sit there and say to him, "lose me and you lose the greatest part of you?" He'd die laughing, and she'd die of shame. But it was true. And she wouldn't say it, not when he was in this mood. "Your friends have nothing to offer."

"I like my friends. They accept a guy for what he is. Know what I mean?"

He was being a brick wall. "Maybe they accept a guy for what they are."

"It's all the same."

"Is it?"

"Maybe we're all the same."

"And maybe not. Maybe one of you isn't like that at all, but likes to lead a group and doesn't care who it is that he's leading."

"Whatever you say, Kim."

She was being dismissed, and she knew she should leave if she wanted to keep any pride, but she couldn't leave. She wanted him. Not this him, but the one who had had to call in the middle of the night.

"We could be friends, but no more sex. If you want that."

"No, I don't think so."

"Well, then, that's your choice."

She would have to leave. There was no way to stay. She picked up her purse, and stood up. He still hadn't moved. "You want this?"

"Yes."

"You're sure – no more calls at night?"

"I said it's best, didn't I?"

"I think you meant it is easiest."

"Whatever."

"You don't care about the difference?"

"Not as long as you're leaving."

"You aren't going to make it Alex."

"You mean without you?"

The sarcasm stung her – and he was right: she didn't have the guts to follow through on that. Still, she knew that he would lose something, and never have it again. Something that mattered. And he knew it too. It just didn't bother him, or so he wanted her to believe. And she did believe it – why should it bother him when he had given up on himself? But one day, he would know what he had lost, and one day he would want it back. And it would likely be too late. And that was the way it was going to be, because he wasn't leaving her with any other option. "Okay, you got it."

"Drive carefully. The roads get slippery this time of year."

"Right." Why did he say things like that now? But it didn't matter. She left, and she hurt.

"Grab on boy what you can scramble for—Don't let the tears linger on inside now."

23

She kept herself from him for a year – almost to the day. And during that time, she dated other men and tried new things, and hoped that the thought of him would eventually go away. It didn't. The new things were new things, and some were great – skiing was terrific – but not replacements for him. And the men . . . she shook her head just thinking about the waste of time that had been – not one of those guys could so much as kiss properly, and not one made her feel anything in the slightest bit interesting, and not one stayed with her even once. Not one could replace him. In fact, they made her want him more. Because she didn't want anyone else's arms around her. Because she wanted to feel something. Oh, she'd had a few interesting talks with them – the sort of thing she always thought that Alex thought she wanted – and she'd gotten into it with them, but that was the subject, not the man. The man, each man, bored her. And the harder they tried, the worse it got, because Alex had never had to try to keep her interested.

So she thought about him for the year, and still didn't know of a way to go back to him. She couldn't go back to him, not as long as that Charlene was with him, and Charlene was lasting, just as Kim had expected she would. That pained her. She knew what that meant for Alex – what it said about Alex's frame of mind. Because it was worse than giving up on himself; it was turning the giving up into a thrill: that was the essence of the S & M, and that was the essence of Charlene. She knew that. She felt it right through her bones, and she would not let anyone dispute it: Charlene was a danger and as long as Alex was choosing her, Alex was lost. She wasn't going back as long as Charlene was around, and there was no reason to think that Charlene would be dumped any time soon. Indeed, there was every reason to think that Charlene would be his life's mate, because they were so right for each other in all the wrong ways.

And there were other reasons for staying away. The complete lack of honesty was one. He knew and she knew what was true and what was not, but he had not and would not confess to that truth. He had to play his games, always circling, never landing, never leaving, but circling, and staying. That one night, almost two years ago now, he had played that game to perfection. He had been so cold and distant – deliberately; he had even invited his friends over to play poker. She'd taken him that night out of desperation, having to have him just to know that she could. *Sometimes a guy likes to be pursued.* Which is fine, but he'd taken a funny road to it. She'd almost left so many times. It had almost backfired, and she had the feeling, even now, that he wouldn't have minded if it had. He had been making sure that she paid a price before she stayed, and if she hadn't been willing to pay, then he wouldn't have wanted her to stay. *We can switch roles you be the guy setting things up.* He'd said that that same night. She'd winced, she'd tried to push it away from them – ignore it – but now, hearing its echo, she still shivered. She knew what he meant, and why he'd said it, and there was no way that she was ever going to accept that from him, because he wasn't that – he wasn't unable, or hesitating, or unknowing; in essence, he wasn't a sheep at all. He simply wasn't letting him live. He wasn't being honest.

And that was the source of her pain. A pain that had seized her at night for weeks after *Love should be a two way street and I don't love you* – it kept coming back, folding itself around her, imprisoning her, and she hated it. And she loathed the fact that it was from him: she anguished because he was inadequate, and she suffered because he couldn't live up to his own emotions. And if it was true – it wasn't true. Men who were not in love did not show and tell their inadequacy *what do you think of me now tired of babysitting we can switch roles* they did not take that sort of risk.

It didn't matter. They were dead, regardless of what she wanted. She couldn't deny that he wanted it over. She knew that he had made his choice in Charlene. She knew that her seduce and conquer tactics would just buy her time. And so she had stayed away.

But then she found herself walking in the mornings to memories of rising to him. She knew again his kisses, his touch, his smell, his hands, his mouth all on her face, her neck her breasts – her nipples sucked, thighs caressed, kissed – all the confusion of wanting felt, all the memories of having back. She was going to see him again. She was going to find the way to walk back into a man's life after a year, and get back what had barely been there then.

And there were other reasons to give it that last chance too. She knew that his attempts meant more than his refusal – *We can talk about this* – that had cost him much more in effort than *I don't want to see you again* had. So it was silly and weak of her to place so much emphasis on the one over the other – the other had value, because the other had risk. Copping out was so easy to do – it took away the risk.

So she would go back, but how was still a question. She wasn't going back begging or insisting. She was only going back to give him the opportunity to ask her back. Because if he didn't want her back … she wasn't Charlene, she didn't have hooks. So how? – she couldn't casually run into him at the bar again, and there was no use in doing that anyway as Charlene or her friends would be there. She could phone, but she didn't have the courage to phone. She had to see his face, because she would know by his smile. All she could do was go over, but when? He would have to be alone – how would she know when he was alone? Patty. She invited Patty over for a cup of coffee.

She hadn't seen Patty much during the past year, and had

wondered if Patty would be of much help. But Patty walked in gushing information.

It seemed that Patty did not like the way things were going for Alex these days, and hoped that Kim would help straighten him out. Patty's main concern was Charlene, and Patty had plenty to say about that set-up: "They can call it anything they want to, Kim, but he leaves her at the bar, and takes other girls home – not that she doesn't manage alright for herself after he's gone, but it bugs me. And this has been more than once now. He's done it a couple of times. Charlene always looks real put out by it, but she's back with her hooks the next night. And I've seen her a few times with other guys. She hides when she sees me. No one can tell me that there's anything between those two. He's just spinning his wheels, and she'll stay. I wish he'd dump her because I'm tired of having her in my house."

And there was more news too: "Alex was evicted in August, you know – it was all Tom's fault, and he's moved into this shack outside of town. It's a shack, I really mean that. It's only one room, and Tony says it's not very well insulated. And it's shared bathroom there, not too close either. He only has running cold water. If two people are in there, it's crowded. I've only been there once, and I hear Charlene won't go there – I think he knew that if he moved into a decent place, like a one bedroom apartment, she'd assume, you know what I mean, that she could move in too and be in there like a dirty shirt. He's too smart for that, so he moved way out there. But we don't see much of him now. He comes in on weekends and stays with her or someone else."

Kim drank it all in. She loved every word Patty said. It sounded like Alex was changing. There was even more reason to see him now. She asked Patty when his days off next week were, and she determined to see him one of those days, whichever day she could get away from the office.

It was Tuesday, and she was sick with excitement as she drove up to his place. She had too many thoughts, and too many hopes, and too many fears. What if – what if he was changing? – what if he looked at her with anger – what if he was breaking with his old ways? – what if he was thinking – what if he wasn't pleased to see her? But nothing could be lost today, and, if she just handled it right, everything could be back to her within two hours. The shacks were ten minutes out of town by car. Five minutes on the highway, and five minutes down the stretch of road that led into the woods. She had a bit of trouble finding the mailbox that Patty had described, but when she saw it, she knew she had found the right turnoff. The road then was narrow and muddy and filled with potholes, as Patty had said, and she had to drive slowly. But a couple of miles down it, she saw the clearing and the shacks. Her heart started beating faster and faster.

There were ten or twelve shacks in a sort of circle. All were fairly run-down looking, and some were quite small. Off to one side was a big shack, the bathroom Patty had mentioned. To the other side was a big house, one that would not look out of place in the richer suburbs. Kim assumed that was the owner's place. Overall, the scene struck her as a forgotten village, feudal-like, with lords and serfs. The only modern sight was that of broken down cars. And then she realized that Alex's wasn't among them.

Her stomach tightened. Her nerves jumped. She'd depended on his car to show her where he lived. – And what if he wasn't home, what if he had gone into town today? She didn't know if she would be able to find the courage to bring herself back here another day. She drove to the big house, and asked the man there where Alex stayed.

"Number six."

"Thank you." She didn't like the man. He'd looked so hard and cold. He made her feel unwelcome. That was one of the lesser delights of knowing Alex: people didn't worry much about the way they treated his friends. But she wasn't justifying herself to each stranger that came alone. She drove to number six, and saw a Volkswagen parked beside it. Was that his, or did he have company? It wasn't Charlene's. She went up to the door and knocked. He answered before she'd knocked three times. "Hi." She watched his face.

"It's you. Come in."

He looked a little stunned, but that was all right. She stepped into his place. The place was smaller than she'd realized looking at it outside. The room wasn't one room, but a nine by ten foot space. It had a table, a single bed, and a dresser. He'd turned the furthest wall into a closet, with shirts and suits hanging from nails. The bed ran the length of one wall, with the table across from it. A walkway of two feet was left between. The bed was unmade. The table was cluttered with junk and dishes. A hot plate sat on it. Apparently he was cooking himself scrambled eggs.

"You want some tea? I just made some."

He motioned towards the tea pot sitting beside the hot plate. She nodded, and looked around for a place to sit.

"Just sit on the bed."

"Okay." She sat down. She watched him – he was still in his robe. He wasn't showing any surprise at her arrival. Indeed, he wasn't showing anything at all. "I would have called, but you don't have a phone here, do you?"

"No. Here you go."

He passed her a mug of tea. "Oh, thanks. Any milk?"

"In the fridge."

He was grinning, and he'd raised his eyebrows in the way he did when he was pretending to be secretive. She laughed a little. "And where is the fridge?"

"Right here."

He bent down under the table, and she saw a fridge, a small fridge, under there.

"It's all I need."

"I bet." He passed her a carton of milk and turned back to his eggs. She watched. She wasn't sure what she should think. He hadn't shown any sign that he was thinking anything at all. He seemed quite natural, as if this was normal, as if they'd not missed a day together. Or as if this wasn't insignificant, and maybe it was. She wanted more of a reaction from him. But what could she do? "Were you just getting up? Am I disturbing your breakfast?"

"No problem. You don't mind if I eat?"

"No, no – of course not." She took off her coat and laid it on the bed beside her. It was quite warm in here considering that Patty thought it didn't have any insulation. He seemed comfortable enough in his robe – she wished he'd put some clothes on. "It's quite cozy."

"Everything is at my fingertips."

"It's warm too."

"That heater keeps this place hot. Sometimes it's like an oven in here, and you can't breathe."

She looked and saw a little electric heater set up under the window at the other end of the walkway. She nodded, and glanced around her again. The place was no palace, but Alex had made it functional, and it was clean enough. "Where's all your stuff?"

"At Mom's. She's storing it in her basement."

"Where does she live again?"

"About forty miles from here."

"Oh. Is that your car out there?"

"The Volks? Yeah."

"You sell the other one?"

"The Camero? No. It's at a friend's, on blocks until I get some work done on it."

"You working on it?"

"Yeah, as soon as I get some time. I meant to get down there last weekend, but I didn't."

"Oh." She looked around some more while he finished his eggs. She still wasn't sure that she should be here, that he wanted her here – if he was indifferent, then she should go; she knew that.

"You still working for our man in government?"

"No. I quit a few months ago."

"Oh yeah? Why?"

"I don't know. Bored I guess."

"So what are you doing now."

"Working at a halfway house."

"With juvenile delinquents?"

"No, with women. You know, coming out of jail and all that."

"Doesn't sound like you like it too much."

"I don't. It was just something, you know, to keep me busy for a while. Well, it sounded better than it turned out to be. I might quit."

"Got another job lined up?"

"There's something I'm thinking about, but I don't know yet."

"What's that?"

"Well, when I was working at Patterson's, we were involved with setting up a sort of mini Peace Corps for some kids in the area. They go to work with the really poor in different countries, under adult supervision. I'm thinking about going."

"You could go – you have the qualifications?"

"Yeah, I have enough administrative experience, and I certainly have the connections. I could go if I wanted. I have enough courses too. I could probably go to Mexico since I speak Spanish."

"Mexico is one of the countries?"

"Mexico, lots of African nations, some in South America. Not Asia yet. They aren't set up there yet."

"Is this a local group?"

"No, it's international. We just introduced them to the area. Patterson really liked the idea, and it made good copy, running around with these kids and sending them off to dig ditches around the world."

"You sound cynical."

"I guess that's why I quit."

"I thought you'd see through politics sooner or later."

"Yeah, well." He looked interested, and he looked proud of himself. And he looked relaxed. This was working out after all –

it wasn't the way she'd expected, but that was all right, as long as they had some connection. "What about you? What have you been doing?"

"Store's always the same. You know that Kim."

"Yeah, I guess it is."

"Rumors say that Griffin will be transferred soon, and I've heard that I'm going to be put in a downtown store which would be okay, but you know how it goes."

"Yeah." She remembered that place. She'd never been able to think of it with any fondness or kindness. It had been so frustrating to be a part of that, because really there was nothing to be a part of there. How Alex had stood it for this long was beyond her. "There were always lots of rumors floating around, and nothing ever seemed to change. There were rumors about Griffin being transferred when I was there."

"He'll never be transferred. He doesn't want to go anywhere else, and someone in head office likes him."

"Is that how it works?"

"You know how it works — it doesn't work; bunch of guys in middle management make all the decisions, and most of them don't know what needs doing."

"Are they all still there?"

"Hobbartz retired last year, and Johnson got a promotion from sales, but the rest of them are still going at it."

He'd finished his breakfast, and was up rinsing the dishes off under the tap. She hadn't noticed that before. It was tucked in between the table and the wall. A little sink and taps. Two taps. He seemed to have running water there.

"You want some more tea?"

"No, I'm fine."

"Want some water?"

"No."

"I'm going to have a glass of water."

Holding a huge glass of cold water, he sat down at the head of the bed, the pillow behind him, his legs under the blankets. She laughed to herself: he'd never liked his legs.

"Shouldn't you be at work or something, or do you have different hours with this job?"

"No, pretty much the same hours. The counselors keep strange hours, but I do administration."

"Once a bureaucrat, always a bureaucrat."

"Thanks a lot." She liked the way he was looking at her. "Sometimes it feels like that though. That's why I'm thinking about changing again. Pushing paper doesn't seem too important, although I know it is. People want everything accounted for, and there are all sorts of letters to send out. I don't know."

"So you're going to change jobs."

"I don't know."

"Sounds to me like you are."

"I don't know if I want to go away for a few years. Maybe there's something else around here."

"So what else is new with you?"

"Not a lot. But what about you?" She was feeling pretty comfortable with him now. "What's brought you to an isolated place like this? I thought you were the life of the party."

"Saving money."

"What for?"

"I don't know yet. I might buy a house, or I may do some traveling – Europe maybe. I don't know what my plans are, but it never hurts to have a few extra bucks in the bank."

"True." She didn't believe him. Not for a second, because he didn't have to go this far to have a few extra bucks in the bank. Going this far – now that she'd seen the place, she was even more convinced – was breaking with the other lifestyle, because he couldn't party here, he couldn't bring girls here, he couldn't do much of anything here but sleep. And nobody was going to drop in on him and hang around here.

"So did you take the day off?"

"Sort of."

"You left early?"

"Yeah, well, ten o'clock is more than early. Let's say I took an early lunch." She was still holding onto her tea mug. She got up and went to the sink to rinse it out.

"So who are you sleeping with now?"

His tone was casual, and she couldn't see his face with her back to him, but she could feel his hand going down her back as if he was smoothing her sweater. She didn't know what to do. She didn't want to tell him no one. It would make him sound too important. She didn't want to tell him someone, because it was a lie, because she didn't want him to think she'd left him. "Gentlemen don't ask questions like that."

"You want to fill this up for me?"

He passed her his glass. She put it under the water. His hand was now going up and down her back. It excited her – even that touch, no more than that touch, and she felt all of her body responding to him. She moved back to her spot on the bed and gave him his water. She wanted him, yes, but she wanted a few things about them settled first.

"So you won't tell me anything?"

"You shouldn't ask." She was so clumsy, she knew it. She couldn't not tell him, and she didn't know how to tell him without sounding like she was stuck on him. "You always ask."

"And?"

He wasn't going to let this pass by. "No one right now."

"So you're still mine, are you?"

He was grinning and his eyes were dancing. She looked away.

"I knew it."

"It's just that you men are a real disappointment to me." She looked back at him. "The lot of you are boring."

"Are we?"

"Yes."

"You think so?"

He was laughing at her. "Yes."

"What else do you think?"

He had ways to drawing her to him. She couldn't put her finger on exactly what it was – maybe his eyes, or his voice, or all of it together, but when he looked at her the way he was looking at her now, he made her feel so much of herself that she had to move to him, and have him. All wonderful intentions of having everything laid out in nice, neat words were shoved away. She sat beside him at the head of the bed. "I think I have cold hands." She put her hands out in front of her.

"You sure do."

"It's driving. The steering wheel gets cold."

"It's smoking. It cuts off the circulation to your fingers and toes."

"Maybe." He was rubbing her hands together, and blowing on them to warm them. And kissing her fingers. He was looking at her over their hands. He looked so good.

"So you want to reconcile."

"Yes." She wanted to slip down into the bed, and put her arms around him inside that robe. She wanted to have him so close that she could smell only him. "Do you?"

"Yes. I guess."

"You guess?" That wasn't good enough. She wasn't risking anything on that.

"We should lay out some rules first."

"Like what?"

"We see each other every couple of weeks, and we both can do what we want to outside of that."

He wanted things the old way. She wanted him to leave Charlene. She couldn't ask him that – he wouldn't, and it seemed that in some way, he was controlling her if not outright leaving her. Anyway, there'd be time for that later. "I want to know if you want me here."

"I want you here."

"Okay."

"So we're reconciled?"

"I guess." She didn't know. She didn't feel reconciled. There weren't enough changes or answers or questions or anything else to please her. But it was one step, and she did feel relief.

"You want to turn on the radio?"

"Why me?"

"Because you're on the outside and you'd have to move anyway?"

"Where is it?"

"Over there on the table."

She saw it. She could reach it without leaving the bed. "How loud do you want it?"

"Yeah, right there, that's fine."

"Anything else?"

"You could turn out the light."

"Who was your slave last year?"

"It shines in my eyes when I sit in bed. I don't know why I turned it on. It's light enough in here to read by anyway."

She turned off the light, and sat beside him again.

"You want some water?"

"Yeah, I'll have a sip." She took the mug and drank the water. And she looked at him. Sitting here with him like this struck her as quite strange. They had made up, and they were going to make love, and she did want him, but something was missing. Some passion, some answers, some sense that their reason for being apart was overcome. None of that was here with them. Maybe she'd made a mistake — maybe she should make a scene. There was just no momentum here. "So."

"I was going to cut my nails this morning."

"What?" She knew what he was thinking about.

"Huh? — nothing. I was thinking aloud."

He was embarrassed. She laughed.

"There's nothing wrong with that."

"No, nothing." She was laughing.

"So you want to come to bed."

He pulled her down underneath him abruptly, almost as if he was diverting her attention from his remark.

"We'll have to get these clothes off of you."

He was undressing her, kissing her. She could taste the cold water still fresh in his mouth. She could feel the tenderness of his touch on her breasts as her shirt came off. He fumbled at his robe until it was gone, and she had his body pressed against hers.

"Slow down. We've got all day here."

He slowed down. His kisses and touch stayed longer. He was building all the wanting in her. She had to reach out to kiss and touch him. "You are good."

"Don't go to Mexico or Africa."

She pulled back a little to look at him. He looked as sincere as he'd sounded. And, somehow, nothing was missing any longer. Things were good with them again – not through trying or working at it, but instantly, because of that plead. It was strange. It was wonderful. She had him, and she was quite ready to float along with them. "Okay."

"Good."

"You're not normal, you know that?"

"Is that a compliment?"

"Probably."

"You're not normal either."

"Probably not."

"Take my word for it."

"I'm not worrying about it." She couldn't think any longer. She was melting into the utter sensations he was so good at creating in her. He was kissing her neck, her ears. He was loosening her jeans. She wiggled out of them.

24

He grinned – he had to stretch his head back, as he sang the Stones' love anthem *Angie*. He was grinning so much. He loved this: tender hooks. And he watched her face – she didn't know which it would be, couldn't know, didn't dare guess, because it could be either. "'When will those clouds all disappear?'" He smiled. She smiled. "You can't say we're satisfied." She shook her head and looked up at the ceiling – what do you do with a guy like this one? – and he kept grinning, kept playing, stopped singing, letting her guess now. Which was it, which did he dare hear in her mind? – *'You're beautiful, But ain't it time we said goodbye?'* or *'I still love you baby, Everywhere I look I see your eyes – there ain't a woman that comes close to you.'*

He swaggered the guitar around. "Where will it lead us from here?" Grinning.

"Cute."

And he kept playing, watching her face, letting the music fill him up. He could hear the words in him: 'All your kisses still taste sweet, I hate that sadness in your eyes. . . . "He loved this, always had, and it had been so long . . . but the power was still there, freeing and feeling – he'd only felt when he'd played, he was sure of it now. And he went up to her, grinning. He leaned right over her, dancing his eyes on hers. "But. . . ." Which would it be? She blushed. "Ain't it good to be alive?" And he jumped back and finished the song off with a blast. It was good to be alive.

"I've always liked that song, actually."

"I bet you have." He laughed – she blushed – he could see it, the girl listening to the music, and he laughed again, taking off with rough chords on the guitar. And he grinned. "So you ever getting up or what?"

"There's not enough space for me to get up, not while you're playing."

"You want more?" And he took off again. With *Start Me Up*. And he wasn't stopping, not while he could feel it again. It had been too long – he hadn't forgotten just hadn't remembered. And that was back: the noise, rushing his skin, beating his heart, scattering everything with a great spiraling speed, making him believe he was alive, making him cry.

And he played it, twisting around in the little space, watching her smile, watching her, her watching him. He never should have stopped. He finished the song.

"Is all you know the Stones?"

"All there is is the Stones." And he kept going, just stopping to turn up the amp and launched into *I Can't Get No Satisfaction*. He'd wound himself up now, tensing every part of his body, and he let it go – And he could hear it all with him: drums bass backup, everything starting up, everything letting loose, everything going to its place. He couldn't hear himself over the guitar. He couldn't remember it all, but he filled in as he went, and more and more came back to him. Chords. Beats. Sounds. And he watched her. She looked amused, playful. He changed songs. He was playing *Under My Thumb*. Kim had turned off the amp. He laughed. "Don't like that much?" And he laughed again, bending over to her. "Maybe I know someone who does. What do you think?"

"I've heard you know some pretty catty people."

"You've heard that, have you?" He'd wondered what she'd heard.

"I've heard that some of the people you know cat around town quite a bit."

"That's pretty catty, Kim." And he laughed and tried to go off again, but there was no sound to the guitar. "Turn it back on." He nodded towards the amp. "I know what you want to hear."

"What do I want to hear?"

"Turn it on and find out" And she did, almost dropping her blankets while leaning over, and she pulled them up so quickly; he laughed. "Think I'll see something I haven't seen before?"

"I thought you were going to play the guitar."

"Yeah." And he thought for a minute, because he couldn't remember how that one went. "Okay, it's like that . . . yeah – one two three four." And launched into *I Miss You Child*.

And he swayed, playing the song through for her, watching her face. Did she think he meant it for the time she went away? – what did she think? He laughed – she wouldn't meet his eyes for more than a second but she kept coming back for more. "No I won't miss you baby, yeah, Lord I miss you child." And he finished it with another swagger. "That's more your style, isn't it Kim?"

"You think so."

"Yup, that's what you want, isn't it Kim?" And she looked away blushing again. He had her.

"Aren't your neighbors going to start complaining now? It's pretty early for rock and roll."

"In this neighborhood?" He laughed. "My neighbors probably aren't sure yet that they're hearing anything. They think it's in their heads. You can do anything out here, you know, and no one is sure you've done it or even been here."

"Charming."

"Best neighbors in the world."

"You might have something there."

"So." He sat down. "You ever getting up or what?"

"Is the concert over?"

"Did you like the morning with the Stones?"

"You're pretty good."

"A little rusty." She didn't need to know he'd been practicing for two or three weeks now. "But it comes back."

"Seems to."

"You should have been there, Kim" He laid the guitar down at the end of the bed and leaned against the wall. He could remember those days – the taste of life. "We were hot, you know, and we were cool We played everywhere, and we got everyone going."

"Did you play gigs?"

"No, not really. We used to go downtown – to town – Saturday nights, and walk around – we were too young to get into the places, even to fake it, but we'd walk around and I'd have the guitar, and we'd talk to people, and we'd end up just anywhere – parties, just wherever the people were going." He could still feel it, the looking at those people, the getting in with them. "Those were the good old days. You know, there were girls there too, and they were about twenty-two, and I was sixteen, seventeen, eighteen, you know, and they were like groupies. It was unreal."

"Older women."

"Yeah."

"And now they're the younger ones."

"Yeah, I guess they were. Even you're not twenty-two anymore, are you?"

"No."

"I guess we're all getting old."

"I guess so."

"And we're getting old hungry."

"Is that a hint?"

"You ever getting out of that bed?"

"Oh, I might."

"Why don't you get up and make us breakfast?"

"As soon as you pass me a robe."

"Oh." He grinned."So if you're so hungry...."

"I guess you've got me there." He tossed her a robe. "So what are you going to make us?"

"What do you have and what do you want?"

"I've got everything, and I want an omelet with bacon and green peppers and onions and cheese in it."

"You're really hungry, aren't you?"

"Yeah – and check the coffee there. It should be through."

"It is."

She poured him a cup and passed it over. He made himself comfortable, and watched her cook – he could still hear the music: *da da da da da da da da da da da da*. He picked up the guitar and listened, strumming along with the sounds. Those days – he hadn't known then that life just came to this, and maybe it was that not knowing that made him so free, that made it all so easy. Because it had been easy, nothing like today. Because he hadn't known it wouldn't go anywhere – hadn't even known that anything ever had to go anywhere, that life was supposed to be one straight line through the universe, that if a guy didn't go anywhere, he wasn't any good. He switched to *Me and Bobby McGee*. "That was the first song I learnt, did I tell you that?"

"No."

"I had an acoustic then. Mom thought a guitar was okay when she thought it was just an acoustic, but I got this one about three weeks later."

"Sneaked it in, did you?"

"Oh yeah." He strummed the strings, caressing them. "I guess everyone learns that song pretty fast." It seemed to him that a guy should fall into the world before he fell out of it because it hurt too much to do it the other way around. "I let her slip away, she's looking for that home and I hope she finds it, but I'd trade all my tomorrows for a single yesterday – why do you think people do that Kim?"

"Do what?"

"Nothing." He'd thought about it enough already – had worn himself out just thinking on it since he'd moved here. Because he was trading all his yesterdays for a single tomorrow, and he didn't know why – because that was what was done. Because that was the only thing there was to do. Because that's what guys did: fell into the world, the one world. It was called growing up. And he was twenty-five, and it was time to grow up. He watched her beat the eggs. He could smell the bacon cooking. He drank his coffee. This was supposed to be enough – maybe he could get Charlene and Kim to set up a schedule, one going when the other was coming; that might be a life worth living. But they did that now, just didn't know it – it wasn't that anything would change, because nothing would change, not really, but somehow it had all changed.

"Watch the bacon for a minute."

"Why? She was putting on her boots. "Where you going? Want me to check the can out before you going in?"

"I'm just going to the car."

"What for?"

"You'll see."

"You going out wearing that, you're brave."

"Well, around here I have to be."

"Walk fast."

"You listen for screams."

"I'll do that." He stood up and leaned over the bacon. It wasn't doing anything. And then she was back with a bottle of champagne. "Where'd that come from?"

"My car."

"Why didn't you bring it in last night?" He took the bottle from her and looked at it. He didn't know anything about champagne, but he thought it must be good if she brought it.

"Because I was saving it for when you told me your news, and you never did, so it never got in."

"Oh. What news is that?" But he knew, and he could feel it already: the hand, plucking him, like that song by Bowie.—*oh, you pretty thing, don't you know. . . .*

And that was another lie. He looked at Kim. "What did you say?"

"I said Patty told me you're moving out and up in the chain. Where are you?"

"Did she say that?" He yawned. "I'm hungry."

"Alex."

"Those eggs burning?"

"I haven't put them on yet. If you don't want to talk about it, that's fine. We'll just have a champagne brunch for no reason."

"I didn't say I didn't want to talk about it. I just don't see what there is so much to talk about." And he didn't. Because nothing had changed. He hadn't changed – wasn't going to change. "It's just a transfer. Actually, it's moving out and down because I'll just be a second assistant. It's just a bigger store."

"Patty seems to think you're being groomed . . . ."

He looked at her, looking bored at her. "I think grooming is for horses." They should be asking us what stars we want to touch – he remembered – *tinker tailor soldier sailor* – and now they weren't even asking, didn't even bother with it. "It's such a long drive, and it's not more money, so it will end up costing me."

"If you don't want it, don't take it."

"Did I say I didn't want it?"

"Pretty much, yes."

"I don't think so." Because it didn't matter much if he wanted it or not. They'd spotted him now, and now he'd go, or he wouldn't go at all. And maybe that was it – no; he wanted to go, since that was the way to go.

He opened the champagne.

"Alex. . . ."

She looked so worried – she wanted him to bare his soul, didn't know yet that he didn't have one – survival of the fittest – *'making way for the homo-superior.'* "What?" Aren't we celebrating?" He passed her the bottle.

"I was going to mix this with the orange juice."

"Sounds good." He picked up his guitar and strummed.

"What's bugging you?"

"And the first one said to the second one there, I hope you're having fun; Band on the run, band on the run.' What do you think? Think I could have made it? That was the first song I learnt on this guitar. Drove everyone nuts for weeks." He leaned over and turned off the amp.

"Did you want to make it?"

"No." He could see that she didn't believe him, that she thought he wanted the stage and the sounds and all the rushes, but she was wrong. Because there was more to it than all of that, and it was that he'd wanted – he'd wanted that to be true, and it had been true, while he played, while he listened. He'd felt it in him – the changing, the opening, the breathing at last. But it had stopped, ceased. Because for no place for it, not in this world. So it wasn't true. "Breakfast ready?"

"I haven't started the eggs. Just a minute."

And she went back to the hot plate, still giving him funny and concerned looks. Because she hadn't figured out it wasn't true yet. As if things could be true when the world proved they weren't. As if wishes were more than dreams, and dreams were more than torments. Only a girl could believe that, because a girl didn't have to stop. And she looked at him as if he had a problem.

"Why do you have the guitar here? I didn't even know you still had one around?"

"Maybe you never looked." She thought she knew everything, and she knew nothing.

"I didn't go through your closets, if that's what you mean."

"It was at Mom's. A kid at work wants to buy it so I'm taking it in tomorrow. No use keeping it."

"Is that why you're so strange now?"

He laughed – he thought he was getting less strange by the minute. He was doing what he should. He was normal. "So where's that OJ you promised."

"Your kind of OJ."

"You got that right." She mixed it up in a jug and passed him a glass. "So let's toast it."

"Just a minute."

"Well, are we going to toast or not?"

She frowned. "Just a minute. This is just about done. I can't let it burn."

He waited until she'd dished out the eggs and joined him sitting on the bed. "So what is a good toast?"

"The way you're talking, I think we should toast horses."

"Been down to the tracks lately? There are some beautiful horses there. Just telling by looking that they've been looked after. Makes a difference." And he'd made her look twice as concerned, twice as puzzled. He laughed and touched his glass to hers. "To horses."

"If you don't want to, don't."

He smiled – chuckled – and drank. Because that was all part of the lie too. A guy could grow up to be president, sure, but a guy couldn't grow up to be anything he wanted to be – it would be easier to be president than to be anything he wanted to be. He ate his eggs. "These are good."

"Thanks."

She still looked so concerned, so puzzled. She wasn't eating. "Your eggs will get cold."

"I'm not hungry."

"Can I have them?"

"Go ahead."

He took her plate and dumped the eggs on top of his. "You're a good cook, you know that? Always have been." And he ate. Things weren't that bad – he didn't know why he was letting himself get down about it. He should be proud, and would be, once he was through this part. "Pass me some more of that OJ will you? It's good." And he gave her his glass.

"Get it yourself."

And she gave the glass back to him. And she glared. He laughed – she took his life more seriously than he did. "You won't get it for me?"

"I don't know how you do it. I really don't."

"Do what?"

"Manage to make absolutely everything you do seem to be just one more step into some dark hole."

"Is that what I do?"

"Yes. You even make a promotion and a new house into a part of the hole, and maybe it is, maybe that's true, but don't pretend it isn't once you've said it is."

He grinned – she'd caught him.

"And it is such a lie. It's almost as if you think you get to go around more than once in this life, so it's okay if you blow it this time around. But this is it. Until it's proven otherwise, this is all you get."

She was up, pacing. She passed – thrusted – him the OJ.

"Here. See if you can't drown the pain a little."

She was just trying to provoke him – rub his face in it until he denied it. But there was no point in denying it. He took the jug and refilled their glasses. "Thanks."

"You sure you don't need it all?"

"Maybe you should have brought two bottles. You know what a drunk I am." Because two could play this game. He could prove anything he wanted to her.

"It's not how much you like it, it's why you like it. And it's why you accept anything that comes your way instead of looking for what you want. I . . . it's so stupid. It's such a waste. I'm fed up."

He shrugged – he hadn't given her the right to be fed up with anything. He didn't owe her anything. She was just a girl – couldn't even claim to be his girl because he'd never given her that, even if she'd offered.

"You just want to wrap yourself up in your pain. You don't even want to try. You just want to dig this hole and bury yourself and bury everything you ever felt or thought or whatever – you don't even try to make your own life yours, and that's what I can't stand."

"So who asked you to stand it?" He looked at her with no expression on his face. "That's just the way it is. Simple.

"Things are complicated, maybe more than you want, and maybe you think holding them down to some sort of fatalistic view that everything comes around because it's supposed to and you don't matter much in the play of things, maybe that's just another way of copping out, just like drinking and chasing around and keeping away from any possibility of any sort of commitment."

"I don't give commitments. I told you that at the beginning."

"That's not what I'm talking about and you know it."

"No I don't. I think that is what you're talking about."

"No, and don't try to put it down to that. I'm talking about taking a job that you don't want. I'm talking about becoming a person you don't want to be."

"Well, I don't see that." He stretched, and made himself comfortable on the bed, folding his robe neatly around him. "Nope, I don't see it."

"You don't dare see it, just like you don't dare think, because if you saw something or if you thought, you just might have to do something about it. But it's there, whether you grab hold of it or not, it's there."

She stopped, lighting a cigarette, glaring, breathing heavy at him with hatred. He shrugged. He wasn't listening, didn't have to listen. She was just a girl.

"How many lies do you have to tell yourself to get through the day? Why don't you stop one day and count them and see if that scares you enough to get your ass in gear?"

She was just a girl who knew nothing about his days. She didn't know what he did, what he didn't do. She only knew what he'd let her see. She didn't know about any of it – didn't know how great it felt sometimes – so she couldn't talk. He had a good life – he had good times. He ignored her, lighting up a cigarette too, drinking his juice.

"How you can pretend that your own life means nothing to you is beyond me. If I were you, I wouldn't want to dig a dark hole. I would do something, anything, just to keep myself out of it."

He poured the rest of the juice into his glass. "Like I said, you should have brought two bottles. There's not much in one of these, and you know how much I like to drink."

"Like to hide is more like it."

"You think so?" He yawned. This isn't doing anything for me, Kim." He reminded her she was just a girl, she had a role to fill.

"I really don't care."

She looked out the window, her back to him. "You should. You want to stay around, you have to fulfill your part, you know."

"Why don't you go buy one of those rubber dolls? Because that's all you need to get what you say you want, isn't it?"

She was just trying to shock him. He shrugged, she smoked. Because he didn't care – he didn't owe her.

"You don't want real people with real feelings, and Lord knows, you don't want to have a real feeling yourself. Yes, I think you should have a rubber doll."

She was holding herself up as some great arbitrator, some great master. "Yeah, you could be replaced that way." And she glared, and sat down at the end of the bed, her back still to him, as if she couldn't look at him.

"You don't even try anymore."

He reached over and pulled at her robe's belt. "You're hanging around to get lucky again, aren't you?" He laughed. He knew how to get to her, how to make her feel him, remember him. "Wearing my robe to keep me tempted? You know how many girls have done that?"

"Fuck off."

He could feel the rush starting in him – the power, and the "I-am-and-you-are." Because he could make her anything he wanted her to be. "I don't keep count anymore, but that's why I bought the thing in the first place. What do you say?" He kept tugging at the belt. "Going to let me use you now? Like I do."

"Go buy a rubber doll."

"You can leave and someone else can come if you want. That's okay with me."

"We all know what discriminating tastes you have in girls, don't we? You are so easy. You are so gutless. You play a thousand games, and you think you have control, but all you have is a thousand games."

"No. I have a good side too."

"You don't even know what that it."

"Maybe I know as much as I want to know. What do you think of that? Maybe I don't need to know anymore than I do, because maybe I'm getting what I want."

"I'm fed up with you I'm fed up with being mad at you. I'm sick of hearing your cop-outs. I'm not talking to you anymore. It's a bloody waste of time."

"I agree with that. He moved his hand inside the robe, and squeezed her breast. "We can have a good time, if you want." She threw his hand back at him. He laughed: she was feeling it, feeling him, because what was he about – sex, fun. "So you don't like me know. That's too bad."

"It's a game, another fucking game."

"You think so? I think it could be fun." He was a sleaze. He smiled. He ran his hand down her back. "Come on Kim, what do you say. Want to get laid. Because that's all you're here for, that's all I want you for."

"You really think this gives you control, Alex?"

"I feel pretty in control, yeah." And he grabbed her around the waist, and pulled her down with him. "So what do you think?" She was glaring at him. He grinned.

"I think this is a game, and I'm not going to play."

"Sure you are." He pushed her away from him. "You're not fun" To make her come to him.

"You're too weird for me."

"Am I weird?" He laughed. He wasn't weird, he just wasn't her kind of guy, and she should see it. "You should meet new people, you know that? Yeah, you should find other guys to sleep with."

"Don't think it's out of any loyalty to you, because if I met someone, you'd be old news pretty fast."

"I'm glad to hear it." And he was: she shouldn't be with him, she should be with guys more like her, guys to dream with her.

Because he knew too much to dream. Didn't dare dream. "So Patty told you about the house too." He'd noticed that she knew. "She didn't leave me much to say." Patty wouldn't think that he would want to decide when what was to be known, and by whom it would be known. He hadn't planned on telling Kim – didn't know what he'd thought. Maybe he'd planned on just slipping into it – this life with a mortgage and an eye on his back – and that way, just slipping out of everything else.

"You could have told me. Patty said you bought it in November."

"Didn't take possession until the New Year." He took a cigarette. He didn't like being trapped into other people's knowings. He didn't like other people putting importance onto things when they weren't important but simply were.

"Where is it?"

"You coming to visit me there?" He laughed and pulled her back to him, gently now. Because now she looked concerned again, not furious. And he was tired.

"You going to invite me?"

You going to wait for an invitation?" He laughed again, and buried his head in her neck. "That would be a first." The girl did want him, and the girl did try to understand – maybe she understood too much, maybe that was the problem. It didn't matter. He'd think about it later when he had the time, the energy. He pulled away from her and rested against the pillow. "It's an old place. Be a while before I can move in. Needs work. Good price though – that's why, a handyman's special."

"Is that why you bought it? An investment?"

She hoped not – he laughed – he could hear it in her voice. She hoped he hadn't fallen that far into the world. And he hadn't. "Maybe I want to be a carpenter, like Christ." Her little eyes opened up and she didn't say a word – didn't know what to say, he knew. He laughed and pulled her to him. He didn't know what to say either – he didn't know why he'd said it. He just wanted something else, something that he wasn't getting, and it had always been this way, and he was worn out. But wouldn't it be nice to be something, be in touch with something . . . something that gave something of the self, something that would let him breathe, that wouldn't make him so anxious all the time? "I'm cold. Let's get under the blankets."

"You're so weird. You change like night and day."

"Do I? He stretched. You don't seem to mind."

"I don't mind you being weird. It's when you try for some . . . I don't know what it is, some sort of false act, role, something, that's when I mind."

"I noticed."

He laughed. He pulled the blankets over them. One thing about Kim: she did like him when he was weird. No one else did. He'd keep her for a while.

25

S o they go ahead, right, and arrange this swap and the other guy ends up with this guy's wife, you get it. He gets together with her and she's real hot for it, you know, 'cause she's been looking forward to this for a long time. She's never had any adventure in her sex life, see? So they get together, and he drops his pants, and she takes a look and laughs. 'Is that all you got to offer?' she says. And the guy says, 'not enough?' and he starts to twist his ears. She's watching this and she's amazed to see that as he twists his ears, it gets bigger. I mean, she's astonished, right? But when he stops and it's still pretty small, she starts laughing. 'That's better, but not by much,' she says. 'You want more?' he says, 'you just say when.' And he keeps twisting his ears and twisting his ears, and it's growing and growing. When it gets to a good length, she says 'when,' and they go to it and have really great sex. She can't get over how good it was. Her husband comes back the next day and asks her how it was for her. 'Great, terrific,' she says, 'and how was it for you?' 'Not bad,' he says, 'but the woman kept twisting my ears.'"

And a *ha ha ha ha*: she smiled weakly as the two guys laughed. She felt like telling them all about how modern dirty jokes reveal modern neurosis in modern men. But then she really couldn't complain as she'd heard much worse in her life – ones about camels and sheep. This was pretty mild – sick, but mild. It was typically male too. They always got stuck on stupid ideas – size didn't matter, and that was a scientific fact, but men would never give up the image of whipping it out and thus proving their manhood. Crass comparisons in the locker room, and other such nonsense. She looked out the window until the jokes were finished. But then his friend started on about something else.

"I mean, there's no incentive in it for us. Why should we promote their product? Why should I take the time and staff and floor-space to put up a display? And why should I keep that display full and neat?"

Kim could think of a few reasons, beginning with the paycheck the cretin took home every week.

"I know we do it, but any product would move out twice as fast if there was a bonus clause in it for us. Do I care if a customer wins a trip or a free shopping spree? Look at the wholesalers. Those salesmen are off to Spain and Portugal and South America and Hawaii all the time. Because their people reward them, and create a little free enterprise spirit in the troops too. I say we should do the same, we should get the same. Don't cut the stuff to the customer, I'm not saying that, but bring back all the promotional contests and stuff like that. It's good for business, and it will more than pay for itself. It will be good for the company too. It would let us show our stuff. There's nothing to motivate us now. There's the quotas and the sales and all of that, and we know we aren't going to get ahead in the company if we don't get the product moving. That makes sense, but hell, we both know how long it takes to move ahead in the first place. Give us more to motivate us for this year, you know. Head office won't put money in on the store level – that's the way it is, and they're cutting their noses off. That's what I'm saying. It wouldn't cost anything, and we would wipe out the competition."

She stifled a sneer. She did not like this guy. His jokes were sick, and his ideas were wrong – if he was looking for some satisfaction in life, he wasn't going to find it in contests. And Alex – he was soaking this up as a sponge does water. His little face was all scrunched up in concentration, and he was leaning towards his friend, looking very intently at him. How could he? She was disgusted; there was nothing here that she saw as even mildly interesting. But then, she knew she wasn't wanted here. "Alex. Excuse me." She smiled at his friend for the interruption. "I have to get going, Alex. There are some errands I forgot about."

"This can be pretty dull for the ladies."

She smiled again at the sickening man, and stood up, looking at Alex. "I'll talk to you later."

"I'll walk you to the door."

He got up and came with her.

"It was nice meeting you."

That was his sickening friend again. She had to turn back to him. "Yes. Well, take it easy."

"We take it anyway we can get it."

"Right." She caught up to Alex at the door. "I'll check with you later."

"Come back later."

He was squeezing her fingers – that special pressure he knew to do so well. "How much later?"

"A couple of hours."

"I'll try." She did want to be with him tonight.

"Here, I'll turn on some lights for you. It will be dark by then."

"Why don't you turn on the lights when your friend leaves? I don't want to walk in here and find him still around. That would be sort of uncomfortable."

"You'll see his car gone."

"Yeah, that's true. I can do that."

"Then you're coming back?"

"Yeah."

"See you then."

"Yeah." He squeezed her hand again, and she left. But she felt happier than she had been sitting there. And she remembered that he had a right to talk to his friends if she was there or not, that many men push women aside when business comes up, that being ignored for a few minutes didn't mean that things were over between them. It wasn't over at all. She just had a few hours to kill, and then she would have all of his attention, which was what she wanted. So what would she do? She drove down to the Classics Theaters.

Lost Horizons was showing. She went in. The theater was almost one fourth full, which was a good turn out for this place. That meant, of course, that a lot of people needed a dark place to think or be alone tonight; the world wasn't turning well tonight. It was funny, this theater was, the way it measured pain by showing classic movies.

The show was starting. Kim didn't care. She'd seen the movie before, and the first part was all snow. She bought her popcorn and sat down in the lobby for a smoke. What was bothering her was not so much Alex's visit with a friend, even though she did want all of his attention when he was near her. It was the nature of the visit, and the friendship. The way he had sat there, as if he was impressed, she saw that he was turning into something new – was turning himself into something new, and she wasn't sure she liked it. She knew she was supposed to like it, even applaud it – he wasn't drink-ing much, he was taking on the responsibility of a mort-gage, he was interested in his work etcetera, etcetera, etcetera; but she didn't like it. And she hadn't liked his friend – that guy sat there begging for the odd pat on the head when he should take pride in what he did for himself and not need any other nonsense, and if his job so lacked satisfaction, then he should move on to something else. — And if he really thought he had ideas that could work, he shouldn't be sitting there bullshitting with Alex, but take them to management. Risk more than his mouth. She hadn't liked him, and she hadn't liked Alex sitting across from him like that.

—Wife swapping as adventurous sex: such nonsense, even for a joke. It broke the rules, no doubt, but that was the only adventure there. But that was typical of what people thought adventurous sex should be. Orgies broke the rules. S & M mocked the essence. All of kinky sex built a thrill out of doing what shouldn't be done, and doing it at a time when utterly opposite acts should be done. Hence all of it was the failure of the real thing in each of those who chose it over the real thing. And Alex was one of those. She closed her eyes and leaned her head against the wall.

The things that she had wanted to do with him . . . she would have shown him the real power of the real thing to thrill him. She'd wanted to revel in his body the way she did in his eyes, smile, charm – the way she did in his eyes, smile, charm – the way she did in the very fact of his existence; she hadn't. She'd wanted to know his body so well through touch that she would never need to look at it again. She wanted to discover a hundred new positions with him. And she'd wanted to know him all wet. And she'd wanted to feel him on hard smooth rocks. And she'd wanted him all over her and her all over him and them so mashed together that the world could not move them apart. And all of it she wanted not to make it better, because it was once so good between them that it would have led them there. All gone, all wasted: she was scared to touch him now.

She hated to think about it, but she knew that their sex life was nothing to get excited over these days. They seemed permanently stuck in the missionary position. They did nothing – and her trembles when they touched, those were from fear as much as from longing. It was always a struggle now, as if they had to break through something each time they came together. And there was no freedom between them now, no freedom holding them together, no freedom letting them revel in each other. No celebration either, only desperation: "Take me, do not refuse me."

She could remember them in the good times. She still giggled and glowed when she recalled him pulling all the blankets over them one summer morning when the sun had intruded so early. He had said that they would pretend it was still night. His voice had been so free of fear and guilt and confusion. He wanted, and he didn't doubt. That instant had been special. He had made the world suit them, and he hadn't apologized or hesitated. Because the world had been theirs, and they had been the world – all of it, there in that bed, under those blankets. And they hadn't needed any gimmicks to get to there, or any kinks to distract them from being there. That had been six years ago. That instant was lost forever.

She knew all the reasons they weren't like that now. And Charlene MacGregor was the image of all the reasons. Charlene had to go. If Alex did want this new respectable lifestyle, why was Charlene still a part of the picture? What did that say about what he was choosing – or had Patty been right when she said that Charlene was very hard to get rid of once she got her hooks into a man? And Alex didn't like to hurt people.

Kim didn't know what she was going to do. She didn't know what she could do. She couldn't take a little wander through his mind and see exactly what was going on there, and then know exactly what to do or say to reach him. She couldn't force him back to the past. She couldn't live in the past herself. She wanted something to come from him, as it had before, in the time when his existence seemed a miracle. And he could do that if he would, because once in a while, even now with Charlene and all, he still did that. Those moments were still possible. If he would. But he wouldn't.

She didn't even know if she wanted him now. She wanted those moments, and he had been those moments, but was he now? He had changed. He'd lost so much of what he had. He'd sat there like a lap dog, listening to someone whose position in the company was no higher than his own. He hit Charlene. He missed – omitted – the very point of living. In six years, he'd done nothing to bring forth all of those special gifts he had within him. And he'd had so many. She couldn't put it in words. She couldn't go up to him and say, "this is what you have forgotten, this is what you have left behind." It wasn't simple cause and effect. It wasn't one thing, or one mistake. It was in some other way that he'd changed. And it was hard to get a hold on.

Charlene had lasted two years, and that was a very frightening fact. One that Kim was going to have to come to terms with.

How different was she from Charlene? Charlene was there for sex – she'd told everyone in town that she was into Alex's body.

But that wasn't the whole truth. Charlene was there because her energies were met by something in Alex. In some way, Alex affirmed everything that Charlene was about, because he was about it too. That was why they worked together, and why they were still together. And, if asked, Alex would admit that. He would admit no such thing about himself and Kim.

So why was Kim there? When she walked back into his home tonight, they would both know that she was there for sex. There was no difference between her and Charlene. Wrong: she would be there for boring sex while Charlene was there for S & M. No, she would end up with boring sex, but she was going there because she wanted all that she had with him before to happen one more time. And she would have sex with him because that was the only way left to be near him.

That wasn't enough, and they would be finished soon unless they broke through that. Kim knew that. And sitting back and suffering silently wasn't her style. She had to do something . . . something that would change it. She stood up and left the theater.

Ray's car was still parked in front of Alex's place. She drove on. There was a park not far from his house, and she stopped there. The sun was setting. She decided to give him until the sun set. That should be sufficient time, and then she would go back there. And then she would talk to him.

She knew how she wanted it to go. She wanted to walk straight on in there, look at him, and have all the right words to summon back in him all the beliefs and emotions he'd shown her before. And, while he was caught in that, she would say: "This is life, Alex. This is reality and don't let it frighten you. You feel what we had as a beginning, and it is a mere hint of what we can have. Go with it. Trust it. Don't shovel it back inside of you. Forget about sociology and your friends and my friends and fitting into each other's world. What is that now? Does that feel as right as this? Feel this, and go with it." And he would.

She watched the sun set. She knew he wouldn't. Because she would never say the things to him that needed to be said – how could she say anything that intimate when she couldn't even risk reaching for his hand? They were so mangled in mistrust . . . he didn't trust his experiences with her, and she didn't trust him at all.

When it was dark, she drove back to his place. She went to the door and knocked. Alex answered after she knocked again.

"Oh, Kim, hi. Yeah, come in."

He was acting as if he was surprised to see her there. She expected him to be sitting in his living room, waiting for that knock on the door. She didn't like this – she sensed that he was going to betray her tonight. "You said to come in when his car was gone."

"I was just thinking here – you know how you get caught up in thought."

She followed him into the living room.

"So what can I do for you?"

She recognized that game: he was putting the onus on her, as if she had dropped in when in fact he had not only asked her over in the first place, but had also insisted – with a little squeeze of the hand, no words – that she come back after his unexpected visitor had left. His favorite game – it made it seem that everything about them came from her when that was not true. "Who was that guy?"

"Ray? I introduced you two."

"Yeah, but who was he?"

"I told you. He's the other assistant at the store. He's a good guy to work with, a real go-getter."

"You like him?"

"You don't sound like you do."

"I don't know him."

"Yeah, well, he probably shouldn't have been telling those jokes in front of you, I can see that, but you know how it is. You want a beer?"

"No thanks."

"Mind if I get myself one?"

"No."

"So where'd you go?"

He was calling from the kitchen. She waited until he was back in the room. "I saw a show."

"What?"

"*Lost Horizons.*"

"Isn't that one of those old ones?"

"Yeah."

"Was it on TV?"

"No. I was down at the Classics."

"You could have saved your money. It's on TV all the time, isn't it? Most of those old shows are."

"I guess so, but they're better without commercials."

"Yeah, that would be true. So did you like it? What's it about?"

"Lots of snow." He wasn't listening. He was chatty and polite and the rest of it, but he wasn't really with her. He was still caught up in thought. What had that guy said to him? "Have a good talk?"

"Oh, yeah. Well, we were just bullshitting, you know, just figuring the place out."

"Solve all the problems?"

"No, but you know, Ray's got some ideas on that."

"I heard some of them."

"Yeah, but he had some more after you left."

"What did you think of them?"

"I thought they were good. I guess that was pretty dull for you to sit through. But you left."

She wasn't sure if that was a sneer or a pout. "I thought you'd rather talk alone."

"Yeah well, I guess it doesn't really have much to do with you now, does it?"

He was pushing her away. He was drawing lines of distinction between them – "this touches me, this doesn't touch you." Her stomach turned over – why did he want to do this now? "It's been a long time since I was in retail foods, and it would be a hell of a lot longer before I go back to it. There's too much crapping there, and no answers."

"Did you think Ray was crapping? I didn't."

"If Ray wasn't crapping, why was he talking to you, not the guys from head office? Has he told them those ideas"

"I don't know."

He was being so casual – dismissive. "You know he hasn't, and you know he hasn't because there's no one in the place who'd want to hear from him."

"You think that?"

Now he was being arrogant, as if she had no right to think. "One level dumps on the level below it in that place, and everyone runs around thinking that's what they are supposed to do their jobs."

"Yeah?"

He was rubbing his chin. He was amused. She wasn't. Everything that she was talking about mattered – this was the very stuff that made the gap between them. All the things he didn't or wouldn't see, all the things that he let control his life, all of that was right here, and she was going to take the opportunity to tell him so. "I don't know what goes on there. I worked there, remember? If you want to be a cog in the machinery, fine, go ahead, but that's all that is wanted of you there, and all that's all that will ever be wanted of you. The place wants hands, not individuals. There's no use thinking about that place because there's no place to take those thoughts to."

"I think Ray and I know a little more about the place than you do."

"I think you and Ray are going to be very disappointed very soon, if you think you can make the place listen to ideas. No one there cares about any of the things that have been learned or studied in the past twenty years. I remember one day what's-his-name? – Myers, Myers walked in and said that he'd been to a seminar on labor relations and that they told him that all employees wanted to be told what to do all the time, that we wanted to be ridden all day long, that the tough hand was the right hand. He was telling Griffins in front of me, and I could see that he was really pleased with it. I thought to myself that that was just par for the course with that company. Sending all middle-level management to a seminar like that. Because the company didn't want to be open to ideas from us. They wanted to run the place, and Myers, he was almost dancing down the aisles with relief. He didn't have to give up any of his petty little power. All of that had just been blessed, and if you want to know, that was the day I decided to quit." She lit up a cigarette.

"Really? That was why?"

He looked interested. He was listening. She had a chance here to make a few points, if she played her cards right. "Yes, because I had too much respect for myself to stay there, under that attitude. It's the way the world works. Either you make something of yourself, or they make something of you, and you keep choosing the latter. Over and over and over." She had his attention. "Why can't you see that that is what is happening. And it's not just at work that you do that. It's in every part of your life." She had a notion that she'd never had before. "Whose idea was the ropes? Yours or Charlene's?"

"What are you talking about?"

He'd stiffened. He'd not known that she knew. "I think you know what I'm talking about. I know what I'm talking about."

"I don't think that's any of your business."

"I think when someone I'm sleeping with starts hitting a person he's sleeping with, it's my business."

"I don't think so."

"Well, I do." She wasn't going to let go of this.

"How long have you known?"

"Since it started. It's a small town, and Charlene has a big mouth."

"Well, it's none of your business. I'm not doing it to you."

"That's right, you're not. But it still says things about you that I don't like to hear." She didn't know what was coming over her, but it felt right, and she was going to do it – it was necessary. She knew that now: he was not going to change unless he was blown out of his old and stinking and stagnant waters. She didn't yell. She kept her voice as soft and as emotionless as she could. "There are two kinds of pleasures to have in this world: momentary pleasures, and long-term pleasures. Momentary pleasure is just that, a few moments, and nothing else. Long term pleasure is building and growing and becoming. The pleasure you get from it becomes a part of you, and it carries you on into tomorrow." She wasn't sure of what she was saying – where she'd heard it? – where it was coming from? "You feel good about yourself, and you learn about yourself. And you feel good from the inside, not just because you've stuffed your body full of drugs, and then given it sensations to thrill it." He looked like he was listening. "But with the other kind, you have to keep looking outside you for thrills, and bigger and bigger thrills at that. And all of that can backfire, because you don't learn the things you need to know to like yourself."

"Well, you're into things like that. I'm not."

"You should be, if you want to live. Copping out isn't going to help you."

"Maybe I don't think I need help."

"If you're hitting someone in bed, you need help."

"Don't knock it 'til you try it."

That was another cop out. "You're going to find yourself sitting in the bar when you're forty, with a beer belly, and you'll look like you're sixty, and you won't have anything to offer anyone but bull-shit about sex. You won't even have what a three year old has. That's where you're going to end up."

"That's my business."

"You want that?"

"You don't understand things, you know. You don' t know everything under the sun."

"That was true enough, but she did believe that she knew more than he did.

"If it feels good, do it."

"That's fine as long as you understand 'feels good.' I don't think you do."

"We're different types of people. You feel good when you think a lot. I like bodies."

His ultimate cop out. She'd gone too far. She lit up a cigarette.

"You smoke too much."

"I don't smoke any more than you do."

"Yes you do. You should see the ashtrays when you leave this place."

"You smoke a man's cigarette. These aren't."

He rolled his eyes.

"Oh, fuck." She looked away.

"Does that mean you're finished telling me about the evils of my life?"

"Yes." She didn't look at him.

"Good."

"I just think that you should remember that grooming is for horses, not people."

"Yeah, well I'll remember that."

"Do that." She didn't know what she was going to do. It was so frustrating to be anywhere near him these days, and had been like that for so long. And he was no help. He wasn't going to take any sort of action under any sort of circumstance – whatever she did or said or cried, he would sit there like a brick wall. She was just banging her head against it. Why was she there? – it was all a set-up, every bit of it. She would have to reach for him. Reach for him or leave him, because that was what he wanted, that reassurance every time, because he wasn't strong enough to reach for her – or not in love enough.

She was drained. She did not want to have to take that risk again. But she wanted him yet – more now than when she'd walked up the stairs expecting to find him wanting her. Because now she couldn't leave without having him, without feeling him wanting her. There was so little left between them, she couldn't leave without knowing that some was still there, and sadly sex was all the connection that they had left themselves.

She stood up and walked over to the window. She hoped – she didn't know what for. But how could she have him? How was she ever going to find a way to move close enough to him to have – make love with him now? She knew he wouldn't make the first move. He insisted she did, now as always. She went over to the couch and sat with him. She watched him drum his fingers against the edge.

"So."

He'd rested his hand halfway between them. She looked at

him. She knew he was waiting. "You're lucky murder's illegal. You know that?"

"Am I?"

"Very."

"I don't blame you."

She snorted and glared at him. She blamed him, for everything – for wanting this. But what was the point? And what was the point of getting into it with him once more? Even if she pushed as hard as she could, all he would say was that he owed no alliance to any moment in time, and was not affected by any moment in time, and that if she was, that was her problem, and she should deal with it. Words sent straight up in the air to pop like balloons but still effective – she'd never prove otherwise; she couldn't tell him what his reality was. But there were other ways, that didn't lean on words, and that weren't concrete, and that were easy. She reached for his hand and played with his fingers.

"So what do you think?"

That was what he always said when he didn't know what to say. She knew what to say, but all of it was taboo, because all of it was tangible. "I don't know."

"Well, if you don't, who does?"

But that wasn't sarcastic. His voice was merely tired. She let that go by.

"You just come here to get laid anyway."

And that was a challenge: agree that she was just another slut in his harem of sluts, or deny it and take all of the responsibility for them. All of it was beginning to weigh too heavily on her. And she knew that two could play this game. With ridicule in her voice, she agreed, "Absolutely."

"I've known that all along."

"I've always thought you've known the truth all along." She watched his reaction. He grinned for an instant.

"You think so, do you?"

"Oh, I think you're a bright boy, much brighter than you let on."

"Do you now?"

"Yes."

"You can get into a lot of trouble by overestimating people."

"Maybe."

"So you want to go to bed, do you?"

He squeezed her fingers, and he grinned again, but it was a game she didn't want to play. So you want – her idea, his assent, as if he was doing her a favor. That wasn't enough from him. "What do you want?"

"I want to be wise."

And that pulled on every part of her that lived, just as he knew it would. How . . . why . . . he created such moments out of nothingness, and then would deny that they existed, but she would know – and he would know – that they had existed, and that was all it took. It was all it would take tonight, that and his eyes, pleading with her not to catch and betray him in that statement, but to hold him because of it. "Okay."

"What?"

"Let's just go to bed, Alex."

"If you want to."

"Fine, I want to." She almost threw her hands up at him, she was so fed up with the games.

"Want me to get a bottle of wine, or something?"

"If you want to."

"It's up to you. Sex is better when you've had a couple of drinks."

"No, it's not." She had to say that, because she could not let another one of his justifications – lies – stand. "You just think it is."

"We don't have to drink then."

"It doesn't matter. It really doesn't matter." And she looked at him, and he looked at her, and they were stuck in some warp – a lagtime between wanting each other and having each other. And all because of the doubt they'd stuck between them – he'd stuck; she knew. She was tired of it. She looked away.

"Come on."

He'd stood up. She looked at him. He bent down and picked

her up – he'd never done that before – and carried her to his room. She rested her head on his shoulder. But she didn't want him now, and she was going on only out of a sense of obligation. The sex itself . . . sex wasn't enough, and hadn't been enough since the moment it had become all they had left, because it wasn't all they had left. That was a lie: I want to be wise. That was what they could have, and should have had, because that was what was in him.

He laid her on the bed, and it all seemed so sad.

26

He knew it was her car, had known the moment he'd turned the corner and spotted it. He didn't even have to get out of his car and look into it. That it was just another blue Honda in a world over-stuffed with blue Hondas, on a street littered with two or three alone, that didn't matter. It was her blue Honda, and she was inside, talking to Patty, and the topic under discussion was him — what else did they have to talk about? His heart told him that, and his palms, sweating too. It was her car, and she was inside and they were talking about him. And he had to go in. They would have seen him by now, and were probably wondering why he wasn't getting out of the car. *Speak of the devil, look who's here. Isn't he coming in? We've scared him off — you've scared him off, Kim.* He turned the engine off and pulled up on the emergency brake. He hated seeing her. He stepped out of the car.

It wasn't so much that he hated seeing her, it was that he didn't know how to see her. She made him nervous, awkward, anxious — she would make the Pope nervous, awkward and anxious — probably wanted to make the Pope anxious, awkward and anxious, because she wasn't happy unless she'd gotten under the skin. As if she was some surgeon whose only moments of life were had on the operating table, pulling the guts out of some poor joker. Suddenly, to see her face seeing him, to be searched out . . . he knocked on the door.

"Coming."

He smiled as Patty opened the door. "Hi there, Pats." She was grinning broadly—relishing. And he didn't know how much she knew.

"Hi Alex. What brings you around? Long time no see, and all that?"

"You don't even offer a guy a cold beer on a hot day? No wonder I don't come around here much anymore." He stepped into the kitchen and saw her sitting in the living room – Patty always kept everyone in the kitchen or the basement, didn't use her living room. Kim was curled up comfy-like in the lazy-boy chair, holding a glass of something – probably iced tea, since she wouldn't even take a beer on a hot day, making him keep ciders and wine stocked – wearing summer shorts and a T-shirt that showed the world that she didn't wear and didn't need to wear a bra. And she was tanned. Looked like she'd been enjoying the summer. Except for now: her face, there was none of the summer's ease there, not welcoming; she looked ready to run, bolt, get away from him. *I want to be wise – It doesn't matter, it really doesn't matter.* He'd been stupid to come in, as stupid as the fool who walked into a brick wall and then had to make everyone believe that walking into a brick wall was the way to spend the day. He took the beer from Patty. "Thanks. So how's it going? Hear from Tony?"

"He called on Sunday."

"So when's he heading home?"

"He didn't know. He'll stay as long as there's work, and he thinks they'll be working through September unless it rains a lot soon."

"Staying put till the last fire's out and the last paycheck's in, is he?" He drank his beer, keeping his eyes on Patty, his back half turned to her.

"Something like that. You going in or standing out here, talking all day?"

And Patty grinned. He took another drink of his beer and grinned too. And he turned around and went into the living room. "So look who's here."

"Hi."

"Hi." He wasn't going to let it lapse, let her or him have time to think about it. "So how's it going?"

"Pretty good."

"I guess I walked in on a hen party." And he grinned.

"Guess so."

But she didn't even smile. "So what have you ladies been up to?"

"We were up at the lake."

"Oh yeah." He sat down and turned to Patty. "See any of the old crowd up there?"

"Not really. Bob and Sue were up there with their kids and that's about it."

"How are they? I haven't seen much of them since the wedding."

"You were the best man, weren't you?"

"Yeah, but that was just a last minute thing when his brother broke his leg. Remember that?"

"Oh yeah. He was still in the hospital. They're doing all right. Three kids now."

"No kidding? I haven't been there since little Rob was born."

"He's a real handful now, isn't he Kim?"

"Looked like it to me, but we only saw him for a minute."

"Oh yeah?" He nodded at Kim, and looked back at Patty. "What's he like? Is he worth getting married over?" And he laughed. "That's the one that caused the wedding, isn't it?" He could feel Kim over his shoulder. She hated him. She saw through him.

"Yeah, but he's a good kid, just keeps you running. Sue says he's the only one of the three that's like that. And you should see this kid. He's in and out of everything before you can move. Bob's always running after him"

"Bob is?" He couldn't see Bob as a daddy. Bob wasn't the type.

"Bob's quite the father. He really seems to like playing with the kids."

"That's good, that's good." And he drank the last of his beer. "That was good too, Patty. What do you say to another one?"

"Sure."

And she left, and he had to talk with Kim. "How have you been?"

"Fine, like I said."

"Oh yeah." He nodded, smiling – he didn't know what he was doing here. "So I haven't seen much of you around. You been on holidays."

"First two weeks of July."

"Oh yeah, that's right." He nodded again. He remembered now: she always took her holidays then. "So what did you do? Go away?"

"Just to the coast."

"Sounds good." And Patty was back with his beer. He took it and drank. "Nothing beats a beer on a hot day." And he looked at Patty. "So." He couldn't think of anything to say. "I thought I'd better stop in and see how you're doing with Tony away."

"That was nice of you. You could drop in more you know. You never visit anymore."

"Well." He didn't know what to say. "I'm a busy boy, you know. I'm in demand." But that was the wrong thing to say. He could feel Kim stiffening beside him.

"How's Charlene, or are you still going with her?"

He glanced at Kim – why did Patty ask that in front of Kim? Kim was pretending to look out the window. "You know me Pats. I don't give commitments." Kim still looked away.

"You still see her?"

He grinned – he couldn't say a word.

"Oh, I see."

"So Pat, where's your little one? I don't see an ankle-biter around."

"She's at Tony's mom's for the week."

"Taking a holiday, are you?"

"Yeah, that's what it's like. She phones just about every night to check on Mommy, but she's old enough to be without me, and Tony's mom doesn't get to see her the way my mom does."

"This is true." He nodded, smiled. He saw Patty look at Kim – so talk to him – and Kim glare back – *fuck off.* "So." He had to get something going here before there was too much going on. "What are you ladies up to tonight?"

"We aren't really up to anything. I was going to start dinner pretty soon."

"Let's go out for dinner. What do you say? Have a real holiday Pat. "We'll go out and paint the town."

"I don't know, Alex."

Patty looked at Kim. Kim didn't move. "Oh come on Pat. Be like the old days. What do you say? You don't want to cook in this heat anyway."

"What do you think, Kim?"

And he had to look at Kim too. "Yeah, what do you say Kim? Come out for dinner with us?"

"I don't think so."

"Now Kim, I said I'd give you dinner, so if you don't go, I can't go either."

He could have hugged Patty. "Yeah. You going to keep Patty stuck in the house?"

"You two are ganging up on me."

"So come along."

"Yeah, Kim. Come along. I'm buying."

"Well now, that does make it an irresistible offer, doesn't it?"

She meant that he never took her out anywhere. "Look at it that way then, but we wouldn't think it was a party unless you came, would we Patty?"

"No. We'd think about you sitting at home, and we'd just eat and have our dinners laying in our stomachs."

"Oh right."

"So you're coming, right?"

"Okay."

"Okay, so let's go." He stood up and waited for them.

"Alex, we can't go dressed like this, unless you're taking us to McDonald's."

"Oh." He stopped. He hadn't thought of that. "So how long will it take you two to get changed? Half an hour?"

"It will take me just about that long to get home and come back."

"Oh." He thought. "Forty-five minutes?"

"Make it an hour and a half. Give a girl some time to wash the sand out of her hair."

And Patty took him by the arm and walked him to the door. He glanced at the clock. "So that makes it seven-thirty."

"Sounds good."

"See you then." And he left, Patty closing the door behind him.

He smiled, bouncing and laughing and singing and humming along with the music all the way home. Because he could see the night unfolding in front of his eyes. First, he'd make reservations for eight-thirty at a nice restaurant in town. And he wouldn't tell them until they were there, and Kim would be surprised that he knew such a place. And he'd remember to pull out her chair, and Pats too, and order a good wine, and not miss a course. And they'd sit and have a slow fancy coffees before they went dancing. And they'd go to a place with a band – he'd have to remember to check the paper before he left, and find out who was where tonight. And he'd take his card, and put it all on that, and they wouldn't run out of money. And she'd get drunk, and she'd remember, and she'd come back to him.

Because she'd see that he was trying too.

He bounced his palms against the steering wheel. Even the music was right tonight – he loved this song playing on the radio, That old time Rock'n Roll. He sang it out: "*don't take me. . . .*"

It was going to work.

The boy was back in town tonight.

He was going to have it back tonight. He knew it, he could feel it growing in him. The stuff that wowed people, the stuff that moved people, the stuff that made life flow in every direction at all times and swept everyone along with it with an incredible speed. He was showered shaved dressed and ready to go by six-thirty, and he was on his way at twenty to seven, with reservations made, and the nightclub chosen. He knocked on Patty's door at five to seven. "Hey, anyone one home here?"

"What you doing here already? My God you look jazzy."

Patty was peering out at him from behind her bedroom door.

"Do I?" He glanced at himself. He looked good. "We're heading to a nice place tonight, so put on your best clothes."

"You should have told us that before."

"You think Kim won't know?" He laughed. Kim would dress, he knew it. "Don't worry about it."

"Get yourself a beer. I won't be long."

"Thanks." Patty withdrew and he reached into the fridge. And he turned on the stereo and sat himself down for the wait. "Hey Pat."

"What?"

"Kim coming?"

"As far as I know."

"Good." He drank his beer. He was sure she'd come, and he was sure she'd be here early too. "You better hurry or you'll make us all late."

"I'm hurrying. Give me a break."

"As long as you know."

"Can't go until Kim's here anyway."

"She won't be long." He drank his beer. "Hey, you mind if I help myself to some Scotch?"

"Help yourself to whatever you want."

"Thanks."

"It's in the bottom cupboard near the fridge."

"I know." He was already there, and he poured himself a good one. "So you almost ready?"

"Alex."

Patty came out into the hall in her robe.

"Sit down, and relax, will you?"

"Oh. Okay."

"I can't get ready much faster. I hurt my back at work – did you know that?"

"No. When did that happen?"

"A couple of weeks ago. I've been off on Comp."

"How is it?"

"Not bad. It only bugs me when I stand a lot, you know, in one place."

"Like at work."

"Yeah, exactly, but I'll probably be able to go back next week."

"You know they say sex gives you a bad back." And he laughed. He didn't know where his thoughts were coming from, and that was the way he liked it.

"Get your mind out of the gutter."

And she went back into her room. He laughed. And he waited, listening to the music, slapping his thighs, walking around a bit. And he grabbed himself another beer. Then Patty was out, dressed. Patty's face always disappeared when she was made up; he remembered that now. "You look nice."

"Thanks."

"So." He went over to the window and looked up and down the road. "All we need now is Kim and we're on our way."

"She'll get here when she gets here. You can't get her here any faster than that."

"Oh, I was just looking." He sat down on the couch.

"Who you kidding?"

"What?" He took a drink of scotch, to hide his smile.

"'What' yourself."

"I don't know what you're talking about."

"Right. And Kim's only coming along because she thinks you owe her at least a dinner for all the crap you've given her. Hell, I'll believe anything."

"Is that what she said?"

"Yeah. Just as she left."

"Well, we're just good friends, you know. She can say that if she wants to." He glanced out the window again. It was seven-fifteen.

"And I'll believe that one too."

"What?" He took another drink.

"You two are like two burrs stuck to each other, you know that? Someone should really pull the two of you apart and make you stay apart until you both admit that you don't want that. That's what should happen."

"Why do you say that? What did Kim say?" He couldn't imagine what she could have said.

"Wouldn't you like to know?"

He didn't know what to deny and what to say, because he didn't know what Kim had said, or what Patty knew. But he was sure that Patty knew plenty. He grinned. "Wouldn't you like to tell me?"

"You want another beer? I have time for a beer, don't I? What time is it – split one?'

"Sure. I can use a chaser for this." He couldn't press her, because he wouldn't admit how much he wanted to know. He lit up a cigarette, and Patty was back with the beer. She passed him the bottle. "So, how's it going anyway?"

"It's pretty boring. I can't do much with my back like this, and Tony's not here, and Courtney's not here."

"Yeah, you're going to miss your call tonight."

"No, she called. She doesn't stay up late, you know. She called about six-thirty, told me what they had for dinner, and said I could go out if I wanted to."

"She's a pretty bright kid for her age, isn't she?"

"I think so. I have some pictures of her from the beach. You want to see them?"

He grinned. What could he say? She went to get the pictures and he glanced out of the window again.

"My mother would tell you that a watched kettle never boils."

"What?" He grinned, shrugged, and took the pictures from her. "When was this?"

"The long weekend. Tony was down for two days. We took her out to the beach for the first time. She'd been swimming before, but just at the pool, and you should have seen her eyes when she saw all that water . . ."

He looked through the pictures. He heard a car door closing. "That must be Kim." He gave the pictures back to Pat.

"It's just the neighbors."

"How do you know?"

"Sound's from the side. Relax. She's on her way."

"Maybe you should call and make sure. I made reservations." But he heard another car door, and that was from the front. "There she is. Let's go." And he grabbed his coat and ushered Patty along with him out the door. They met Kim standing beside her car. "We've been waiting for you."

"How are we going?"

"What do you mean?"

"I mean, whose driving?"

"I am." He had his keys in his hand."

"I think I should drive."

"What do you think Pat?" Because he knew what Kim was thinking, and she was right, but he didn't want to admit it. "Think we should let her drive?"

"Yeah, I do."

"Okay." He opened the door to her car. "You're driving. Patty, you can sit in the front, and I'll sit in the back." He scrambled in. He liked this little car. It was a good car for a girl.

"So where am I driving to?"

"Fourth and Oak."

"Fourth and Oak? You mean like in town?"

"Yeah, that's right. And put your foot down hard, because we have reservations for eight-thirty." And he leaned back against the seat, making himself comfortable. "And put on a tape. It's lonely back here."

"Where'd you make the reservations?"

"You'll see."

It was called 'The Attic', and it was supposed to be filled with antique chairs and couches and tables and lamps and plates. Kind of place Kim would like. Food was supposed to be good too. He was going to show her the sort of night she was used to.

The night went by fast – too fast – and he'd had too much to drink, and too much to eat, and he couldn't keep his eyes from swishing around in his head, and his thoughts from swishing around behind them. He'd eaten and he'd talked and he'd danced and he'd laughed and he'd drank, and he'd poured out his energy and made the night happen. And it had been a good night – no one could deny that. He'd had them all going – everyone sparked. The waitress, the people at the next table, and those tourists – he'd taken pictures for those two girls, and sat with each too, so they'd have pictures when they got home and then everyone had sat together and the host (probably the owner, the way he walked around the place) had taken a shot. And they'd all gone dancing together after dinner, and he'd danced with everyone, Kim too. He'd been charming – he'd charmed everyone.

Patty had had a good time too. He hadn't seen her up like that in years. She'd laughed and danced – danced until her back told her not to anymore – and she'd talked to the two tourists, telling them all about a city that she didn't know anything about, and she'd talked to the other couples, telling them what was in store for them if they ended up with kids. And she'd smiled, and danced with him, and talked to him. She'd loosened up; she'd been fun.

Kim – she couldn't drink because she was driving, and he couldn't ask her to drink because she was driving. But she seemed to be having a good time – she'd smiled on cue whenever anyone looked at her – even at him, for a flash, before she looked away. She'd talked a lot. She knew a lot more about the city than anyone else there, but she worked there too, and the rest of them were from out here. But she knew the spots. And she talked, and she danced and she laughed. She'd had a good time. But no thanks to him – he'd felt her all night slipping away from him, staying a few steps away from him. And there really wasn't anything that he could do about it. *It doesn't matter. It really doesn't matter.* She was right. He'd known it before she said it.

Because it couldn't matter. Because it had always been a lie, a dream. Because he was a washout. Because he didn't know how to do it – not the doing because he could always do the thing, but the it, whatever the it was. It. If someone would tell him what it was, he could do it, but he'd never learned – nothing taught. The ways of the world were taught – the pull of gravity – but nothing said about out there, beyond, where life was. Because then everyone would go there. Just like everyone came to him. He smiled and rolled over, hitting his face against the back of the seat. "This fucking car's too small."

"What's he doing back there? If he gets sick. . . ."

"He won't. Alex never gets sick. Not once."

"Well, if he does, he stays in it until he cleans it up. I thought he'd passed out."

"Oh, he's just half sleeping there. He's fine. Don't worry about him, Kim."

"Yeah, don't worry about me Kim." He stared at the back of her head. She wasn't worried about him, he knew, she was worried about the car seat. And he couldn't blame her – he'd just never expected to meet refusal in her face. He would have, if he'd thought, but it had never gotten as far as thinking because it had always been there: she believed, and he'd believed she'd believed. *I want to be wise.* Ripped out of him, discarded by her, and that was right, because he didn't need that in him – had no use for it – and she should know that – should know that he wouldn't be that because people were born into that or not born into that and there was no more to life than that. But he could still hear that song floating in his head: *Reason to Believe* by Rod Stewart. He'd danced with Patty, a slow dance for her back. She'd always done that for him. He looked up at her. She was talking with Patty. Memories – so much was tangled up with her, like beads in her hair. "I guess you don't know the value of things until they're gone."

"What did he say?"

"I didn't catch it Kim."

"Oh. Is he still awake?"

"Sort of."

If I listen long enough to you, I'd find a way to believe that it's all true—she wasn't giving him that chance anymore. "Serves me right."

"What's he doing?"

"Don't worry. He won't get sick. He's harmless."

"Yeah, maybe that's his problem."

'Still I look to find a reason to believe.' "I had that once, you know. Not everyone has that."

"Had what Alex?"

"It was like Romeo and Juliet. It was. It was so honest. It was true, it was." 'Someone like you makes a way to believe that it's all true.' "But I guess you got to learn the pain before you can know the other. Like one goes with the other. Is that what it is Kim?"

"I don't know what you're talking about."

"Don't you remember us?" He remembered them – always would. Kim, on top of him, her hair encasing him, her face so caring, with that little bit of sadness for him. He remembered. And he remembered the weight of her body too, on his, and the way she smiled – she never wore perfume, didn't need it. And she didn't need a bra, and she didn't need any make-up – *If I'd listened long enough to you, I'd find a way to believe that it's all true.* He should have listened. "You just don't know that you really want something until she's gone." – she hadn't even let him touch her tonight, she'd gone to the washroom for the slow dances. "I blew it." He sank into the seat. "I could have had it all, and I blew it." She'd had such a gentle touch, she'd touched him as if he was porcelain. "Don't you remember any of it Kim? Don't you remember what it was like?"

"Why haven't you passed out? Why don't you pass out?"

"Don't you remember what it was like?" He could remember her face, so scared *do you care at all Alex?* And he'd cared, and he'd been sincere – she'd made him sincere, and she'd made him feel, and she'd given him love and it was all gone now. Swept away by the tide. "But how did you forget it. It was so true."

"I wish we had a beer to give him. That would do him in."

"I think it's kind of interesting."

"Right. Alex, why don't you just sleep? We aren't too far from home now, so just sleep."

Her breasts, her body – the woman was boneless, the way she moved. Pure energy and flesh. "I'm going to bed." Her hands were on him, pulling open his shirt, and her flesh was on his flesh and he could feel her heart beating inside of her, and he had her, and he kissed her because he knew she loved to be kissed. . . .

"Alex. Alex. Wake up. Christ. First, you won't sleep and then you won't wake up. Alex."

It was such a harsh voice, not like the one in his dreams. He rolled over, away from the hands.

"Alex, come on."

"I've got my clothes off."

"No, you don't. Now come on. You have to get out of my car. You aren't sleeping here tonight."

"No." He pulled his shoulder away. "I'm fine."

"I don't care if you are or not. You're not sleeping here. Now come on. Your bed's about thirty yards away. Wouldn't you be more comfortable there?"

"I'm fine." And he remembered where he was: her hands were stroking him, and she was kissing his stomach, and he was losing his mind in her. . . . "Come on. Yeah." And the other voice was quiet, and he slipped away from it. "Don't go away."

"Alex." He kissed him, little kisses on his cheek, forehead. He rolled over to her and put his arms around her. "You don't need your clothes. Take them off."

"Are you awake now?"

"Take them off. He tugged at her shirt. "I have mine off."

"No you don't. Now wake up."

And she kissed him. "Okay, I'm awake." He put both his arms around her and pulled her close to him. "Are we home?"

"You are. Now get up, and you can go in the house."

"That was a fast trip."

"You slept. Now come on."

She was half out of the car, pulling at him. "Where?"

"To your bed. You can sleep there."

"Where's Patty?" He remembered the night now.

"I dropped her off on the way. You can pick up your car there tomorrow, but we didn't think you should drive."

"Oh."

"Come on now. You can sleep in your bed."

He stepped out of the car and fell into her.

"Wait a minute."

She propped him up against the car. "What?"

"Didn't you have a coat?"

"Yeah, it's in there somewhere."

"I'll get it."

"Okay." He waited, breathing the cold air, and his mind cleared a bit: they were home, and they were awake, and they were alone, and they both knew where it went from here. She stood up and he leaned on her, leaning against her until he had her under him, and he kissed her. A long kiss, and again, and again, and she was kissing him . . . the dream was real.

"Okay, you got your keys?"

"Um." He kissed her again – she liked kissing, she'd stay."

"Alex?"

"What?"

"Can you walk to the house on your own?"

He could, but he wasn't, because she wasn't leaving. "Where's the house?"

"Okay, it's this way."

And she put his coat around his shoulders, and, holding him (holding him up, she thought) walked him to the house.

"Give me your keys."

He passed them to her.

"Which one's for the house?"

"This one." He picked out the key and passed it to her, kissing her again – he knew he had to bring out the wanting in her, had to get her to remember too.

"Alex, don't."

"Why not?"

"Just don't. I can't get the door open when you're doing that."

"Okay." He let her open the door. She couldn't get in. He took the keys and opened it himself. "There. Come on." And he took her by the hand and went to his room, and laid down on his bed. But she waited at the door. "Come in."

"I'm going to get going."

"No." He didn't move but just looked at her. Because she believed too, underneath it all, and he knew it and she knew it and she'd find a way to stay.

"You can't sleep like that."

"Why not?"

"You still have your coat around you and your shoes on."

"So take them off." He wanted her to undress him, and to strip for him, just like she had before. Because if she stayed, she cared, and if she cared, she believed.

"For crying out loud."

But she undid his shoe laces, and took off his shoes for him. And she sat down at the end of the bed.

"Well, thanks for dinner."

"Stay with me."

"Alex."

It was a moan – "no, stay." Because he wasn't asking too much. He was only asking that she love him like she did all the times before. "Please, for me?"

"Don't you know that you're killing me?"

He didn't want to kill her, but if she left it would kill him, because no one else believed in him, and no one else loved him, and no one else could touch him the way she touched him. . . . "There's never been anyone but you. I haven't had anyone since you." And that was true, and she would know it – the spirit of it, because no one else mattered, and she knew it, and had known it all along or she would never have stayed.

"Alex."

"All the pain will go away if you stay."

"Yours or mine?"

He grinned – she could always catch him and that was how he knew she loved him.

"You always do this to me."

"Stay." She couldn't leave him. "Stay for me."

"It's always for you."

"Please."

"Alex."

"I haven't had any loving since you, and that was so long ago Kim."

"I don't want to get into this."

He had her hand. He pulled her down onto the bed to lay beside him. And he kissed her.

"Okay, I'll stay."

She'd found the way, she was loving him again, forgiving him and believing in him and wanting him again. He breathed. He relaxed. "Do anything you want to me tonight. Make love to me tonight. Next time, it will be for you."

"Alex."

"It will, I promise." He laid back – he wanted her to want him, he needed her to want him. He waited. She took off her shoes, top, skirt. She had a beautiful body, slim and firm and tanned. And she crept over to him, unbuttoning his shirt, slipping it off his shoulders. Her hands, so gentle, almost like a breeze. "Your touch. Where'd you learn to touch like that?" Because no one was like her. He'd wanted that touch all night, searching him, finding him. He let her touch him all over, taking off his clothes, and then he had to touch her. And he kissed her, her shoulders, breasts, ribs. "I love you." Her magic was pouring through him. She was bringing him all that wondrous confusion. She was making him believe too.

27

One look and he saw that last time was still in her eyes, in her smile – even more alive now than it had been that night, as if time kept up the drunkenness, as if she didn't know (didn't want to know) that he'd sobered up with the day. He smiled to himself – he'd expected her to come looking for more of the same, expected her to try to tie him to that. But she was dreaming, and he knew how to wake her up to a few of the realities of life. He left the door open for her and went back into the house. He sat down. She stood halfway into the living room. "So what do you want?" As if he didn't know – she didn't know, she wouldn't admit it to her to herself. But her smile was gone. He smiled.

"I phoned. You said to come over."

"You didn't say what you wanted on the phone. I thought you'd tell me when you got here." I want to get laid. I like good sex. What else is there? – she wouldn't say it but that was all there was, and she was here because she didn't get it anywhere else.

"I didn't know I had to have a reason to come here."

"Didn't you? Well, it doesn't make any difference to me anyway." And he lit up a cigarette, yawning. She came into the room, sitting down on the chair opposite him. Watching him, disturbing him. He liked that, and he liked the hint of fear in her eyes too.

He looked at the television.

"What's this?"

She was being polite – hadn't learned yet that politeness wouldn't do it for him.

He shrugged. "Some show."

"Any good?"

"Not really. It's TV, isn't it?" But he kept watching it, and she kept watching him. "You want to grab me a beer there? You can grab yourself one too, if you want. I don't have any wine or anything else in the place."

"If you want me to leave, you could just be honest about it."

"Did I say that?" He shrugged, he smoked. "Doesn't matter to me. If you want to stay, stay."

"Haven't we been down this road before?"

"Have we?" He stared at her, his face blank. "Maybe we didn't go down it far enough."

"What does that mean?"

"It doesn't 'mean' anything." He smoked, looking back at his TV. "You could get me that beer if you want to stay."

"Fuck."

But she headed to the kitchen, throwing exaggerated looks over her shoulder at him on the way. He waited until she was almost there. "Make sure you get one out of the fridge. I don't want a warm beer." And she stopped for an instant, her shoulders seized up, annoyed. But it was true: they were two different people, and he didn't expect her to know much about him, his life, his wants. But she was going to learn.

"Here."

She gave him a beer. "You didn't get yourself one?"

"I don't like beer."

"There's a keg of wine there, in the fridge. I guess you could help yourself to some of that."

"Yeah, I saw it."

"It's Charlene's but I guess you can have some. You help yourself to other things that belong to her."

"Do I?"

"Seems that way to me."

"Does it?"

And she sat down again, smoking, glaring, hoping. He knew her – knew she thought she could take him again and make him into what she wanted again, but it wasn't going to happen. Because he was Charlene's. He'd found the perfect woman in her – someone who accepted him for what he was, someone who went with him into it. He drank his beer. "Wine too cheap for you?"

"Something like that."

"Thought it might be."

"Did you?"

"Yeah." He grinned – she knew what he was saying, what he was doing, and she couldn't stop him. He stretched. "I'm tired. I'm heading for bed." And he stood up and left, moving the scene to the proper stage. And she followed. Just like he'd known that she would. He dropped his clothes and got into bed. She was standing in the doorway. "Did you turn off the TV?"

"Your TV."

"Well go turn it off. I'm not buying a new picture tube just because you're lazy."

"You won't be. You'll by buying one because you're lazy."

"No, you see, that's what girls do."

"Is it?"

"One of the things. There are other things too."

"Spare me from the list."

"You don't need to know it anyway, do you?" He grinned, not smiling. She didn't please him, didn't do the things that pleased him, wasn't going to either. And that was fine, because she wasn't staying.

"No, I don't."

"Well, I don't need to know the things you think girls do." He folded his arms across his chest, still grinning, not smiling. "So, the last time you were here, I guess I was pretty drunk."

"You'd sobered up in the car."

"Had I?" He laughed, dismissing that.

"You unlocked the door pretty easily, in the dark."

"You learn to do that."

"I guess you'd have to."

She came into the room, and sat down at the edge of the bed, looking at him carefully, looking for that weak spot. He grinned – it wasn't there tonight, he'd eradicated it. Because he thought it was over. They did not fit, and that was in the cut, and she would have to see that, and see it now, because there wasn't going to be a tomorrow. "So what happened, anyway? I don't remember much."

"You don't?"

"It wasn't exactly yesterday, was it? You can't expect me to remember every lay, especially when I'm drunk."

"It wasn't all that long ago."

"Your tan's faded. Must have been a season ago."

"Alex."

"So, what happened? You going to tell me, or what?" Because she couldn't tell him if he didn't remember, because there were some things that didn't exist if they were denied.

"What do you think happened?"

"Oh." He grinned, he stretched. "I think you seduced me again, got me drunk."

"That wasn't quite the way it went."

"So what did we do? Did we have a good time?"

And he laughed, dismissing the idea that they could have a good time together. Because he didn't need – didn't want and didn't like – his sex all wrapped up in a mythical emotion. "So did you thrill me? What did you do for me?" And she glared – she couldn't say it, *what you begged for*, because he wasn't begging now. "It seems to me you wanted me pretty bad there."

"I was just going to leave—"

"Sure you were."

"I was."

"Right." He laughed. He was getting into it now – pounding

her, taking it all away from her and forging it into something else, something it should have been all along. Because he never should have gotten weak, and he wasn't going to let her remember him as weak. "Get off it."

"Get off it yourself, whatever it is you're on."

"I'm not on anything."

"You asked me to stay. That was the way it went."

I haven't had any loving since you – he'd been loaded, out of his mind. "So tell me what you did for me? – did you go down on me for a change, did you, or did you make me do it for you, like you do?"

"Alex."

"Can't talk about it? Just into doing it?" He grabbed her hand and pulled her down beside him. "So you want to get it on, do you?" He pinned her down with his hands. "What do you think?"

"Let me up."

"Why should I?" He was grinning at her, over her. "You're here to get laid."

"Alex."

"I'm not always nice Kim. You know that. You know all about me. You know what I like." And he did like it, more than he liked it before. Because he was proving it – the difference, the objectionable – to her. "It's fun." And he leaned over and bit her breast, hard, through the cloth. "We're going to have some fun tonight. What do you think?"

"I think you can think again."

"No? Fine." And he let her up, and lit up a smoke. He could take her or leave her – she wanted to be taken.

"So what do you want me to say? Want me to ask if you feel like a man now? Fine. Feel like a man?"

"What does a man feel like? You tell me." And he sneered at her. Because she thought she was more of a man than he was. "I'm not a fag, you know. I've never had a man. What does it feel like?"

"Cute."

"No, I want to know. What does it feel like when I go into you?"

"What the hell is your problem?"

"You tell me – that's what you do, isn't it? I don't think I have any problems. I think I just want a good time." He remembered the hours she'd spent telling him about his problems, laying it all out for him, nice and simple so that an idiot could understand. That was all wiped out now. And he had more to wipe out before he could be through tonight. "So who you been making it with, Kimmy? You never tell me anything about your sex life."

"Alex."

"Where'd you get so good?" Because that night was the best night he'd ever had, and he didn't have to believe it all came from love. "Where'd you get all your experience? Not here. Let's see, we make it what? – fifteen or twenty times a year? And it's been what? – about seven years now, so that's what, a hundred and forty times. That's nothing. A couple of months, three or four. So where you been practicing?"

"You're vulgar, you know that?"

He laughed – he wanted to be vulgar, he wanted to be everything he was and everything she wasn't. "I just want to know where you got so hot."

"Maybe for once you were inspiring."

"For once, is it?" He laughed.

"Yeah, for once."

"I bet you have more experience than I do."

"Bet whatever you want. You know the truth."

"What's the truth, Kim?" Because truth could be anything he wanted to make it, and she knew it, because if he didn't share it, then it wasn't that way. He grabbed her down again. "We just made it the way you like it last time—"

"Memory improving, is it?"

"—sweet and slow, the way you like it so this time's for me. What do you say?" He pushed his hands under her top. "Why don't you do a strip tease for me? Get me excited for a change?"

"Fuck off."

"Wait a minute." He pulled out his cigarette and hers too. "Better." Both hands were free. "Now you can get up in the light and strip."

"Dream on."

But she was the one who was dreaming, because she thought she could make him into anything she wanted. "You invited yourself over. Least you could do is try to excite me. Because you don't, you know. I don't like it slow and sweet. Take off your clothes and let me see you." He wanted her to turn herself into a sex object – the objectionable – for him, to do it his way. "See if you can excite me."

"Go to hell."

"Oh, I will, one day."

"And you'll be right at home."

"Why not?" He let her go. "It's getting boring, Kimmy. It's getting dull. You don't even want to see if you can arouse me," because she was going to have to face the fact that only one thing excited him.

"Don't call me Kimmy."

"No? It's just a term of endearment."

"It's belittling."

"'Belittling.'" He laughed. "Okay. What you going to do, baby, strip or let me get some sleep?"

"What do you think?"

He thought she was still hoping, still looking for that way to make him sweet and slow. "Them's the choices girl. Pick one."

"What are you trying to do?"

"I'm trying to have some fun for a change."

"I don't think that's all there is to it."

"You wouldn't, but then you don't know much." She'd made it complicated, if she could. He wasn't going to give her the chance. "Are you going to deliver, or not? Because I'm getting tired here."

"What do you think?"

He thought she'd have it her way or no way, and that was fine with him. He rolled away from her, pulling the blankets up around his neck. "Fine. Then let me sleep."

"Alex."

A hand strayed onto him. He shrugged it off. "So you going to let me have you? You taking off your clothes?"

"Alex."

"You want me to take them off, do you?" He rolled back to her, and tugged at her shirt. "You want me to take them off, do you?"

"What do you think?"

He thought she wanted them off slowly. He thought she still thought she could turn it all around and make him putty in her hands. He thought she still believed she could tie him to the last time. She reached for a cigarette. He grabbed the package from her hands. "That's a good idea. Nothing else going on here."

"Fuck, you're impossible."

"I got some leathers in the closet. We could get something going Kim. What do you say. That would excite me." She glared. He grinned, winking.

"Would you get off this crap?"

"Well, if you're not into it, you may as well pass me a light there." He took a cigarette out.

"Get it yourself."

"Think I should just take what I want?" He grinned, grabbing her. "Is that what you think Kim? I can get into that." And he forced her down on the bed – she wasn't resisting, she still thought she could change him – and rolled on top of her. "I'll take you. I bet you'd like that. I bet you dream of it."

"You'd lose."

"All you girls fantasize about it. We all know that."

"Still reading all the wrong magazines?"

"You'll like it." He started undoing her buttons. "Let's see what there is to see, shall we?" He laughed.

"I wouldn't do that if I were you."

"Tough talk, tough talk." He kept her down with one hand – she could have gotten away, he knew, but she was still waiting for him to change – and took the shade off the lamp. "Let's really get a good look at you here."

"Let me go."

"I could phone some friends. You'd like that too. I bet you could have ten guys like me for breakfast." He pulled her top open, and looked at her breasts. "Small but sweet, eh, Kim?"

"Let me go."

"You want me to?"

"Yes."

"Okay." And he let her go and turned out the light. "Then I'm going to sleep, so you can just leave." And he rolled over again, putting his back to her. He knew she'd come to him, she'd let him take her his way. He was waiting, getting excited. It didn't take long. A hand pulled him back onto his back. "So you want it."

"What do you think?"

"Let's see if your headlights are out." And he turned the light back on. She'd done up her top. "Kim." He undid it again, peeling it off of her and throwing it on the floor. She glared at him. "Look. They are." And he grabbed her down, wrapping his legs around her now, holding her down. "Let's see the rest of you." He reached his hand down and unzipped her jeans, pulling them open. "These have to come off if you want to get laid."

"You really think you can play this game."

"Games make it fun, Kim." He bit her breast. She slapped his face. "That's not nice."

"You didn't want nice tonight."

"You think you can turn me on?" He grinned. "Try."

"No."

"Oh." He laughed. "Know you can't, is that it?"

"If you want to be seduced, there are easier ways to go about it."

"Not as much fun." He grabbed her again, now pulling her

jeans down. "I bet you're wet." He laughed in her face, his hand going into her. "You are. You like this."

"Dream on."

He laid back again, keeping her pinned in his legs. "Let's see you then." He looked her over, watching her squirm. He toyed with her breast. "Starting to sag, dear. Better exercise more."

"That hurts."

"Does it?" He kept doing it. She didn't stop him. "So you don't want to spice up our sex life?"

"Spice or destroy?"

He laughed. "Then pass me that smoke. May as well just smoke and go to sleep."

"Go ahead."

"You don't excite me."

"So you've said."

He pinched her waist. "Getting fat. Better diet."

"Go to hell."

"No. I think I'll get this show going." He pulled her jeans off of her and tossed them and the panties too. "You see, Kim, women are pleasure vehicles, and when I say spread 'em, you spread 'em." He grabbed her thigh, pinching. "You got that?"

"I doubt it."

"You'll learn." He squeezed her thigh hard, and started moving his hand up to her hair. "You came over for this."

"I doubt it."

"Sure you did."

"No."

"Fine then." And he let her go. "Leave." Because he knew she'd stay. And she did. She didn't move.

"Alex, I—"

"Staying, are you?" He ran his hands down her sides. "You want me to take you, do you?"

"You know better than that."

"There ain't no sweetness here, Kim. You got to learn that."

"Do I?"

"You learn it yet?"

"No."

"Well, you will." He rolled on top of her, forcing her legs open with the strength of his – she wasn't resisting, she wanted him. "See, this is how it is. You got me horny now. I'm going to take you." He held her down with one hand – she wasn't trying to get away – and opened her up with the other. He lifted and entered her. "We're going to do it, right now. What do you say?"

"Get out."

"Push me out. Let's see your muscle tone. Push me out." He started moving, rocking. "Can you push me out you think?"

"Get out."

"Go on, try. Squeeze as hard as you can." But he fell out. "Oops. Just a minute here."

"That sort of makes it academic, doesn't it."

And she was glaring. "If looks could kill." He laughed. "We'll try that again. This is interesting."

"No, we won't."

And she was gone, slipped away from under him. She lit up a cigarette. "Sure, we can stop for a smoke if you want."

And she gave him another look – a cold hard look, hating now. A thrill ran through him. "Trying to kill me?"

"Wishing you were dead."

"Sure you are. Come back here." But she stood up, out of his reach, and starting picking up her clothes. "What are you doing?" Because she couldn't get dressed yet. He hadn't finished.

"Tap dancing."

She already had her panties and top on, and she was quiet. He watched. She did up her shirt – she was leaving. She was honestly leaving him – she was pulling up her socks, reaching for her jeans, and she didn't say a word. He knew he shouldn't be amazed – he'd just given her plenty of reason to leave him – but . . . she was just walking out, without a word. He leaned towards her. She didn't even seem to know he was there. "Is it over?" He barely knew he'd spoken—barely heard himself, barely believed that he'd had to ask, because he didn't believe it was so suddenly, so quietly over.

"Over?"

She whispered. She didn't seem to know what it meant.

"Over? Yeah, over."

She was just standing there, holding her jeans. She didn't believe it either.

"Yeah, over. I guess."

"But...." She was gone from him, not seeing him, not hating him, not aware of him. He hadn't meant that, hadn't thought that. "Don't you have something to say?" Because she could hate him, that would be okay, but she couldn't stay so far away. "Don't you have something to say?" Because she should be raging, telling him not to be this, not leaving him in this.

"Kim?"

"at last"

28

She hasn't bothered hurrying – scurrying – back to him. She sees no reason. She knows his mind, knows how it works, knows what he'll say: "I don't think we should see each other anymore." It was his only possible reaction to her, because if he couldn't control her, he would have to leave her. As he had each time. As he would . . . ineluctably.

And so there shall be no more mores, when mores are all she wants from him, from life. She doesn't want to hear that. She's letting time pass by simply to avoid hearing that – another season, as he would say. And maybe another yet; she may let winter turn to spring. She doesn't know. She only knows how much she doesn't want to hear that. Because sorrow hurts too much. Sorrow hurts most of all. Rage and pain and anger and even humiliation all hurt, but can be tossed off with the right effort, the right action. Sorrow allows no action. Sorrow sticks and aches. Sorrow molds itself into the soul, in the very spot of the love that died, and remaining because the love never comes back. Because sorrow is not believing. Sorrow is walking into the ocean's depths in the middle of the night.

So she keeps his words away, and tries to hope that love can come out of despair. And she remembers that there was a closeness at the end of that night. And she prays that time has let him find a new reaction. Perhaps he has thought or felt, or somehow found the courage to put some value onto her and them again. Or perhaps God has come across that spare miracle. But as she thinks, she knows that she doesn't believe it. Believing started too long ago, with too little to feed on since.

And so she finds it's Christmas, with no presents to exchange, and then it is the New Year, with no plans made or to make. It aches and hurts inside of her, and she knows that that is sorrow. Not needing a call to come, it crept in as she gave up hope. And so there is nothing to lose, nothing to gain. It is time to know – hear, how alone she is.

All alone, she knows already, alone and sad. Still, some thoughts flicker through her mind, a word or two of hope. Maybe, she thinks, he heard a word or two, or if not, at least felt the desperation behind the words and knows now not to force it to an end. Or maybe he does value the good, the joy – maybe he heard her belief in that, and didn't sneer. But there is no energy to hold up these thoughts. The sorrow stays.

It is all his decision now, and one likely made, and therefore nothing she says or does or hopes or dreams matters one bit, and thinking on it more and more will not matter one bit. She knows that. She hates that. Thinking and deciding has not been his strongest point. He has not learned to start with what he feels or has felt, but runs to some standard, some reference – any reference, and usually one that excludes her from him: "Let us look, Kim. Oh, we do not compute. See there, on the screen, we do not compute. So what if I have loved you for moments, for many moments, for incredible moments? So what if I have experienced with you delight and excitements that scared me, that I have been so in love with you that I have been silly with it in my blood. Yes, I have manipulated, nearly schemed, to be with you. And I have held you, seduced you, been willingly – so willingly at times it seemed I begged – seduced by you. But you see, there it is, we do not mix. We mustn't see each other anymore. Logical."

That makes her scream, loud and long. It is an outrage the stuff that makes the blood boil. And when she leaves as she must, it will seem to him that she is agreeing: "Oh yes, Alex, logical. You are of your kind, and I am of another, and although I too have felt the beauty of our meeting, I know that we cannot do. What is a moment in a lifetime? I have simply been blinded by silly silly emotions – I am a woman, what can you expect? But I won't let it happen again. Ta-ta." To say – to even allow such agreement to be implied – to let one thing that could be construed as agreement with his attitudes exist – she couldn't. She doesn't stop at disagreeing with him, she violently objects to his ideas. For him to want too many rules and guidelines and safety rings is more than to protect himself from mistakes, it is to forget to live. Because life is wild, and everyone must take the chances when chance is kind enough to offer them, and if it turns out that love goes to where it is least expected, then you trust that, and go with it, thanking God along the way. You do not go running back to safety. You will the way into existence. If you cannot will that, then you have no life worth living, no chance at life worth living. And when there is love, but not the guts for it, you should suffer long and hard. And worse: when you say you haven't the guts for it, but you have been the one to show the way to me, opening undreamed of possibilities, you should pay in blood and tears and pain. When you, who are life itself, forgot to live . . . there should be a special place in hell for you.

She knows that there's no such place and that he will feel no such pain. He will end them quietly, without a fuss, and then he will return to live his little life, turning into a decent "company-man," joining the store's baseball team, and, later on, the bowling team, and marrying his Charlene – or one just like her; and then, when he has grown tired of beating her up and calling it love, they can join the wife-swapping in the neighborhood, and think themselves sexually adventurous. And he will never say that he is dead. It will all be wasted on him.

She will not create a scene this time. Part of her listens to the doubting whispers: "if he is all that I say he is, then he is right and this is best; I don't like myself – what I have become – when I'm around him; he will be better off without me creating dissension in his life – no, not better, because with me goes also the possibilities; he will have it easier – those two must not be confused.

Still, she remembers that he was not hiding behind sex or booze or any excuses when they were at the door. He had left his little power games and was open and honest and sincere – was trying. He was tender and sweet and all – he was scared, but willing. And she had said what needed to be said. She is too pessimistic. Doesn't she want to hope? But can she go through it all again? There's been too much, for too long. The outcome's been waiting. Ineluctably. And she's tired.

So she readies herself for the worse. The challenge is to be sure he knows that if he says "no," it will stay "no." She will not come back this time, there will be no more reconciliations, he will have to live with his decision. She will not act against it. Because the games have to end. The stuff in her for that is all used up now.

She phones. He says to come now. She says yes. She feels ready; the resolutions are made, the scene written, and the strength for it as strong as it will ever be. And strength it is going to take, because no matter how inevitable it seems – or how inevitable he has made this day – it goes against her entire being. She will hate every moment of it, every word every look every sound. And not to fight back – the idea makes her scream. Quiet acquiescence has not been her style. Yet, he will sit there, stuffed with all his calm reasoning, being firm, and being wrong, and she will take it. Because there is no point in disputing the process when the result is due.

She checks her make up in the mirror and leaves. It is the last visit. The morning is snow-hushed, no cars and no people disturbing it but her. Even the children freed from school seem to respect it and stay quiet, inside. And the dogs and the cats and the birds and all else too. All but him – she knows that as soon as she sees him, he will destroy all peace, and she is all too quickly at his house. She parks, and gets out of the car. She takes in a deep breath of the cold air. She wants to stay there and enjoy this morning, for it seems to her to be one of the rare mornings when the world has fallen away, and beings can just be. She would like just to be, for a change, without stress, concerns, without him. But his house is across the street. She goes to the door and knocks.

"So you made it."

He is abrupt, unfriendly, irritated. He is slopping around in his robe. She knows all she needs to know. "I said I would be here."

"And you always do what you say."

He is sneering at her, because he isn't going to do what he said – he is going to betray her, as always, she feels it run through her. Sick, she follows him into the house. He sits down on the couch, his breakfast in front of him.

"I have to go to work soon."

She sits down opposite him and closes her eyes for a moment. He's rejected her already. Again, he hasn't bothered with the words and reasons, but has ensured that there is no time for them to get together. "When?"

"I should be there by eleven."

But it is only nine now, and that leaves time for anything. She can still hope and pray. She relaxes. She plans to be nice, and to hope, and to find the way to change his mind. "I interrupted your breakfast."

"There's some coffee in the kitchen. Help yourself."

"No. Thanks. I had enough at home."

"Yeah, they say too much coffee isn't good for you."

"Bad for the nerves I've heard that." She's not talking to him, and he's not talking to her. They're talking around each other, because neither wants this, but for different reasons. She doesn't want it over, and he doesn't want the bother of ending it. But he has to end it, or start it; he has to take responsibility for one or the other. She watches him eat. He still has impeccable table manners.

"You eat already?"

"I had a muffin at home." She hadn't. She hasn't kept down food since she decided to call him.

"You should have a better breakfast than that."

"I wasn't very hungry."

"I'm always hungry in the morning."

She shrugs, and glances at the television. The sound is turned down, but the picture is on. She sees some sort of interview is taking place, but she doesn't know the show or the people.

"You ever watch that?"

"I'm usually at work by now."

"You aren't working today?"

"I'm going in later." The look he gives her, as if she's some sort of lazy bureaucrat – she hates the way he can make her justify herself to him all the time, anytime. "I work late many nights."

"You should watch this show. You would learn something."

"That's another attack, she knows, on the person he makes her be – one she's never claimed to be, never wanted to be for him. "What's it on?"

"One guy's from the Middle East. He's talking about the PLO."

"So is he for or against it?"

"He's talking for it. I told you he comes from there."

He sounds impatient with her, when he's the one who doesn't know, and he's making her tell him that. Don't tell the Israelis that."

"No?"

"They like to think they're from there too."

"Oh."

And he's made her prove that she's the person he says she is, and he's the person he says he is, and now he can go on and say what he's planning on saying, resting in the fact he's proven it. He sets her up.

"So sit here and watch this."

He pats the spot beside him on the couch. Yes: now he has divided them, he can be kind, nice – he can even ask for forgiveness, even be sad for it all. It's a mockery and she can't stop. She moves over to the spot, and her heart drops: it's over, and there is nothing she can do, no way to stop him. Maybe one way.

The voice is droning on from the television; "Our position hasn't changed, even in face of that recognition. Why should it? We were right. . . ." She doesn't listen. She has to know what she will do – she's falling apart now. She doesn't have a lot of time. If she wants him – she wants him. All reason and dignity and idealisms are gone; she needs to have him. Because she cannot stand the moment when she will never have him again. But how? He is going to break them up, and she isn't going to touch him now. He would laugh, and scoff, and she wouldn't be able to stop him – she would die, she'd be so shamed . . . but she has to do something. "Alex, I came over to talk, remember?"

"And so you want to get right to it. That's good."

He turns off the set, and nods at her, almost business-like. She shrugs. "You have to go to work too."

"Right."

"So." I have to get changed."

"I'll wait here."

"No, you can come."

She follows him to the bedroom, but leans against the door jam. He takes out his pants and starts to brush them with the lint brush.

"So you want to talk."

But she doesn't want to talk. She knows that they have to talk, because they have to get things settled between them – there must not be another rerun of that night, for her sake, and for his. But she knows what will happen next, and she feels sick – she can't stop it. She takes a breath and sighs – she doesn't want to help this happen. "We're supposed to. You're supposed to have come to a decision about the whole thing."

"I've thought about it a lot."

"And," she knows, and she hates it.

"It doesn't work between us. I don't love you. I don't think we should see each other again."

She takes it as she would any blow: she relaxes her muscles to let it move through her. She sits down on the bed. What can she say to that? She looks up at him. He's not brushing his pants now. He's dropped his robe. He's not wearing anything. He's naked, and he's talking about breaking them up.

"Anything else isn't fair to you."

Fair? – she blinks and looks at the wall. She can't believe – doesn't he know that there is such a thing as privacy and a thing as intimacy and times and places for each? – is this one of his little messages? – is he that insensitive? But she has to say something, and she has to talk sensibly now, while looking at that view. "I've heard that from you before, and you haven't exactly lived by it. It's beginning to bore me."

"Well, that's the way it is."

He's dressed. "As long as you know that."

"I do. I just hope you can accept it this time."

So sanctimonious, so patronizing – *I'm trying, I'm learning about love – I haven't had any loving since you – take me – don't go away* – she did not deserve that remark. "Don't worry about me, just be sure you mean it, that it comes from whatever is in you that has meaning, because this time it sticks. This time, I won't be back."

"Good."

"Fine." It is time to leave, time for the dignified exit, with head held high and pride intact. She doesn't move. He is tucking in his shirt.

"Anything else?"

She isn't going to be dismissed like this. She is not an errant schoolgirl, she is not a fly buzzing around his head, she is not a slut who has stayed too long. She is someone he loved – loves. And maybe, if he just understands more – understands her, and her part in them, because she never meant to make him feel less. "Do you know why I bitched at you the way I did?"

"Never thought about it. I guess it made you happy."

"No it didn't. It made me safe. It gave me distance from you. You wouldn't believe how much I don't trust you."

"I haven't given you lots of reasons to trust me."

He understands, he doesn't care, he will not make the effort. It is time to leave. Her limbs won't move. There has to be something she can say. . . . "I thought you should know that."

"Okay. You told me."

There has to be one thing that would change his mind. "I won't be back this time. This time it sticks."

"That's what I want."

"That's what you have."

"Good."

"Goodbye then." There's nothing left.

"Yeah, take it easy."

And so she leaves, sickened, dazed, but not surprised. She'd known what would come when she'd called. What she hadn't known was how much she would hate it, how wrong it would feel. The pain has hit her – the outrage, the screams, the sorrow, all there but somehow not real. It is as if she has stepped into someone else's life – life without him cannot be her life. She tries to shrug away the pain. She tells herself that it was best, that she gave it all she could, that she took the risks, that she did not allow fear to blind her, that losing is not as bad as never having had him would have been, that she leaves him with so much more than she had when she met him, that life without him would have always remained a frustration, that he would stay potential and never be reality, that this is not her fault. And she remembers her friends telling her not to love so wildly, to find tranquility and not the heavens in a rush. But none of it moves the pain. Because she knows that it is a waste, and that it was wrong. She knows she wants all those moments back, and all the fire and feelings and strength too. And she wants his smiles to give her the world again. And she wants his hands . . . she doesn't want comforting crap.

But could he give her that? She remembers that the man who gave so much is not now, is changed, is wasted. Whatever he had, he lost – forgot – neglected – misunderstood? So there is nothing left to believe in now, and only the sorrow left to feel.

She does not sleep that night, or the next, or the next. Work is a blur; life, a moan. And when she finally sleeps, she only sleeps to wake to flowing tears; the sleep refreshes the sorrow, refreshes the tears. She curses him: he is a fool, a coward, a gutless wonder who should never be allowed joy or love, or happiness of any kind, who should be drunk, who should stay drunk, who must not ever have anything to offer anyone again.

She is suffocating. No breath, no air, no space. All she can know is her pain — for him to have brought her to this, to have denied her so much pleasure and joy, to have shown her all the possibilities and let her taste all the freedoms, to have given her all her memories, and then to have wasted it, refused it . . . there is nothing but those facts. She cries, she writhes under the pain. The waste of it all, the unlivable waste of it all, she cannot let go of that.

Because she had believed in what she felt, and in what she saw him feeling — what he said he felt. She had not walked into it blindly, she had watched him. She had not been wrong, not wrong enough to be this wronged. Because all those nights and all those feelings could not come out of sex, but had to come out of loving. No night could be explained away his way. Still, he is gone, and that too may be the result of loving. But the tears dissolve her thoughts again, and she cries until she is too weak to think.

Days go by, then weeks, and she functions in the world again. Yet it is not her world, not her life. Her life is crushed away, because her life came from believing in something that cannot be believed in now. And she doesn't know that she can ever believe in anything again — he twisted reality away with a whim, he turned love into lust, he turned trust into hate, he told her that everything she had known was true was false, and she'd lost her way of knowing. Faith just slipped away into a mass of unknowns and unknowables. All became suspect — all became potentially betrayed. And now she had chores and hours left to her, but life cannot come from those.

But she had believed in them for as long as she could—

29

Home. Sanctuary. Refuge. Exile. Called by any name, it stays sweet. Forgiveness, indulgence, grace: she's still as sweet as he'd remembered, as sweet as a deep deep breath of pure air. He smiles. He'd forgotten too much of this – her joy in him, unmistakable, her caring, her light because she has light in her. She's one of the rare ones who have some strange source of light in them. And she likes him – loves him. He stretches, reaching over to her as if he had just awakened from sleep. "Well?" He wants her to stay with him a while.

"What?"

"You're falling asleep."

"No I'm not. You're the one who's passing out."

"I don't pass out on two beer."

"Five."

"You were counting, were you?"

"You'd thought you'd slipped those by, didn't you? I knew what you wanted when you went to the kitchen."

"Why don't you slip into the kitchen and slip me one more?"

"You're lazy."

"It's a day to be lazy."

"Tuckered out, slipping into the kitchen, smuggling beers, are you?"

"It's your turn."

"My turn?"

"Sure. You've got me two, I've got me three. Your turn. Keep it even. Even distribution of labor.

"I think you're just lazy."

"Don't you want to be nice?"

"You always have to put it like that, don't you?"

"Does it work?"

"Yeah."

"Then that's the way I'm always going to put it."

He smiles, drifting away into his smile: she will always be nice to him, always. He grazes her leg with his hand as she goes by, and he sits up to watch her walk. He likes her walk – always has, he remembers. And he remembers all the other things about her that he has always liked: her cooking, her laugh, her weird sense of humor, her hands – her willingness, wanting, above all, her wanting. He's grinning. Because that is the secret of Kim: wanting. And he's touched it in her. Even today, when she had the right – the chance – to cut him down with one look, she didn't. She wanted him, and she came with him. No past. No hate. Because she wants. And he can still feel it coming from her, wave after wave, look after look: wanting, accepting, choosing. He couldn't resist if he wanted to. And he doesn't want to – it has been so long. . . .

"Where are you today?"

"Huh?" He starts up and sees her holding his beer out to him. He takes it and drinks. "I'm here."

"The hell. You've been laying there, grinning to yourself all afternoon."

"Have I?" He grins.

"You sure have. It's making me nervous."

She doesn't know – he laughs – she's never known herself. "It doesn't take much to make you nervous."

"Who knows what goes on in your mind."

"'Who knows what evil lurks in the hearts of men?'"

"Something like that."

He pulls her hand and she sits down beside him on the chair. She's funny, she's dear, he kisses her cheek – she doesn't know herself, doesn't know what she can do. "Maybe I'm figuring out how to take over the world. *I'll give you television, I'll give you eyes of blue, I'll give you a man who wants to rule the world.*" She'd like that.

"Making plans?"

"Maybe."

"Going to let me in on them?"

"Oh, I don't know." He plays with her fingers, dancing his eyes on hers. "Can you be trusted?"

"Probably."

"Probably not."

"Thanks a lot."

"You just want to play queen to my king."

"Can you think of anyone better for it?"

"Oh, we're feeling confident today." He laughs and hugs her. She has never guessed – not to bet on – how much she means to him – never played that card.

"I'm just stating facts."

"Oh, is that what you're doing?"

"You weren't thinking that anyway."

"No? What was I thinking then?" He knows she won't guess-won't dare to guess.

"Probably something from the gutter."

"That's a nice thing to say, or are you hoping?" He laughs, hugs her fast – she's blushing, she was hoping.

"Then what were you thinking?"

"I was thinking. . . . " He smiles, rolling his eyes around for a moment, flirting with her mind: what was I thinking Kim? – guess it. See, the sun's in the west."

"Yup. It's time for you to cook."

"Nope. You're cooking."

"It's your job. I'm a guest here."

And she went back to her chair, and stretched out slowly, inch by inch, like a queen. As soft as silk. "You haven't been a guest for years. You're part of the place. You don't get service, you get to cook." He watches her, smiling, watching her hear him. Because he wants her to feel it too: they have never been apart, not really, just in time, not in them. Because they are perfect together. Because they are meant to be together. "I only know how to make liver and onions."

"You've been living off that for all these years?"

"Yup. Liver and onions and bacon sometimes. Every night you don't cook for me."

"Then you'd better get your heart checked."

"Why's that?"

"That stuff will kill you. Do you know the cholesterol that's in that stuff?"

"Liver? It's good for you."

"All organs are high in cholesterol."

"All?" He laughs, watching her blush again.

"I knew your mind was in the gutter."

"Well, you know me." And she does. He lays back in the lawn chair. She does know him, even knows he wants to rule the world. He lets the sun hit his face. He feels good now. He drinks his beer. "So what are you making us?"

"Why don't we just order in?"

"You're lazy."

"Who's lazy?"

He watches her in her chair, her body lifting slightly when she laughs.

"You're lazy."

"What if I said 'I haven't had a home cooked meal for so long, and I can remember all those meals you've made for me, and they were so good, and don't you want to do something nice for me?"

"Try saying it and find out."

"Don't you want to be nice to me?"

"You're really pushing this nice bit. I want you to know that."

But he does know it, and he knows he can keep pushing it, because she loves him, and she's just proving it for him. "Be nice to me."

"I'm so hot – do you know how hot an oven is in August?"

"Hotter than in December?"

"It's one of those freaky laws of physics. Let's just order a pizza or Chinese."

"But I do that all the time. I want you to cook."

"I thought you ate liver and bacon all the time."

"When I don't have Chinese or pizza."

"You're going to make me move, aren't you?"

"Yup."

"You're not nice."

"You would be if you'd cook."

"I told you, you're pushing that."

"I think there's a couple of steaks in the freezer, but I guess it's too late for that, isn't it? I should have thawed them and barbecued."

"Yeah, you should have."

"Tomorrow. I'll cook tomorrow. You cook tonight." He likes that idea: a bunch of tomorrows for them.

"Probably rain tomorrow."

"I'm getting really hungry."

"You're going to make me move."

"Yup."

"Damn. So what have you got in there?"

"I don't know – make your spaghetti, or those pork chops. You made really good pork chops once, with apples. I remember."

"You have pork chops out?"

"No. What about that veal you make? That sounds good too." He remembers everything. He's floating in those memories – she was so good to him.

"You have veal?"

"You could go to the store."

"Or you could."

"Go see what I have, Kim. See if there's anything there." She stands up. She's going to cook – she's so sweet. "There's a fan in the living room. You can move it if you want."

"Gee thanks."

She shakes her head at him. He grins and grabs her hand, holding it tightly for a moment, smiling at her, searching her eyes. She wants him too, he can see it in her; she's only seeing him right now, not the house, the sun, nothing but him. He lets her hand go. "And could you grab me another beer?"

"You're not going to make it to dinner."

"I wouldn't pass out on your cooking."

"You'd better not, or you'll eat it burnt and cold."

"Okay, that's fair." He smiles, and finishes his beer, giving her the empty bottle.

"Sweet."

"Thanks." She takes the bottle, and goes into the house. He lays quietly – floating in her, she is so nice to him, when he doesn't deserve it. She's back with his beer. "Don't cook if it's too hot."

"I'll make something that doesn't use the oven."

"Good idea."

"I don't know why you want something hot anyway. We should just have sliced meat or something. Deli food."

"Is there any there? I think there's some spam in the cupboard, if you just want to cut it up."

"I think I can do better than that, Alex."

He knows she can. It's the reason he wants her to cook for him. The screen door closes behind her. He settles in with his beer – she'll be about half an hour, forty-five minutes. He feels so good – it has been so long . . . months, winter and spring and nearly all of summer without her. But it was all back with one smile. He smiles – but it makes him wonder; it dazes him, dazzles. Because she is so good to him. There has to be a miracle in it – one smile and it's all back, for both of them; there is a miracle in that. And he knows better than to question miracles. *I'll give you television, I'll*

– 378 –

give you eyes of blue, I'll give you a man who wants to rule the world. If he could give her that – she makes him feel as if he can. It has been so long . . . if he could give her that, then he could give her back what she gives him. This ease, this excitement – he needs it, wants it – this is the ease and the excitement that makes a man's home his castle, and she gives it to him. He gets up and goes to her. "How's it going?"

"You have fresh vegetables. I'm impressed."

"I was by Mom's the other day, and the garden's good."

"These are really fresh. I'm not cooking them. I'm going to put them all in a salad. It will be great."

"Sounds great. He picks up a slice of tomato and eats.

"Good, isn't it?"

"Been nibbling, have you?"

"Testing. It's called 'testing' when a chef eats."

She's grinning at him over her shoulder. He laughs. "That's how you girls get fat, all that 'testing.'"

"Tomatoes?"

"Maybe not." He shrugs, and slips up behind her, putting his arms around her waist. "Nope. You haven't put on any weight."

"You remember, do you?"

He does remember, everything. "Of course."

"The important things, right?"

"I remember it all." And he hugs her, remembering: she was so good to him – the best to him – she believed in him, knew him. "You need a hand here?"

"Not really."

"Got it all under control, do you?"

"You've got more than you said – you could go to the store and buy hamburger buns, if you wanted to help."

"Are we having hamburgers?"

"Well, you've got hamburger, so I thought we might. It's a pretty good summer dinner, hamburgers and salad. Sounded like a good idea to me. What do you think?"

"You're getting ideas, Kim?" He laughs — he has a few ideas of his own.

"I was talking about dinner."

"What makes you think I wasn't?"

"Oh, I don't know Alex. I don't know."

"It's because your mind's in the gutter." He laughs, he holds her. "Isn't that right? Confess."

"I thought you wanted dinner."

"Salad done?"

"Pretty much."

"We could just take it and go to my room."

"Alex."

"What?" She wants him, he knows that.

"It's too hot."

"Okay, we'll go to the shower."

"What?"

"Haven't we done that before? You're going to like this Kim."

"Sounds dangerous."

"No, it's fun. You're going to love this."

"Why don't you just get an air conditioner for your bedroom?"

"Because that would be no fun." He swings her around a little. "What do you think?" But he wants dinner first. "Right after dinner, we'll try it."

"Let go of me if you want dinner."

"Okay." He lets her go and sits down at the table. "So how long's it going to be?"

"Twenty minutes, I don't know"

"I forgot my beer."

"Why don't you go back outside and finish it, and relax?"

"Am I a distraction?"

"No, it's just nice out there. Why not be out there?"

Because he loves being in here, watching her be his wife. "You didn't bring that fan in. Want me to get it for you?"

"No." I'm not using the oven, so it doesn't matter. I put it on in there, to cool the place off."

"That's good." Sex in front of the fan – it's the summertime version in sex in front of the fireplace. He laughs. "Sounds good Kim."

"We can eat in there, or out on the porch, whichever you want."

"In there."

"I thought you were getting out of my way."

"I'm going to grab my beer. I'll be right back." He brushes by her on his way, grabbing her for an instant. She's titillating, provoking, because he doesn't really believe it yet – the ease, the simplicity, the instant of them. He doesn't dare to believe it, just hope in it. And he's giddy with it, silly with it, like a little boy *is it real Mom, can I keep it Mom?* He grabs his beer and goes back into the kitchen. She's standing in front of the frying pan. The burgers are beginning to fill the air with their aroma. He slips up behind her again, wrapping her up to him in his arms. "So we're reconciled." But it's a question, and she knows it.

"I didn't put hemlock in the salad, if that's what you mean."

"That's a good start." He laughs, giggles. She's right: he can't ask for more than this; he can't ask about tomorrow, because tomorrow could crush them. "Let me get you a drink. What are you having there? Cider?"

"Yeah. The lite."

"Do I have that?"

"Apparently."

"Oh." He didn't buy it, unless he bought it by mistake. But he won't say anything, nothing that could send her off on a thousand thoughts that wouldn't do them any good. "I must have been thinking calories when I bought that."

"It's good."

"Then it was really smart of me, wasn't it?" He laughs – he can do things right, just not when he's trying to. He pours her cider for her, and sits down again, watching her. She's so pretty, and tanned — she went two or three shades darker just sitting out there with him, he's sure of it. And she's smart — she should be able to see through him, and he's sure she does, and yet she stays. He can't believe it, and he knows it's true. "So you haven't said much about what's going on with you. Who are you sleeping with now?" Because it's been months, and she's too sexual to have stayed with him.

"Alex."

"Well."

"You're not supposed to ask things like that."

She's blushing — he's caught her: she hasn't been with anyone else but him, not in eight months. It's all true: they are true, real. He reaches out and grabs her, swinging her over to him. She's blushing, he's laughing, he loves her. "So you're mine mine mine mine, are you?" He searches out her eyes, making them meet his.

"I think you're drunk drunk drunk drunk."

"It's the only way I'd have you Kim." Because the only way he can have her, the only way having her could mean anything.

"You're going to have burnt hamburgers, that's what you're going to have."

"Okay." He lets her go. He finishes his beer, watching her cook for him. She's so sweet — "Why do you stay?"

"You really want to know?"

He's not sure, but he's asked. "Yeah."

"Because you aren't boring."

"I'm not?" But he's always thought he'd bore her, that he wouldn't be enough for her. "How aren't I?"

"Well, I can't sleep through this relationship. Some of my friends, they can sleep through it — not sex, but maybe sex too. I mean, why wake up when you haven't bothered waking up at any other time?"

But he doesn't know what she means. "I don't know. . . ."

"Okay. You're bizarre, right? You aren't predictable. You aren't boring — you have some spark. Maybe it's imagination, I don't know what to call it – you aren't reasonable, that's for sure, but . . . I guess I don't know either, but there's something in you that isn't in everyone else. I don't know. I wonder too."

And she's looking at him, as if trying to read the answer on his forehead. He waits, but she just shrugs and goes back to the frying pan. *Bizarre* – he thinks about it. He's never felt bizarre – tried for it. He's just felt scattered and confused – and used too, because he's never been too sure why she stays. But she thinks he's bizarre and unpredictable, and she likes it. Is he? How is he? – is that the secret of him? Because he's always known he has a secret, and he's never known what it was. He watches her.

"You didn't get the buns."

"Use bread. I have bread."

"So what do you want on your burger?"

As if she hadn't said a word. "Everything. Mustard, mayonnaise, the works." He picks up his beer, but it's empty. And then the doorbell rings—

"Alex."

She's on full alert. He sees it in her eyes. She's thinking that it's his girlfriend, that there's going to be a scene, that this night is going to be destroyed. He grins – he's better than that. He called Bonnie as soon as they got here, and he told her that he wouldn't be around tonight. He's no fool, and Bonnie's not fool enough to come around after he's said that; Bonnie wants to stay a while. "It's okay."

"Are you going to answer it?"

"Just relax." He gets up, laughing, shaking his head at her – she has such little faith, as if he doesn't want tonight as much as she does. She is going to feel so guilty in a minute.

At the door he finds Corrie and Wendy. He almost laughs. Anyone else might have mentioned to Bonnie that he was at home and that a strange car was in the driveway, but not these two. They'd never be able to explain to her what they were doing here, because they shouldn't be here. "Hi there. How's it going?" And he keeps them out with a story that he's probably heading down to the bar later, and will see them there, or maybe he'll see them at Corrie's. And they smile and leave, and he goes back to Kim.

She's not in the kitchen. She's on the back porch, with her purse beside her, ready to leave. He goes out to her, grinning – he's caught her, she has no faith in him when she should. "What are you doing out here?"

"What do you think?"

"I don't know. That's why I'm asking." He leans against the door. Blocking the way into the house.

"I think you know."

"You can bring your stuff back in and stay a while, if you want. It's safe." He laughs, and holds her as she goes by. "You are silly." Because she could have anyone he knows for lunch on her worst day.

"I don't like scenes."

"You're silly." He lets her go and follows her back into the house. "So is dinner ready yet?"

"Yes, except that you don't have any salad dressing."

"A good salad doesn't need dressing." He gets out two plates. "So we're eating in the living room, are we?"

"Or outside."

"In there. Too many mosquitoes out there this time of night." He's nonchalant, casual. "You want another cider there?" He has his plans. He's smiling.

"I haven't finished this one yet."

"I think I'll just have a milk with this. I'm getting tired of beer." It's not true. He's saying it for her. Because she'll like him for it. "Pass me a glass there."

"Here."

"Thanks." And they get their dinner together, and take it into the living room. "We can eat Japanese style. How's that sound?" He puts his plate and glass down on the coffee table, and slips over to turn on the stereo. "A little food, a little music . . . maybe a few glasses of wine. I have some red wine out there. Should I get it? What do you think?"

"I'm fine. It's cooled down in here, hasn't it?"

"Yeah, it has." He hadn't noticed, but she's right. It's not too bad in here at all. In fact, it's about right. "This looks good." He picks up his burger and eats. The night is working perfectly. Just the waiting is left now: eating, relaxing, drinking watching the sun go down. That's all that's left for him to get through, and then he'll have her. He watches her. She eats very neatly. He's always liked that about Kim. He listens to the radio.

"And we'll be back with more of our top hits of the '70's—yes, you've got a commercial message."

"Is it a long weekend?"

"No. Why?"

"I just thought they only had those on weekends."

"Had what?"

"Those oldies things. Didn't you hear that?"

"No."

"That's what they're having tonight. Seventies songs."

"Oh. Probably just a summer special. You thought you had Monday off for a moment, didn't you?"

"Well, a guy can hope." He laughs.

"Not for three weeks."

"Yeah, I guess there is Labor Day coming up."

"Yeah."

He drinks his milk. "So do you want to listen to this, or do you want me to put on a record?"

"Leave it on. We can remember being young."

"Don't be depressing, Kim."

"It is depressing Alex."

"Yeah, but you don't have to remind me." He goes back to his food, eating his salad. And it's good—fresh in his mouth. He relaxes. Tonight is going to work. And he listens to the song coming on.

'*Every night, I'm laying in bed, holding you close in my dreams.*' He freezes — he knows this song, and it's close, too close. He jumps up — it's off.

"But I like that song."

"Oh." She's grinning. She's seen too much. He turns the stereo back on — there's nothing to lose. She knows it all now, better than if he'd let it play, and he would have, but he'd been unguarded . . . and the song plays on, confessing more: "*you get the best of my love*".

He eats and drinks until the last 'sweet darling' dies away. But maybe it is okay for her to know — maybe she should know, because he has tried to give her the best of his love. He's tried at least that much. He just doesn't know — he has never known — how to. Because loving doesn't come easily. To give himself . . . there just isn't that much to give. But she always thought . . . there are things he wants to talk to her about, things she can help him understand. He finishes his dinner and goes into the kitchen to get the wine. And he decides he will talk to her. He goes back to her, settling down behind her on the floor, curling around her. "So." But he doesn't know how to start. Because dreams carry a bit of a guy with them, and dreams have a way of sticking — nightmares take hold like tapeworms in the gut. Yet it is silly too, to get upset about them.

"What?"

"What do you mean?"

"You're looking awfully intense suddenly."

"Am I?" How can he be sure of her? — how can anyone else? She seems, but that is as close as he can get to her mind. "I didn't tell you about my dreams, did I?"

"What dreams?"

"I had a couple of freaky dreams. You know how you remember them when they're really weird."

"Yeah."

"Like, these were really weird. In one, I was a soldier in a war."

"God help your side."

"Thanks a lot."

"I'm only kidding. Go on."

"I was in this war, see. I was on a raft on some river, and I was wearing a uniform, and we were sitting there – there were two other guys with me. Anyway, suddenly there was gunfire, and the enemy was crawling all over the banks of the river, and there was no way they could have gotten there that fast. You know how dreams do that. So we start shooting back. I had this rifle, like from an old Western, a Winchester, something like that. And I was aiming straight, but the bullets, they wouldn't go where I was aiming them, you see. That was the weird part. They wouldn't go straight. They'd swerve, right around these enemy guys. You get it?"

"Like in baseball."

"Exactly." He wants a cigarette. He lights one. "So what do you think?"

"It ended like that?"

"Yeah."

"You woke up?"

"I was trying to get under the raft, because I knew we were all going to get massacred, and I woke up. And then I had this other one. In that one, I had this car. Vintage car, and it was a beaut. It was old, but in mint condition, and it had all the latest stuff, and even some James Bond stuff. It was just beautiful, and it handled like a dream. And I was driving along – I'd just touch the pedal, and we were out of sight. It was just incredible."

"A dream car. I get it."

"Yeah, I guess that's what it was, but you'd only dream it. You wouldn't think it during the day. Anyway, I was driving along, and there was this guy with me, and for some reason, we started trying to kill these two other guys with the car. I don't know why, but we had to do it in the dream. So we start going down this hill, and these guys are at the bottom of it, and we know we've got them. Right in our sights. And we're cheering, and going and cheering, and then the car took over. Like, it wouldn't do what I was doing to it – it steered itself, and moved itself, and we were trapped in it, and we knew it was on their side, you see. And then it started going for a tree. It wanted to kill me. And it was picking up speed, and like we were on a collision course and it wouldn't stop. I was hitting the brakes and jerking that wheel around, but I couldn't stop it, so I jumped out, and woke up. So what do you think?" He waits, watching her.

"I think you've been reading Freud or something, and you're putting me on."

"I'm not. Those dreams are real."

"You'd better hope not."

"Why? Why do you say that?" He's watching her, and he can see that she knows something that she's not telling. "What's wrong with them?"

"Tell you what, I'll tell you later."

"Later? Why not now?"

"Later. Trust me."

"Don't you see anything in them? I mean, they stay with me."

"I'll tell you later if I do?"

"Why not now?"

"Because you said something interesting about a shower earlier, and I'd rather get into that."

She grins, she kisses him.

"What do you say?"

What can he say? He kisses her. She tastes like wine. It's the only time he likes wine. "You're going to love this."

30

T his . . . this . . . this is . . . this says a lot." She puts the receiver back in its cradle. "I don't believe this. I'm too old to be doing this." She lifts the receiver once more and starts to dial. On the fourth number, she puts it down again. "I can't" She stands up and walks around the room. "So why can't I? I should. This is not me. I don't hide. I don't cower at a thought. I don't believe that he has done this to me." She goes back to the phone.

She knows what is stopping her. It's him, and his endless fears. She knows him too well. She knows that since his last touch was a loving one, his next must destroy that one. He will have to reject – not merely her, but the loving itself. He can't live in love. He does not have what it takes to risk himself over and over again, or even once. Yet . . . he fills her with all the things she wants to be filled with, and she won't leave that. She goes to the window.

"So what's a little grief? The risk is going to be there always, with him, or with someone else. It's fear, and I can't give into fear. It may not be there, that's true – it was that the last time we were together. Eight months apart, and in three seconds, all that we had ever had was there, as if those eight months had not happened. It was alive. It was strong. It can do it.

But she knows him, and she knows them, and she knows what the next outcome will be. because it is more than fear: it is dread, and a strong dread, firm from eight years of history. Together and apart to together and apart to together and apart to . . . to the belief that the apart will stick, and the together won't happen again, because the apart hurts, and the together is less and less able to overwhelm the hurt. But wanting can overwhelm the hurt – or is it needing?

She picks up the receiver, and then sits down, still holding it, not remembering it. She hurts. She has not avoided any pain. Not having him is not having him. It makes no difference if it is brought about by his gutless rejections or her equally gutless avoidance of his rejections. It makes no difference . . . she doesn't know what to do.

She has weighed all of this out in her mind too often not to know it by rote. Whatever his problem is – she doesn't care to analyze it any longer, she doesn't care if it's the result of his lifestyle, or of his self-image, or of the lack of love in the home, or merely the natural outcome of living in this world – the fact remains that he runs from love the way a cat runs from a dog. That is fact one.

Fact two is that he loves her. And, given fact one, he must love her a lot to have shown it at all. And he most certainly has shown it; she has all sorts of evidence to support this fact. The last encounter was just more evidence – the strongest evidence to date. Because after eight months and after the Christmas scene, and after the scene that brought on the Christmas scene, after all that pain, after knowing he was the cause of all that pain, after successfully escaping the entire situation, after ending it, no sane human being welcomes it back, and no human being can get it back, unencumbered by that past, unless it is love. No other power could do it. Lust wouldn't even bother. Lust would find fulfillment in a less complicated setting.

Fact three: she loves him. The evidence supporting fact two does an equal job for fact three. But she doesn't need to call on such for fact three. She knows it each time she thinks of him. She knows it each morning, when she wakes thinking of him.

That men are not like buses is fact four – and anyone who can think that has never never loved – never never will. She cannot imagine people who think that – the insensitivity, the laziness. As for his idea that she should find someone closer to her in lifestyle, it does not impress her – he impresses her, and she wants him, and she will not settle for less than him, and even a president or a prince would be less than him. He stirs her soul. Buses don't.

His favorite little sentence will always be fact five. He will say it, and she will swell with pain.

Cementing all these facts together are his little beliefs. Ones developed over the years, through experience. He believes that as long as she cares for him, he does not have to act, she will. He believes that she will always come back to him, she has. Power of the least interest. He knows he has complete freedom, she can't disprove it.

So she is trapped in his freedom, and that she will not stand.

But there is so much that has become so tedious – and this phone call shows all of it. Because having him should not be a test of strength, and going to him should not be an ordeal. She should not have to announce her belief in him each time she sees him. She hates that, and the trepidation and suspicion and inaction that comes with it. She hates his feeble will (what else is a poor self-image) and she hates the coward she feels she is becoming. She nearly hates him – she hates the him he chooses to be some days. But most of all, she hates the boredom. This man was supposed to teach her the ways to touch the sky, but instead she waits on pins and needles to see how he will be and she is bored with it. It has worn thin.

Thin thin thin thin thin, but the potential is always there – *I want to be wise* – old man. Hope can be dragged up yet again – has to be because if he would only try to be what he said he wanted to be, then they could be what she wants them to be. There is a chance. *You get the best of my love – oh, sweet darling* – it's probably true, she probably has. She dials.

Tom answers on the third ring. She recognizes Tom's voice from the time he lived with Alex. "Yes, hello. Is Alex there?"

"Yeah, hold on."

She's thinking: if Tom is there, answering for Alex, a party is probably going on, in which case, she is intruding. She won't find her Alex, but that other one.

"I don't know. A girl . . . yeah."

She laughs: Tom isn't smart enough to put his hand over the mouthpiece, but at least he doesn't recognize her voice. Alex can't beg off the call.

"Yeah, hello."

"Alex?" It doesn't sound like him.

"Yeah, who's this?"

"It's Kim."

"Oh, I didn't recognize your voice."

"You sound funny too." He sounds irritated. Cold and casual.

"So what can I do for you?"

"Just thought I'd call and see what's new and exciting with you."

"Not much – nothing you'd think."

That is resentment – she has done nothing to deserve that. She tries to force a play. "How's that?"

"Some people don't find the same things exciting."

He's building walls – he has some sort of chip on his shoulder – she doesn't have to take this. "I suppose that's true."

"Then it must be, right?"

She lets that go by, and braces herself with a deep breath. "I wanted to see you."

"Is that right?"

"I gather you're busy right now."

"Yeah, I am."

He's closing doors. She's not going to let him do it so easily. "So when won't you be busy?" Her voice tells him she's irritated.

"I don't know."

"Make a guess." He is the one who brought them back together – she doesn't have to take this.

"I'll get back to you on it."

"No, you won't." If he insists she be pushy, then she will be pushy. She doesn't care if his new little girlfriend is there or not. From what she's been able to ascertain, this Bonnie is all too much like Charlene anyway, or at least Julie thought so. "Just say when now."

"I don't keep a calendar, you know."

"If you can't figure out one day, then maybe you'd better start."

"Well, I can't."

"I have heard that too much pot has that effect on the brain."

"What effect is that?"

"Memory goes."

"Oh?"

"Tomorrow night?"

"No good for me."

"When."

"Later."

"Exactly when is later?"

"After ten."

"After ten when?"

"Later."

"Does that mean after ten later tonight, or what?"

"Yeah."

"Tonight?"

"Okay."

"Bye-bye."

"Yes." She puts the receiver down. She's trembling and her heart is racing – what he can do to her, what he puts her through. Even now, she doesn't know if he wants to see her or not, but that is the name of the game. She wants to hit him. She thinks he will likely hit her: *I don't want to see you again.* And why not, because she sure as hell didn't get back together with him to come back to this crap. She lights up a cigarette.

He doesn't know her – that is the fact that bothers her the

most: he doesn't know her at all anymore, because he hasn't bothered trying since she met him at the store. He's turned her into a nagging bitch. She never wanted to be a nag. She wanted to share things with him, but he made that impossible. And he's still doing it.

She stabs her cigarette out. Sitting around here, thinking on it on and on is not the answer. She gets her coat. She's leaving. She's going to visit with her friends until it's time – and if she has a good time, who know – maybe she won't show up at all tonight.

Promptly at ten, she parks her car in front of his place. There is a strange green car, one of those small domestic makes, sitting in the driveway – Bonnie's car?—is the party still going on? She turns off her engine and lights. It could be anyone's car, she knows that, but what it if is Bonnie's? It's another hassle, another doubt. It could be a scene she doesn't need. Julie had said that Bonnie was a lot smarter than Charlene, 'the same but with brains." But Alex wouldn't let that happen. He wouldn't be that stupid. She calms herself and goes to the door.

Rex answers – one Rex who cannot be called sexy Rexy because it would be just too cruel. Rex is not one of Alex's best friends. Indeed, she has only met Rex once, and that was over three years ago. She's not pleased to see him now.

"Yeah?"

"Alex here?"

"Sure. He's in bed."

She doesn't believe what she just heard. What is he doing? She's imagining the worst scenario possible: he's in bed with Bonnie. The ultimate insult, the ultimate rejection, the ultimate escape. Even if he's not in bed with her, if he's gone to sleep, it is still insulting, it is still a rejection. She closes her eyes for a minute. She doesn't need this, or want it, but if he has gone to sleep, she'll wake him up. She won't take it from him. She goes into the house. Rex is in the living room.

"You want a beer?"

Sitting and drinking with Rex, it's not the way she sees herself. "No thanks." But what's she supposed to do? March into his bedroom? – *Onward Christian soldiers, marching as to war. . . .* It was beginning to feel like that. She sits down on the couch. Maybe Alex will come out of his room. "So how are you Rex?"

"Hey, do we like know each other?"

"I met you once a couple of years ago."

"You have a good memory."

"Yeah. When did Alex go to bed. He invited me over earlier."

"Yeah, he said someone might drop in. He said he had the flu and went to bed."

"Oh?" She doesn't know what that means. Did Alex ask Rex to waylay his visitor or what? In Rex's wasted mind, anything could mean anything. "I thought there were some people here. A party going on."

"Everyone headed down to the bar."

"Oh."

"I'm going down as soon as my old lady calls. You want to get a ride?"

"No, thanks." She is going to go in and see Alex, even if she does look like the cheapest little whore doing it. She stands up. "I think I'll check on the invalid."

"Nice talking to you."

"Yeah." She goes down the hallway. Alex's door is closed, another perfect sign. But she knows he's alone, because Rex wouldn't have let her get this far if he wasn't. She knocks, gently.

"Come on in."

His voice sounds quite cheered. She opens the door and peeps in. "Alex?"

"About time you got here."

She sees him laying on his bed, with a couple of books opened up in front of him. And he's smiling. "You sick?"

"No."

"Rex said you didn't feel well."

"He doesn't know what he's talking about."

"Oh." She walks into the room.

"Close the door behind you."

"Right." She closes the door, and sits on the foot of the bed. She doesn't understand this.

"You want some wine?"

He gestures to a bottle of wine and two glasses sitting on his night table. Now she knows: this is a set-up. He went to bed to get rid of everyone, and he's stayed in here because Rex is taking up the rest of the house. Of course he's not sick, but he did tell everyone he was. And he did it all for her. But should she appreciate this or insist on something more honest, something easier for her? "Sure."

"I've been letting it breathe."

"Oh." She laughs, and she relaxes. She's going to let it be for now. What else can she do? His eyes are all open and blue and smiling, and he's smiling too. He's being all she could want him to be.

"I was just reading these books."

He passes her a glass. She drinks, and looks at the books. "How-To's?"

"Yeah, I've got to start fixing this place up, like I planned when I moved in. I really can use some new shelves and the bathroom's starting to rot. The place is really old, you know. I think the porch needs some work too. I should have gotten to that last summer, but now it will have to wait. I'll work around here though."

"Sounds good." She's never heard him talk so much before.

"I got to keep the value up. I might want to sell."

"Oh yeah?"

"I might do some traveling – New Zealand maybe."

"Yeah? What is she supposed to say? What is all of his enthusiasm about?

"I'm just thinking about it. So what's new with you?" What have you been up to lately?"

"Not much. I've been pretty busy at work."

"I read about that in the papers. You guys are expanding to include juveniles?"

"No, not quite. We're taking over the facilities, not building. It's more consolidating."

"That's good."

"It's supposed to save money. That's why it's happening. It's part of the cutbacks. It's not too exciting."

"You don't want it?"

"I think it means that we'll be overworked, and some of our people are going to be unemployed. But that's the times. What about you? You just planning rebuilding or what?"

"Went to the races yesterday."

"Win anything?"

"Nah. Well, I won one on two, but lost on the rest so I didn't walk out even."

"Bet on the long shots?"

"No, they didn't look good. I bet the percentages."

"I've always wanted to walk in there and bet on a real long shot and walk out rich."

"Can't be done. You have to bet the percentages. I was going to make this bet, and then I changed my mind. If I had stuck to that, I would have come out ahead. I should have. Got to go with your guts sometimes."

He's so animated; she's amazed. He hasn't been like this for a long time, but each gesture, each expression, every inflection of his voice, all tell her what he felt when he was there – what he feels about everything.

"If I had gone with that, we could have had a really nice wine tonight. I would have gotten you to pick it out."

"This is fine." He is absolutely overflowing with all sorts of good feelings. She doesn't believe it – she can't absorb it – she isn't ready for this. "I thought there was a party going on here when I called."

"Some people were here. They went to the bar."

"I wasn't sure who was here when I got here."

"You saw Rex's car? I told him it was a girl's car. It's a girl's car, isn't it?"

"I didn't know whose it was."

"Just his."

He's reassuring her. She smiles.

"Did he clean up out there? I told him to."

"Why's he here."

"He's staying for a couple of nights, until he finds a new place."

"What happened to his old place?"

"He was living back east. He's just back here, looking for work."

"He seemed to have cleaned up. At least I didn't notice any real mess out there."

"He's pretty good about things like that. That's why I'm letting him stay."

All the gestures in his eyes and smile tell her that he's enjoying that little bit of power. She laughs. "You'll have the cleanest place for the next week."

"Should."

"You're terrible."

"Let's have some more wine."

He fills up her glass. He's smiling still, right at her, and his blue eyes are ready and sparkling. And she wants him. She toys with his shirt collar.

"So, you want to use me, do you?"

His voice is lusty. She laughs and falls back onto the bed. "You're looking pretty ready to be used."

"I make it easy for you, do I?"

She keeps laughing. He is leaning over her, holding her down by the shoulders. She remembers: women are pleasure vehicles. She tenses. She watches him. But it is okay, because his eyes are still bright and kind. He bends down to her. What? – he touches her lips with his tongue, so lightly, very lightly. She barely feels the graze. She wants to lift up to him, and make it a touch, a kiss. He sits up again.

"Come here."

He takes her hand, and scrambles them both up to the head of the bed, flopping the pillows behind their heads. There is some sort of energy in him tonight. She doesn't understand it, but finds it appealing.

"I want to show you something."

"What?" She expected sex, but he's reaching for a book.

"Look at this."

He's pointing to a picture of an old fashioned style cabinet, with stained glass windows, and spindled legs.

"I could make this."

He's looking at her intently, not with any childlike glow in his eyes, but with determination. He is serious. He is sharing something with her now that matters to him, and she can feel that meaning coming out of him and waiting on his words. She looks at the picture again. So that is his dream. Or a beginning.

"So what do you think?"

"Um." He's so fragile. And this yearning in him is fragile too. *I want to be wise. This isn't that – this doesn't even reach for that,* but this is a step, and who is she to deny him his enthusiasm? "When are you going to do it?"

"Not right away. I'll do some other stuff first, but I'll get that done."

"I guess you would have to practice first."

"I thought I'd turn the garage into a workshop, and start making furniture there. I have the time, if I want to."

"Sounds good." So this will be his way of becoming more than he is. It's a nice enough cabinet, one anyone would enjoy having. *But here in my heart, I give you the best of my love* – everything he did was like that. Not small scale, but tiny movements. He is so fragile.

She takes the book away, and refills their glasses with wine. "We'll toast those plans then."

"You want to stay?"

He is still intent. His eyes search hers. He is so vulnerable sometimes, she has to hold him. "Of course I want to stay."

"You'll stay all night?"

Does it bother him that she doesn't always? "If you want me to."

"You going to take off these clothes?"

Now he is teasing – he has what he wanted, and he is relaxed. "You going to help?"

She's just sitting there, waiting to get laid — putting in her ten minutes of social pleasantries, and pretending this is his saving grace — not even putting in her ten minutes, but reading a paper to pass the time because he bores her so. But he's not to see that. He's supposed to buy it, so. But he's not to see that. He's supposed to buy it, believe it, thank her for it. As if bowing to the queen.

Queen Kim:

Take love from sex. What would remain?

Alex:

Sex, a good time.

Queen Kim:

Wrong, as usual. Nothing would remain. You see, sex alone is sleaze, and sleaze, like its good friend slime, won't remain in your hands, but slips away through your fingers. Nothing would remain.

Alex:

What nonsense—

Queen Kim:

Take sex from love. What would remain?

Alex:

A monk?

Queen Kim:

Wrong as usual. Everything would remain.

Alex:

Everything?

Queen Kim:

Always having to help you see, its such a drain on me. Sex is nothing. Take nothing from something, and what would remain?

Alex:

I see. (Shall we take sex from us and see what would remain?)

Because he knows that loving means doing and not just in bed. And just as he knows he can't (not won't, can't: is not able to and so cannot possibly) love her because he can't (not won't, can't: is not able to and so cannot possibly – cannot even begin to imagine how to) meet her in that doing, he knows that she doesn't (not can't, doesn't: makes no effort to and so does not want to) love him because she doesn't (Not can't, doesn't: makes no effort to and so does not want to – has never made any effort to) meet him any doing but in bed. She's twenty-five now: no family, no house and husband, no kids – not even shared coffee in the morning because she doesn't stay until the morning much anymore, when she comes around at all, which isn't much anymore. It's just sex, all of it, all of them – always was; the rest of it was just satins and silks for her to get laid in. A lie. A lie laying on top of another lie. Two lies lying and calling it making love. He laughs.

"What's funny?"

"Nothing." Let's take the lies from us and see what would remain. Nothing would remain. You see, if you take two lies away, you don't find the truth.

"You've been awfully quiet today."

"Have I?"

"You've hardly said a word since I got here."

"Don't have much to say, I guess." Let's take the love away, and see if you remain. "You've been reading that paper since you got here."

"Oh. No, just looking through it."

"Looked like reading to me."

"If it's bugging you. . . ."

And she folds the paper up and puts it back onto the coffee-table – yes, I'll take the satins and silks away and see what remains. He reaches over to her and presses his hand onto her stomach. "This bugs me more. You've put on about ten pounds, maybe fifteen."

"Five."

"Well, it shows like ten."

"Too much Halloween candy."

"Don't tell me you went out. Don't you think you're getting a little old?"

"No, that was sort of the problem. Nobody went out. Apparently the elementary school put on a party that everyone gave to, but no one told me about it, so I was stuck with seventy little chocolate bars."

"So you pigged out."

"I can't say 'no' to chocolate."

"Yeah, you just give into your animal instincts, don't you? I'm not surprised. Sounds like you." And he lays down, laughing, smoking, wrapping his legs around her. "You got to remember one thing: you got to keep yourself sexually attractive there, or you won't find anyone who will give in to his animal instincts for you." And he tightens his grip around her.

"You trying to knock the breath out of me, or what?"

"Suck in your stomach and you'll look better."

"Until I go to breathe."

"Then you'd better lose it."

"And before Christmas, or I will be ten or fifteen pounds overweight."

"Yeah, all that food around you, I'll bet you'll just dive in. Right?"

"It's hard to say 'no' to plum pudding."

"I bet."

Queen Kim:

When is lust love?

Alex:

When it's yours.

So, are you going to lay down here with me?" And he reaches out his hand, and she lays down with him. "You should go into the kitchen and get us a *Playboy* to look through. Let's see if we can't get something going here."

"What?"

"Sometimes it turns me on, you know. We should give it a try. What do you think?" And he stokes her breasts, and yawns. "You're sagging a bit, aren't you?"

The punch-line never ends. And the horror never ends. Both go on and on and on. Oh, they wait, sometimes, hiding in a closet, until they're quite sure you believe again, and then they pop out: Surprise! But it's no surprise, because you never quite believe again, and you never quite stop looking over your shoulder. "Alex" – just to touch him, to coax him back, to stir up one memory in him All the pain will go away if you stay, just one. Because she knows that this is only here because that is here too.

"Aren't you going to get that for us? I'm sure I left it on the table in there."

"No, I'm not going to get it."

"Well, if you can't start me up, we can't go anywhere."

"If you start me up, If you start me up I'll never stop.' She remembers, and she remembers hoping it was true. 'If you start it up, love the day when we will never stop, never stop, never, never, never stop.' And she would have. She would have loved it forever, loved him forever. But that's not his song. "*Hide In Your Shell*," that's his song, and wouldn't it be wonderful to just say that and leave it at that? just to sum it up? But summing it up dismisses it, and that she's not ready for, not yet.

"Well?"

And he's good at it. Not a muscle twitches on his face – his grin doesn't drop, not at all, and his eyes meet hers, coldly, of course, toying with hers. He's good. If she hadn't been there for all the moments before—I haven't had any loving since you and that was so long ago; she should have left that tonight, but she knew it was true, as she knows that this isn't. "Well what?"

"Are you going to get me going here or what?"

And he squeezes her shoulders, a mock touch from a mock man. "Don't"

"I thought you liked it when I touched you."

When the touch brings them together, not when the touch is used to tear them down, and he knows it: he knows the difference, and he exploits it – her. And he's going to keep doing it, keep singing the punch-line, until the room is so full of it that not an inch of air will be free of it, and she won't be able to breath for it. He's done it before.

"I don't see the point of this."

And he stretches, yawning. "Alex—"

'What? Are you going to do something to get me going here? You could strip – do a little tease for me Kim?"

And he nudges her. And she just lies there, inert: they were not just sex, they are not just sex – just sex doesn't walk into a room after pain and absence, and by itself – by walking into that room, no more than that – dismiss that pain and sorrow. And just sex isn't still wanting years later. Just sex doesn't have that sort of power. Doesn't need it, because it doesn't need any one person. But she shouldn't even have to think this—just by making her think, defend, he's won. That's his purpose.

"No, eh? Well then forget it."

And he gets up, stretching, and moves to the chair. Leaving her laying there – to leave her laying there, deliberately, because it makes her look like sex, it makes her look like one of those damned *Playboy* pictures; it turns her into some sort of obscene offering to sex. She sits up.

"You just don't turn me on anymore."

"Try making love with an ax over your head." She didn't mean to say that. It just slipped – spat – out.

"What?"

"Nothing." But she should tell him: I can't make love to you – I can barely bring myself to reach over and touch you, because I know that even if you accept that touch, even if you respond with love, this will come, because this always comes, Alex. This never ends, and knowing that just wears me down, bruises me.

"If you have something to say, say it."

– Don't you have something to say? And she'd said plenty that night, and for what? It didn't end this. "You're the one doing all the talking."

"I don't have anything to say."

And he lights up a cigarette. He's so casual, so pompous. She's almost trembling. She is not going to let him do this again, because if he does it again, he'll do it again and again. As he's been doing it and doing it and doing it, until he's made himself right.

"I just don't think you should come around here looking for sex all the time."

And he's right: she came over looking for sex. But she didn't make that true, he did. Because it's all he will give, so it's all she can have – if he would give roses and dinners and chocolates and rings, she'd come over looking for them, but he doesn't; he gives sex, and so ... and maybe he's right: maybe it has come down to being just sex, but if that's true, it's a truth he's created, not her – this is not her doing, but she's the one who always has to scream inside, hurting and dying. "Is that what I do?" And she looks straight at him, without a smile. She's daring him, testing: how far will he go?

"Yeah."

"Really?"

"That's the way I see it. It's all we do."

"Ever stop to wonder why?" She knows he cannot say 'it's all we want,' because I want to be wise is still between them.

"I used to find you attractive, I guess. I don't know – maybe we're just a habit, like smoking. I don't know why I smoke either."

"Maybe you should find out."

"Why I smoke?"

"He's so cold, so cute, so firm, so distant – he uses it all as a club and she's supposed to . . . what? He doesn't know what he does to her when he does this, doesn't know that she can't fight this, that she can't turn it back on him because she won't say those words: you love me and you're scared of it, and if you blow it, maybe you'll never have it again, just maybe never again – 'I haven't had any loving since you . . . I want to be wise.' "No." "I just don't find you sexually attractive anymore."

Crunch, squish, splattered – that's what he's hoping for with that, that's his reason for saying it, and she's not going to let him do it, not this time. She's not a bug for him to step on, not a pest . . . And she's not going to cry (she could have him in a second if she cried because then he could say "I had to, you were crying.") because that is just another way to choke. No, this time, she was going to do something to stop this, something.

"So."

Something. Somehow – raise up like some David and tell him what he remembers, and what was – get them the epitaph WAS at least: make him admit what he knows. Because she knows it's over, but she won't let him pretend it never was – he's sitting there, pretending it never was.

"I mean, you can come around if you want to – don't feel rejected, but don't come over looking for sex all the time. Okay?"

And that's the escape hatch: the invitation to come again another day to see what mood he's in. And she could do it: walk out, and come back and likely find him 'receptive.' But it's not enough, because this would still be coming.

"So. Are you going to leave or talk or what?"

"I'm not to feel rejected?" She is going to pin him down like a butterfly. "What should I feel then?"

"You can come around, if you want."

"You know, I really don't feel rejected. You've put too many cobwebs in my mind for me to feel that." She takes out a cigarette.

"I don't know what you're talking about."

"Cobwebs, I'm talking about cobwebs. I'm talking about the fact that when you say 'leave,' I remember you saying 'I haven't had any loving since you,' and when you say 'I don't love you,' I can remember you saying 'I love you.'"

"Well, you know, I get drunk sometimes."

"You can tell anyone you want anything you want about us, but not me. I was there. I know what's happened and what you felt. You can tell your friends that you have a hot one coming around, looking for sex all the time, if you want to tell them that, but don't, don't ever, try to tell that to me, because I'm one half of us and I know what's happened." She smokes. She's trembling – she can't know what he felt, not well enough to tell him. No one can. And to deny a denial – to tell a storm that is really sunshine; the world will think her crazy. But she knew, knows, and he's not going to run away anymore.

"I don't think I ever said I loved you."

"August last year, to start—"

"I was drunk."

"You'd sobered up quite a bit in the car. You knew what you were doing. You were almost thanking God for the chance to do it. I was ready to leave, and you were insisting that I stay."

"I just wanted sex."

"You want dates and times and places and direct quotes, Alex?– because I'll give them to you."

He has no doubt that she can, and no doubt that she will. "You'll just be telling me when I was drunk, and when I wasn't." Because he will not let her even if he cannot stop her. Because she cannot make him believe things that cannot be true. But he's sweating – there has always been something dangerous about her.

"How many years back would you like me to go?"

"You don't have to bother at all."

"No. You're going to learn a little about yourself and how you operate."

"I know all about myself. You've told me all about me." And

he sneers, hoping she remembers all the things she's said over all the years: you're full of shit – she's said that in a thousand ways.

"You know, you do the same things all the time. Even tonight. When I don't find someone sexually attractive, I don't go laying about on couches with them – I don't bother to find out if they find me sexually attractive or not. It doesn't matter to me, not one bit, not unless I want them. In fact, I don't usually let that kind of situation develop with someone I don't find attractive, because I don't want their touch at all. It turns me off."

"Maybe that's what I'm telling you."

"It would be a lot easier to believe if you didn't have to know if I want you first, before you say it. It would really be a lot easier to believe then."

"I was just trying to get in the mood."

"How far back do you want me to go? – to your accident? Even then, I walk in expecting maybe a polite thank you for my interest in your health, and what do I hear? 'What took you so long?' as if we had never broken up and I not only had a right to be here, but a duty. And you've been doing it ever since. You call your friends over for a poker game and say 'sometimes a guy likes to be pursued,' and 'we could change roles, and you could set things up.' And then I see you with that slut, and you call me up in the middle of the night and say we should talk, and I go over to talk, and it's night and day again: you're closed off like a brick wall. I don't see you for a year, and I go up to that shack, and it's 'don't go away.' After a year. That's not just sex. That's not sexual attraction. Sexually attracted people don't say things like 'I'm trying to learn about love, I've met hippies.' don't you ever say that it's all sex, that it's all me, because it wasn't. And that time at the bar: we were pretty much finished, and I expected to find you dancing in the streets, but no; it's 'I'll never forget knowing you, and I'll always remember every moment between us.' And it's always like that – once you stood there, 'I don't think we should see each other anymore,' naked. Which message did you want me to pick up on?

And you do it all the time. You double-play reality as if you were sharpening a knife, and it's not going to happen anymore. It's done." She hates this – she loves his hands, loves his touch, but his hands will never be enough, and he's right: it's all they have. "I'm not coming back, because this won't stop until I stop, and I can't take anymore."

"Just don't be here when I get back." He grabs his coat and leaves, jamming his feet into his boots as he walks out the door. Because if he gives her one more minute, she's going to say too much. Because she is about to say why he has not spurned her.

It's cold outside, even for November. He turns his collar up against his neck, and walks down the driveway down the street. His hands are stuffed into his pockets, fists. It's a clear night, crisp. It's a perfect night, the lights boasting out into the darkness. He stops and breathes in deeply, wanting to replace her with that cold clean air. He's glad it's over between them. He walks on again, towards the bar.

She was going to say it – he knows she was going to say it: you want me because you don't want you. You can't let go of me because you don't hold onto to you. Because she was betraying them, revealing him in them. I want to be wise in a moment when he felt he could; I'm trying to learn about love in a moment when he felt he could; I'll never forget knowing you in a moment when he knew what knowing her meant – doesn't she think he remembers too, can feel it again too? He walks on, smacking into the cold.

It's better that it's over, because it was never meant to be – a guy can't get out of what he is. Alex knows that. As he knows that there can be too much consciousness of being, too much thought, too many desires. The world isn't cut out for desire – she would have him hate the world, his life, his days and nights and every minute he's had without her, but he doesn't. You double play reality but he doesn't because there is only one reality, one real world for him. And he's not absurd in it – sexually attracted people don't say things like 'I'm trying to learn about love, I've met hippies' – she made him sound obscene, a joke. He cringes. But he's not the absurd one, because he's not the one who comes crawling over, looking for sex. And sex was all she really ever wanted, because it was all she really got and she kept coming. He isn't going to miss her. And he can let go of her, because he does have himself.

She sits in her car, in her driveway. She knows she'll never see him again – the pain in his eyes, he'll never forgive her. And maybe that's good; maybe it had to come to that. Because she would go back, if he'd let her. She'd believe it all all over again, if he gave her one reason. But he won't, because the person she fell in love with doesn't exist anymore – maybe never did, but was a phantom, a hope. She doesn't know. But she does know that today Alex has too many years lived one way, and only moments lived another. Years have a way of grinding up moments. But those moments were his best – I want to be wise; it could have been so fine. . . .

Acknowledgments

Writers are always facing blankness: the empty page. It is so much easier to do so with a lot to say. In my family, I have been blessed with unconventional parents and gifted brother who undoubtedly helped me become more aware of possibilities, of various points of view. They also stayed enough out of the way that I grew fairly self-ruling in my experience. For this I am grateful.

I have had wonderful teachers, in both high school and university, Mike Josiah, Roy Miki, Don Rubin. And I found friends who never stopped encouraging me: Celeste, Karen, and of course, Donald.

But this book would not have reached beyond me without the support of my publisher and editors. They took it the last mile, and I thank everyone at *efg publishing*.

I have alluded to some of the explosive music of the era, music by *The Eagles, The Who, The Rolling Stones, Supertramp,* and *David Bowie.* This music permeated the minds of a generation, becoming the filter through which many experienced love and loss and, yes, sex. Had they chosen different songs, would they have had different outcomes? I am amazed at these artist's talents, and grateful for their gift of music.

About The Author

Wrapping herself up in the hopelessness of it all, she turns to the song and dwells behind blue eyes where dreams are empty and hours are lonely. The Who felt it too, felt it better. Does it have to be this way?

I was born in a small town in the interior of British Columbia, from which I was rescued when my father decided he had at last seen enough snow, and we moved to the coast. My rescue was accomplished only over my loud and long objections. I was about to discover that the safeness and sameness of our small town came at a cost. I literally went from reading Harlequin romances to the writings of Fritz Perl and Carl Rogers: my mother had returned to university and she left interesting books around. That was when I knew I wanted to understand how relationships worked, but the truth of it, and not some tidy and polite version. I didn't yet know that fiction was the best format to explore human experience. That came at SFU. (Simon Fraser University, Burnaby, British Columbia.) The writings of Faulkner told me that even in safeness and sameness, truths could be found. The ordinary could be revelatory. We just had to look. I've been looking ever since. There is something in everything.

(Vivian)

Notes on Typefaces

Body text is set in *Espinosa Nova*, an award-winning type family for designing books released in 2010 by the Mexcian foundry, LetraCase. The font is a reconstruction of the typefaces used by Antonio de Espinosa, the most important Mexican printer of the sixteenth century and probably the first type designer in the Americas (1551).

Chapter 31 injections in the text are set in *HK Compact,*, while main titles on the title pages are set in *HK Grotesk*, two sans-serif typefaces issued by the Dubai-based company, Hanken Design, Subtitles, chapter numberings, and other elements are set in *Quincy*, a type family by the Utah-based designer Connary Fagen.